Jezebel's Dust

Also by Fred Urquhart

Novels
TIME WILL KNIT
THE FERRET WAS ABRAHAM'S DAUGHTER
PALACE OF GREEN DAYS

Short Stories
I FELL FOR A SAILOR
THE CLOUDS ARE BIG WITH MERCY
SELECTED STORIES
THE LAST G.I. BRIDE WORE TARTAN
THE YEAR OF THE SHORT CORN
THE LAST SISTER
THE LAUNDRY GIRL AND THE POLE
THE DYING STALLION
THE PLOUGHING MATCH
PROUD LADY IN A CAGE
A DIVER IN CHINA SEAS
SEVEN GHOSTS IN SEARCH
FULL SCORE (edited by Graeme Roberts)

Edited Books
NO SCOTTISH TWILIGHT (with Maurice Lindsay)
W.S.C.: A CARTOON BIOGRAPHY
GREAT TRUE WAR ADVENTURES
MEN AT WAR
SCOTTISH SHORT STORIES
GREAT TRUE ESCAPE STORIES
THE CASSELL MISCELLANY, 1848-1958
MODERN SCOTTISH SHORT STORIES (with Giles Gordon)
THE BOOK OF HORSES

Other
SCOTLAND IN COLOUR (with Kenneth Scowen)
EVERYMAN'S DICTIONARY OF FICTIONAL CHARACTERS
(with William Freeman)

Jezebel's Dust

Fred Urquhart

WITH AN INTRODUCTION BY
COLIN AFFLECK

Kennedy & Boyd
an imprint of
Zeticula
57 St Vincent Crescent
Glasgow
G3 8NQ
Scotland.

http://www.kennedyandboyd.co.uk
admin@kennedyandboyd.co.uk

First published in 1951 in London by Methuen.
Text Copyright © Estate of Fred Urquhart 2011
Introduction Copyright © Colin Affleck 2011

Front cover photograph © Kim Traynor 2011
Back cover photograph from Fred Urquhart's own collection
Copyright © Colin Affleck 2011

ISBN-13 978-1-84921-094-2

Introduction

Fred Urquhart had one of the stranger careers in Scottish literature. His revealing and original first novel, *Time Will Knit* (1938), made a considerable impact, due to its candid picture of working-class life in Edinburgh. He was hailed by Janet Adam Smith in *The New York Times Book Review* as the latest addition to the "white hopes of Scottish literature." [1] When the book was re-issued as a Penguin paperback during the Second World War, it sold more than 70,000 copies. Urquhart went on to publish another three remarkable novels and 13 volumes of short stories (as well as many uncollected stories) that include many brilliant examples of the genre, so that he has been justifiably described as the greatest Scottish short story writer of the twentieth century. He received high critical praise throughout his career, particularly from other distinguished writers, such as George Orwell, Stevie Smith, Francis King, Allan Massie and Iain Crichton Smith. And yet, success in terms of financial viability always eluded him, so that he had to spend much of his time working as a reviewer, publisher's reader, book editor, literary agent (briefly) and London scout for Walt Disney (even more briefly). Somehow he never sold enough books or stories, despite his reputation and the enthusiasm of his supporters.

This situation may be partly due to his being domiciled in England between 1944 and 1991, so that – despite the fact that he mostly wrote about Scottish characters – he was increasingly cut off from the Scottish literary scene, as it developed an identity that sought to be entirely separate from England. At the same time, his work had a decreasing appeal in England, with changes in fashion among critics and readers. Furthermore, the nature of his writing, which is always highly readable and seems straightforward, although it actually explores profound social and psychological issues, meant that it did not attract much attention from academics. In response, Urquhart developed a theory of "elimination" to explain how certain writers receive a lot of publicity and promotion and therefore high sales, while others are overlooked. It seems more likely that he suffered from bad luck, such as difficulties with publishers and changes in the market for short stories. As a result, even before his death in 1995, his work had begun to fall into obscurity, despite his once having been automatically included in lists of the leading British short story writers.

It is thus particularly pleasing that two of his novels are again being made available to readers who are interested in enjoyable fiction with high narrative values; fiction that can tell a story in a comic way, while respecting the integrity of its characters and reflecting deeper concerns; fiction that reveals the nature of Scottish society as it was, and in some ways still is, concentrating particularly on poor, powerless and vulnerable people.

The (mis)adventures of Bessie Hipkiss and Lily McGillivray begin in *The Ferret was Abraham's Daughter* (published in 1949, and now reprinted), to which *Jezebel's Dust* (published two years later) is the sequel.[2] It is not necessary to read the first book in order to appreciate the present volume – Urquhart makes sure that enough explanation is provided – but, in order to get the full story and the fullest enjoyment, it is best to do so.

In *The Ferret was Abraham's Daughter*, Bessie Hipkiss (nicknamed the Ferret) is living with her working-class parents and siblings in the Calderburn housing estate in Edinburgh. She escapes from the reality of her life by going to the cinema and fantasising (in an amusingly overblown style) that she and her family are the exiled royal family of France, who have been restored to their throne. She also takes up with the flighty Lily McGillivray, who introduces her to peroxided hair and the pursuit of men. Meanwhile, the Second World War ineluctably approaches. Following family difficulties, the 15-year-old Bessie flees at the end of the book (and on the last day of 1939) to a new life as a maid in Mrs Irvine's boarding house.

The first page of *Jezebel's Dust* shows Bessie (who has replaced her hated surname with Campbell) in her new situation. It is now 3 June 1940, the last day of the Dunkirk evacuation, but Mrs Irvine and some other landladies are about to have a lavish tea party. Their conversation (and gluttony) immediately shows the falsity of the official (and still popular) picture of a nation united in adversity. Referring to the now famous statement made by the new prime minister three weeks earlier, Miss Laidlaw complains, "I must say I didn't like it when Mr. Churchill said he had nothing to offer us but blood, toil, sweat and tears. I didn't like it at all. I'm a one for my comforts, and I don't care who knows it." As a conscientious objector, Urquhart was sceptical about the war and the mythology (or propaganda) surrounding it, although this book is less explicitly anti-war than some of his writings. The tea party scene is also the first of several in which the xenophobia of the British is displayed, with Mrs Munro exclaiming that "the French have let us down …. You should never trust foreigners."

Jezebel's Dust takes Bessie through an eventful period, beginning in Edinburgh in the aftermath of Dunkirk and on to London in 1942, with a flashback to the later days of the Blitz. A review in *Books of Today* noted that, in conveying the mood of this wartime period, "the book assumes considerable documentary significance as a picture of how ordinary people reacted to 'our finest hour.' Many of the incidents have significance both as personal comedy and as social history."[3] This is all the more true the further removed we become from the 1940s and the more distant from the real attitudes of people at that time. Urquhart shows the reality of daily life as it carried on, affected but not overwhelmed by the convulsions of history. The process of social change, speeded up by wartime conditions, meant that old controls diminished, so Lily can exclaim, "What does it matter what folk say!"

One of the topics of wartime conversation that appear in the book is the concern about the possible presence of Fifth Columnists (secret supporters of the Germans). These references had a personal significance for Urquhart, given that he had been suspected of being one in 1940, while staying with a friend, Mary Litchfield, in Cupar in Fife. He wrote various accounts of the incident (reflecting the lasting impact it had on him), including this:

> Shortly after Dunkirk Mary's house was raided at ten o'clock in the morning by six policemen and a policewoman, and she and I .... were held prisoners until late in the afternoon while the police searched the house .... We were not told at the time, but we heard afterwards that somebody in Cupar had reported we were Fifth Columnists because of the many strange visitors we had – mostly students from St Andrews and members of the Fife Labour Party!" [4]

Urquhart was sometimes seen as a "proletarian writer," a much-used term in the 1930s and 1940s, because he came from and wrote about the working class (although his work did not display the political propagandising of the proletarian school). It is not surprising that the working-class Edinburgh characters in these novels are so convincing, because many of them were based on Urquhart's relations, friends and neighbours. Harrisfield is really Granton, on the Firth of Forth, where Urquhart's maternal grandparents lived at West Cottages. Although Urquhart was born in Edinburgh in 1912, his father's work as a chauffeur took the family to rural areas of Scotland, including Fife, Perthshire and Wigtownshire. However, in his childhood he spent holidays and some longer periods staying with his grandparents in Granton. Later he and his family lived in near-by Fraser Grove. Calderburn, where the Hipkisses, Lily McGillivray, Dirty Minnie and the other neighbours stay, is based on Wardieburn, a council housing estate next to Granton, built in the early 1930s. [5]

One of the most striking aspects of Urquhart's works is the colour and vivacity of his characters' language. Whether he is writing about country people in north-east Scotland, as in many of his short stories, or about the citizens of Edinburgh, he captures precisely the way they speak. He attributed this ability to his having learned to listen closely to people from infancy, when, rather than going out to play, he preferred staying in the house and listening to the conversations of the grown-ups (particularly women).

In these novels the dialogue of the working-class Edinburgh characters is particularly convincing. They use a recognisably real mixture of Scots words, slang, catchphrases (such as "Och, why worry! Use sunlight!" which was derived from a soap advertisement) and Americanisms (picked up from Hollywood films, on whose stars the young women try to model themselves). There is particularly clever use of accurate dialogue to reveal the essence of the female characters. Reviewing *Jezebel's Dust*, Compton Mackenzie praised the "quite exceptionally good dialogue and a remarkable talent for depicting women young and old." [6] J. D. Scott referred in the *New Statesman and Nation* to "the brilliant reality" of the depiction of "the girls, the lively, bedizened, boy-hunting trollops whom Mr Urquhart loves with a pure and holy love." [7]

Urquhart's characters also demonstrate the self-consciousness of members of the Edinburgh working class when talking in their normal way in front of middle-class people who consider it "common." Mrs Moore tries to talk genteelly in front of Mrs Irvine, but in the flow of her narrative she soon returns to using more expressive terms and words such as "skedaddled" and "chums a' bubbly wi' a Pole." Mrs Irvine is evidently an example of someone who has gone up in the world, but who sometimes lapses back into using Scots words.

The lives of Bessie and Lily are transformed by the arrival of Polish troops in Edinburgh. Urquhart was fascinated by the interaction between the Scots and the exotic wartime visitors in their midst, particularly the Poles. During the war he wrote a number of stories featuring Polish soldiers in Scotland. The novella "Namietnosc – or The Laundry Girl and the Pole"[8] was written in late 1940 in Cupar, where Urquhart had observed the effect of the arrival of a detachment of Polish soldiers on the local women. As he put it, "In 1940 the Polish soldiers came to Cupar, and I studied their love lives in the blackout…" [9] "Namietnosc" is Polish for passion, and that is what Nettie the laundry girl finds with Jan the Polish soldier. In October 1942 a Polish translation was serialised in *Dziennik Zolnierza (The Polish Soldier's Daily)*. It was well received by the readers, some of whom suspected that Urquhart was really a pseudonymous Pole.

Some other stories at this time treated relations with the Poles as a source of comedy. In "Beautiful Music," Lizzie, a farm maid, practises saying the Polish for "I love you," in the hope of landing a Polish officer. Three women railway porters gossip in "Mrs Coolie-Hoo's Pole" about a genteel married woman who has "got a Pole." Mrs Coolie-Hoo is less colourful than Mrs Irvine, but her Pole also calls her "mummy." Among the gossip in the public wash house that is the setting for "Dirty Linen" is talk of Mrs Jackson going with a Polish sergeant, a cause of criticism and envy. [10]

In *Jezebel's Dust*, Urquhart's attitude to his Polish characters may seem quite harsh. With the exception of Josef Rolewicz, who is quiet and stolid but reliable, the Polish officers are depicted as arrogant, selfish, effete, violent, cowardly and (in one memorable case) sinisterly, if hilariously, masochistic. There may be a political element in this. Until after the war Urquhart considered himself to be a communist, and in this he was encouraged by Mary Litchfield, a communist former school teacher with numerous connections in Scottish and British literary, artistic and theatrical circles. He stayed with her in Cupar between 1939 and 1940. Her wartime letters to Urquhart show her dislike of Poland, which was shared by many on the Left because of its (unsurprising) opposition to the Soviet Union, and Urquhart shows the Poles – unsympathetically – as explicitly anti-Russian and anti-communist. At the same time, Litchfield was on civil terms with many of the Polish soldiers based in Cupar. It was there that Urquhart first came into contact with the

Poles and Litchfield gave him more information in her letters about their effect on the town. It was also she who arranged with the editor of the Polish soldiers' paper for publication of Urquhart's novella. Her ambiguity about the Poles may have been transmitted to Urquhart.

It must be pointed out that Urquhart is not very complimentary about any of the groups that he deals with, whether Edinburgh landladies or GIs, although there are individuals who appear in a good light, so his depiction of Polish soldiers should not be seen as malicious. It is also notable that Bessie's obnoxious father is made to express anti-Polish sentiments, which makes the reader more sympathetic to the Poles.

The first impression of *Jezebel's Dust* that a reader will receive is of a lively comedy, full of memorable characters, amusing dialogue and references to popular culture (especially films). The passage of almost 60 years means that the book will also prompt nostalgia among some people, especially if they knew the Edinburgh of the past, with mentions of shopping in Patrick Thomson's, dancing at the Palais de Danse, the Store van, various long-vanished cinemas, and so on.

However, the book also has serious intentions. Some reviewers, missing these, accused Urquhart of sentimentality, a charge that was sometimes made against him by a few critics throughout his career. Nothing could be further from the truth. Urquhart sympathised with the poor people, the children, the women, the old people, the prisoners of war and the other vulnerable people that he wrote about, but he never sentimentalised them. He sometimes explicitly shows the absurdity of sentimentality, as when Mrs Irvine describes Bessie's appalling siblings as "two poor little innocent children," immediately followed by a description of Jenny's usual misbehaviour. Urquhart's means of expression may often have been comic, but he saw the tragedy of life too.

A clue to this lies in the epigraph of this book – a long, complex quotation from John Donne's Sermon LXXX – which may seem an unexpectedly solemn text to be found at the beginning of a largely comic novel. The thrust of it is that all people die and decay, including the notorious Jezebel, "who painted and perfumed this body." Therefore, "*Jezebel's* dust is not Ambar"; that is, unlike amber, her remains are not preserved as a valuable substance, with reputed medicinal properties, but have crumbled and vanished. And yet, despite this inevitable bodily decay, God holds out the promise of bodily resurrection. Urquhart was not religious, so the quotation is not to be taken literally, but it indicates the moral force underlying the social comedy.

When Bessie is in hospital, Mr Powys, an elderly bibliophile, leaves with her (presumably by mistake) a copy of Donne's works. She and Norman puzzle over Sermon LXXX – particularly the words "Jezebel's dust is not amber" – but they can't make out what it means. [11] This is ironically amusing, since they are major characters in a book to which this text is intended by the author to be particularly relevant. Bessie means to ask Mr Powys about it, but she "never had time," which is also ironic, given the text's reference to the insubstantiality of the temporal.

At the end of the book, after a judge has described Lily as "a painted Jezebel," Bessie recalls remarks made by Mr Powys, including, "Nothing in temporal things is permanent, and nobody is perfect," which is a combination of another direct quotation from Sermon LXXX and a paraphrase of part of its message: that everything human is imperfect. She also remembers Mr Powys saying that Lily's downfall was due to society allowing wars, which have inevitable consequences. It seems that Mr Powys is introduced to voice his author's opinions.

Urquhart does not take a moralistic approach to sexuality, which, sometimes taking unorthodox forms, pervades the book. Bessie's sexual experiences are described, sometimes from her point of view in terms reflecting the romantic fiction she reads and sometimes in objective detail. In addition, sly allusions to sex of various sorts are scattered about (Lily tells us that sailors are "aye ready for any kind o' fun!"). He does, however, have an interest in exposing hypocrisy and narrow-mindedness, which were vices that he saw as particularly prevalent in Edinburgh (and which he said led to his deciding to stay elsewhere). In those terms he sometimes takes a moral approach to his characters. Thus, there is a contrast between Bessie, who is basically good (as far, at least, as any of Urquhart's characters can be good) but is led astray, and Lily, who, despite the vivacity and force that make her a delight to the reader, is fundamentally bad: a hypocrite, liar, thief and gold-digger. Bessie's flaws are an over-active imagination and a lack of will, but these are not tragic flaws, whereas Lily's are: she is the tragic figure and they both get the fate they deserve in these terms. However, Urquhart ultimately does not judge Lily; using the expression that she previously used about herself, Bessie comments that Lily "never had a real chance." Even Lily's hypocrisy is depicted as so blatant as to defy criticism; as she remarks, "What I said and what I'm goin' to do are two entirely different things." She may not be resurrected in the religious sense, but the character continues to live because her author has drawn her so vividly.

Bessie's character develops in this book. At its start, she still has "bewildered eyes," but she gradually grows up. There are fewer fantasies about her being Madame Royale, daughter of the King of France, although there is a spectacular example in a cinema when she forgets herself and cries out in French. She comes to terms with real life, eventually dismissing her royal day dreams as "a lot of havers," and she is eventually able to criticise and feel sorry for Lily, having achieved a degree of independence; but as well as becoming more sensible, she has become harder, as is seen when she thinks that Lily should have held onto a married man in whom she had her claws.

Bessie finally achieves an American apotheosis – the dream of so many young women of her time – and she thinks of her life as a fairy story. She may seem to have been given a fairy-tale ending, but there is still an element of irony. Is she really happy ever after, or has she just exchanged one environment with noisy children and petty snobbery for another? It is significant that the very last words of the book are "On and on and on with the story!" – the demanding cry of Bessie's little sister Jenny that echoes through *The Ferret was Abraham's Daughter*. The implication is that, just because the book ends at a particular point, Bessie's story is not really over. Given Urquhart's unstoppable narrative drive, Jenny's words could have been his motto.

Colin Affleck

1   *The New York Times Book Review*, 31 July 1938, page 8.
2   Urquhart began making notes about Bessie Hipkiss in the early 1940s and she first appeared in print in the short story "Barbara of Shallot" (*The New Statesman and Nation*, 31 October 1942), which became the basis of an episode in *The Ferret was Abraham's Daughter*.
3   *Books of Today*, December 1951, pages 11-12.
4   From the typescript synopsis of a proposed autobiography.
5   Urquhart first used Harrisfield and Calderburn to stand for Granton and Wardieburn in *Time Will Knit*. He had written about life in Calderburn in the short story "Backgreen Concert," in which Mrs Moore, a minor character in the novels, appears. Another story, "Dirty Minnie," introduced the particularly memorable title character (slatternly but sympathetic), who re-appears in the two novels. Both stories are included in Urquhart's *The Clouds Are Big with Mercy* (1946).
6   Quoted in an advertisement in *The Observer*, 18 November 1951.
7   *The New Statesman and Nation*, 17 November 1951, page 570.
8   Included in *The Clouds Are Big with Mercy*.
9   From the typescript synopsis of a proposed autobiography.
10 These three stories were included in Urquhart's *Selected Stories* (1946).
11 Urquhart had noted "Jezebel's Dust is Not Amber" as a possible title before he had begun this book. He had a remarkable talent for choosing intriguing titles, which usually came before the story or novel.

For

PETER WYNDHAM ALLEN

The World is a great Volume, and man the Index of that Booke; Even in the body of man, you may turne to the whole world; This body is an Illustration of all Nature; Gods recapitulation of all that he had said before in his *Fiat lux,* and *Fiat firmamentum,* and in all the rest, said or done, in all the six dayes. Propose this body to thy consideration in the highest exaltation thereof; as it is the *Temple of the Holy Ghost:* Nay, not in a Metaphor, or comparison of a Temple, or any other similitudinary thing, but as it was really and truly the very body of God, in the person of Christ, and yet this body must wither, must decay, must languish, must perish. When *Goliah* had armed and fortified this body, And *Jezebel* had painted and perfumed this body, And *Dives* had pampered and larded this body, As God said to *Ezekiel,* when he brought him to the *dry bones, Fili hominis, Sonne of Man doest thou thinke these bones can live?* They said in their hearts to all the world, Can these bodies die? And they are dead. *Jezebel's* dust is not Ambar, nor *Goliah's* dust *Terra sigillata,* Medicinall; nor does the Serpent, whose meat they are both, finde any better relish in *Dives* dust, than in *Lazarus.* But as in our former part, where our foundation was, That in nothing, no spirituall thing, there was any perfectness, which we illustrated in the weaknesses of Knowledge, and Faith, and Hope, and Charity, yet we concluded, that for all those defects, God accepted those their religious services; So in this part, where our foundation is, That nothing in temporall things is permanent, as we have illustrated that, by the decay of that which is Gods noblest piece in Nature, The body of man; so we shall also conclude that, with this goodnesse of God, that for all this dissolution, and putrefaction, he affords this Body a Resurrection.

JOHN DONNE: *Sermon LXXX.*

PART I

MRS. IRVINE was having a tea-party for some other Edinburgh landladies. Massive bosom encased in a white silk blouse, she toyed with her cameo-brooch as she surveyed the tea-table. 'Everything looks very nice I must say, m'dear,' she said to Bessie Campbell, her young maid-of-all-work. 'I'm glad to see that you've put the potato scones down near Miss Laidlaw's place. She has a passion for them. My godfathers, I whiles tell her that she'd eat them to a band playing.'

'Too true!' Bessie giggled. 'I mind the last time she was here, she——'

'Oh, you've forgotten the chutney, Bessie,' Mrs. Irvine cried. 'Run and get it, like a lamb, and bring the tea-cosy at the same time.'

'Ay, okay,' Bessie hastened away.

'Bessie,' Mrs. Irvine stopped her.

'Bessie,' she said. 'You must learn to say "yes". You must never say "ay, okay". It's common. You must remember you're not living in Calderburn now. You'll have to learn to speak like a lady.'

'Like me,' she laughed, although Bessie knew perfectly well that she meant what she said.

'Yes, Mrs. Irvine,' Bessie said, and she scuttled away to bring the required objects.

But about ten minutes later when she was putting on her new navy-blue dress, she thought: Mrs. Irvine has a right nerve, too, to say anything about the way I speak. She speaks real broad herself sometimes. I've heard her when she gets into a puggy, she forgets to be so lah-de-dah then. And swears like a trooper, too, when she likes. . . .

All the same Mrs. Irvine was all right, Bessie reflected, smearing eye-black on her sandy eyebrows. Mrs. Irvine had been right good to her ever since she ran away from home six months ago. Of course, in a way it was Mrs. Irvine who had egged her on to do that. She might not have had the gumption to do it if she hadn't had Mrs. Irvine's to come to. Anyway, she was real comfortable and it was a nice job, although there was a lot of hard work in connection with it. Looking after half a dozen boarders day in and day out was no picnic. Washing all those dishes and scrubbing floors and making so many beds. . . . In a way she had been better off at home where she'd had only her father and the two bairns to look after. In a way. She'd aye had time, too, at home to have a bit read now and then. But of course there was her stepmother now to be reckoned with. . . .

Ay, there was dear Mabel, she thought, stepping back to see how she looked. Dear Mabel with all her gush and her blarney, winding her father round her wee finger. Bessie Campbell scowled first at the thought of her stepmother and then at her reflection.

It was high time she did something about her hair. It was getting too streaky. All that gingeryness at the roots, she'd soon be a red-head again if she didn't watch out. She'd have to have another go at the peroxide-bottle. But she hadn't time now, she sighed, looking at the clock, she'd have to rush and lay the tea for the lodgers.

No, boarders, she corrected herself. Mrs. Irvine said it was common to call them lodgers. 'In our class there are no lodgers, Bessie. Lodgers are just common working people. But in our class they're always boarders or paying-guests. I like paying-guests myself, but I always compromise—just in case they're behind-hand with the rent or anything like that.'

Bessie took a last look at herself. She looked all right. Not as good as she would have liked to look, but well enough. She saw a thin girl of almost sixteen with large, bewildered eyes. She had plastered her face liberally with powder, hiding

2

her few remaining freckles, and vivid scarlet lipstick made her large mouth look even larger.

You look all right, hen, she assured herself, hurrying to the dining-room. Maybe you're not as glamorous as Ginger Rogers, but you're glamorous enough. She hoped that Lily McGillivray would be satisfied when she met her.

She and Lily were going to see Margaret Lockwood and Rex Harrison in *Night Train to Munich*. Margaret Lockwood wasn't one of Bessie's favourites. She'd rather go and see Bette Davis or Ann Sheridan any day, but she hadn't been to the pictures for a fortnight, so was determined to go. It all depended, of course, on what kind of mood Lily was in. Lily had been keen enough to go when she'd seen her on Sunday and they'd arranged it. But you never knew what other plans Lily might have cooked up in the meantime. Lily was a right funny one sometimes. One minute she'd be all out for going after boys, and then the next you'd think she had just come out a convent. Especially these last two months since she'd married Tommy Hutchinson, you'd think butter wouldn't melt in her mouth. Even though Tommy was safely away in the navy, somewhere in the middle of the Atlantic or the Mediterranean, Lily would get all high-hat and act as if she had never looked at another fellow in her life. Her that had aye been such a one for the lads. . . .

It was changed days, Bessie reflected, banging the cups and saucers on the table. Lily had been such a spark when they'd worked together in Andrews' Bakery. She'd had one lad after another, and she had always been at her to get a lad, too. But ever since she married Tommy . . .

'Bessie,' Mrs. Irvine popped her head round the door. 'Bessie, I wonder if you'd make the macaroni-cheese for Mr. McQuarrie and Donald before you go out? I'm busy with my visitors, and I haven't got time. It'll only take you a minute or two, dear. It won't keep you much longer.'

'Okay, Mrs. Irvine,' Bessie said. 'I—I mean all right.'

Mrs. Irvine smiled and gave a little nod.

'Where are you going tonight, m'dear?' she said.

'Well, we're supposed to be going to the Playhouse to see

3

Margaret Lockwood in *Night Train to Munich*,' Bessie said. 'But you never know with Lily. She might. . . .'

'I wish you wouldn't go out with that Lily McGillivray,' Mrs. Irvine said. 'She's not the right sort of chum for you at all, Bessie. She's a very common girl. I never liked her, I must say. I've always felt she has a bad influence on you. I told you that when we all worked in Andrews' together, and I'm not going back on my words one inch. She's a right bad little hat. And getting married to that poor simple sailor! She just did it to get a marriage allowance from the Government. My godfathers, he'll rue the day he ever set eyes on her.'

'And so will you,' she said.

'Aw, I dunno,' Bessie muttered, fiddling with the fringe of the table-cloth. 'Lily's not bad.'

'You mark my words,' Mrs. Irvine said. 'Lily McGillivray was born under an unlucky star. I've studied her horoscope, and no good'll come to her or anybody connected with her.'

'Well, I cannie help it,' Bessie said. 'I've known Lily ever since we were bairns. We played together and went to the school together, and we've aye been chummy.'

'That's no reason why it need continue,' Mrs. Irvine said majestically. 'You must remember that you're living in a different class of society now. You'll have to cut yourself away from all these encumbrances.'

'Well, I must go back to my guests,' she said.

She closed the door, but she opened it again almost immediately. 'And by the way, Bessie,' she said. 'Don't be too late in coming in tonight. You were very late last week, and I don't like it. It's not the thing for a young girl like yourself to be out to all hours in this blackout. It was maybe all very well when you were living in Calderburn, but I feel I've got some responsibility for you as long as you're living with me.'

'Besides, it gets the house a bad name,' she said.

'Okay, Mrs. Irvine,' Bessie said.

4

'My, what a lovely spread!' Miss Laidlaw said. 'I don't know how you manage it, Mrs. Irvine, with this awful war on. Where do you get all the stuff? My goodness, you must spend all your time in queues!'

'Oh, we manage,' Mrs. Irvine said. 'We manage.' She inclined her head and said: 'Try another of these cakes, Mrs. Dallas.'

'I wonder if I should dare!' Mrs. Dallas giggled and touched the frill of her black georgette blouse with hesitant fingers. 'I don't think I should, I've had two already!' She giggled again, and her hands flew up and screwed the roll of hair at the nape of her neck.

'Go on!' Mrs. Irvine said. 'Might as well be hung for a sheep as a lamb!'

'That's what I say.' Miss Laidlaw reached for her third piece of jam-tart. 'These days you never know where your next meal's coming from, so you might as well eat all you can when you get the chance. You never know the moment when a bomb might fall on you!'

'You're cheerful, aren't you,' Mrs. Munro said. 'What I always say is: Those that speak in jest. . . .'

'Yes, and with all this awful business at Dunkirk,' Mrs. Dallas said, twisting her pearl necklace until Mrs. Irvine thought she might break the thread. 'It's terrible. Goodness knows what's going to happen to us all.'

'Oh well, when it comes, let it come.' Mrs. Irvine prepared to pour more tea. 'There's no use looking for snow before it comes on, as my old granny used to say.'

'Try one of these meringues, Miss Laidlaw,' she said.

'I've had one.' Miss Laidlaw's large damp face, smeared with pink powder, creased into a smirk. 'I wonder if I dare take another?'

'They're exquisite,' Mrs. Dallas cried. 'They're simply gorgeous. I don't know how you do it, Mrs. Irvine.'

5

'I just hope you don't feed your boarders like this,' Miss Laidlaw said. 'My goodness, if you did you wouldn't have much profit.'

'That's just what I was thinking,' Mrs. Munro remarked. 'What I always say is: A house that's rough with food is never rough with money.'

'Oh, I wouldn't say that,' Mrs. Irvine said. 'I never stint with food, and yet I'm always able to put a little past for a rainy day. It comes of being a good manager, of course. Some folk just haven't that knack. Either they starve themselves and have a big bank account, or every penny goes down the drain.'

Mrs. Munro's scraggy little neck shot forward like a tortoise's from its shell, and she said: 'Well, what I always say is: If you don't save up for your old age yourself nobody else will. I for one have no intention of spending my last days in the poorhouse. I wouldn't accept a penny from charity. Not a penny.'

'Saving up for your old age is all very well,' Mrs. Irvine said. 'I'm all for it. But at the same time, you want to enjoy yourself while you're young enough and able to have your fling.'

Mrs. Munro sniffed, but before she could think of a suitable retort, Miss Laidlaw cut in: 'I'm all for having your fling, too, while the going's good. But at the same time I don't see why one's boarders should benefit. I feed mine adequately with good plain food, but I don't coddle them. After all, I don't keep boarders for the fun of the thing.'

'None of us do,' Mrs. Irvine said. She held out a plate of fancy cakes to Mrs. Munro. 'Another cake, m'dear?'

Mrs. Munro's brown-mottled claw hovered above the plate. 'That pink one looks nice,' she said. 'But yet—you know I fancy this marzipan potato!'

'You're like one of my boarders,' Miss Laidlaw said. 'Jenny Wishart, you'll have heard me talk about her very likely. She's an awful girl—a real fast piece, you know, always out with different men—and I really don't know why I keep her, except that she always pays her board regularly on the dot. Well,

6

whenever we have cakes for tea—not that I believe in giving my lodgers cakes, mind you, but sometimes on a Sunday as a special treat we have them—well, whenever we do, Miss Wishart always grabs the marzipan potato before anybody else can get a look in. I've had to speak to her about it several times. There are other people at the table as well as you, Miss Wishart, I've had to say. You should try and not be greedy. It's not becoming in a young girl like you.'

'Some of them are terribly greedy,' Mrs. Dallas said, rolling the frill of her blouse between finger and thumb as she scanned the plate Mrs. Irvine was holding out to her. 'I have a couple of Art students just now, and they really are the end. They're never satisfied with what they get. Always wanting more. I told one of them that he was like he had a tape-worm. It's not natural, I told him, always being hungry like that.'

'That's what I tell Miss Wishart,' said Miss Laidlaw. 'I'm sure none of your students are as bad as her. She's just like Oliver Twist. She upsets the whole house with her continual demands for more. I heard her say the other evening to young Porteous: "One plum again, chum!" So I just yoked her about it. Miss Wishart, I said, if you're not pleased with the food here you can go elsewhere. I could be doing with your room, I said. And out she'll go at the toot, too, if there's another cheep out of her.'

'I wouldn't stand for one of my boarders behaving like that,' Mrs. Munro cried, pressing her thin lips together. 'What I always say is: Give them an inch and they'll take an ell. But they know better than try any of their tricks with me. They get their set meals at set times, and if they're not there to get them, then that's their lookout. It's no use any of them coming grumbling to me about it. I just tell them: "It's all written on the board." Breakfast at nine sharp, lunch at one and high tea at six o'clock. Then a cup of tea and a scone at nine, if they're in for it.'

'I don't give mine anything after seven-thirty,' Mrs. Dallas said. 'But of course we have *dinner* then.'

'We're not all as classy as you!' Miss Laidlaw giggled. 'Of course, you have a maid to help you.'

7

'That reminds me,' she turned to Mrs. Irvine. 'How's *your* little maid doing? What's her name again—Bessie? I just caught a glimpse of her as I came in. How's she getting on?'

'Fine,' Mrs. Irvine said. 'She's taking shape nicely.'

'Does she ever go near her people?' Mrs. Dallas leaned forward.

'Oh, yes, I made her make it up with them,' Mrs. Irvine said. 'I didn't approve of her running away from home like that. It put me in an awkward kind of position, y'know. So I went to see her father. He works in a pub just round the corner from here. I go in sometimes to have a little drop of gin. Not that I ever indulge!' She gave a booming laugh from the depths of her tight corsets. 'But I go in occasionally to get a wee drop gin for my nerves. You know how it is with this war and all the work with my boarders. The constitution needs a little fillip now and again!'

'Indeed it does,' Miss Laidlaw said. 'I always like to have a bottle of stout in the house in case my heart troubles me. And in case there's an air-raid. Manys and manys the time——'

'Yes, I went in and saw Mr. Hipkiss,' Mrs. Irvine continued as majestically as the *Queen Mary* under full steam. 'And I said to him: "Mr. Hipkiss, I don't like this way of doing at all," I said. "I hope you'll not be too angry with Bessie," I said, "but she's just a young thoughtless lassie, and after all we were all young once," I told him. "So I'd like you to make it up with her, Mr. Hipkiss," I said. And so they did. She goes home about once a fortnight to see them, but of course there's no love lost between her and her stepmother. And I can't say that I blame her. Mrs. Hipkiss is a—well, to say she's a tartar is putting it mildly.'

'But I thought her name was Campbell,' Miss Laidlaw said.

'That's what she calls herself now,' Mrs. Irvine said. 'It was her mother's maiden name, so there's no harm in using it. She doesn't like her own name. And I can't say that I blame her either. You know what young girls are and what daft notions they get. But she'll grow out of it.'

'Oh, yes, she'll grow out of it.' Mrs. Munro shook her head of wispy grey hair and pressed her rimless glasses more firmly on her small pointed nose. 'What I always say is: Once a girl has to battle with life——'

'My godfathers, that reminds me!' Mrs. Irvine rose. 'I told her to put on the macaroni-cheese for the boarders' supper before she went out. I must look at it before it's burned to a frazzle.'

'I wouldn't dream of giving my boarders "kitchen" for their supper,' Miss Laidlaw said when Mrs. Irvine returned with a heightened colour and panting slightly. 'I simply wouldn't dream of it. All mine get is a cup of co-co-a and a biscuit. It's quite enough for them.'

'Well, I don't know,' Mrs. Irvine said. 'Time was when you could be choosey with boarders, and if they didn't like what they got they could lump it. But things are a bit different these days. I'm down to two, you know. Two, and this is a big house and takes a lot of running. My godfathers, I never thought I'd be reduced to two boarders, otherwise I'd never have given up my old flat and taken on this house. I don't mind admitting that I'm worried to death about it, wondering how I'm going to pay all the rates and taxes. I've only got old Mr. McQuarrie left, and young Donald with the clubfoot that's coming out for a doctor. All the others have been called up.'

'Thank goodness, my boarders are all ladies,' Mrs. Munro said.

'Oh, they might get called up, too,' Mrs. Irvine said. 'You never know these days. After all, Ernest Bevin more or less said that women would be called up as well as men.'

'I never could abide that man, Attlee,' Miss Laidlaw said. 'I can't abide any of that crowd. What right had Attlee to say that he could take property of any kind? He's got a damned cool cheek, if you'll excuse my language. I don't like any of these Socialists in the new Government. That Attlee and Herbert Morrison—what right have they to be spouting about sacrifice and equality and all that?'

'Well, things look bad,' Mrs. Irvine pointed out. 'Especially with this Dunkirk business. It's a terrible thing when we've got to this state.'

'I know things look bad,' Miss Laidlaw said. 'I must say I didn't like it when Mr. Churchill said he had nothing to offer us but blood, toil, sweat and tears. I didn't like it at all. I'm a one for my comforts, and I don't care who knows it.'

'Ah, but we've all got to make our sacrifices,' Mrs. Munro said. 'What I always say is: If you don't work hard for a thing you don't appreciate it when you get it. Look at Mr. Churchill himself. My word, how that man has worked to get where he is now! And he's had a hard struggle with everyone against him. We'd be a lot better off today if we had listened to his advice years ago and put *That Hitler* in his place.'

'Yes, Mr. Churchill's a wonderful man,' Mrs. Dallas sighed sentimentally. 'He'll pull us through all right.'

'Well, all I can say is: he'll have a lot of pulling,' Mrs. Irvine said. 'For things are *very* bad. I wouldn't be at all surprised if we were invaded.'

There was a shocked silence, then Miss Laidlaw cried: 'Mrs. Irvine! Do you know what you're saying, Mrs. Irvine? My goodness, you'd think you were a Fifth Columnist.' And she laughed to show that she was joking, although there was a tremor of doubt in her laughter and in the looks which she darted at the other ladies.

'Well, I might as well say what I think,' Mrs. Irvine said. 'As long as we still have freedom to say what we think, for by God, if old Hitler comes across here there'll be no freedom of speech left. And that day might be nearer than any of us care to think. I don't like this Dunkirk business at all. First there was the Belgians surrendering, and then this mad gallop across France. The Jerries are seemingly sweeping everything in front of them.'

'That reminds me, it's six o'clock,' Mrs. Munro cried in alarm. 'We'd better listen to the News.'

They switched on the radio, and almost as soon as they heard the announcer, Mrs. Dallas whispered: 'It's Alvar Liddell,' but Miss Laidlaw shushushed her and said: 'It's

Stuart Hibberd. I know Stuart's voice almost as well as I know my own.'

'. . . for the 3rd of June, 1940. The evacuation of the B.E.F. from Dunkirk has been completed. A quarter of a million British soldiers have been rescued together with 112,000 Allied troops, but all their equipment has been lost. . . .'

They sat in stunned silence, and listened to the bitter end.

'My godfathers,' Mrs. Irvine said at last. 'That means that now we're completely surrounded. Old Hitler'll start to invade us at any minute.'

'Who'd have thought six weeks ago that things would come to this?' Mrs. Munro cried. 'I tell you what it is—the French have let us down. What I always say is: You should never trust foreigners.'

III

Bessie Campbell was fuming as she hurried to meet Lily McGillivray at the Wellington Monument at the East end of Princes Street. Not only had Mrs. Irvine made her late by asking her to prepare the macaroni-cheese for the lodgers— 'I'm damned if I'll call them boarders to suit her, the old bitch!'—but she had infuriated her with her remarks about Lily.

After all, she had chummed about with Lily for years and years, and it was none of Mrs. Irvine's business. Mrs. Irvine was like her father: too fond of poking her nose into things that didn't concern her. That had always been one of the troubles at home: the way her father went on about Lily, saying 'She'll land up by being a tart,' and 'You keep away from her, my lassie, or you'll live to regret it.' In a way, maybe her father had some right to say things like that, but Mrs. Irvine had no right whatsoever, and the quicker she learned that the better.

Stuck up old besom with all her airs and graces. And the way she was aye going on about 'you're living in a different class of society now.' It fair made you sick. Especially when

11

she called these dried-up old hens of landladies, who came to visit her for tea and a gossip, 'a better class of people than the kind you've been accustomed to.'

Bessie sniffed with indignation as she got off a number six tram at the Post Office and hurried across Princes Street to the Monument. It was two minutes past six on the clock above the North British Station Hotel. She was late, but apparently Lily was later, for there was no sign of her among the crowd milling around the Monument. Bessie stood as close to it as she could get and leaned her back against the wall of the Register House. She thrust her hands deep into the pockets of her short scarlet jigger coat, and scowled at the toe of one of her bright red shoes.

She was still smarting because Mrs. Irvine had not asked her to have tea with the visitors before she came out. It wasn't that she liked any of the old hags, mind you, it was just that she didn't see why she should have tea in the kitchen while they had theirs in the sitting-room. After all, she was as good as them, wasn't she? Her father would likely say 'a damned sight better,' but that was neither here nor there. You would have thought that Mrs. Irvine would have had the decency to ask her—especially since she and Mrs. Irvine always had their meals together. Really, Mrs. Irvine was a right funny one sometimes. One minute she was all chummy and ready for a joke, and then the next she would go all hoity-toity and shove her neb in the air as though she were Lady Muck herself.

'Hya, Ferret, you look as though you'd lost a shilling and found a sixpence!'

Lily McGillivray's greeting and the raucous giggle which followed drove Mrs. Irvine's shortcomings from Bessie's mind.

'Don't tell me ye're worried about the news from France,' Lily jibed. 'Everybody's that down in the mouth about this business at Dunkirk. You'd think it was the Judgment Day or somethin'. My father's been goin' his mile about it, sayin' the bloody French have let us down. Of course, my auld man's aye shootin' off his neck about something. I told him it was high time he was up in Parliament runnin' the War for us. Jesus Christ and General Jackson, we'd get a shock then!'

'Me! I haven't got time to worry about the war,' Bessie said. 'I've got ower many other things to take up my attention. That auld besom Irvine's been on the war-path again tonight.'

'I told you,' Lily said. 'I told you she was an auld tartar and that you were a bloody fool to take a job wi' her. I never liked the woman. A two-faced twister, that's what she is. I'll aye mind the time in Andrews' when she turned on me tooth and nail and said——'

'Come on, it's a quarter past six!' Bessie grabbed Lily's arm. 'There'll be a queue at the Playhouse if we don't hurry up.'

'Och, ye're no' wantin' to go to the picters, are ye?'

'Of course, we're goin' to the picters,' Bessie said. 'You know fine that we arranged to go and see Margaret Lockwood.'

'Och, I'm no' in the mood for the picters.' Lily teetered on her high heels and looked at the groups of young soldiers and civilians standing around the Monument.

'But you promised, Lily!'

'Ay, but that was last week and a lot of things have happened since,' Lily said. 'All this evacuation at Dunkirk for instance. I don't think it's right for us to go to the pictures when this is happenin'. It's no' patriotic, my auld man says, when sae many men have been killed and drowned.'

'Huh, ye're surely awfie pally wi' yer auld man if ye're listenin' to all his palavers,' Bessie said.

'Well, there's somethin' in what he says,' Lily ruminated, eyeing a hefty soldier in a kilt, who was standing a few feet away and glancing at them every now and then. 'He says we might get invaded at any minute. Things are real bad, he says, and you never know the moment.'

The soldier began to walk backwards and forwards in front of them, his kilt swinging, and his glengarry cocked at a jaunty angle.

'You'll better get your rifle out, Ferret,' Lily giggled. 'You'll maybe soon need it. By God, it'll be the day when

I see you crouchin' behind the barricades, takin' pot-shots at Jerry!'

Bessie pushed out her lower lip and sighed with resignation: 'Well, what're we goin' to do if we're not goin' to the pictures?'

'Och, just wait a wee and we'll consider it,' Lily said, re-arranging the scarf on her head and drawing her peroxided curls further out on her cheeks. That done, she thrust her hands deep into the pockets of her jigger coat and pushed out her behind.

The kiltie stopped his perambulation to light a cigarette. As he bent forward to the match flaring in his cupped paw he winked at the girls.

Lily giggled and thrust back her shoulders. 'I tell you what,' she said in a voice loud enough for the soldier to hear, 'let's go across to Rutherford's Bar and have a drink.'

'Oh no,' Bessie cried. 'No, I wouldnie dare. My father would kill me if he found out. And so would Mrs. Irvine. Besides, I'm ower young, they wouldnie serve me. And they wouldnie serve you either if they knew ye were just seventeen. It's only because ye look aulder that ye get away wi' it.'

'Och, you look aulder, too,' Lily said. 'C'mon, nobody'll be any the wiser.'

But Bessie hung back, and at the same time the kiltie waved a greeting to another soldier at the edge of the pavement and strode away with a swing of his kilt.

'Look what ye've done,' Lily said. 'That one was all set to pick us up, but ye've frightened him away with yer silly shillyshallyin'. Ye'll just have to get used to goin' into pubs, Hippy, if ye're goin' to come out wi' me.'

'You know fine that I dinnie like pubs,' Bessie said. 'The only time I ever was in one was that time Big Ginger the vanman at Andrews' pushed me in and made a pass at me. The dirty big brute, and him wi' a wife and three bairns!'

'Och, worse things than that'll happen to ye before ye get much older,' Lily said, scanning the crowds with an anxious eye. 'We've gone and lost that kiltie, anyway, wi' you openin' your big mouth too wide. How was he to ken we were under-age for pubs?'

'Anyway,' she said, 'I'm a married woman now and can go into a pub if I like."

'Well, I dinnie like,' Bessie said.

'All right, all right, keep your hair on,' Lily said. 'C'mon, let's take a bit dander along Princes Street and see what we can see.'

'I wish it was the winter-time again,' she said, as they pranced arm-in-arm past Woolworths, shoulders thrust back and behinds stuck out jauntily. They threaded their way slowly along with the crowd, their too-high heels making them walk in a slightly knock-kneed manner. 'I'm at my best in the blackout. You feel freer-like in it. I wouldnie have let that kiltie get away so easy if it had been the blackout.'

'I don't see what you're needin' to pick anybody up for,' Bessie said. 'You that's got Tommy and all.'

'Och, Tommy's away in the middle o' the ocean and he'll likely be away for months and months,' Lily said. 'What do you expect me to do, Hippy? Sit at home and knit socks like an auld granny?'

'I wish you'd stop callin' me Hippy,' Bessie said. 'I've told ye time and time again that I've changed my name to Campbell.'

'You and your daft notions!' Lily jeered. 'Hipkiss you were born and Hipkiss you'll die—unless ye get married, of course. Which I very much doubt, if ye keep goin' at the rate ye're goin' at. Terrified even to wink at a felly. I don't know what's come ower ye lately, Ferret. You used to have more spunk in you. I'm sure when you worked in Andrews' you were after the lads as often as I was.'

'Och, I know,' Bessie sighed. 'But I never seemed to get anybody I really *liked*.'

'There was that Jim Whatsisname,' Lily said. 'You liked him all right—until ye took a scunner at his name. What was it again? Stinky or something?'

'Smellie,' Bessie said. 'Jim Smellie. I couldnie have married a felly with a name like that.'

15

'Och, what does it matter what their names are? So long as you get one that'll marry ye so that ye can get an allowance from the Government. Jesus Christ and General Jackson, it'll not worry me if I never see Tommy Hutchinson again so long as I get my money regularly every week.'

'Aw, Lily, what a like thing to say!' Bessie was so horrified that she stopped in the middle of the pavement.

'C'mon, dinnie be a sap!' Lily pulled her arm, taking the opportunity at the same time to smile at three Norwegian sailors who were passing. 'You know fine I don't really mean it. Tommy's all right, I guess. Still, at the same time you're only young once and you might as well have a bit of fun while the going's good.'

They continued their walk, prancing in a seemingly aimless fashion, although Lily kept her eyes open for every likely man that passed. And there were a number—soldiers, sailors, civilians, and on scarcely a face was there any sign of the tremendous historical event which was shaking Britain at the moment. Although uniforms predominated, it might have been any crowd out for a stroll in the main street of any great city on any summer evening in peacetime. Young people prevailed, and each looked as though he or she was out for any kind of adventure. Heads were continually being turned, and looks and winks were freely exchanged.

'It's Friday night, and Friday night's pay night and everybody's out on the randan,' Lily said, squeezing Bessie's arm.

'What a lot of funny uniforms there are,' Bessie said.

'Ay, there's a lot o' foreigners. They seem to have sprung up all of a sudden. Norwegians and French and all sorts. I suppose some o' them have come from Dunkirk already.' Lily turned to look at a soldier in a drab olive-green uniform with peculiar mauve facings. 'Now, what can that one be? You could tell he was a foreigner even without the uniform. He has a funny flat sort o' face.'

'Maybe he was a Pole?' Bessie said.

'God knows,' Lily said. 'I thought they'd all been killed in Poland—that is if you're to believe everythin' you hear on the wireless—but nothin' would surprise me.'

16

'Nor me,' Bessie giggled.

They had reached the West End. They stood for a few minutes outside Binns' huge windows and looked at the display. 'Fancy you in that red and black rigout!' Lily said. 'You'd be a smasher!'

She turned and watched the crowds passing. 'Well, I suppose we'd better just go back again,' she said, cleeking her arm into Bessie's. 'We'll just walk along Princes Street two or three times, then if nothin' turns up we'll go into the Golden Sallymander and have some fish 'n' chips. It's a bit early to click yet, but we're bound to click wi' somebody in the Sallymander sooner or later.'

IV

About eleven o'clock Bessie put her key in the door, opened it quietly, and was slipping stealthily upstairs when Mrs. Irvine shouted:

'Is that you, Bessie?'

Bessie hesitated, wondering if she should continue upstairs as though she had never heard. There would be a chance then that Mrs. Irvine would think it was Mr. McQuarrie—she would know it wasn't young Donald, who made a terrific thumping with his game-leg. But before she could do anything the sitting-room door opened and Mrs. Irvine came out.

'What a like time of night for a young lassie to come in at!' she cried. 'My godfathers! You young girls! If I'd dared come in as late as this when I was your age, my father would have ham-strung me.'

'Well,' Bessie began. 'I really couldnie help it. It was Lily. . . .' But before she could say any more, Mrs. Irvine said: 'We've got three new boarders.'

'Three!' Bessie clutched the banister.

'Three French soldiers,' Mrs. Irvine said. 'Or officers, I should say. Three very nice young gentlemen. Fair charmers! They kissed my hand and everything until I felt like the Duchess of Dantzig. I just wish my daughter in New York

17

could have seen her auld mother extending her hand and receiving just like Queen Mary herself.'

'Fancy, three French soldiers!' Bessie said softly.

'Officers, m'dear. Don't forget that!' Mrs. Irvine said. 'My word, I'll have something to blow about to Mrs. Munro now! Yes, one of these billeting-officers brought them, and he told me he'd have more for us within the next day or two. He took down all particulars about how many the house would hold and everything. He said we might have to put up more beds and put two or three in a room. It looks as though you and me are to be kept busy, m'dear.'

'Well, away with you!' she said. 'Get some sleep, for you'll have to be up early in the morning to prepare everything for them. They want their breakfast at eight. Sharp.'

Bessie would have lingered for more information, but Mrs. Irvine said: 'Scram now when you're told! Another cheep out of you and I'll be asking awkward questions about what kept you out to this time o' night.'

Bessie giggled softly to herself when she reached her small attic-room. Awkward questions right enough. If Mrs. Irvine just knew the half of it. What a night she and Lily had had. And now this coming on top of it!

Three French officers . . . what would they be like? As she undressed quickly and dropped her clothes on the chair beside the bed, she conjured up pictures of tall, dark, handsome men with sweeping moustaches and flashing eyes who would bend over her hand and murmur 'Enchanted, madame, enchanted!' And she picked up the hem of her thin nightgown and swept a curtsy, saying: 'Voila, gentlemen, voila!'

But no, that wouldn't do, she thought, getting into bed and snuggling down. Princesses didn't curtsy to officers. They just stood as straight as they could and gave them a fish-like look as they put out their hands to be kissed. For she would have to remember that she was Elizabeth, Duchess de Braganza, Madame Royale of France, and that these blokes were her subjects. She would receive them in the powder-blue drawing-room, sitting on a gilt chair, and she would say: 'What news from Paris, messieurs? Does France stand where she did?'

And then she would tell them to be of good cheer and that all would soon be well again and the war would be over and her father, King Robert I, would soon be returning from his long exile to make France a great country again.

The officers sprang to attention, and one of them shouted: 'Vive le roi!'

Madame Royale inclined her head, smiling slightly. 'And now, gentlemen, I shall not detain you,' she said. 'I know you are tired and have had a long journey. I shall arrange for you to have audience with His Majesty tomorrow morning. . . .'

The sound of Mrs. Irvine coming upstairs and switching off the light in the passage broke into her fantasy.

Bessie sighed and pounded her pillow into a more comfortable shape. It was like what she had said to Lily tonight: 'You know, Lil, I scarcely have time to call ma soul ma own these days, what wi' one thing and another. If it's no' Mrs. Irvine yellin' *Bessie, hurry up and get thur beds made,* it's one o' thae bloody lodgers shoutin' for his breakfast or for his boots to be cleaned or somethin'. I get right fed up sometimes. I never seem to have a minit to masel'. You know what a lot I used to read? Well, I never get a book opened frae one week's end to the next.'

'I cannie even get peace to think,' she had said as they went into the Golden Salamander café.

'Ach, why worry, Ferret!' Lily said, prancing ahead and stretching her neck in search of a table. 'It's only daft folk that think. Lookit ma faither worryin' his brains into train-oil aboot the war and the way it's bein' run. I tell you, Bess, it doesnie pay to think. The folk that get on best in this world are the ones that never worry and barge straight ahead.'

'Well, I dunno,' Bessie said. 'I like to be able to sit and sort of let my mind wander. You know . . .'

'Here's a table,' Lily cried. 'C'mon, park your arse before somebody else nabs it.'

The Golden Salamander café was a popular rendezvous for a certain section of the youth of Edinburgh. Early in the evenings it was simply an ordinary café where people had supper or high tea, but about eight o'clock its clientele started to change. In twos and threes, girls like Bessie and Lily flounced in and commandeered tables where they sat, drinking coffee after coffee. Although they chatted and giggled to each other, all the time they watched the door with avaricious expressions. Every young man who entered was sized-up, and if found worthy of attention there was a great deal of ogling and giggling until some contact was made. Because of the war, most of the pubs closed at half-past nine, and after that the male population drifted in in greater numbers. The Golden Salamander did not close until ten-thirty or eleven, and for the last hour it was crowded to capacity. Often a queue waited patiently at the door, hoping that some of those at the tables would rise and go away into the blackout so that they could take their places even for only a few minutes. It was seldom, however, that those already seated gave up their tables. Once in, they were there until they had to be almost forcibly ejected by the manager and the commissionaire at closing-time.

Being early and having obtained a table in a good position, Lily was all set to make the most of it. She unpinned the garish silk square she was wearing over her head and threw it back on her shoulders with a royal air.

'Cheer up, Ferret!' she said. 'We'll soon be dead!' And she tittered as she beckoned a waitress and ordered fish and chips and coffee.

'I think I'll have tea,' Bessie said diffidently.

'Tea! What d'ye want tea for?' Lily said, and then as soon as the waitress had gone: 'It's common to drink tea, ye silly mug. All the classy folk drink coffee.'

'I dinnie like coffee,' Bessie said.

'It's not what ye like, it's what other folk like,' Lily said. 'You'll have to mind that, Bess, if you're ever to get anywhere.'

'I dinnie care,' Bessie said.

'I thought you that was so grand, thinking you're royalty and all that, would have liked to do the classy thing,' Lily giggled.

Bessie stuck out her lower lip, but she said nothing. Once in a burst of confidence she had told Lily about some of her

20

day-dreams: how her family did not really belong to Edinburgh at all but were the Bourbon royal family exiled from France since the Revolution. Lily had hooted with laughter, and Bessie had regretted it ever since. But, thank goodness, Lily hardly ever remembered about it; she was usually too full of her own affairs.

'Lookit that Raf felly with the wallopin' walrus moustache!' Lily nudged Bessie with her knee. 'Across in that corner with the wee pug-nosed bitch in pink. Lookit the way he's gazin' at her, as if he could eat her. My God, he's welcome to her, too. He'll get indigestion if he doesnie watch out. She should ken better than wear pink with that sallow complexion.'

'Ach, you're jealous!' Bessie said.

'Jealous my foot!' Lily said. 'I wouldnie have him in a gift. That moustache! *Feech,* it would be like bein' kissed by a bicycle!'

She attacked her fish and chips, shovelling them into her mouth without looking at her plate. 'No, this is more in my line,' she said, nodding at the door.

Bessie turned and saw two Norwegian sailors threading their way between the tables. One of them, a large blond young man with two or three soft chins, stopped and looked around in a calculating way. There were still several vacant tables, but he disregarded them. Hands thrust into the top of his tight trousers, he looked boldly at all the ogling girls. His small, dark companion plucked his elbow and motioned towards an empty table in a corner. But the large sailor said something in a guttural voice, laughed, and came up to the table where Lily and Bessie were sitting.

'Sit here, yes?' he said, bowing with exaggerated politeness over the back of the chair he was already drawing out.

'Okay by us!' Lily said.

'Okay, okay!' The large sailor laughed and pushed his friend into the other seat. He sat down himself, spreading his huge thighs firmly, and he beamed at the girls. 'Me, Olaf,' he said, thumping his broad chest with the flat of one large golden-haired hand. 'This—Eric!'

'Olaf, Eric!' he said again.

'Me, Lily Hutchinson,' Lily said in a loud voice, pointing to herself. 'This my friend, Bessie Hip—Bessie Campbell.'

'Lilee? Bessee?' Olaf grinned, delighted with himself. But the small sailor looked around sulkily, twiddling his cap between his knees.

'We are *good* girls,' Lily giggled.

Olaf made a sneering face. 'Norwegian sailor no like goot girls.'

'Oh, but we have our moments,' Lily said, and she winked. 'Haven't we, Bess?'

'Too true!' Bessie giggled in imitation of Lily.

Eric looked even more sulky. 'No like girls,' he said. 'No like Scottish girls.'

'Ach, away with you!' Lily said. 'You haven't had time yet to see whether you like them or not.'

'Olaf like Scottish girls,' Olaf said. 'Olaf lo—ove Scottish girls.' And he pressed Lily's knees between his own.

'Here, here, you're too fast a worker!' Lily cried, and she gave him a playful slap on the arm.

Bessie sat silent. She never knew what to do on occasions like this, and she envied the way Lily was able to laugh and banter with Olaf. She knew that her role was to draw the sulky dark sailor into conversation, but she could think of nothing to say. It was bad enough when it was English or Scots fellows—though you could always speak about the weather to them—but what could you do with foreigners? She realised that here was a chance to emulate Bette Davis or Hedy Lamarr. They wouldn't sit like this, staring at the pepper and salt dishes; they would break into fluent Norwegian and wave their hands and look languorous. Or they would just look languorous, and the sailor would do the rest.

But this sailor didn't look as though he were going to make any effort. He sat hunched in his chair, twirling his cap round and round. Bessie rubbed her sweating palms against her knees, aware that Lily's toe was tapping her ankle. 'Go on!' Lily was saying to Olaf. 'You say that to all the girls.'

Bessie reached over and took Eric's cap from him. 'Ship?'

she said, trying to speak in a loud voice like Lily. 'What do you call it? Ship?'

Eric repeated the name of his vessel in a bored voice. Bessie giggled and said it after him. 'Nice ship?' she said. 'Nice ship! Nice girls!'

Lying safely in bed, she thought again of what uphill work it had been. She had been glad when the café had filled up and she had been able to let her attention stray to the other tables. All the time Lily and Olaf had laughed and wrestled playfully with each other, Lily's voice getting louder and louder as she said: 'Now, less of it, sailor! Less of it! You don't know me that well yet!' And so it had gone on until closing-time, with Eric scowling at the table-cloth or into his coffee cup. So that Bessie had been furious when Lily had nudged her and whispered: 'There's that kiltie again. See, over there with that awful-like dame with the red bandeau. You'd have thought he'd've picked up somethin' better, wouldn't you?'

Yes, if it had been that kiltie, Bessie thought now, she would have had a better time. At least she would have known what to talk to him about. It was all very well for Lily— all that Lily cared about was to have her as a stooge. Lily always managed to pick the best ones for herself. And Lily hadn't lost much time in making a date with Olaf for the following evening. Trust Lily, her that was a married woman and all. But *she* always got landed with the dumb ones. Thank goodness, he hadn't tried to make a date with her.

Still, she thought, pushing away the sheet from her hot shoulders, maybe she would get on better with the three French officers. Surely they wouldn't be as dour and donnert as that Eric. And one good thing: she'd be able to speak to them in their own language.

'Parly voo France, monsieur?' she said to the tallest and best-looking one.

'Mais oui, madame,' he murmured, bending over her hand, which was blazing with diamonds and emeralds, and kissing it. . . .

But there was nothing glamorous about any of the French officers at breakfast the next morning. They were bleary-eyed and looked as though they had slept in their uniforms for a week. They were small men with nothing spectacular about them. I wouldn't turn round in the street to look after one of them, Bessie thought. And they may have made a great fuss over Mrs. Irvine, kissing her hand and all that, but they certainly did not make any fuss with her. 'Hurry up, please!' one said sharply. 'We are late. Please to have breakfast one half hour more early tomorrow.'

Usually Bessie did not bother about her appearance until the late afternoon, but this morning she had done her hair with great care and put on powder and lipstick. The officers ignored her, however; they spoke rapidly to each other, gesticulating with every few words. And one, the shortest one who had complained about being late, kept thumping the table to emphasise what he was saying. The name 'De Gaulle' was repeated again and again.

'Well, I dinnie think much o' them,' Bessie said to Mrs. Irvine after they had rushed out, still haranguing each other.

'Och, I think they're very nice,' Mrs. Irvine said. 'We'll get used to them once we begin to understand their lingo.'

All forenoon as she dusted and cleaned and ran errands, Bessie rehearsed the scraps of French she still remembered from her schooldays and from her reading of the novels of Alexandre Dumas. 'Allons, mes enfants!' she murmured as she washed the lunch-dishes. 'C'est la plume de ma tante! Tiens!' But in the afternoon all these were scattered from her mind as though by one sweep of a gigantic brush. The billeting-officer arrived with two more boarders.

'Lieutenant Klosowski,' he said. 'And Lieutenant Rolewicz.'

The Polish soldiers clicked their heels and bowed stiffly from the waist. 'Madame,' the dark one said, bending over Mrs.

Irvine's hand and kissing it. He stepped back and sprang to attention. 'Klosowski,' he said. 'Dmitri Klosowski.'

Bessie stood in the shadow of the kitchen door and peered along the passage at them. Mrs. Irvine smiled and inclined her head regally. 'How do you do?' she said in a very loud voice, enunciating each syllable as though she were speaking to a deaf person.

The tall blond Pole, who was very handsome, despite his sullen olive-greyish face, the colour of shagreen, and a deep scar on his forehead, bowed over her hand and kissed it. He, too, sprang to attention. But he did not speak, and the dark lieutenant waved his hand at him, smiling so that he showed three gold teeth, and said: 'My friend. Rolewicz. Josef Rolewicz. He does not spik ze Engleesh.'

'Ah, but he will learn, he will learn,' Mrs. Irvine said, and she smiled condescendingly as she led the way upstairs.

Bessie tingled with excitement as she went back to the sink. Lily can keep her Norwegian sailor, she thought, plunging her hands into soapy water and scrubbing industriously at a pot. That Olaf's just a common or garden sailor, but these blokes are officers. And she hurried through her work, singing *Tonight my heart will sing the sweetest song of them all ta ra ti ta titita la la la at evenfall.* . . .

'Well, we're fairly doing it!' Mrs. Irvine cried, bursting into the kitchen. 'Five officers in the house! We're getting fair international!'

'Mind you,' Mrs. Irvine said, rolling up her sleeves and preparing to fry fish for high tea, 'I don't know whether we should be glad or sorry about it. I suppose it's just a sign of the times. Our own boarders are taken away with one hand and we get foreign boarders shoved on us with the other. I haven't made up my mind yet whether it's a good thing or not. This damned war has a lot to answer for. It takes our own poor lads away and dumps them down in some foreign country and dumps these poor foreigners down here—not able to speak the language or anything. We'll just have to try and be as nice to them as we can, Bessie.'

'Too true!' Bessie giggled.

'Mind you, it's going to be difficult,' Mrs. Irvine said, slapping fish into sizzling fat. 'None of them speak very good English—and that Josef one doesn't speak it at all! I shouted as loud as I could to him and spoke as slow as I can, but he never gee—ed his ginger. He just stared at me with those big solemn eyes of his. I hope they're not all as dumb as him!'

But there was no sign of dumbness about any of them when they gathered round the tea-table. Bessie's ears were strained almost to bursting point as she tried to make out what they were all saying. The three Frenchmen gesticulated and shouted to each other at one end of the table; the two Poles talked rapidly and moodily at the other. In between, uneasily, Mr. McQuarrie and young Donald did their best to appear at ease among the aliens. Young Donald aired his French, passing pepper and salt politely, and when his French failed he imitated Mrs. Irvine in talking in an unnaturally loud and slow voice. But Mr. McQuarrie, napkin tucked into the top of his dark waistcoat, gave most of his attention to his food.

'Lot of damned yaps,' he muttered to Bessie as he passed her in the passage after the meal. 'I don't know what the world's coming to.'

Donald, however, was quite pleased with the foreign invasion. He clumped into the kitchen later that evening and sat down with some text-books at the end of the table. 'D'you mind if I sit in here?' he asked Bessie. 'I've got to prepare for a little exam on Monday, and I can't hear myself think in the sitting-room. I don't mind them talking; it'll improve my French and maybe I'll be able to pick up some Polish. But they've got the wireless on as well, and I can't concentrate for it.'

'It's okay by me,' Bessie said. 'I'll not disturb ye. I've got all thur dishes to wash, and that'll keep me quiet for a good while.'

Donald opened one of his text-books, but after reading a few lines he said: 'What do you think of the new arrivals, Bessie?'

26

' I think they're all right,' she said. ' They seem nice enough fellies.'

' You'd better watch them,' he said. ' They'll be giving you the glad-eye before you can cough! '

' Ach, away! ' she giggled.

' You'll have to watch the Poles especially,' he bantered. ' I hear they're hot stuff with women.'

' Ach, I can take care o' myself,' Bessie sniggered.

' That's what you think! ' he grinned. ' Anyway, they'll brighten the house up a bit—though I hope they don't stay in every night and keep that wireless blaring with foreign news bulletins.'

When she had finished washing the dishes, Bessie looked at Donald to see that he was safely deep in study, then she went along to the sitting-room. Mrs. Irvine was away to a Spiritualist meeting, so Bessie knew she had nothing to fear from that direction. The roar of the wireless greeted her as she neared the door. She stopped for a second, touching her hair while she rehearsed her excuse: 'I've just come to get last night's *Evening News*.' Then she gave a light tap and went in.

The room was empty.

Bessie gaped with dismay. She peered into the dusk to see that none of them was sitting in the shadows. But there was nobody. She sighed and went to turn off the radio. But before her hand reached the switch she decided that she might as well have some dance music. It was no fun in the kitchen with Donald sitting there poring over his books. She leaned against the radio, twirling the knobs and staring vacantly into space.

' Jairmany calling! Jairmany calling on the nine-metre band! '

' That bloody Haw-Haw! ' she cried, and she turned the knobs furiously until dance music filled the room.

She was jazzing up and down, pretending that she was dancing with Robert Taylor in the Brown Derby in Hollywood when Donald opened the door.

' Hello,' he said. ' Nobody here? '

'No, they're all away,' she said. 'They all went and left the wireless on.'

'And the lights were blazin',' she said in an effort to take Donald's attention away from her dancing alone. 'Blazin', though there's no need for them yet, and the blackout's no' up. They want us to have the polis here complainin'. We'll have to get Mrs. Irvine on their track. They'll have to learn to economize like the rest o' us.'

That night when Bessie was going to bed, Lieutenant Klosowski passed her on his way to the bathroom. He stood aside to let her pass, but the corridor was narrow and she smelled the wave of alcohol that came from him. 'Good eveneeng,' he grinned. 'Veree nice night.'

Bessie smiled foolishly and sidled past him. He was not much taller than herself, but his solid body made him appear much larger. His lean dark face with its high Slav cheekbones seemed to loom over her, and instinctively she shrank against the wall.

'Veree nice Scotch girl,' he said, flashing his gold teeth, and he put out his hand and touched her arm.

'Och, away!' she giggled.

And she hurried up the last stair to her own room. She glanced down and saw that he was watching her. 'Good night,' he called, and he took a step towards her.

'Good night,' she cried.

She shut the door behind her and leaned against it, surprised to feel that her legs were trembling. And even after she was in bed she could still see the Polish officer's brown brooding eyes boring into her with a catlike intensity, as though he were going to strike.

VI

The following evening, being Sunday, Bessie went to see her father and stepmother. It was two or three weeks since she had visited them, and she would not have gone tonight if Mrs. Irvine hadn't insisted upon it. 'It's high time you

paid them a wee visit, m'dear,' she said. 'Otherwise, they'll
be blaming me for keeping you here.'

Bessie was annoyed, for Lily McGillivray had telephoned
and told her to meet her at nine o'clock. However, she decided
to make the best of it. It would be a good excuse for getting
away early, she thought as she got off a number eight tram
at Harrisfield Square and started up the hill towards the tenements at Calderburn.

A group of youths and girls met her on the brow of the hill.
'Hya, Hippy!' called one of them, a girl from a neighbouring
street. 'Haven't seen ye for ages. Where're ye hidin' yersel'
these days?'

'Oh, I'm working in a hotel,' Bessie said in the voice she
kept for speaking to the boarders. 'Got an awfully nice job.
A lovely job.'

'Some folk ha'e a' the luck,' the girl said. 'Well,' she
turned to hurry after her companions, eyeing Bessie up and
down as she did so, 'I'll be seein' ye! See and no' do anythin'
I wouldnie do!'

'No fear!' Bessie said.

She heard them laughing and some of the youths hooting
after her, but she did not give them the satisfaction of turning
round. She held her shoulders straight and pranced on.

Goldengreen Street was just the same as usual. Radios
brayed from open windows. Some boys were playing football at the top of the street. A number of women and a few
men leaned on windowsills, gaping down into the street,
shouting greetings to the passers-by. Bessie did not look upwards as she turned into the entry of number sixteen. She
opened her handbag and pretended to be fumbling inside it
for a key, so that she would not need to glance at the windows
across the street where she guessed that Mrs. Moore and Dirty
Minnie would be watching her. Every second she expected
to hear a raucous shout: 'Bessie! Hey there, Bessie Hipkiss,
are ye blind!' But she got safely into the entry without
interruption.

Mabel Hipkiss opened the door. 'Oh, it's you, is it?' she
said.

'Ay,' Bessie said, brushing past her stepmother.

'So it's Her Ladyship herself, is it?' her father said, looking up from his newspaper. 'My God, we're honoured the night, aren't we, Jenny?'

Jenny Hipkiss looked up from her seat on the hearthrug. 'It's Stinky Bessie! What did ye bring me, Bessie? Have ye brought sweeties?'

'Ay, I've got some in ma bag.' Bessie bent to kiss her small sister. 'How are ye, hen? Are ye still a guid wee girl?' she said, brushing Jenny's hair back from her forehead.

'Where are they?' Jenny squealed. 'Gi'e them to me quick afore Billy comes in! He's no' to get ony, isn't he no', Daddy? He's a bad bad boy!'

'All in good time, all in good time,' Mabel Hipkiss said. 'Give the bag to me, Bessie. I'll give her them tomorrow. She's had enough sweets for one day.'

'No, now! Now!' Jenny cried.

'Do what your Mammy says, my wee hen,' Bert Hipkiss said.

Jenny lay back on the rug and drummed her heels. 'I want them now,' she cried.

'Well, you're not getting them now,' Mabel said, putting the bag at the back of a cupboard well out of Jenny's reach. 'Sweeties are getting too scarce to be gutsed down like this. You'll have to learn to save them, my lady. They'll be getting put on the ration one of these days.'

'I dinnie care, I want them NOW!' Jenny shouted, drumming her heels harder.

'Now, now, ma wee doo!' her father said.

Jenny sat up on her hunkers, and a cunning smile came over her four-years-old face. 'I want them now,' she said. 'Or else! Or else I'll say a BAD word.'

'Jenny!' Bessie was shocked, although she knew her small sister's tactics of old.

'Do you want some tea, Bessie?' Mabel said. 'We've had ours, but I can easy make you a fresh pot.'

'Well, I suppose I could,' Bessie said. 'But if it's any bother——'

'I could be doing with another cup myself,' Mabel said, going into the scullery to put on the kettle.

'I wanta sweetie!' Jenny screamed. 'I wanta sweetie! You buggis!'

'Aw, Jenny, ye know that Bessie doesnie like to hear ye say thae bad words,' Bessie said, bending over her. She looked at her father. 'D'ye no' think we could let her have just one, Da?'

'You heard what your mother said.' Bert picked up his paper. 'Now, Jenny, that's enough, my wee hen, you'll get a sweetie tomorrow, if you're good.'

While Bessie drank her tea, Mabel Hipkiss plied her with questions about the boarding-house and Mrs. Irvine. 'Is she still going to as many Spiritualist meetings?' she said.

'Just once a week,' Bessie said.

Her father guffawed. 'Once too many in ma opinion. Ye'd think she'd get more to take up her attention. Goin' and listenin' to a lot o' daft havers about spooks and spirit-controls and other planes! The daft auld geezer! I hope you don't go to any o' them with her, my lady?'

'Well—er—I've been once,' Bessie said.

'Ay, and once is enough,' he said. 'Once is too often, if ye ask me.'

Bessie said nothing. In all she had attended four Spiritualist Circles with Mrs. Irvine, each time hoping to get in touch with the spirit of her dead mother. But she did not dare tell her father that. In any case, each attempt had been unsuccessful, so she was determined to say nothing about it until she had something to tell. Besides, she would not say anything before *that woman* who sat so calmly now in her mother's place at the other side of the fire from her father.

'We've got five new boarders,' she said, eager to change the subject. 'My goodness, it's a lot of extry work. It seems to me as if I've never been out o' that sink for days and days. Still, they're all nice fellies, and I dinnie mind doin' it.'

'More students?' Mabel said.

'No, the 'varsity'll be closing in a week or two,' Bessie said. 'It's officers.'

31

'Officers!' Mabel cried. 'Well, I never!'

'What kind of officers?' Bert asked.

'Oh, we've got all kinds,' Bessie said. 'Poles and three Frenchies, and the billeting-officer said he'd be back next week wi' more.'

'Dunkirk,' Bert said.

He folded his paper and lit his pipe. 'They haven't taken long to get here. I must say it takes thae foreigners to get crackin' when there's anybody after them wi' a gun. The war hardly started before we had all sorts o' high-rankin' Poles here—counts and colonels and God knows what! And now it seems we're gettin' the rank and file, all commandeering the best billets while our own puir lads are still lyin' at railway-stations or cramped up in wee boats waitin' to get into harbour.'

'Well, after all, Bert, you can't blame them,' Mabel said. 'Just look at what the Poles have gone through since the war started. They must feel in need of some comfort. Poor souls, I'm sure they're all right.'

'Ay, they seem nice enough fellies,' Bessie said, although she was unwilling to find herself on the same side as her step-mother.

'Oh, I suppose they're all right,' Bert conceded. 'I've nothin' against them. But I was just thinkin' it was funny that they should all come here and grab the best places. A month or two ago it was the Danes and the Norwegians, now it's the Poles and the French. The whole country'll soon be overrun wi' foreigners. God knows how many o' them are Fifth Columnists. Hitler's clever, mind, and he's not goin' to lose an opportunity like this for infiltratin'. We're entirely surrounded now, and that clever bugger knows that if he can get help from inside he's got us in the hollow o' his hand.'

'Oh, you said a Bad Word!' Jenny cried.

'You attend to your comic like a guid wee lassie,' Bert said.

'Maybe you're right, Bert,' his wife said. 'I can see that it's a grand chance for the Fifth Column.'

'Aw, I'm sure none o' our Poles are·Fifth Columnists,' Bessie said. 'They're really terribly nice fellies. That

32

Lieutenant Klosowski is a perfect gem, and he's got such lovely manners. I had a long talk wi' him last night. He said what a nice place Edinburgh was, and he asked me if I'd show him round on ma next afternoon-off. He's goin' to teach me Polish.'

'He'll teach you somethin' else if you're no' careful,' her father said. 'Now, look here, my girl, you keep away frae those Poles.'

'But there's nothin' wrong wi' them. You couldnie find a nicer, pleasanter felly than Lieutenant Klosowski. Mrs. Irvine says that she's never met such a perfect gentleman. The way he springs up and opens the door for ye, and bows and everythin'. . . .'

'By God, they're clever,' Bert said. 'Get the women on their sides, and that's more than half the battle. I can see that it's high time I came up and had a bit word wi' Mrs. Irvine. It would be wicer-like if she attended less to her spiritualism and more to her lodgers. She should stop worryin' about what's on the other side and think a bit more about what's happenin' on this.'

'It's high time you got another job, my girl,' he said.

'But——' Bessie's mouth fell open in a whine, preparing for an argument. Before it could start, however, six-years-old Billy Hipkiss burst into the room.

'Hya, Ferret!' he cried. 'I saw ye comin' in. I was playin' football wi' the gang, but ye were too high-and-mighty to see me. What've ye brought us?'

'She brought sweeties!' Jenny cried.

'Where are they?' Billy shouted. 'Hand them over. Quick! I havenie got much time to waste. The gang are ready to start a new match.'

'You'll get no sweeties here tonight, m'man,' his father said. 'And you're not goin' out again either. You're in for the night. It's about time you were in bed.'

Billy stuck out his lower lip and backed to the door, but his stepmother had her hand on the handle.

'Yes, it's time all little girls and boys were in bed,' she said.

'It is nut!' Billy shouted, clenching his fists and glaring

33

at her. 'Who are you talkin' to, anyway? Who's afraid of you? You're just ma Steppy, and I'm no' takin' orders frae you. I'll go to bed when I like.'

'You'll go to bed right now,' his father said. 'It's too late for you to be stravaigin' the streets. It's a quarter past eight.'

'My goodness, is that the time already?' Bessie cried. 'It's time I was away.'

'But you've only just come,' Mabel said.

'Billy, you go and get your face and hands washed like a good boy,' Bert said. 'You, too, Jenny.'

'I'm no' goin' to ma bed,' Jenny cried. 'I'm goin' out wis a gang. I'm goin' out wis anuzzer gang. I wouldnie go wis Billy's gang.'

'Nobody would have ye,' Billy jeered.

'Billy!' Bert stood up and jerked his thumb at the scullery. 'Away and wash yourself. Or—we'll have to arrange about gettin' you evacuated again.'

'I'm no bein' evacuated,' Billy shouted. 'It's only kids that get evacuated. I've been evacuated once and that was enough for me.'

He moved sulkily into the scullery and rushed some hot water in the sink. 'I'm no' washin' ma knees,' he shouted. 'If I wash ma face n' hands that's enough.'

'Come on, Jenny,' Mabel said. 'We'll get you washed, too, and then you'll be a clean wee girl to say good night to Bessie.'

'I want Bessie to tell me a story before she goes,' Jenny said. 'A long, long story.'

'I havenie time the night, pet,' Bessie said, standing up and arranging her hair before the mirror.

'You have so time,' Jenny said. 'Just a wee story, Bessie. A wee wee story about a guid wee girl that gets her face and hands washed—but not her neck!—and then goes away over the roofs wis a witch on her broomstick. And they comes to a desert island and the witch says we'll have a picnic and they eat sweeties and . . .'

'I'll tell ye a story the next time I come,' Bessie said. 'That's a promise.'

'What's that ye're puttin' on yer face, Ferret?' Billy said, standing in the doorway, drying himself.

'You mind yer own business, nosey!' Bessie said.

'No wonder the kid's askin',' her father said. 'Have you had a right good look at yourself lately?'

Bessie stared at him. 'What's wrong with me?'

'You may well ask!' Bert said. 'Not content wi' havin' your hair the colour o' a piebald pony, you've got it bunched up on top o' your head like a heather-besom.'

'But that's the latest style,' Bessie said. 'This is the way Carole Lombard has it in her new picture.'

'Well, it may suit Carole Lombard, but it certainly doesn't suit you.' Her father guffawed. 'All you little tuppence-halfpenny bitches are alike. You think because you've got your hair like one film star and your eyebrows like another that you're the whole cheese. You think that all you've got to do is waggle your little arses and some millionaire'll fall into your laps. An ordinary working-man's not good enough for any of you—though I notice that you're all bloody glad to grab one whenever the poor sucker shows that he's taken in with all your paint and powder. Like that bitch, Lily McGillivray, goin' and hookin' a poor simple sailor that should still be taggin' at his mother's apron-strings. I saw her the other night, and she had the nerve to shout "Hello there, Mr. Hipkiss, are ye comin' out with me to see a bit o' glamour!"'

Bert spat into the fire. 'Glamour! By God, Hollywood'll have a lot to answer for at the Judgment Day.'

'I hope you're not seein' anythin' of Lily McGillivray these days,' he said. 'Or Lily Hutchinson as she calls herself now.'

'I havenie seen her for weeks,' Bessie said. 'Honest, I havenie.'

'Well, must you go?' Mabel said, bringing Jenny back into the living-room and preparing to undress her. 'You've hardly been here any length of time.'

'I've got to be back to help Mrs. Irvine with the boarders' supper,' Bessie said. 'I told her I'd be back at nine o'clock.'

'It's a pity you can't wait to hear J. B. Priestley on the

wireless,' her stepmother said. 'He's going to speak about Dunkirk after the nine o'clock news.'

'Ay, Dunkirk!' Bert Hipkiss sighed and picked moodily at his little black moustache. 'Dunkirk—that's all we've been hearin' for days. And I doubt we havenie heard the end o' it yet by a long chalk. God knows what'll happen next.'

VII

'Mrs. Irvine's no' expecting me back till ten or half-past, but it was a guid excuse for gettin' away,' Bessie said to Lily. 'So don't you go and gab to anybody that ye've seen me the night.'

'My, what a liar ye are, Hippy!' Lily tittered, cleeking her arm into Bessie's and drawing her into the throng moving Westwards along Princes Street.

'I am not,' Bessie said. 'I'm not such a liar as you.'

'Me? I never tell lies,' Lily giggled. 'I just tell folk what I think they want to hear.'

'Seriously though, Hippy,' she said. 'Whether I'm a liar or not doesn't matter, but I've noticed you two or three times comin' out with muckle whoppers. I've been taken-in myself often. I've got to hand it to you, you fairly do it in style. Mind you, I don't think ye *mean* to tell lies, but you just sort o' touch things up. See what I mean?'

'I do nothin' of the kind,' Bessie said.

'And I'll trouble you to mind your own business, Lily McGillivray,' she said.

But secretly she felt rather proud, as they went into the Golden Salamander, that Lily should trouble to compliment her on what Lily evidently regarded as an accomplishment. For she was not conscious in any way of deviating from the truth. Everything she said was coloured by her imagination, and before she knew where she was her tongue had run away with her. And by the time she had finished she believed her story even more strongly than her listeners did.

The Golden Salamander was crowded, and the only table

36

they could get was one at the back. 'I hate bein' stuck away here,' Lily grumbled, taking off her short coat and draping it over the back of her chair. 'Ye can't see anything. And nobody can see you either!'

'And it's too near the Gents,' she said, swelling her bosom and pulling down the neck of her dress as far as it would go. 'I feel fair embarrassed.'

'Ach, it's all right,' Bessie said, anxious to mollify her. 'Where's Olaf the night? I thought ye'd ha'e been out with him.'

'Olaf!' Lily spat. 'He's like all the rest o' thae sailors. He had to get stuck on guard-duty. Though what guard they can do in Leith Docks beats me.'

'Two coffees, please,' she said to the waitress without waiting for Bessie to say what she wanted. And not listening to Bessie's mumbled 'I'd rather have tea,' she craned her neck and looked around.

At practically every table there was somebody wearing a foreign uniform. Lily pursed her lips when she saw that most of them were already talking to girls. She sighed with resignation and looked towards the door. Whoever came in next would be almost bound to sit at their table.

'Did ye hear about Mamie Proudfoot in Goldengreen Avenue?' she said to kill time.

'No, what's happened to her?' Bessie said.

'She's had another bairn.'

'Fancy!' Bessie said.

'Ay, I came up in the tram-car wi' her auntie,' Lily said, 'and she told me Mamie's just had a wee lassie. That's the second.'

'Fancy!' Bessie said. 'And her no' married!'

'She's such a nice quiet lassie, too,' Lily said. 'You'd never think she had it in her to do a thing like that. I saw her with a felly I wouldn't 'a' spat on, but I never thought anything about it.'

Lily broke off to smile at a Danish soldier who was going into the lavatory. 'Did ye get a load o' that?' she whispered. 'That was a fine big hunk o' beef for ye!'

37

Bessie giggled.

'Mamie's such a *clean* like lassie,' Lily went on. 'Terrible clean and wee. She doesnie come up to ma shoulder.' She paused, watching the door of the Gents. 'Though she's maybe a bit too stout,' she said.

'Fancy, I can hardly believe it,' Bessie said.

'The second time, mind ye!' Lily said. 'You could excuse it the first time, but when it happens twice—well, that's just prostitution.'

VIII

Bessie shut the front-door softly behind her and turned round to find Lieutenant Klosowski watching her from the sitting-room doorway.

'Good eveneeng,' he said, bowing. 'Good eveneeng, Bessee.'

'Hello,' she said, moving towards the stairs. Despite her remarks to her family about his niceness, she was vaguely afraid of the Polish officer.

'You have been out, yes?' he said. 'Veree nice night for a walk. Beautiful Edinburgh! Nice place, nice girls! Many beautiful Scotch girls!'

Bessie grinned and put her foot on the first step. The Lieutenant moved towards her. He had arrived in a creased battle-dress, but tonight he was wearing a smart well-cut officer's jacket and tight khaki riding-breeches. His belt and riding-boots were highly polished. And he looked more rested than he had done yesterday. He's not a bad looking fellow at all, Bessie decided, although his slanting eyes looked at her in such a queer way.

'Come to the sitteeng-room and talk,' he said, putting his hand on the banister as though to stop her from going farther.

'Och, I must get away to ma bed,' Bessie said.

'Bed,' he said, and he laughed: 'Bed! I must go to bed, also. But later.'

'Come and talk,' he said. 'Dmitri is lonelee.'

'But—but what can we talk about?' Bessie said.

38

Klosowski shrugged and made an airy motion with his hands. 'Talk! Talk about all sort of things. Bessee will teach me to spik Scotch, yes?'

'Aw, some other time,' Bessie giggled. 'I'm ower tired tonight.'

'Ow—er?' he said. 'Please?'

'Too tired,' she said.

He laughed. 'You will teach Dmitri to spik Scotch good, yes?'

She nodded. 'Well, good night,' she said, but she lingered.

'Dmitri come to bed, too,' he said, and he sprang on to the stairs, standing close behind her.

'Oh, the light!' Bessie cried, and she darted into the sitting-room and put off the switch. 'Mrs. Irvine gets fair furious when the lights are left burnin'.'

She tried to walk as calmly as she could upstairs, but all the time she had to restrain herself from breaking into a run. Lieutenant Klosowski followed so closely behind her that she could feel his body pressing almost into hers.

'Well, good night,' she said again when they came to the final flight of stairs.

Klosowski put his hand on top of hers on the banister and squeezed it. 'Sunday night in Edinburgh not veree gay,' he said. 'Better other nights, yes?'

'Ay, it's never very bright on a Sunday,' Bessie said.

'But other nights? Yes!'

'Sometimes,' she said.

IX

Lieutenant Klosowski was not far from Bessie's thoughts that night and the following day, but he was soon forgotten in the rush of other events. Or rather, he was submerged by them. For he would not allow himself to be forgotten, but waylaid her at every possible opportunity and talked to her, all the time eyeing her slyly and smiling with anticipatory greed. But she did not have time to worry about him or

39

to delve much into the meaning of such attention. She would not have minded if it had been one of the other officers. His sullen friend, for instance, whom Mrs. Irvine had already nicknamed 'Joe Pole'—even though he was so quiet, Bessie would have loved him to show some interest in her. She hung around them all, hoping to be taken notice of, and she giggled coquettishly whenever one asked her to do something. She gaped so much that Mrs. Irvine had to reprimand her continually: 'Get on with your work, lassie, you haven't time to stand about looking like the lost sheep on the mountain.'

Gape and giggle as she might, however, Bessie was scarcely noticed by most of the boarders. It was Mrs. Irvine who received all the hand-kissing and the heel-clicking. But Bessie lived in a continual state of hope that somebody wonderful would arrive and fall immediately for her charms.

There was every chance that it might happen. On Tuesday another three foreign soldiers were brought by the billeting-officer. The house suddenly became a madhouse of uniforms and harsh masculine voices. Mr. McQuarrie and Donald Findlay, who had been used for some time to being waited upon hand and foot, now thought themselves lucky if they received any consideration at all.

Young Donald was driven more and more to the kitchen to do his studying. 'I'm gettin' fed up wi' the sight of him,' Bessie said to Lily on the Friday evening. 'I dinnie ken what I've done to deserve this! A laddie wi' a game-leg talkin' to me and takin' up all my time when there's as many big fine-like blokes in uniform in the house!'

'Och, why worry! Use sunlight!' Lily giggled. 'Ye might as well practice on Donald and then you'll be all set for the right one when he comes along!'

'But I don't know what to say to him,' Bessie said. 'He just sits there wi' his head buried in his infernal books all the time and I never get a cheep out o' him. I'll be damned glad when he goes away for his holidays. Maybe Mrs. Irvine'll let his room then and we'll get somebody else. Somebody like —well, somebody like your Olaf, say!'

'Olaf! That big bum!' Lily sniffed. 'Och, he's away wi'

his boat, and I suppose that's the end o' him. Not that I care. I met a terrific Pole last night. An absolute smasher.' She gurgled and gripped Bessie's arm. 'His name's Tadeusz Gabanski, and do ye ken, Hippy'—she gurgled again—'I think he wears corsets!'

'Naw!' Bessie said.

'I'm sure he does. He's that tight-waisted and walks so straight. But he's an awful nice felly and that generous. He's goin' to take me to the theatre on Saturday night.'

'The theatre,' Bessie breathed. 'Fancy!'

'He's booked seats for the orchestera stalls,' Lily said. 'The orchestera stalls! Jesus Christ and General Jackson, I'll be fairly cuttin' a dash that night.'

'Gosh, I wish I was you,' Bessie said.

'Y'know, Bess, I was thinkin' I'll get another job,' Lily said. 'I'm right fed up wi' working in the Rubber Works. It's not classy enough for ma taste, and if I'm goin' to go steady with Tadeusz, well——'

'Another job?' Bessie said.

'Och, why not? I have to have a job, for the allowance I get from Tommy would hardly keep me goin' in cigarettes. So why should I no' have a job I like? And I cannie expect Tadeusz to pay for me all the time. It wouldnie be *honest,* would it?' And Lily opened her eyes very wide.

At first there was a great deal of chopping and changing with the new arrivals. Some of them stayed only for two or three days before they were moved to camps in Perthshire, or Fifeshire, or Cupar Angus and other towns in Scotland. But by the end of June Mrs. Irvine more or less had a settled collection of 'steadies,' and she was able to say to other land-ladies: 'Yes, we have ten boarders now. Ten! We're quite a little United Nations of our own, for I must say we all agree beautifully. Oh, beautifully! There's never a wrong word. I see to that. If there was to be the slightest hint of quarrelling I would be up in arms at once. But there's never any need for me to even begin to lay down the law.'

In such a house of soldiers Mrs. Irvine became a General directing operations. It was: 'Bessie, bring Captain Van

Klee's despatch-case from his bedroom,' or 'Bessie, didn't I tell you to give Major Barbier his breakfast half an hour earlier?' or most often: 'Bessie, Bessie! Where is that lassie? She's aye here when she's not wanted, but at other times she's mooning around. Get the table laid, the gentlemen'll be here before we know where we are.'

Bessie was, as she said to Lily, fair run off her feet, even though they now had a charwoman, Mrs. McNeill, who came daily and did most of the rough work. But she seldom complained. She loved being in the thick of it all, listening to strange conversations which she hardly understood, finding out the different characteristics of the various boarders, and listening to Mrs. Irvine comparing one with another. Bessie loved to repeat it all to Lily: 'Fancy, Lil, this new Pole, Lieutenant Leja, uses scent! Honest to God, he does. I wouldnie ha'e believed it if I hadnie seen him with ma ain eyes, sprayin' himself wi' some terribly fancy French scent— I forget the name o' it, but he has a muckle bottle on his dressing-table, and I whiles take a wee dab o' it. See, smell! Isn't it gorgeous! Well, I caught him one day, and he was as bold as brass about it. He just looked at me and said, "Bessie like nice smell, no?"'

If at first Mrs. Irvine was like a General among all her officers, as time went on she adopted the role of a Queen. As she got to know them better, she dropped her haughty manner and grew expansive—though, at the same time, in many ways more regal. In the evenings she sat with her officers and discussed politics and other subjects. Bessie was furious at being relegated to the kitchen, usually with piles and piles of washing-up to do. But whenever she could, she hovered around in the passage, listening to the laughter and snatches of conversation coming from the sitting-room where Mrs. Irvine would sit sipping gin or whisky with her guests. Occasionally, on great occasions, Bessie was allowed to join them in order to listen to Mr. Churchill or some other personage make an important speech on the radio. It was what Mrs. Irvine called 'educating' her, for she said: 'Bessie, things are happening so fast in the world these days that you've got to take some interest in them.

We're living in great historical times, and a young lassie like you should take note of them.'

These important radio speeches became so frequent that before very long Bessie found that after she had finished her evening chores she could slip into the sitting-room and sit quietly in a corner and nothing was said. The officers ignored her, anyway. And Mrs. Irvine, burning with patriotism and zeal for 'equality,' would just nod benignly at her and continue her conversations, implying that Bessie would benefit greatly if she listened to her wisdom.

Lieutenant Klosowski and 'Joe Pole' were never in the sitting-room on these occasions. Often as she sat knitting, listening to the radio or watching Mrs. Irvine and Mr. McQuarrie play cards with the officers, Bessie wished that Klosowski or Rolewicz would remain in—even if it was just for one evening! They would have livened things up a bit. But they went out every night, and usually returned very late. Sometimes after she was in bed, Bessie would hear them thumping upstairs, talking loudly, and she knew without seeing them that they had been drinking. Apart from Donald, they were the youngest boarders, so Mrs. Irvine treated their shortcomings with greater leniency than she might have done otherwise. Mrs. Irvine had a very maternal feeling for blond, handsome 'Joe Pole,' and it was he who first started to call her 'Mummy.' It was practically the first English word he learned. At first Mrs. Irvine was called 'Madame' by all the boarders, but 'Joe Pole' either could not or would not call her this, so Mrs. Irvine said: 'You'd better call me "Mummy." After all, I'm auld enough to be your mother!' Before long she was called this by all the boarders. Even Captain Van Klee, the oldest officer, a blond greying Dutchman of forty-eight or so, would shout appealingly: 'Mummee, mummee! Veer is mine boots?'

Old Mr. McQuarrie was inclined to spit. 'These damned foreigners are like a lot o' bairns,' he would grumble. But he did not allow his insularity to prevent him from accepting gifts of cigarettes and tobacco, all of which the foreigners had in abundance. Although this made him spit even more. '*Where*

43

do they get their money?' he would say. 'I'm sure none of *our* officers are able to buy all these grand things on their small allowances. It takes these damned foreigners to come here and buy everything up. They're like locusts, I tell you, like locusts devourin' everything they see in front o' them. They'll have Scotland stripped bare before we can cough!'

Mr. McQuarrie's, however, was the only dissentient voice. Mrs. Irvine and Bessie were charmed with their guests. And so were all the other landladies of Mrs. Irvine's acquaintanceship. 'They're delightful gentlemen,' old Mrs. Munro said. 'Simply delightful.' And she insisted upon bringing her two 'star' boarders to Mrs. Irvine's one evening for tea and biscuits. 'Just to introduce them to another Scottish home, my dear,' she said. 'After all, these poor boys are far away from their homes—if they've any homes left after what these dreadful Russians have done—so it's up to the likes of you and me to entertain them as best we can. What I always say is: Give honour where honour's due, for these lads have been fighting *That Hitler* for a longer time than we have. And who knows —somebody like ourselves may be entertaining our own Boys like this in a foreign land one of these days.'

'That's so,' Mrs. Irvine said. 'Though I doubt, m'dear, that it'll be a good while yet before that happens, what with the way things are just now.'

'Don't be such a pessimist, Mrs. Irvine,' the other landlady said, primming her lips. 'I'm surprised at *you*. We'll just have to put our faith in Providence *and* Mr. Churchill. *He'll* pull us through, I'll be bound. He's a fighter if ever there was one. We may be surrounded just now, with *that man* getting his landing-barges ready for an invasion and all, but it won't be for long, I can tell you. France may have fallen, and those Belgians and their dirty tyke of a king may have gone over to the enemy, but we'll pull through somehow. Yes, we'll see *That Hitler* hanging high yet.'

44 .

x

One evening in July Bessie went to the cinema alone. Lily McGillivray was going out with Teddy Gabanski, so had no use for Bessie. Lily was now working in a chemist's shop in Leith Walk. 'It's a real classy job,' she told Bessie. 'I'm at the scent counter. Christ, Hippy, I never knew there was so much scent in the world till I came to work here! You should try and get a job in a shop, too, Bess, it would be far better for ye than workin' yer fingers to the bone for that auld bitch, Irvine. You wouldnie be so tied-down. You'd have every night to yersel', and lookit the fun ye could have!'

Bessie was thinking about this as she took her seat. The 'big' film, *The Philadelphia Story*, with Cary Grant and Katharine Hepburn, had only a few more minutes to run. Bessie hated to see the end of a film before she saw the beginning, so she closed her eyes and tried to give herself up to her own thoughts. It was virtually the first time she had been able to relax for a week. If she was getting any fun out of it, it wouldn't be so bad, she thought. But there wasn't much fun in cleaning Captain Van Klee's boots and helping Mrs. McNeill to change the sheets on all the beds. None of them ever paid her the slightest attention, except to say 'Goot morn-eeng, Bessee,' or 'Goot night, Bessee.' I might as well be a wee dog, she reflected bitterly, for all the notice they take of me—except that Dmitri.

She wriggled her shoulders against the back of her seat as she thought of the dark, slant-eyed Pole. He still hovered around her at odd moments, although recently even he seemed to have other things to take up his attention.

Now, if she could just be like Lily, what a rare time she could have! Lily was out with a different boy almost every night. Lily was supposed to be going 'steady' with Teddy Gabanski, but that didn't prevent her from having dates with all kinds of other fellows like Free French sailors and Czechs

45

and other Poles. Bessie sighed, wondering what Lily's secret was. If Lily was in her place in the boarding-house she would have the whole lot of them eating out of her hand no matter what Mrs. Irvine might say—even that big dumb cluck, 'Joe Pole'! Lily would never be forced to come to the pictures on her own.

Still, it was a relief in a way not to have Lily whispering and giggling beside her. Bessie felt more at home on her own in the darkness. It was like the time at the beginning of the war when the kids were evacuated and there was nobody at home but her father, and she had gone to the pictures two or three times a week on her own. Nobody to order her about or disturb her but her father, and give him his due he hadn't bothered her much. Gosh, how things had changed since then. She could hardly believe she was still the same girl, so much seemed to have happened.

The cinema organ had begun to play a medley of popular tunes, and she hummed in time with it. . . . *Moon at sea, moon at sea . . . Tell me that my love's a true love, though he sails away with my heart . . . Wait for me, wait for me . . . Tell him that there'll be no new love. . . .* Oh, if only some big sailor like Cary Grant would take a room with us, she thought. If only when she got back Mrs. Irvine would pop her head out of the sitting-room and cry: 'Put clean sheets on the wee back-bedroom bed, Bessie, we've got a sailor coming tonight. . . .'

The News Reel started with a blare, jerking Bessie out of her day-dream. But although her eyes and ears were focused on the screen, the events pictured stimulated her mind on another track. Most of the reel dealt with the Fall of France. As a commentary there were recordings of speeches by Winston Churchill and General de Gaulle. Bessie had already listened to these on the radio, but with the camera picking out scenes and events the words she had listened to in the cosiness of the sitting-room took on new meaning. 'I grieve for the gallant French people who have fallen into this terrible misfortune,' Churchill thundered. 'Nothing will alter our feelings towards them or our faith that the genius of France will arise again.'

46

And then General de Gaulle, stiff as a marionette at the microphone, speaking as if he were dealing in butter and eggs and not in men's lives: 'I, General de Gaulle, now in London, call on all French officers and men who are at present on British soil or may be in the future with or without their arms . . . whatever happens the flame of French resistance must not and shall not die. . . .'

Bessie remembered that the evening they had heard these words on the radio, little Captain André Porel had sprung up, clenched fist held high, and shouted: 'Vive la France!' And Mrs. Irvine had tuttuted with mingled approval and censure and said: 'Mind, Captain, we're not Bolshies here! I'm all for vive la France, but I'm for none of that clenched fist stuff.'

'Vive la France!' Bessie muttered, and she, too, clenched her fist.

And then she forgot that she was a girl of sixteen sitting in a cinema in Edinburgh. She became a virago. She sat straight up in her seat, a shiver of cold excitement tingling down her spine. Once again she became Elizabeth, Duchess de Bourbon-Parma, Madame Royale of France. . . .

The screen flash-backed to scenes taken a year before, while Churchill's voice kept them company: 'Today is the fourteenth of July, the National Festival of France. A year ago in Paris I watched the stately parade down the Champs Elysees of the French Army and the French Empire. Who can foresee what the course of other years will bring? Faith is given to us. . . . When the day dawns, as dawn it will, the soul of France will turn with comprehension and with kindness to those French men and French women . . . who in the darkest hour did not despair of the Republic. . . .'

'Ah, ma belle Paree!' Bessie sobbed. 'Ma belle Paree. . . . Vive la France!'

Tears were streaming down her cheeks, but she made no move to check them. Waves of icy excitement were sweeping over her. She stood beside Churchill on a balcony, looking down at the soldiers and guns and tanks going past. . . .

'Ma belle Paree,' she sobbed.

'That's a little Frenchy,' a woman a few seats away whispered to her neighbour. 'Puir wee soul! It must be gey hard on her.'

'Puir wee soul nothin'.' The other woman turned belligerently in Bessie's direction. 'This place is gettin' over-run wi' thae bloody foreigners. Let them go back to their own countries, that's what I say. Wasn't it the French that let us down!'

'Ay, now that I think o' it, you're right.' The first woman's sympathy was quickly changing into spleen, and she leaned past her neighbour to stare at Bessie.

Bessie put her handkerchief to her mouth to stifle her sobs, then she rose and walked as majestically as she could along the row and into the aisle.

She stayed for some time in the Ladies, powdering the tear-marks from her face and trying to recover her composure, and then she went back to another seat as far from the two women as she could get.

But she could not enjoy *The Philadelphia Story* for thinking about the incident. It was the first time for weeks and weeks that she had remembered that she was a Royal Bourbon, and here this had to happen! Maybe her father had been right when he had said once: 'Your imagination'll run away with you one o' these days, my lassie, and get ye into a hell of a lot of trouble. You're like yer Mother and yer auld Granny before her—too damned fond of living in a world o' yer own. It's high time you snapped out o' it. Otherwise, ye'll suffer for it. . . .'

XI

Bessie came out of the cinema about nine o'clock and meandered slowly down Clerk Street. She was at a loose end. She did not want to go back to the boarding-house for some time yet. If she did, she would just get some jobs to do. And after all, it was her night off.

She did not like walking alone. She missed Lily's arm in hers and the rattle of Lily's tongue. It was not any fun watching the passers-by when you were on your own; you had nobody to laugh with about them. And even the shop windows did not seem to have anything much to take up her attention when Lily wasn't there. It was no fun looking at things if you hadn't somebody to whom you could say: 'Gee, but I'd like that,' or 'Gee, but wouldn't I look smashin'·in that frock!'

She was staring lackadaisically at some evening dresses in Patrick Thomson's window when somebody touched her shoulder.

'Good eveneeng, Bessee!'

Dmitri Klosowski clicked his heels and bowed from the waist, saluting her with a proprietary smirk. 'You are surprised to see me, yes? I gave you leetle fright, no?'

'Well,' Bessie giggled. 'Well, in a way. . . .'

'You look at dresses?' he said. 'Veree nice dresses.'

'Ay, they'd be nicer at half the price,' she said.

'Please?'

Bessie flushed. 'I mean—er—Och, how'll I explain it? They're awfie dear.'

'Dear?' he said, and he grinned. 'Dear! Like Bessee?'

'Och, away!' she giggled.

'You like dress, Bessee?'

'No' half,' she said.

'Which dress you like, Bessee?' he said. 'Best dress?'

'I like that yin best,' she nodded at a pale blue taffeta.

'Dmitri will get it for you,' he said.

Bessie laughed and gave him a dig with her elbow. 'Ay, and the band played!' Then, horrified at such familiarity, she drew away from him.

'Tomorrow,' he said, nodding. 'Shop shut tonight.'

Bessie giggled. 'What a case ye are!'

'Case?'

'Och,' Bessie floundered. 'Forget it!'

'No, not forget,' the Pole said, and he nodded solemnly. 'Come back tomorrow when shop opens.'

He put his hand on her elbow, and she was astonished at the strength of his fingers. He held her as though in a vice.

'Where go now, Bessee?'

49

'Oh, I was just taking a walk.'

'Dmitri walk with you,' he said, and he turned her in the direction of Princes Street. 'We go for drink, yes?'

'Och, I wouldnie dare,' Bessie giggled.

'Bessie go to pub? Nice pubs! Rare pubs!' Dmitri laughed, rolling the rs of 'rare' in imitation of the Scots voice.

'No, I never go to pubs,' Bessie said.

'Go to Golden Sala—Mander, yes?'

'Okay,' she said.

Gee, this would be one in the eye for Lily, she thought, prancing sedately beside Dmitri, trying to fit her step to suit his long almost goosestepping stride. Lily was bound to be at the Golden Salamander with Tadeusz Gabanski. What a shock she would get when she saw her coming in with her own Pole! Bessie thrust back her shoulders and held her neck stiffly, looking haughtily at other girls who were alone.

Because of the shortage of petrol some of the old horse-cabs had been resurrected in Edinburgh. One of them passed now, clop-clopping over the cobbles of the North Bridge, the cabby flicking his whip on top of the box, looking for a possible fare. 'That's right funny, isn't it?' Bessie nudged Dmitri. 'Makes you think you're back in the year dot!'

'Dot? Please?'

'Aw, skip it!' Bessie said. 'It's just an expression.'

The Pole looked after the cab, eyebrows drawn together, trying to figure out what Bessie's meaning had been. He gripped her arm tighter and squeezed her against him.

'You can ride horse, Bessee?' he said.

'Me? No!' she giggled.

'You would like to ride horse, Bessee?'

'Ach, I'd be feared I'd fall off.'

'I will teach you to ride horse, Bessee. One day soon.'

'Ach, away!' she tittered.

They had turned into Princes Street and were walking past the North British Station Hotel. Bessie looked enviously at two women in evening-dress who were going in the main entrance escorted by a stout Polish colonel.

'You will love riding horse with Dmitri,' Klosowski said, and he clicked his tongue enticingly as though he were astride a horse at that moment.

'Ay, but would the horse love it?' Bessie sniggered, and stopped at the edge of the pavement at the top of the Waverley Steps. 'Let's cross here. It's no fun walkin' along this side o' Princes Street. All the talent walks on the other side.'

'Talent? Please?'

Bessie bit her lip, wondering how she could explain that 'talent' was the expression used for young men and women who were out looking for 'pick-ups.' But before she could find the easiest words, the wailing of the siren filled the air.

'Christ! An air raid!' she cried.

Dmitri drew her back on to the pavement. 'We go to shelter this side,' he said, and keeping his fingers firmly on her elbow he propelled her towards the Air Raid Shelters in Princes Street Gardens. People were pouring into the nearest shelter beside Sir Walter Scott's monument, so Dmitri hurried her along to the next. 'In here,' he said.

They moved to the back of the shelter and stood there, watching people come in. It was darker at the back, and it was only when Dmitri put his arm around her waist and drew her against him that Bessie understood why he had been in such a hurry to get her into a shelter. Now she remembered that several times when the air-raid warning had sounded when Dmitri was in the boarding-house he had just laughed at Mrs. Irvine's alarm and said: 'Klosowski in Warsaw. Klosowski not afraid of air-raids. Edinburgh a safe place. Edinburgh well guarded. Not like Warsaw—boom, boom, boom! Warsaw veree bad, but Edinburgh chickenfeed!'

Remembering this and feeling once again the slight nervousness that he always excited in her, Bessie tried to draw away from his encircling arm. But the press of people was so great that she could not move. People were jostling against her from all directions, almost smothering her. And Dmitri's arm was as firm and immovable as an iron band round her waist. 'Not afraid, Bessee?' he looked down at her, his dark face appearing even darker in the shadows of the shelter. 'Air-raid over veree soon. Nothing will happen. One bomb in middle of sea perhaps.'

Just then there was a distant explosion. 'My God, it's a bomb!' a woman cried. 'He's kept his word all right. He said he wis goin' to bomb us night and day, day and night——'

'You are the one!' a soldier sang with merriment. 'Only you beneath the moon and under the sun. In the silence of my lonely room, I dream of you . . . Night and Da—ay! Day and Ni—ight. . . .'

'Ay, it's all very well for you to make a laughin' matter out o' it,' the woman cried. 'Singin' there as though ye were at a concert. But ye'll be singin' on the other side o' yer face if a bomb lands right on top o' us.'

'Ach, it's all right, missis,' an elderly man said. 'There's nothin' to be feared for. They'll be awa' up beside the Forth Bridge. It's it they want to bomb and no' puir simple souls like us.'

The soldier went on singing, and several other people joined in. But the woman wailed: 'How do ye ken they're tryin' to bomb the Forth Brig'? If they'd wanted to bomb it, they'd ha'e bombed it long ago. No, no, that Hitler wants to keep the Forth Brig' intact so that his train'll pass ower it when he comes here to gloat on what he's done.'

'He's still got to do it yet, missis,' the elderly man said. 'He'll no' gloat yet a while, believe you me.'

'Too bloody true!' several people shouted.

'For we'll hang up our washing on the Siegfried Line!' the soldier sang, and the others joined in.

'I wouldnie mind if I hadnie thur bairns wi' me,' the woman said in a lull in the singing. 'It would be terrible to get bombed wi' them in an air-raid shelter.'

'Better to get bombed in an air-raid shelter than to get bombed in the open street, missis,' the elderly man said. 'Now, hold yer wheesht like a sensible wumman! Ye're just excitin' the bairns. They were all right until you started to have hysterics aboot nothin'.'

'Now then, my wee hen!' the woman cried to the hidden child whose howls began to drown every other sound. 'Now,

now, my wee hen, if ye greet like that we'll never be able to hear the all-clear.'

'All-clear go soon,' Dmitri said, bending over Bessie. 'My wee hen!' he laughed and pressed her against him even more firmly. And suddenly he placed his mouth to hers, forcing his tongue between her lips until she felt that she would suffocate. She tried to pull back her head, but Dmitri's other hand, which had been caressing the nape of her neck, tightened.

When at last he drew his lips away, Bessie sagged against him. Her head was spinning. She had never been kissed with such ferocity in her life before. She struggled to think of something to say, furious at being kissed in public, and with such force—even though her reason told her that nobody could see them in the darkness and that people were too intent on themselves and the air-raid anyway.

'Aw, stoppit!' she said, putting her hands on Dmitri's chest and trying to push him away.

'Bessee no like Polish kiss?' he said.

Before Bessie could say anything the all-clear went. In the ensuing rush for the fresh air she extricated herself from Dmitri's embrace. And when they got outside she was careful to walk about a yard away from him. It was only as they crossed Princes Street that he managed to put his hand on her arm again, and they walked in silence to the Golden Salamander.

XII

Once inside the café, Bessie's self-confidence returned, and when she saw Lily and Tadeusz at a table she skirled: 'Ay there, Lil! I see the bomb didnie fall on *you*, anyway!'

'No, it was somewhere down beside Leith Docks.' Lily took her handbag off a chair and pulled it out for Bessie. 'I don't mind tellin' you, though, that I was right feared for a while. I was scared stiff,' she said, looking Dmitri up and down coyly.

Bessie introduced them. Gabanski and Klosowski clicked their heels at each other and stood to attention, eyeing each

53

other warily. Dmitri kissed Lily's hand and bowed over her with a flourish. 'Feared?' he laughed. 'No, no. Scotch girls are never feared. Scotch girls are good sports, yes?'

'Ay, sometimes,' Lily said.

'Air-raid here nozzing!' Dmitri shrugged his right shoulder almost up to his ear and flashed his teeth at Lily. 'But in Warsaw! Ah! Boom, boom, bang!'

He broke into a spate of Polish to Tadeusz Gabanski, and for a few minutes the two men gesticulated and spoke excitedly. Lily took the opportunity to whisper: 'Where did ye pick this up? Christ, Bess, I must say I like your taste. He's a smasher!'

Bessie sat back and tried to look like a woman of the world. 'I know how to pick them,' she said airily.

'Coffee, Bessee, my wee hen?' Dmitri leaned over her in a proprietary manner.

'No, I'd rather——' she began, then she nodded: 'Okay.'

'Okay!' Dmitri laughed. 'Okay, my wee hen!'

'Please?' he turned to Lily. 'My wee hen—what means it?'

Lily giggled. 'Ach, it's just an expression that folk say— mostly to wee lassies. It means—well, it means "dear."'

'Dear?' Dmitri frowned. 'Dear like dress?'

It was Lily's turn to look puzzled. But Bessie said: 'No, that's a different kind of dear. A wee hen is—well, it's a wee bird. A bird that lays eggs.'

'Eggs?' Dmitri looked from one girl to the other, then he said something to Tadeusz, at which both men laughed uproariously, slapping their thighs.

'Dear? Eggs?' Dmitri shrugged and spread out his hands. 'Scotch vords veree difficult sometimes for poor Polish soldier. No un'erstan'.'

'Well, it's like this,' Lily said. 'A hen lays eggs. A hen is a lady bird, like me and Bessie. The other bird is a cock.' She looked around to see that nobody was paying too much attention, then she gave a low: 'Cockadoodledoo!'

Realization dawned on Dmitri's face. 'Ah, you hen! Me cock!' he cried. And he leaned over Bessie, slapping his chest and saying: 'Dmitri cock, yes? Dmitri veree nice cock, yes?'

54

Bessie blushed and looked at the table, but Lily saved her further embarrassment by saying: 'Oh, by the way, Bess, d'you remember tellin' me about Mamie Proudfoot and her two bastards?'

Bessie screwed her brows together. 'Mamie Proudfoot? I cannie remember sayin' anything about her to you.'

'Och ay, two or three weeks ago,' Lily said. 'You told me all about her havin' another wee lassie and her no' married.'

'Oh, her!' Bessie took a cigarette from Tadeusz' case and tapped it on the back of her hand. 'No, I never said anything about her. It was you that told *me*. You said you had come up in the tram-car wi' her auntie and she had told you.'

'Oh, what a liar you are, Bessie! You say things and then forget you say them.' Lily's eyes opened wide with shock, and she tried to transfer her amazement to Tadeusz and Dmitri. 'She's a terrible lassie this! You can't believe one word she says! Really, Bess, liars should have good memories.'

'But I never told you about her,' Bessie protested. 'It was you that told me.'

'Away ye go!' Lily said. 'It was you that told me. I remember distinctly. You told me that Mamie had had two bairns and that you had seen her with the man and all. Honestly, Bess, you'll have to do something about your memory.'

'But I never,' Bessie said.

'Of course you did. I remember it distinctly.' Lily shrugged her shoulders as much as to say to the Poles: 'What can you do with her?' 'Well, what I was goin' to tell you,' she rattled on before Bessie could get in another word, 'was that I met Mamie hersel' this morning, and she told me she is so married to the man, so none o' her bairns are bastards after all!'

'But, Lily,' Bessie said diffidently, 'it was *you* that told me.'

'Och!' Lily sighed with exasperation. 'Your memory's not worth a damn!'

Bessie opened her mouth to continue the argument, then she subsided and studied the glowing end of her cigarette. Maybe Lily was right . . . maybe she *had* told her. . . . She tried to remember back to meeting Mamie Proudfoot's aunt on a

55

tram-car. Had she? She knew the woman well by sight: a big stout woman who was always in a hurry, so much so that Bert Hipkiss, watching her from the window once, had remarked: 'That's a right hashmagundy! She's aye on the hop like a blue-arsed flea!' But had she been in a tram-car with her recently? She vaguely remembered the conversation she and Lily had had about Mamie, but which of them had said what was now beyond her. So if Lily said she had said it, well——

All the same, she was not going to let Lily get away with her implications to the Polish soldiers that she was an habitual liar, so she said:

'Dmitri's goin' to teach me to ride a horse.'

Lily, who was sipping her coffee in a genteel manner in order to impress the Poles, spluttered into her cup and had to lay it down.

'What!' she cried.

'Yes, he's going to teach me to ride a horse.' Bessie simpered at Dmitri, who winked at her and put his hand on her knee. 'Aren't you?'

'Of course, my wee hen!' Dmitri's fingers clasped round her knee and stroked it.

Bessie tilted her chin at Lily. 'Just picture me gallopin' round Inverleith Park on a horse, Lil!' she said.

'Heaven help the horse!' Lily said, patting her hair and smiling at Tadeusz. 'You'll be like a sack of tatties bouncing up and down!'

'Bessee go on horse one day soon,' Dmitri said. 'Then——' He clicked his tongue against the roof of his mouth and jogged up and down in his chair. 'Bad horse! Veree bad horse! Get whipped!' And he pushed up Bessie's skirt and slapped her bare thigh.

'Here, here, that's enough!' she giggled with embarrassment and pushed his hand away.

'Whip for bad horse!' Dmitri said. 'Whip for bad mans!'

'Whip for Russian mans,' Tadeusz said harshly. 'Dirty moujiks!'

'Ay, these dirty Bolshies stole all Teddy's estates away frae

56

him,' Lily said. 'He had great big estates, acres and acres o' them, and when the Russians came they swept everything in front of them, burnin' and pillagin'.' Her breast heaved with indignation as she recited what Tadeusz had told her again and again. 'Teddy was a Count,' she said almost defiantly to Bessie and Dmitri.

Tadeusz stroked his little blond moustache with one hand and flourished his long black, silver-mounted cigarette-holder with the other. He sat very straight in his chair as though he had been poured into his uniform and was afraid by bending to burst through the seams. Bessie remembered Lily's story that he wore corsets, and she looked to see if she could discern any sign of them. 'Russian mans very bad,' he said. 'Gabanski kill all Russian mans some day. Line against wall and shoot! Shoot!' He leaned back and looked down complacently at his immaculate riding-boots. 'But first give them the whip.'

'Russians veree bad,' Dmitri agreed. 'Stalin and Hitler—*Pah*!' He practically spat across the table. 'Communists bad in all countries. Shoot! Shoot dirty Reds!'

'Your father's a bit of a Red, isn't he, Bess?' Lily said, and she giggled. 'You'll have to watch and not introduce him to yer boy-friend!'

'Oh, I wouldnie say that,' Bessie said. 'He's no' a Red at all.'

'I've heard my father say different,' Lily said. 'Him and yer auld man have had many an argument about politics, and my faither's aye said yer Da was an arrant Bolshie and would end up by bein' lined against a wall.'

'Well, maybe he used to be a bit o' a one,' Bessie mumbled. 'I mean—he was never a Communist or anything *bad*. He just used to shoot out his neck a bit about the conditions o' the workin' classes and things like that. But I haven't heard him lately.' She sat up and glared at Lily. 'No, I haven't heard him lately. So don't you go and carry any tales around, Lily McGillivray.'

'You're never at home to hear what he says,' Lily said.

'I'm at home often enough, anyway, to know that my Da's

all for the War,' Bessie said. 'So don't you say otherwise. Whatever he is, my Da's not a Fifth Columnist.'

'I never said he was a Fifth Columnist.'

'No, but ye were hintin' as much.' Bessie dabbed the end of her cigarette fiercely into the ash-tray.

'There ye go again!' Lily said. 'Lettin' yer imagination run away wi' you!'

The Polish soldiers had been listening in silence to the argument, but now, finding the girls' quick Scottish voices beyond his comprehension, Klosowski thought it time he heard his own voice again. 'Polish soldier shoot all Russians,' he said. 'One day soon.'

Tadeusz Gabanski nodded in agreement. 'Soon!' he cried, waving his cigarette-holder as thought it were a banner. 'Go back to Poland and shoot all bad mans.' He sighed sentimentally. 'Poland . . . poor Poland! Gabanski had leetle sister. Girl like you,' he said to Bessie. 'No know what has happened to her. Russians came one day and—*kaput*! All gone. House burned. Papa and Mamma killed. Little sister taken. Gabanski had to run away fast.'

'Poor Teddy,' Lily murmured, and she took his hand and played with his fingers. 'Ay, they've had a bad time o' it, puir fellys,' she said to Bessie.

'Bad time, yes! Veree bad time,' Dmitri said, and he started to speak in Polish to Gabanski. For a time the two men gesticulated and talked, and the girls listened. Bessie puffed another cigarette and tried to look as though she understood everything the Poles were saying. She nodded every now and then in agreement, and whenever their voices got louder and one of them would wave his hands madly or thump the table she would giggle to Lily and say: 'What cases they are!'

After a while Lily got bored. She stared moodily at the dregs of her coffee. 'Ach, it's all very well for them,' she said in a low voice to Bessie. 'But how would they like if *we* had a conversation on our own like this? I wish to goodness they'd speak English. Ye never know what they might be sayin'.'

58

Gabanski and Klosowski were deep in some tactical problem; Gabanski made great play with the knives and forks on the table, arranging them in groups and pointing first at one and then at another, all the time barking out weird-sounding words at Klosowski. He would be some five or six years older than Dmitri, who was twenty, so his words were listened' to with flattering attention by the younger man. Lily fluffed up her hair from her shoulders and turned round to survey the other tables. 'Ach, this is no' much fun,' she muttered. 'I don't see why they need to play at soldiers when *we're* here.'

'Too true!' Bessie said, but she kept a fixed smile on her face and watched the Poles, looking at every expression on their faces as though this would help her to understand.

'Good evening.'

Heels were clicked behind Bessie. Gabanski and Klosowski broke off their conversation and sprang to attention. Bessie turned and saw Lieutenant Leja standing stiffly at her back.

Introductions were made. Leja bowed coldly to the girls, drew out a chair and sat down. Lily's boredom vanished, but only for a few seconds, for Leja began immediately to talk in rapid Polish to the others. The heads of the three men were drawn together, and the girls were completely ignored.

Lily took in Leja's permanently-waved red hair, his eyeglass and his beautifully-tailored uniform, and she kept simpering at him. But seeing that no notice was likely to be taken of her, she picked up her handbag and rose. 'Comin' Bess?' she said.

'Well, I don't think——' Bessie hesitated.

'C'mon,' Lily said.

'Well, I must say this is no' my idea o' a picnic,' Lily said when the girls went into the cloakroom. 'It's no' fair of them to ask us out and then to behave like this. Who's this other guy, anyway?'

'He's one o' our boarders,' Bessie said. 'He's the one I told you about that aye eats oranges in his bed.'

'What!' Lily tittered. 'Oranges in his bed!'

'Ay,' Bessie nodded. 'Though we never see the oranges,

59

mind you. The greedy brute keeps them all to himsel'. You'd think, wouldn't ye, that oranges bein' so scarce he'd share them wi' the rest of us.'

'Ay, ye'd think so,' Lily said. 'But he looks a greedy bugger. He's that cauld and fish-like.'

'Oh, he's greedy all right,' Bessie agreed. 'He's terrible mean about everything. Mind you, give them their due, the Poles are not greedy at all. Dmitri and " Joe Pole " are terribly generous. But that Leja—he wouldnie share anythin' with anybody. Not even his bed.'

'I don't think any self-respecting body would want to share it wi' him,' Lily sniffed.

'He made a great how-d'ye-do when Mrs. Irvine asked him if he'd share a room with one of the other officers,' Bessie said. 'He fair got on his hind legs and said no, he wanted to be alone.'

'Like Garbo!' Lily giggled.

'We have a terrible job, y'know,' Bessie said. 'We've had to put two beds in most o' the rooms. Dmitri and Joe Pole share a room. And Major Barbier and Captain Porel share one, too. But that Leja—no, he's so high and mighty he must have a room to himself.'

'Och, it'll keep him from quarrellin' with anybody,' Lily said.

'I don't know about that,' Bessie said. 'He'd fain like to quarrel with the Frenchies. About politics mostly. It's funny how the Poles and the Frenchies don't seem to like each other. There's been two or three arguments in the sitting-room at nights, and it's aye been that Leja that's been at the bottom o' them. It's taken Mrs. Irvine all her time to keep the peace, but she's managed so far. I must say she's the boy for them! They just fair fawn on her like wee dogs—especially the Frenchies. They's aye sookin' up to her.'

'Auld bitch,' Lily commented.

'You'd think Leja would give some oranges to Mrs. Irvine, wouldn't ye?' Bessie said, slapping powder on her face and then brushing most of it off again with her puff. 'She's that good to him in other ways. I must say she gets fair mad about it. Especially when she sees the mess he makes on the sheets. They're all stained wi' orange juice.'

'I'd make him wash them himsel',' Lily said. 'That might take some o' the stiffness out of him. He's a right pansy, if you ask me.'

Bessie giggled. 'He's the one I told ye about that uses all the scent.'

'Scent!' Lily closed her handbag with a sharp snap. 'Dinnie talk to me about scent! I'm fed up wi' the way the Poles are buyin' all the scent. Sometimes I think they must have baths in it! D'ye know, Hippy, we've had to go down to the basement in the shop and rake out all the old bottles o' scent, the Poles are buying them up that quick. I've sold gallons and gallons of toilet-water to them, too. I whiles wonder where they get all the money.'

They took a last look in the mirror to see that they were all right, then they pranced back to the restaurant. 'And fountain-pens!' Lily said. 'The Poles are buying every fountain-pen they can lay their hands on. We have none o' those Blue Cardinals left, and we cannie get any more from America as long as the war lasts. The Poles are the only ones that are able to afford to pay the price for them. God help any puir Scots felly that wants to buy a pen. He has to put up wi' a cheap one out of Woolworths.'

'That reminds me,' Bessie said. 'Have ye heard from Tommy lately?'

'Tommy?' Lily sounded as though she were trying to remember who he was. 'Oh, ay, I had three letters from him this mornin'. Three! He must spend all his time writin'. They dinnie seem to do much work at sea, I must say. He's sent me screeds and screeds. I've got them in ma bag here, but I havenie had time to read them yet. I'll maybe read them in ma bed when I'm havin' a long lie on Sunday mornin'.'

When they got back to their table they found the Polish soldiers on their feet, ready to go. Dmitri grinned and took Bessie's arm. Lily cleeked her arm into Gabanski's and then the other one into Leja's, smiling at him with artificial brightness. But Leja disengaged himself and strode ahead of them.

61

Going back to the boarding-house in the tram-car, seated between Klosowski and Leja, Bessie smiled from one soldier to the other, and she glanced continually at the other passengers to see if they were noticing that she had been out with two Poles. Dmitri's thigh was pressed tightly against hers, and he pawed her knee every now and then. But he spoke all the time to Leja.

In a sense, Bessie was relieved that his attention was taken up with the other officer. And when they reached the boarding-house she took the opportunity to run in ahead of them. She was halfway up the first flight of stairs before Klosowski had shut the door behind them. 'Good night,' she called.

'Ah, Bessee!' Dmitri made a movement as though to check her. 'One moment, please! Not go to bed yet.'

'I must,' she cried. 'I've got to be up early in the morning.'

'But, Bessee——'

'Good night,' she called again, and she ran quickly up the other stairs to her own room. She sighed with something like relief as she shut the door behind her, and she stood for a second, listening in case he had followed. Then, almost without thinking, she turned the key. It was the first time since she came to live with Mrs. Irvine that she had ever locked her door.

XIII

The following afternoon when Bessie was in her bedroom, Mrs. McNeill, the charwoman, bawled upstairs: 'Bessie, are ye there, Bessie?'

'Ay.' Bessie pushed her head over the well of the stairs and looked down at Mrs. McNeill's large moon-face beaming up at her.

'Here's a parcel for ye,' Mrs. McNeill screamed. 'From P.T.'s. What have ye been spendin' yer hard-earned money on now?'

'I havenie been spendin' it on anything,' Bessie said, rushing downstairs. 'Gosh, what can it be?' She held the large flat

cardboard box in her hands and looked curiously at the label:
Patrick Thomson, Ltd., North Bridge, Edinburgh. It was
addressed to 'Miss Bessie, c/o Mrs. Irvine.'

'Oh,' she cried. 'I wonder——'

Mrs. McNeill, a huge shapeless figure in a tight floral overall,
leaned her breasts against Bessie's shoulder, panting with
excitement: 'Well, open it quick, lassie, and dinnie stand
there gapin' as though ye'd swallowed yer tonsils!'

'I wonder——' Bessie said, and she tore off the string.

She was right. It was the pale blue taffeta dress she had
admired. Nestling amongst the tissue paper was a card with
'To my wee hen from her devoted cock, Dmitri,' written in
large sprawling letters.

'Well!' Bessie gasped.

'What does it say?' Mrs. McNeill's fat red fingers grabbed
the card from her. 'I wish I had my specs wi' me.' She
screwed up her eyes and peered at the writing. 'Govey Dick,
but he's got a right funny kind o' fist, hasn't he? Whae is
it, Bessie? One o' yer lads?' She guffawed ribaldly and
nudged Bessie. 'I've had many a love letter in ma time,
though maybe ye wouldnie think it frae the look o' me now,
but my Christ, I've never had yin like this!'

Bessie stood with the box in her arms, blushing with mingled
embarrassment and excitement, and before she could do anything Mrs. McNeill, giving her hands a perfunctory wipe on
her thighs, pulled the dress from the tissue paper and shook
it out. 'My Christ, but isn't it gorgeous! Ye'll look a right
topper in this, Bessie.'

Mrs. McNeill held the dress in front of her and gave a few
skips. 'It fair puts me in mind o' ma ain young days when
I was crazy about dancin'. *Oh Abie, Abie, Abie my boy!*' she
skirled. '*What are you waitin' for now?*'

'Ay, but that song was long afore your time, Bessie,' she
sighed, folding the dress and laying it back in the box. 'It
was all the go just after the last war when I used to go to
dances wi' my fyongsy—Mr. McNeill that was, God rest his
soul!—and I never missed a dance when the band played it.
Eh, but it was a right guid song and had some guts in it.

No' like some o' the wishywashy songs they ha'e nowadays. I mind I once sang it at a concert.'

'Did you?' Bessie said, smoothing the skirt of the dress.

'Ay, did I!' Mrs. McNeill shook back her massive shoulders, folded her hands on her stomach, and stared straight in front of her. She held her grey head with its array of steel curlers very stiffly on her short fat neck and sang:

> 'All the family keep on asking me
> Which day, what day,
> I dunno what to say.
> Abie, Abie, Abie my BOY!
> What are you waitin' for NOW?'

'I was a riot,' she said. 'Ay, I was presented with a box o' chocolates by the minister. I mind as though it was yesterday. A great big box of chocolates tied wi' blue ribbon, and it had Gladys Cooper's picter on the lid. And Alfie—Mr. McNeill that was—proposed that very night. So the family were able to stop sayin' "What day, which day?" after that.'

She chuckled. 'Well, come on, dinnie stand there, lassie. C'mon upstairs and we'll try the frock on!' And she pushed the astonished Bessie in front of her and hustled her up to her bedroom, singing: *'You promised to marry me one day in June! It's never too late and it's never too soon. . . .'*

'But I've got the boarders' tea to lay,' Bessie protested. 'Mrs. Irvine said——'

'Ach, forget the bloody boarders for a wee while,' Mrs. McNeill cried. 'And Mrs. Irvine'll not be back for an hour yet, anyway. There's plenty time to get it all done afore she comes.'

'There ye are now!' Mrs. McNeill stood back, arms akimbo, and surveyed her handiwork. 'Ye're a perfect dabber!'

'Ay, it looks real nice, doesn't it?' Bessie looked down at the dress and turned round slowly, rustling the full flared skirt. She stood on tiptoe and tried to see as much of herself as she could in the small mirror.

'Awa' along to Mrs. Irvine's room and ha'e a decka at

64

yersel' in the big wardrobe-mirror,' Mrs. McNeill said. 'Eh, but it puts me in mind o' auld times right enough when ma heart was young and gay!' She laughed. 'Ma heart's light enough yet, Christ knows, but ma feet won't let me!'

Standing in front of the mirror in Mrs. Irvine's room, Bessie sighed with a mixture of pleasure and annoyance. It was just like Mrs. McNeill to be here at the very moment when the parcel arrived. Bessie would have liked to have opened the box slowly and to let her imagination linger over the dress as she put it on. But she had been hustled so quickly into it that still she had not fully realized what it all meant.

Really, it's right good of Dmitri, she thought, stretching her neck over her shoulder in an endeavour to see how she looked from the back. I thought he was just joking. I'm sure I don't know how I'm going to thank him. . . .

'My godfathers, Bessie, what's this?' Mrs. Irvine's voice made her jump.

She turned round guiltily. 'It's—it's a dress that Dmitri—I mean Lieutenant Klosowski—has given me.'

'Lieutenant Klosowski?' Mrs. Irvine advanced into the room with the majesty of an outraged lioness. 'A dress that Lieutenant Klosowski's given you. I don't like the sound of this at all.'

'I saw it in P.T.'s window last night,' Bessie mumbled, 'and Lieutenant Klosowski said he would buy it for me. I thought he was just jokin', but a wee while ago it came, and——'

'Joking indeed!' Mrs. Irvine sniffed. 'It doesn't look much like it, does it? My word, that dress must have cost him a pretty penny. Really, Bessie, you can't accept such an expensive present. Unless——' she paused, bosom swelling. 'Unless you've been up to any tricks! Have you?'

'Tricks?' Bessie said. 'Oh no, Mrs. Irvine, honest I haven't.'

'I should hope not.' Mrs. Irvine took off her hat, placed it carefully on the bed, and smoothed her hair. 'We all know what these foreign soldiers are. I wouldn't trust one of them an inch. Not an inch!' she said. 'So you'll just give him the dress back.'

'But——' Bessie's mouth fell open.

65

'Yes, you'll give it back, my girl. Go and take it off before it gets crushed. Thank him very much for it. Say you're most grateful and all that, but you can't accept such expensive presents from a stranger.'

'But I——'

'You'll do what I say, Bessie.' Mrs. Irvine waved her out of the room. 'Get it off at once and hurry up and get the tea ready.'

'But I——' Bessie gulped. 'But he'll no' be pleased if I give it back.'

'I'll deal with him,' Mrs. Irvine said.

'But I don't *want* to give it back,' Bessie cried. 'It's a lovely dress and it suits me and——'

'You'll do what I tell you,' Mrs. Irvine said. 'Or I'll have to have a word with your father. I will not have such ongoings in *my* house.'

'But there wasn't any ongoings,' Bessie said sulkily. 'I just admired the frock in the window and he said he'd get it. I never thought he meant it.'

'Get the frock off at once and get the tea ready,' Mrs. Irvine said. 'I'll deal with Lieutenant Klosowski.'

Bessie folded the dress carefully and laid it back amongst the tissue paper, but she did not put on the lid. She stood for a few seconds, touching the frills of the skirt with tender fingers. . . .

XIV

Bessie was careful to keep out of the boarders' way at tea-time. She did not want to see Klosowski at any cost, for she did not know what she could possibly say to him. Usually she was in a hurry to clear away the dirty dishes, but tonight she put off for as long as she could, and when at last she took a tray sulkily to the dining-room she crept past the sitting-room door.

She was furious at Mrs. Irvine. Putting her spoke in where she wasn't wanted, the old bitch. By God, she has a right nerve, and it would serve her right if I gave notice. I've a good mind to tell her to stick her job where the monkey stuck the nuts. She'd know then where she was with this big house to run herself and all these boarders and only Mrs. McNeill to help her. . . . She wouldn't be so keen then on trying to diddle a poor lassie out of a nice present that a fellow had given her out of sheer good-heartedness. It was just like Mrs. Irvine, the narrow-minded old besom, to see evil where there was none. What if he *had* kissed her? It was just in fun, wasn't it? Lots of lassies got kissed by fellows and nothing was thought of it.

Bessie dumped the crockery into the sink, regardless of whether she broke anything or not. Just let Mrs. Irvine complain about a cup being chipped! By God, if she did she would fairly cheek back at her: 'And what right have you, Mrs. Irvine, to say whether I'm to keep the dress or not? Lieutenant Klosowski gave me the dress, and I'll trouble you to mind your own bloody business. . . .'

Ay, that was the way to talk to her. Bessie scowled as she ran the hot water into the sink. She was damned if she would give the dress back—although very likely by this time Mrs. Irvine had done the damage and spoken about it to Dmitri. She wished now that she had phoned Lily and asked her what she should do. Lily would have been sure to tell her to stick to the dress. 'Of course, ye're not to give it back, Bess. The idea! Just you tell the interferin' auld bitch to mind her own business. And you pack yer bags at once and come away. Dinnie stay another minute in that house where ye're no better than a slave.'

Yes, she should have phoned Lily, Bessie ruminated, swirling the cups vindictively and banging them on the drying-board. She would have been better to phone Lily than to have wasted time in having a wee greet to herself, making her eyes all red and nipping.

Now if Mrs. Irvine had had Lily to deal with, it would have been a different story. Lily would never have taken the likes of this lying down. Lily would have been up in arms at once and told Mrs. Nosey Irvine just where she got off. . . .

'Bessie!' Mrs. Irvine bustled into the kitchen.

'Ay,' Bessie muttered sulkily.

'Bessie, Bessie!' Mrs. Irvine laughed. 'My, what a forgetful lassie you are to be sure! How often have I to tell you not to say "ay," but to say "yes"? At this rate, I'll never get you educated properly!'

Bessie did not answer. She rubbed the plates furiously with the dish-rag and put them on the board.

'I've spoken to Lieutenant Klosowski, Bessie,' said Mrs. Irvine, bending down and rummaging in the cupboard where they kept the boot-brushes and polish. 'I told him I didn't think it quite the thing for a young girl like you to accept expensive gifts. But he was that nice about it, saying he thought such a lot of you and how hard you worked and all that, that I hadn't the heart to tell him to take it back. And so!' she laughed again and emerged triumphantly with the brown boot polish and a duster. 'And so the upshot was that I said you'd be delighted to keep the dress and that you'd thank him personally as soon as you saw him.'

'Oh, Mrs. Irvine!' Bessie nearly dropped a plate into the sink. 'Oh, Mrs. Irvine, do ye mean . . .'

'Yes, you can keep the dress,' Mrs. Irvine said. 'But——' She drew in her chin majestically. 'But I don't want you to make this a precedent. I don't really approve of it. But Lieutenant Klosowski's such a nice fellow and he's got such a way with him that—well, I think it would have hurt his feelings if you had shown you were displeased. So you'll just have to thank him nicely. But let him know that it's not to happen again. Don't let him run away with the idea that you're a girl who accepts things lightly.'

'Oh no, Mrs. Irvine,' Bessie breathed, her eyes wide with injured innocence.

'I'm sure that Lieutenant Klosowski didn't mean any harm in giving you the dress,' Mrs. Irvine continued, hoisting her foot on to a chair and rubbing her shoe with the brush. 'And I'm sure you meant none in accepting it. But it's what other folk would think that was worrying me. You know how narrow-minded some folk are.'

'Oh yes, Mrs. Irvine, I know,' Bessie said, nodding vigorously. 'But I never thought——'

'I know you didn't, m'dear. But other folk are not to know that, and they would think all kinds of evil of you. So it's better not to give them any cause, if you see what I mean.'

'Yes, Mrs. Irvine.'

'The trouble with you, Bessie, is that you look so simple that folk think they can take a loan of you. I know that there's a lot more in you than meets the eye, but folk that don't know you just take you at your face value.' Mrs. Irvine gave her shoes a final rub with the duster. 'You'll have to watch yourself with young master Klosowski. After all he's a foreign soldier—even though he is an officer—and foreign soldiers have to be watched very carefully. Klosowski's not the kind that gives evening-dresses away in presents without expecting something in return. So watch your step, m'dear.'

Mrs. Irvine straightened up. 'And just you come to me, Bessie, at the first sign of trouble. Remember that. Don't hesitate. Just come to me and I'll deal with any situation— no matter how bad it is.'

'Yes, Mrs. Irvine.'

Mrs. Irvine put away the boot brushes and dusted her hands. 'That's that!' she said. 'Now, what about hurrying up with those dishes and coming to the Circle with me?'

'Aw, I don't know. . . .' Bessie hesitated. 'I've an awful lot of things to do, and——'

'And you want to try your dress on again!' Mrs. Irvine laughed. 'I was young once myself, so I know what it is. But the dress'll keep, m'dear, the dress'll keep. Just you run upstairs and put it in your wardrobe, and then get yourself ready and come along with me. It's a while since you were at a meeting of the Friends and, who knows, tonight we might be successful in getting in touch with your Mother. One never knows about these things. This might just be the moment when she's on a plane near ours, and we might get through to her.'

'Do ye think so?' Bessie said eagerly. 'D'ye really think so, Mrs. Irvine?'

'One never knows. We'll see if we can get in touch with her through my guide, Ali Ben Hassim. Ali's been away for a sort of holiday, y'know, on another plane, but the other guide we had these last two or three weeks said at last week's Circle that likely enough Ali would be back this week. I feel that if anybody can get us in touch with your Mother it'll be him.'

'Oh, do ye really think so?' Bessie exclaimed. 'Honestly, Mrs. Irvine?'

'Honestly,' Mrs. Irvine replied. 'Ali is really terribly good about getting in touch with people. Mind you, and this is strictly between ourselves, I don't think he's as good as another guide I used to have—Dr. Varconi—you'll remember me telling you about him—but he's the best guide I've had since Varconi went to a Higher Plane. So I think you'd better come with me, m'dear, and we'll get Ali to seek our your mother.'

'I would like you to get your Mother's advice about that dress,' she said. 'It would set my mind at rest if she just set her seal on it and said it was all right for you to have it.'

Bessie rushed upstairs and, although she ached to linger and stroke the dress, she put it on a hanger and put it in the wardrobe. But she promised herself, as she threw a silk scarf over her freshly peroxided hair and rubbed lipstick on her mouth, that she would put it on when they came back from the Circle.

'Captain Van Klee was to have come with me tonight,' Mrs. Irvine said as they went out. 'But he found at the last minute that he couldn't manage. I'm fair disappointed, for I was looking forward to introducing him to the Friends. My word, if ever a man was psychic that one is! He gars me shudder sometimes, I see such a psychic aura round him.'

'Ye wouldn't think it to look at him, would ye?' Bessie giggled. 'He's that big and solid.'

'Solid or not, he's psychic,' Mrs. Irvine asserted. 'And I won't rest content till I've taken him to a Circle. I must say he's awful interested in everything I've told him about my Faith. He never laughed or scoffed or anything the way lots of men would do. My late husband, y'know, Gilbert Irvine was a great scoffer. But of course, Captain Van Klee's a different kettle of fish from Gilbert in every way. Gilbert was a devil for the bottle and was never happy, as you know, unless he was properly soused.'

Bessie was on the point of saying that she had noticed a number of gin bottles in Captain Van Klee's room several times, but before she could bring it out, Mrs Irvine swept on:

'Captain Van Klee was very interested when I told him that a great English Admiral was one of my ancestors and how I was always trying to get in touch with his spirit. He was very interested indeed. The Dutch have aye been a great sea-faring nation, y'know, and they admire people who've got the tang of the sea in their blood. So I'm really disappointed that he wasn't able to come tonight, for I've a funny feeling in my bones that Ali Ben Hassim'll have come back from that Higher Plane with some news of Sir Francis Drake.'

xv

Both Mrs. Irvine and Bessie were disappointed with the Circle, however. Ali Ben Hassim was still away on another plane, and an Hindu guide, Lubra, new even to Mrs. Irvine, got complete control of the medium, Mrs. Baines.

Mrs. Baines did her utmost to get Lubra to get in touch with Francis Drake, but Lubra apparently thought that Mrs. Irvine wanted news of a sailor in the modern navy, for he kept saying: 'Frankie's ship is quite safe. It is somewhere off the coast of Africa, I can't tell you exactly where, but Frankie is all right and nothing will happen to him in this war. He will be torpedoed once, but he will be uninjured. Do not worry about him, but worry more about yourself. Your Aunt Rosie, who is very happy indeed on this side, says you are to beware of air-raids.'

'In the first place, I haven't got and never had an Aunt Rosie,' Mrs. Irvine said on the way home. 'And in the second place, I know better than him to watch out for air-raids. My godfathers, if Lubra was down here just now he would know

71

what air-raids really are with That Man continually sending his Messerschmitts 109's over here to annoy us. I don't need Lubra to tell me to take care of myself.'

'It's a pity about not getting in touch with your Ma, m'dear,' she said. 'I doubt we'll just have to rest content till Ali comes back. That Lubra's a complete washout, and I hope he's not going to be here long to bother us. If he is, I must have a few words with Mrs. Baines.'

Bessie was surprised to find that she was not as disappointed as she might have been. The truth was that she had been a little bored during the meeting. Sitting in the darkness round the table, her outstretched fingers touching Mrs. Irvine's on one side and a nervous old gentleman's on the other, she had not paid particular attention to the medium's attempts to get the proper answers from the spirit guide; she had been dreaming about the pale blue dress, picturing herself wearing it at some wonderful dance to which Dmitri had taken her. . . .

As soon as she and Mrs. Irvine had had a cup of tea and a biscuit, Bessie went upstairs and tried on the dress. For a long time she mooned about the room, holding up the skirt with both hands while she did little dance-steps. Then, hearing sounds that showed Mrs. Irvine to be preparing to come upstairs, she took it off quickly, hung it with loving care in the wardrobe, and got into bed.

But she did not put off the light. Whenever she got an opportunity Bessie took one of the books from Mrs. Irvine's bookcase to her bedroom. Most of the volumes were devoted to spiritualism, but a number dealt with another subject which had interested Mrs. Irvine at one time—famous courtesans and the spell they had wielded over Kings and Emperors and great statesmen. Bessie had read one of these, *Ten Great Courtesans of History* from cover to cover several times, and she could repeat passages almost verbatim, but she never tired of dipping into it. Tonight she opened it at the pages dealing with Madame de Pompadour, and propped it up on her knees. Then she took a small bottle of nail-varnish from the table beside her bed and started to varnish her nails. Holding each finger over an old copy of the *Edinburgh Evening News* in case the varnish got on the sheets, she read again about the famous French-woman who had held such sway over Louis XV. But gradually her eyes strayed from the page and, lying back on the pillows, she was soon in a dream-world of her own. . . .

Jeanne Antoinette Poisson. . . . Bessie knew enough French to know that 'poisson' was 'fish.' No wonder Madame de Pompadour had changed her name! She really must remember this the next time Lily twitted her about calling herself Campbell. She would just show Lily that no great woman in history had ever got anywhere with a daft-like name and that they had all changed their names as quickly as they could. What would Dmitri say if he ever found out that her real name was Hipkiss? He would get a right laugh, wouldn't he? Except that Dmitri didn't seem to be the kind of bloke who would laugh at another's misfortune. No, Dmitri was a perfect gem of a fellow. It was really terribly good of him to give her this dress. Fancy him keeping his promise when there was really no need to keep it. And after the way she had laughed, thinking he was joking. . . .

What if he really meant that he would teach her to ride a horse? He probably did. Jees, but wouldn't it be wonderful to sit on a horse's back and gallop and gallop. . . .

Madame Bette de Carlos, the world-famous beauty, whom rumour has it is the power behind a certain Balkan throne, swept out of her hotel in Madrid and mounted her milk-white Arab stallion—no, that wasn't very ladylike—Madame de Carlos mounted her milk-white mare. Leaning forward, she patted her steed's silky neck, then gathering up the reins, she looked at Prince Dmitri and called: 'I am ready, *mon vieux*!' Her escort, already astride his coal-black stallion (it was all right for a man, a man could control a beast like that better than a woman could) laughed and applied his spurs to Nero's shining sides. Then with a thunder of hooves and gay laughter they galloped madly through the great park where fashionable ladies and gentlemen looked after them with admiration. 'There goes Madame Bette and her beau! *Mon Dieu,* what a beauty she is! A woman who holds millions of lives in the hollow of her dainty . . .'

There was a gentle tap at her door.

Bessie sat up with a jerk, knocking the book off her knees. 'Ay, what is it?' she called. And thinking it was Mrs. Irvine, who had crept upon her unawares, she quickly put the bottle of nail-varnish on the table.

The door opened, and Dmitri pushed his head around.

'Hello, Bessee!' he grinned, and he sidled in and shut the door, keeping his hands behind him for a few seconds.

'What are ye doin' in here?' she gasped. 'My goodness, if Mrs. Irvine comes up here, she'll raise the roof.'

'Mrs. Irvine too busy in own room.' Dmitri took off his black beret with one hand and drew a small comb through his smooth black hair with the other. 'Beautiful night,' he said, bowing. 'Beautiful Bessee! Dmitri wanted to see Bessee. Did Bessee like dress?'

'Ay, it's lovely,' she said quickly. 'It's really lovely. Thank you very much. I was goin' to thank you when I saw you in the mornin'.'

'Bessee like it?' Dmitri advanced into the room, holding his beret in front of him and twisting it between his fingers.

She nodded, clutching the bedclothes to her breast. 'Yes, it's lovely,' she said again. And she stared at him, wondering what she should do.

'Bessee put it on to show Dmitri,' he said.

'Aw, not tonight,' she said in a low voice, terrified that Mrs. Irvine would hear. 'I'll show you tomorrow. You'd better go now. I'm just goin' away to sleep.'

'Not sleep yet,' Dmitri smiled. 'Veree early yet. Dmitri is lonely and wishes to talk with Bessee.'

'Aw, not tonight,' she whispered. 'Mrs. Irvine'll be up in a minute, and goodness knows what she'd say if she found you in here.'

'Door is locked,' Dmitri said. 'Mrs. Irvine is too busy to come.' He grinned. 'Bessee put on dress to show Dmitri?'

'Och, I cannie,' she exclaimed, terrified at the way he was approaching the bed with sinister feline movements. 'I really cannie.'

'Cannie?' He gave a low laugh. 'Where is dress, Bessee?'

74

'It's away,' she said, but instinctively she glanced at the wardrobe.

'In here?' Dmitri opened the wardrobe-door and laughed. 'Nice dress!' he said, taking it out. 'Put on, please.'

'No! Och no, I couldnie,' Bessie cried, so terrified that she did not notice that she had raised her voice. 'I couldnie try it on tonight.' And she made a convulsive movement to the back of the bed.

The Pole held the dress in front of him and leaned over the bed. 'Come, Bessee!' he said. 'Come, my wee hen! Put on dress for Dmitri. Lovelee dress! Lovelee, lovelee Bessee!'

He reached out and pulled her nightdress. 'Come, Bessee, my wee hen!' And the next instant he had slipped his arm around her bare waist and pressed himself against her, lunging on to the bed.

The blue dress fell in a heap on the floor, but Bessie was too agitated to notice. She felt only Dmitri's smooth face pressed against hers, his avid mouth, and his warm searching hands. And then waves of excitement tingled through her, and Mrs. Irvine and everything else was forgotten.

PART II

I

BESSIE'S father joined up as a lorry-driver in the R.A.O.C. at the beginning of September, 1940. Hitler's much prophesied 'blitz' on London had started. Bombs were falling with ferocious intensity. Fires were raging as they had not raged since the Great Fire of 1666, and public attention was caught as it had been caught by no other disaster—except possibly that of Dunkirk—during the war so far. Those who had experienced air-raids on a minor scale did their best to imagine what it must be like. For the first time the Public realized that it was the people on the 'Home Front' who were to suffer most in this war and that it was not to be another period like 1914-1918 when they could sit back comfortably and talk with sentimental hypocrisy about 'Our Poor Boys over there.'

Possibly it was this that made Bert Hipkiss enlist, for he said: 'I don't hold with this war. And I'm no hero. But if I don't join up just now it'll not be long before they come and nab me. Anyway, things are gettin' so bad in my line—most pubs'll soon have to close down because they can't get the booze to sell—that I would soon get my Books. So I might as well join up while I can still choose what mob I want to go into.'

Although she joined her stepmother in a tearful farewell at the Waverley Station, Bessie was rather relieved to see her father go. It meant that Mrs. Irvine could no longer hold over her the threat of 'I'll have to see Mr. Hipkiss about this.' With her father safely out of the way, she told herself, she

77

could now do what she damned well pleased. But she wept loudly and kept repeating: 'I wish ye werenie goin', Da.' And Mabel and she vied with each other in promises to write to him as often as they could. 'I'll write every night, Bert,' Mabel snivelled. 'Even though it's just two or three lines to let you know that we're all okay.'

Through the mist in front of her eyes, Bessie was astonished to notice that her father looked absurdly young as he leaned out of the carriage-window, and she was horrified to catch herself thinking: 'If I didn't know he was my father I believe I could fall for him. He's really not a bad-looking fellow at all.' Of course, she remembered, he was only about thirty-six or thirty-seven. He couldn't be much older than Big Ginger, that vanman at Andrews' who had tried to come funny with her.

She and Mabel were still twisting their little balls of hand-kerchiefs in front of their noses and mouths after the train had disappeared out of the station.

'Well, we'll be seeing you, Bessie,' said her stepmother as they waited for a tram-car at the top of the Waverley Steps. 'You'll have to come down and see us oftener now that your Da's away, so that you can get all the news of him. And I'm sure the bairns'll look forward to seeing you. You're not to make yourself a stranger, mind!'

'No, I'll come down every time I get a night off,' Bessie promised.

She kept that promise on her first night-off, and she and Mabel were carefully friendly and polite with each other. But on her following night-off she had a 'heavy date,' so she could not go down to Calderburn. And something happened to prevent her from visiting her stepmother and the children on her next free evening, also.

She wrote several letters to her father, however, telling him that they were all well and that Billy and Jenny were behaving themselves. And she promised to start knitting him a pair of socks just as soon as she could get any spare time.

Bert had been posted to an army camp in the south of England, and about three weeks after he had gone, Bessie

78

met two of their neighbours, Mrs. Moore and Dirty Minnie, in Princes Street. Bessie was coming out of Woolworths when the two large blousy women pushed the swing-doors from the opposite direction, almost knocking into her. For a second Bessie had an impulse to turn and run, but Dirty Minnie, after a gasp of surprise, had already recognized her.

'Hoy there, Bessie!' she cried. 'Fancy meetin' you, hen! It's wee Bessie Hipkiss, Mrs. Moore!'

'I've got eyes in ma head,' Mrs. Moore retorted, taking in every detail of Bessie's appearance from her bright auburn hair to her vivid apple-green coat and high-heeled black patent shoes.

'My, what a swell she is, isn't she, Mrs. Moore!'

'Ay, fine feathers make fine birds,' Mrs. Moore sniffed. 'What have ye been doin' to yourself, lassie?'

'Well——' Bessie simpered. 'A gentleman friend thought my hair would look better if it was its natural colour. . . .'

'But that's no' yer natural colour,' Mrs. Moore said. 'I've known ye since ye were a bairn, and yer hair was never as bright a red as a' that.'

'Oh, I don't know,' Bessie said, preening herself. 'It's maybe a wee thing touched up, but it was aye red.'

'Sandy I would 'a' called it,' Mrs. Moore said. 'However, I suppose you ken best.'

'And how are ye, Bessie?' Dirty Minnie asked, and she leaned against a counter, hands folded on her ample stomach with black oilskin message-bag dangling, and prepared herself for a long gossip. 'We havenie seen ye down at Calderburn for a while.'

'No, I've been terribly busy,' Bessie said. 'In fact, I'm in a bit of a hurry just now. I'm just doing a bit of shopping for Mrs. Irvine, and she's expecting me back, so——'

'Och, there's no rush,' Dirty Minnie said. 'We've got all day in front o' us, haven't we, Mrs. Moore?'

'Speak for yersel',' Mrs. Moore snapped. 'We're no' all as lucky as you wi' lodgers that never worry whether ye're there to feed them or not.'

'Ay, I must say I'm gey lucky wi' my lodgers,' Minnie said. 'I whiles think it's them that run the house and no' me.'

'Have you still got as many sailors?' Bessie said. 'Ye were aye a boy for sailors, Minnie!'

'No, she's gone up in the world since you used to bide at Calderburn,' Mrs. Moore said, and she nudged Minnie with a fat elbow. 'Haven't ye, hen?'

Minnie giggled and coyly touched her greasy black beret with one dirty hand.

'Minnie's got Poles lodgin' with her,' Mrs. Moore said.

'Fancy!' Bessie said.

'Ay, and I'm no' the only one that's got Poles,' Minnie remarked. 'Have ye seen that Steppy o' yours lately?'

'Mabel?' Bessie said. 'No, I havenie seen her for weeks. I keep meanin' to come down and see the bairns, but I'm aye up to the eyes in work.'

Mrs. Moore sniffed and looked at Dirty Minnie. 'Of course, it's none o' our business,' she said. 'I ken that. But still, I was aye a great pal o' yer puir mother's and although I've often no' seen eye to eye with yer faither I've nothin' against him.'

'No, he's a nice felly,' Minnie said, nodding her head in time with Mrs. Moore's. 'It's a damned shame that a nice felly like that should have to go away to the back o' beyond wi' the army and such on-goings should go on in his own house.'

'Mind you, as I've said already, it's none o' our business,' Mrs. Moore said, glaring at a woman who was pushing past her to get to the counter. 'But I think it's about time that a wee bird whispered somethin' to yer faither.'

'Whispered what?' Bessie said.

'Ay, it's about time,' Dirty Minnie agreed.

'The brazent impiddence o' her to bring the felly to the house!' Mrs. Moore primmed her lips. 'She surely knows that folk would see him goin' out and in.'

'See who goin' out and in?' Bessie said.

The two stout women looked at each other, shaking their heads with indignation.

'The Pole that your Steppy's goin' with,' Mrs. Moore said at last.

Bessie's mouth opened wide and stayed open. 'The Pole that Mabel's goin' with!' she gasped.

'Ay.' Mrs. Moore held her head to the side and sniffed. 'Three times at least have I seen him goin' in, and twice have I seen them comin' out together. Yer puir Da wasn't away in the army a week before that high-and-mighty Mabel brought the Pole home as bold as brass.'

'I think ye should write to yer Da about it, Bessie,' Dirty Minnie said. 'It's not decent.'

'No, it's not decent,' Mrs. Moore repeated. 'However, as I've said, it's none o' our business. Well, we mustnie keep ye, Bessie,' she said. 'I ken that you're in a hurry. So run along wi' ye, hen!'

'But——' Bessie bit her lips, sucking in the lipstick. 'What do ye think I should do, Mrs. Moore?'

Mrs. Moore looked at Dirty Minnie for guidance, but her crony was bending over the counter, raking amongst the cards of cheap brooches.

'Well, there's maybe nothin' in it,' Mrs. Moore said. 'After all, we've only *seen* her wi' the Pole. I think maybe we should hover a blink and say nothin' to yer puir Da in the meantime. He'll have plenty to worry him, I'll warrant.'

'Ay, he will that,' Minnie agreed. 'Bein' in the army'll be no picnic.' She held up a bright brooch shaped like a butterfly. 'How do ye think this would look on ma black lace blouse?'

'Yer black lace!' Mrs. Moore nudged Bessie and guffawed. 'Listen to her! The next thing we hear, Minnie, ye'll be out paradin' wi' a Pole yersel'!'

'Ay, a telegraph pole!' Minnie giggled ribaldly.

II

One evening a week later Bessie met her stepmother in Princes Street with a Polish soldier, but whether it was the same Pole or another one she did not pause to enquire. She pretended not to see Mabel, for she was as anxious as her

81

stepmother not to be seen. Bessie had her arm round Joe Pole's waist, and he had his arm round her shoulders and was looking down at her as they walked along.

A few days after his assault on her virginity, Dmitri Klosowski had been sent to Cupar to take part in some Polish Army manœuvres there. He told Bessie and Mrs. Irvine that he would be away for only a week. At the end of the week, however, he wrote to Bessie to say that it would be some time yet before he would be able to return. The letter was almost obscene in its primitive English, and Bessie did not dare show it to Mrs. Irvine. She delivered his message and hoped that Mrs. Irvine would not demand to see the letter. A few days later Mrs. Irvine herself received a letter which said that it would be at least a month before he came back and would she keep his belongings carefully and he would pay her for the rent of the room when he returned.

At first Bessie was sorry when he went. She was sorry because it meant that she could no longer flaunt him as an escort in Princes Street and especially in the Golden Sala-mander, and she knew she would be subject to pitying looks from Lily and jibes about 'So ye werenie able to keep yer Pole!' But at the same time she was relieved. It was a relief to know that she could go to bed without either locking her door or lying awake, listening for quiet tiptoeing outside her door and then *that*. Although it had happened only twice, Bessie was in no doubt about what it all meant. It was wonderful, of course. Far far better than she had imagined from any of the books she had read or what she had heard. But she knew that it was *wrong*. Nice girls like herself didn't do things like that with men until they were safely married, and by doing it she realized that she had put herself on the same level as girls like that Mamie Proudfoot, whom Lily spat about so vehemently. She wanted desperately to talk about it to Lily, but she dared not, knowing that Lily would be horrified. And of course it was out of the question to even mention it to Mrs. Irvine.

For a few days Bessie went around in a day-dream in which she saw herself in Poland—after the war was over, of course—

82

being feted everywhere as 'the beautiful Madame Dmitri Klosowski.' She went to balls, theatres, great dinner-parties, and everywhere she was the centre of attraction and people raved about Mme. Klosowski's 'lovely soft Scottish voice.' Then Klosowski went to Cupar, and her day-dream receded before an onslaught of doubts and alarm. What if he didn't come back? What if he didn't mean to marry her like he'd said? What if he had a wife in Poland already?

She didn't think this possible—after all, Dmitri was terribly young—but at the same time you never knew with these Poles. As Mrs. Irvine said, 'You can never really trust foreigners.' And so she was delighted when she got his letter.

But her delight was mingled with apprehension. She was delighted that Dmitri still seemed to be keen on her, but she was apprehensive about what would happen when he returned. Because about three days after Klosowski had gone to Cupar, something took place which put a different complexion on the whole affair.

After washing the tea-dishes Bessie was leaning against the sink reading a serial in *Cynthia's Circle*. This was a twopenny paper which she got every week and which she never failed to read from cover to cover no matter what other things she could not find time to do. Her mother had always got it, and Bessie had been reading it since she was seven or eight. This week's issue had huge letters on the front cover: DOES SYLVIA DARLING MAKE THE GRADE? Bessie was deep in the adventures of Sylvia, who had been a mill-girl but was now married to an earl, when the door opened and Joe Pole came into the kitchen.

Bessie jumped with surprise. 'Aw, I thought it was Mrs. Irvine,' she said.

Rolewicz clicked his heels and bowed, but he said nothing. He stood there, a slight smile on his usually sullen face, playing with the linen handkerchief protruding from the sleeve of his well-cut tunic.

Bessie grinned and moved away from the sink, smoothing her hair. 'It's warm, isn't it?' she said in the loud voice she always used when addressing Joe Pole. And she wondered what he could possibly want. He was usually out at this time

83

in the evening. Of course, with Dmitri being away perhaps he was at a loose end. . . .

'Not out tonight?' Bessie said, pausing between each word. 'Nice night for a walk.'

Rolewicz inclined his blond head and smiled again. Bessie picked up some cups and hung them on hooks on a shelf. She felt uneasy. This was the first time Joe Pole had penetrated to the kitchen. Indeed it was the first time she had ever found herself alone with him.

'You want Mummy?' she asked. 'Mummy is out. She will not be long.'

'Mummy?' Joe Pole shook his head. He smiled ingratiatingly: a slow charming smile that lit up his whole face and made Bessie's stomach flutter.

He pointed at her, then he pointed to himself and said: 'Cinema?'

Bessie stared at him. 'Cinema?' she said.

He nodded. 'Bessee . . . come . . . wis . . . Joe?'

'Och, I couldnie,' Bessie cried. Then, flustered, she repeated slowly: 'No, I cannot go. Mrs. Irvine is out, so I have to stay in the house.'

'Tomorrow?' he said.

'We—ell!' Bessie giggled. 'Tomorrow! Yes, I wouldn't mind.'

'Playhouse?' he said. 'New Victoria?'

'Och, anywhere you like,' she said, and she fluffed up her hair and looked coyly at him. 'It's all the same to me where we go.'

'Please?' he said. He frowned like a small boy trying to figure out some difficult problem.

'Let's see what's on this week,' Bessie said, and she picked up the *Evening News* and scanned the advertisements for cinemas on the front page. Joe Pole moved towards her and looked over her shoulder. He did not touch her, but her every nerve tingled with the sense of his nearness. She looked up and saw him scowling at the newspaper, his lips moving soundlessly.

'I see that Ray Milland and Ellen Drew are at the Palace

in *French Without Tears*,' she said. 'I've seen it before, but I wouldn't mind seeing it again. Let's go there.'

'There!' he said. 'Yesss!'

'Tomorrow?' he said.

'Tomorrow,' she said.

They stood and looked at each other for several seconds. Then Joe Pole took the *Evening News* from her and sat down in the old armchair beside the fire. He disregarded Bessie completely and scanned the paper as though he understood every word. An expression of deep concentration settled on his face. Occasionally he would put up one hand and touch a little blond curl dangling over his right temple or he would put his finger inside the collar of his tunic and ease it away from his neck.

After a few minutes Bessie picked up *Cynthia's Circle* and tried to get on with her serial. But she found difficulty in following Sylvia Darling's adventures any longer; she kept glancing at Joe Pole, and whenever he caught her eye they smiled, then both would look quickly at their papers.

The following evening he took her to the Palace, to the best seats, and throughout *French Without Tears* he held her hand. He made no other move, however, except to take her elbow politely when they were crossing streets. And when they parted at the foot of the stairs he took her hand and kissed it, then stood back and clicked his heels, and said: 'Good night.'

Every evening after that, if he did not take her to a cinema or to a café or for a walk, he sat in the kitchen. He said practically nothing. He seemed content to be there with her without any conversation. When they walked together Bessie would prattle out of sheer nervousness, but Joe Pole merely smiled every now and then, walking stiffly beside her. Bessie felt that it was her duty to teach him English, so wherever they went she would point out things and name them very slowly and clearly: 'Shop. House. Boy. Little boy. Siren-suit. Basket. Aeroplane. One of ours. Hurricane—och, no, I think it's a Spitfire. Yes, Spitfire!' All of which Joe Pole would repeat like an obedient child. Despite her coaching, however, his English did not improve very much—unless when he wanted to make himself understood, and then Bessie discovered that he knew much more than she had given him credit for. After a time she realized that he did not say much because he was naturally a silent person, so she contented herself with prancing along beside him, revelling in the envious looks she got from other girls.

She had known him a fortnight before he even attempted to kiss her. It was on the same day as she got a second letter from Klosowski to say that his stay in Cupar would be longer than he had thought. And so when she was saying good night to Joe at the foot of the stairs and he made what was for him a rather more definite movement, Bessie leaned against him, took his face in her hands and drew him down and kissed him.

'But he's that slow,' she complained to Lily. 'Honestly, Lil, you'd think he'd know that a lassie likes a bit o' canoodlin' sometimes.'

'Och, you're better to leave him alone,' Lily advised. 'Once he gets started he'll maybe be too quick. Better to be slow than sorry is what I say, and I know a lot more aboot men than you do, Hippy.'

Joe Pole might be slow, but once he had made up his mind about something he worried away at it. One evening, sitting in the kitchen, he said: 'Why paint hair, *kotka*?'

Bessie giggled. 'Because I like it that way, see! It suits me better to be a blondie.'

'Joe not like it,' he said.

Bessie shrugged and said: 'Well, I can't help it. I never liked my own shade. Red hair doesn't suit me, especially sandy-red the way it used to be.'

'Joe likes red hair,' he said.

Bessie made a face at him and went on reading her book.

The next night when they were going to a cinema, he said quite suddenly: 'Red hair iss nicest for Bessee. Red hair iss immoral.'

'Ach, get away with you!' Bessie slapped his arm playfully. 'Don't you go and say I'm immoral or I'll—I'll scratch your eyes out!'

86

Joe grinned. 'Bessee scratch Joe in cinema, yes?'

Bessie sniffed and gave her head a toss. She had discovered that Joe Pole had a small vice: he liked to be scratched.

'You leave the subject o' my hair alone, and we'll see about the scratchin',' she said.

'Joe likes red hair,' he said stubbornly. 'Red hair iss veree immoral.'

'Look here,' Bessie began.

'Immoral iss . . .' Joe struggled for a word. 'Red hair iss temper!' he said, and he nodded vigorously. 'Yesss! Tem-per-a-ment! Bessee has temperament, so Bessee should haf red hair, yes!'

Bessie said nothing, but she thought a lot on the rest of the way to the cinema, and once inside when Joe took her hand and murmured: 'Little *kotka* scratch Joe, yes!' and made miaowing sounds, she drew her nails gently at first and then with greater violence up and down the back of his hand.

She was terrified to dye her hair again, however. She remembered the row she had had with her father the first time Lily had persuaded her to peroxide it. And so when Bert Hipkiss announced that he had enlisted, Bessie felt a sense of release. She knew she should be ashamed of this, since her father might never return to Edinburgh alive, but on the day following their tearful leave-taking she dyed her hair a vivid henna.

III

When she saw for herself that her stepmother really had a Polish soldier, Bessie wondered why Lily had not mentioned it. She lived opposite to them and knew practically everything that happened in the street. It wasn't like Lily to miss such a chance.

Of course, she reflected, she had not seen much of Lily lately. She had been too busy with Joe Pole, and Lily had been busy with Gabanski. It was a fortnight since they had met. Still, it was curious that Lily had not mentioned it one of those times when she had telephoned. You would have thought that Lily would have been simply dying to tell her. Except that, come to think of it, Lily had not even telephoned for about ten days.

Bessie was puzzled. It wasn't like Lily to remain silent for so long. Had anything happened to her? Maybe she had got a new boy-friend. . . .

As soon as she got Mrs. Irvine out of the way, Bessie telephoned the chemist's where Lily worked. 'Can I speak to Mrs. Hutchinson, please?' she said in her politest tones.

'Mrs. Hutchinson? I'm afraid Mrs. Hutchinson doesn't work here any longer.' And the receiver was slammed down before Bessie could do more than gasp.

Full of curiosity, she wrote a letter to Lily at once and addressed it to Goldengreen Street. But it was three days before it elicited a response. The phone rang. Bessie, answering, heard the drop of two pennies in a public call box, and then a voice saying: 'Can I speak to Miss Campbell?'

'Miss Campbell speaking.'

'Oh, is that you, Bessie?' Lily cried. 'Howlin' Jesus! I didnie recognize your posh voice.'

Bessie simpered into the mouth-piece. 'Where are you, Lil? I phoned the shop and they said you had left.'

'Ay, I left a week ago. And damned glad I was to get away, too! It was a helluva place, and I was fair . . .' Lily's next words were inaudible, and Bessie heard a lot of banging and raised voices. 'Hello!' she called. 'Hello! Are you there, Lil?'

There was more banging and shouting, and then Lily said: 'Are ye still there, Bessie? Honest to God, a lassie can't even phone in peace these days. D'you know that I waited twenty minutes to get in to this box? Twenty bloody minutes. There was a wee whippersnapper o' a lassie in here—she couldn't be more than thirteen—and d'you know, she was in here for twenty minutes and looked as though she'd be in for the duration, so at last I just opened the door and said 'Lissen, are you goin' to be in here all day? This is a *public* box,' I said, 'and I'll trouble you to finish your conversation and give other people a chance to make theirs.' I tell you what it is,

Bess, some folk have no sense. I might 'a' been wantin' to phone the polis or the doctor or the fire-brigade or somethin' important, but this little bitch didn't seem to care a scrap. But I shifted her quick, I can tell you. Well, would you believe it, that was her back to say she'd left her handbag. I'd handbag the bitch! Really, some o' these young ones are the bloody end. What right has a lassie o' that age to be phonin', anyway?'

'Too true,' Bessie agreed.

'But I shifted her,' Lily cried. 'Yes, I sent her away wi' a flea in her ear all right. Really, the wee bitch, if looks could 'a' killed!'

'Well, tell me about the shop,' Bessie said. 'What did ye leave for?'

'Och, it's a terrible long story and I couldn't tell ye here. This box is too public. No, I couldn't tell ye here. There's an auld wife standin' outside glowerin' in at me, and I'm sure she's listenin' to every word. I tell you what—can you meet me some place tonight?'

'Well, I could try,' Bessie said. 'I'll have to ask Mrs. Irvine if——'

'Och, just tell her you've got to go out. Tell her it's a matter o' life and death. Can ye meet me at six o'clock? Six o'clock at the Caley Station, and see and no' be late. The main entrance o' the Caley Station. Well, I'll have to fly now and get Teddy's lunch ready for him, and this auld bitch is startin' to tap on the door. Really, some o' these auld ones! Can they not leave a lassie in peace to phone for five minutes? Well, cheeri-bye, Bess, see you at six!'

'Cheeri-bye!' Bessie said.

She was late in reaching the Caley Station and she found Lily in a bad temper. 'Jesus Christ and General Jackson, Hippy!' Lily cried. 'Whatever made you choose a place like this to meet at? I'm fair choked standin' here with the smoke from thae engines! You might 'a' picked a better place.'

'But you said the Caley Station,' Bessie said.

'Me! I never did.' Lily threw away her cigarette and

cleeked her arm into Bessie's. 'However, we'll not quarrel
about it. Here you are, so let's make the best o' it. Well,'
she said without pausing for breath, 'I've left the shop, and
a bloody good riddance it was too. Honestly, the cheek I had
to put up with. You'd never credit it, Bess, all that I had
to stand from that wee sammy-dreep o' a manager. D'you
know he threatened to get the polis? The polis! Now, I
ask you!'

'Fancy!' Bessie exclaimed.

'Yes, you may well say. And all I did was to take a loan
o' five bob out the cash-register.' Lily's voice was full of
injured innocence. 'I meant to put it back on the Saturday
when I got my wages, but that sleekit wee bugger found out
and raised the devil. Really, the way he went on about it,
you'd 'a' thought I'd robbed the till or somethin'. And me
just takin' a loan o' five bob that was due me, anyway, in
wages. My Christ, I told him what I thought of him and his
job. He got a good piece o' my mind, I can tell you, before
I walked out on him. And then, d'you know, he had the nerve
to try to stop the Broo givin' me any unemployment money?'

'Oh, fancy!' Bessie gasped. 'He did not?'

'He did that,' Lily said. 'He rang up the manager o' the
Broo and told him I was little better than a common thief
and that it was the nick I should be gettin' instead of unemployment benefit. Imagine the nerve o' the man! Tryin' to
do me out of my Broo money that I've paid into for years
and years.'

'I aye said he wasn't a nice man,' Bessie said. 'I've often
thought when you told me about him that he sounded a right
bad hat.'

'Well, I'm rid of him now, anyway,' Lily said. 'Good
riddance to bad rubbish is what I say! I just hope he and his
auld shop get hit by a bomb the next time Jerry's over here.
That would learn him to accuse an innocent lassie and try to
stop her gettin' her Broo money.'

Lily giggled suddenly. 'D'you know, Bess! You'll die
when you hear this! Teddy wanted to go after him with a
knife.'

'Naw?' Bessie stopped dead in the middle of the street, and the driver of an oncoming tram clanged his bell furiously.

'Ay, Teddy wanted to slit his throat.' Lily gurgled breathlessly once they were on the opposite pavement. 'I had an awful job calmin' him down. Teddy's really terrible quick-tempered, y'know.'

'Oh, by the way,' Lily continued as though it were an afterthought, 'Teddy and me are livin' together. Teddy got the offer of an awful nice flat in Learmouth Crescent so he took it, and I just thought I might as well go and bide with him. It's really an awfully nice flat, and I was gettin' a bit fed up with livin' at home. You know how my father keeps narkin' about the war. Well, it was gettin' on my nerves. So I just thought: Och, to hell, I might as well take the chance when Teddy asked me.'

'But—but what about Tommy?' Bessie gasped.

'Och, Tommy!' Lily shrugged. 'There's time enough to worry about Tommy when he comes home on leave—if he ever comes home! I don't think there's much danger o' him gettin' leave if his boat's somewhere in the middle o' the Pacific. Of course, this is such a funny war that you never know what'll happen. I must say I wouldn't like Tommy to come bargin' in on me some day. Though I don't think there's much danger o' that,' she said. 'My mother has enough gumption not to give him my address, and he'd never find it out for himself.'

'But what if he should?' Bessie murmured, awestruck at the thought. 'My goodness, he would fairly kick up a shindy!'

'Och, we'll just have to take the risk,' Lily said. 'In a way, I wouldn't mind if he came home and found out about me and Teddy. I was right fed up with Tommy Hutchinson, anyway, even before he went away this long voyage. The only good he's ever done me was to get me the allotment-money from the Government. I would miss that, now that I'm not workin'.'

'Oh, Lily, what if they ever found out?' Bessie's eyes widened with alarm.

'Found out what, ye silly bitch?'

'Found out that ye were livin' with Teddy and drawin' the money from Tommy's allotment.'

'Ach, that's none o' their business,' Lily said. 'I'm Tommy's wife, and if Tommy likes to make me an allotment that's up to him. The Government have nothin' to do with it. And it's none o' your business either, Ferret. It seems to me that you've got enough to worry about on your own account without pokin' your nose into my affairs. My Christ, I wouldn't like to be in your shoes when Dmitri Whatsisname comes back from Cupar and finds you carryin' on with that Joe—and after him givin' you a lovely blue frock, too!'

'But I—but I never asked him to give me the frock.'

'Maybe not,' Lily said. 'But he's not likely to think about that. All that he's likely to think about is that he gave you a frock and what has Joe got to do with it. You'd better get your thinkin' cap on, Bess, and have a good one ready for Dmitri when he comes back.'

'Och, he's not likely to be back for a while yet,' Bessie said. 'I had a letter the other day to say he wouldn't be back for two or three weeks yet.'

'That reminds me,' Lily said, 'I've never seen this famous frock. When are ye goin' to put it on?'

'Well, it's a dance-frock. I can hardly wear it unless I was goin' to a dance. I wish now it had been some other kind o' frock that I could 'a' worn oftener. Every time I see it hangin' in the wardrobe I wish it had been simpler. It's terrible low in the neck. I'm a bit feared to wear it in case folk say . . .'

'What does it matter what folk say!' Lily blew her breath out sharply with irritation. 'Just thumb yer nose at them! I tell ye, Bess, ye'll never get on in this world if ye bother about what folk think o' you. To hell with them all! C'mon, let's go to a dance next week, so that you can get a chance to wear it. You bring Joe and I'll bring Teddy and we'll have a whale of a time. What d'ye say?'

'Well,' Bessie said. 'It would be fine, but——'

'Next Friday night,' Lily said. 'We'll go to the Pally.

92

Friday night's always a good night at the Pally. We'll have a rip-snorter of a time, eh? Is that a date?'

'Okay, it's a date,' Bessie said.

'Oh, and before I forget,' Lily said, 'I'd better give you my new address. Look, you'd better write it down.'

'Be sure and address any letters to the Countess Gabanski,' she said.

IV

It was only after she left Lily that Bessie remembered that she had never asked her pal what she thought she should do about her stepmother's Pole. She decided, however, to put it off until she saw Lily at the Palais de Danse. It was better to let matters slide in the meantime. After all, there might be nothing in it. . . . And, as Lily said, she had enough to do to worry about her own affairs.

Bessie spent the whole of Friday afternoon having a bath, dusting herself with powder, scenting herself from Lieutenant Leja's stock, varnishing her nails and arranging her hair in three or four different styles. Finally she decided to pile it in the Edwardian manner on the crown of her head. Then she put on the pale blue evening-dress and stood back to see the effect.

'Govey Dick, but ye're a daisy!' Mrs. McNeill, who had been dotting out and in Bessie's room to admire or advise every few minutes between spasms of frenzied but not very effective work, stood in the doorway and gazed at the result.

'Am I all right?' Bessie asked anxiously.

She felt very naked, and she tried to hitch up the low bodice.

'Ye're lovely, hen. Simply lovely!'

Bessie held out the dress and danced a few steps humming *South of the border . . . Down Mexico way . . . tra la la in a veil of white by candlelight she knelt to pray. It was fiesta and we were so gay . . .*

'*Ay, ay, ayay!*' Mrs. McNeill joined in. 'Eh, hen, but ye're a smasher!' she exclaimed. 'I wish I was goin' with you to see the fun. I'm fair full o' envy. Just think o' it, at my age!' she giggled.

93

'What am I goin' to wear with it, I wonder?' Bessie said. 'I cannie wear my green coat, it would clash too much.'

'Wear your wee jigger-coat,' Mrs. McNeill said.

'But it's scarlet! D'you think blue and scarlet . . .?'

'Can ye no' get a loan o' somethin' from Mrs. Irvine? I'm sure she must have somethin'.'

'But Mrs. Irvine's twice my size,' Bessie protested.

'Ay, I'd like to see you in her musquash coat. It would be like a bell-tent on ye!' Mrs. McNeill guffawed. 'Ye'd be like a wee moose lookin' out from under a divot! Still, hen, she might have somethin' she could gi'e you a wee loan of.'

'Aw, I don't like to ask her.'

'Och, why not? She can only say "no".' Mrs. McNeill waddled to the door before Bessie could prevent her and shouted downstairs: 'Mrs. Irvine! Are ye there, Mrs. Irvine?'

'Yes?'

Mrs. McNeill leaned over the banisters and screamed: 'Have ye got a minit to spare, Mrs. Irvine? Come on up and see our wee glamour girl! C'm up and see us sometime like Mae West!'

'I'll Mae West you!' Mrs. Irvine laughed, coming into the room. 'My godfathers, Bessie, I must say you do look nice. Quite a picture!'

'That's what I was tellin' her,' Mrs. McNeill said. 'All she needs now is a coat or a cloak or somethin' to put ower her, and we were wonderin' whether you had anythin' sort o' suitable like. . . .'

'Well, I don't know. The only thing I have is my fur coat, and she would be fair drowned in it.' Mrs. Irvine pursed her lips. 'I wonder now . . . yes, there's that old black lace shawl that used to belong to my mother. . . .'

'Black lace! The very dab!' Mrs. McNeill cried.

'Mind you, it won't be very warm,' Mrs. Irvine said. 'I don't think it's really suitable. It's more fit for an auld wife. . . .'

'Och, it'll be fine,' Mrs. McNeill said, and she was out of the room before Mrs. Irvine could say another word. 'Where is it?' she called up the stairs.

'Yes, I must say it looks very nice.' Mrs. Irvine nodded with admiration. 'It goes very nice with your red hair.'

'Doesn't it!' Mrs McNeill exclaimed. 'She's just like the vamp in yon picture I saw once. What was it called again? Something glory. . . .'

'We're for no vamps here,' Mrs. Irvine said. 'So you don't need to put any ideas in her head, Mrs. McNeill. She's got too many ideas of her own already!'

'I wish I could mind the name o' that picture,' Mrs. McNeill mused. '*Glory in the Morning*? Was that it? No, that was one I saw last week, and this one was months 'n months ago. *What Price Glory . . .*?'

'That was years and years ago,' Mrs. Irvine said. 'I saw that in the Synod Hall before Bessie was born!' She sniffed. 'But it'll not matter much which picture it was, we're for no vamps here, as I've said already.'

Bessie giggled and wrapped the lace shawl first this way and then that way around her.

'I must say your red hair does go very nice with the black,' Mrs. Irvine conceded. 'Mind you, I'm not saying I like your hair that colour. If I've told you that once I've told you a dozen times. But I'll say it once again, and then that'll be an end of it. Now, are you sure you'll be warm enough in that shawl?'

'Och, yes,' Bessie said. 'It's quite warm tonight.'

'But it'll be a lot colder when you come out of the Palais de Danse,' Mrs. Irvine said. 'Not that you're to be late, remember! I must have a word with Joe Pole before you go, and tell him to keep elders' hours. And you be careful with that shawl, my lass! I wouldn't like it to get lost now after having had it all these years. I've aye had in mind to keep it for wearing in my old age in my bath-chair.'

'Just imagine you in a bath-chair!' Mrs. McNeill tittered. 'Away wi' ye, woman! Ye're too active to ever have the patience to sit in a bath-chair. You'll be nippin' aboot on your pins till the last gasp, or I'm a Dutchman!'

Mrs. Irvine's bosom swelled slightly. 'Have you finished cleaning Lieutenant Leja's room yet, Mrs. McNeill?' she

95

asked. 'Because if you haven't, it's high time you did, or he'll be on top of us before very long. And are you going to help me with the tea-dishes before you go, Bessie? Or do you think it would soil your dress?'

'Oh no, Mrs. Irvine, of course I'll help you,' Bessie cried.

'Come on then!' Mrs. Irvine led the way downstairs. 'And remember what I've said. Heaven help you, my girl, if anything happens to that shawl!'

v

Bessie felt rather nervous in all her finery as she walked through Nicholson Square with Joe Pole. Although she had often imagined herself dressed like this, it was the first time she had ever owned a dance-frock or anything even approaching it, and it was a bigger strain than she would have believed. Really, the way people turned to look! You'd think they had never seen a lassie going to a dance before! She felt herself blushing all the time. She was glad that she wasn't alone and that Joe's enormous figure was striding beside her, his hand reassuringly on the black lace covering her bare arm. She looked up at him every now and then, and she giggled and passed remarks out of sheer nervousness. But Joe, immaculate in his best uniform, black beret slanted over one ear, marched with a dead-pan expression as though marching through a desert or one of his native forests. The Polish Eagle on his beret bleamed; the thin gold bracelet on the wrist which gripped Bessie's arm flashed. Before coming out he had smoothed French violet powder over his face and polished it in so that his complexion looked even more shagreen-like than it did usually.

Bessie was so aware of the stares of the passers-by that she unconsciously quickened her steps towards the tram-stop opposite the La Scala cinema, but Joe suddenly stopped her with great firmness, saying: 'We will get taxi, Bessee.' And before she could prevent him he had hailed a horse-cab which

96

was standing beside the air-raid shelters in the centre of the square.

'Och, it would be better to get an ordinary taxi,' Bessie exclaimed.

But the cabby had already tipped his ancient bowler and was urging his horse towards them. 'Really, Joe, d'you think we should?' Bessie said half-heartedly as Joe opened the cab-door and almost lifted her in.

She sank back on the musty horse-smelling cushions and arranged the black lace shawl around her shoulders. She didn't know whether to be pleased or displeased. It was fine to be riding in a cab, but at the same time she knew that she would feel even more conspicuous than she had already felt when walking. There was something so old-fashioned about a horse-cab that people turned to look at it, and it wasn't like a motor where nobody saw you; it was open to the wide so that you were in full view of everybody.

Still. . . . Bessie settled herself, determined to make the most of it. She had dreamed so often that she was a princess riding in a state coach through cheering crowds. . . . Maybe this wasn't quite the same, but it was near enough. She had a handsome officer seated beside her, anyway, holding her hand. It just showed that dreams did come true sometimes, even though they maybe didn't turn out exactly in the way you thought they'd turn out. . . .

It was a beautiful October evening, and the greenish sky was flushed with pink. The cabby whipped up his horse and prepared to turn into College Street, but Joe jumped up and shouted: 'No, no, Princes Street! Princes Street. Go along, please!'

'It's longer and it'll cost more,' Bessie expostulated. 'We'd be quicker to go up College Street.'

'Get there too soon,' Joe said, sitting back and expanding his chest with pleasure. 'See Princes Street in nice *drotsky*. Beautiful Princes Street! Polish soldiers adorrre Princes Street. So gay!' And he laughed and squeezed Bessie's hand.

Bessie smiled and sat back to enjoy the drive. After all, it wasn't every night that she drove in a carriage. And it would be fine to go along Princes Street, for there was a chance then that somebody from Calderburn would see her. 'Fancy, did ye see wee Bessie Hipkiss driving along in a carriage! Ay, I seen her wi' a Polish officer. A General I think he was. It takes her, doesn't it! They say he's got a great castle and that's she's goin' away to bide in it after the war's over. . . .'

Looking at him, nobody would have thought that Joe had been a farmer in Poland before the Nazi invasion. 'Nice farm,' he had told Bessie. 'Veree nice farm. Cows, hens, horses . . . all gone now. Dirtee Germans! Dirtee Russian mans!' As far as Bessie could gather, it had been a large farm, almost a small estate, so she had had no hesitation in boasting to Lily that it was even larger. After all, she had to be upsides with Lily and her Count. There was no getting away from it that Joe was a better bet than Dmitri Klosowski, who had been a mere journalist.

The thought of Dmitri and the pleasant clop-clopping of the horse's hooves and the motion of the cab recalled to Bessie his promise to teach her to ride a horse. Come to think of it, stranger things had happened. Here she was riding in a coach with an officer! Who knows that maybe before long she would be galloping around on horseback?

But that would mean the return of Dmitri, and she did not want him to come back yet. Bessie shivered and drew the lace shawl tighter around the back of her neck. She did not want Dmitri to come back *ever,* horse or no horse. . . .

Such a wave of gloom descended upon her that she could not enjoy their drive along Princes Street. The crowds milling on the pavements, the great variety of foreign uniforms which gave the cold Northern city an almost Viennese air, a military band playing in the Gardens—hidden in the valley behind the war-time precautions of air-raid shelters where gay flower-beds had once bloomed—none of these could rouse her from her sudden feeling of terror and desolation. She huddled in the corner of the cab, afraid to look at the pavements in case she would see Klosowski's dark face and slanting eyes. And she held Joe's hand with almost claw-like intensity as though it were an anchorage. . . .

'Huh, it takes some folk to get here in style!' Lily greeted them when they reached the Palais de Danse in Fountain-bridge. And she swept Bessie into the ladies' cloakroom, saying: 'Christ, Ferret, is that yer Granny's shawl you've got on!'

'What's wrong with it?' Bessie demanded. 'Really, Lily McGillivray!'

'Gabanski to you,' Lily said. 'The Countess Gabanski. Don't forget that!' She giggled and took Bessie's arm. 'Och, there's nothin' wrong with the shawl, Bess. I was just joking. It looks real nice.'

'It's Mrs. Irvine's,' Bessie said. 'And I've got to be terrible careful with it. I don't think I dare leave it in the cloakroom in case it gets pinched.'

'Well, what else are you goin' to do with it?' Lily said. 'You can't wear it in the dance-hall. It's a lot safer in the cloakroom than lying on a chair in the hall.'

'I thought maybe somebody could hold it while I was dancin',' Bessie murmured.

'Lissen, Hippy, d'you think I'm goin' to be daft enough to stand and hold your shawl while you and Joe are on the floor?' Lily guffawed. 'Think again, hen! I'm determined not to miss a dance. No, you leave it here. You'll get a ticket for it, and it'll be all right.'

Bessie handed the shawl with misgivings to the cloakroom attendant. Then they powdered their faces and rejoined their escorts. Gabanski, like Joe, looked as though he had stepped from a bandbox. He was profusely scented and powdered, and he kept flourishing his long cigarette-holder with one elegant white hand.

Lily took his arm and pushed through the crowd towards the dance-floor, but Bessie held back. She felt even more naked than she had felt on the street. She was acutely aware that most of the girls were not in evening-dress. 'Just a minute, Lil!' she cried. 'Let's go on to the balcony first. We'll get a better view there.'

'Don't be daft, Ferret,' Lily jeered. 'What good'll a view do us? We didn't come here to get a view. No decent felly ever goes to the balcony. It's just the pansies that go there.' She giggled ribaldly and swept ahead with Gabanski, saying something which made him roar with laughter.

The dance-floor was crowded, and all the couches and tables around were fully occupied. The girls and the Poles pushed their way right round the floor, looking for a place to sit down, but they could find nothing. 'Ah well,' Lily said. 'We'll just have to watch and grab the first couch we can. Comin', Teddy?' And she put herself into his arms and they joined the dancers.

Bessie found a vacant space to lean against a pillar, and Joe stood beside her, watching the dancing with a brooding face. 'D'you want to dance?' Bessie asked.

Joe shrugged. 'No understan' this dance. Polka, yes! Tango, yes! But no understan' fox-trot.'

'Okay by me,' Bessie said. 'I'd rather watch.'

She hummed in time with the orchestra: *Tra la la la the night we met, there was music and da di di da. There were angels dining at the Ritz, and the nightingale sang in Berkeley Square.* . . . 'Enjoyin' yourself?' she said.

'Please?' Joe said, bending over her.

Bessie giggled and arched herself against the pillar. Two Polish soldiers a few feet away were watching her and talking about her in quick excited Polish. She looked at them from the corner of her eye. They were small under-sized runts, proper moujiks with privates' uniforms far too large for them. But she might as well make Joe a wee bit jealous. . . .

'Gosh, it's hot out there!' Lily returned, fanning herself with her handbag. 'I'm absolutely pechin'! Teddy fair pushes you through it like a steamroller!'

Gabanski laughed and lit a cigarette. He held out his case to the girls. 'No' just now,' Lily said, but Bessie took one. Almost before either Gabanski or Joe had got their lighters out, one of the Polish privates had struck a match and was preparing to come forward. Bessie laughed as she held her cigarette to the flame of Joe's lighter.

'You might 'a' tried to get a table while you were standin'' doin' nothin',' Lily complained. 'See, there's a vacant one there!' She rushed towards it. An elderly Polish officer with a closely-cropped grey head and an eye-glass was sitting alone on the couch beside it. 'Do you mind if we park here?' Lily turned on the full battery of her charm at him.

He sprang up, clicking his heels and bowing. 'Delighted,' he said. 'Delighted.'

'But Teddy's not,' Lily muttered to Bessie, and she giggled as she sat beside the elderly officer, smiling at him with wide innocent eyes.

Bessie was going to sit beside her when the band struck up a tango. 'Please!' Joe gripped her arm and led her on to the dance floor.

'I cannie tango very well,' she said. 'In fact, I don't think I can tango at all.'

'Joe teach you,' he said, and he pushed her expertly into the centre of the floor.

Despite his coaching, however, Bessie was hot and bedraggled by the time the dance ended. She had difficulty with her long flared skirt and her handbag, and she had to hold her head back too far because the smoke from her cigarette got in her eyes. She was relieved when they rejoined Lily and Teddy. They found Lily talking with animation to the grey-haired officer, while Gabanski stood beside the couch, glowering. 'Come, Lilee!' he said, and he took her arm and pulled her to her feet when the band struck up *Oh, Johnny!*

Bessie sat down and spread out her skirt. 'I think we'll sit for a while, Joe,' she said, and he smiled and sat on the arm of the couch. The elderly Colonel edged into his corner to make more room, and he said something to Joe. They spoke for several minutes in Polish, and Bessie looked from one to the other, smiling. By the time Lily and Gabanski returned, friendly terms had been reached, and the Colonel sprang up to give Lily his seat.

'I think we'll sit this one out, Teddy,' Lily said. 'It'll give us a chance to look round.'

Gabanski and Joe spoke a great deal to the Colonel while

the girls watched the dancing. On the packed floor, Bessie noticed there was only about one British soldier, sailor or civilian to every five foreigners, whether Pole, Dane, Norwegian, Czech, French or wearing uniforms that she did not know. Here and there she saw girls whom she knew by sight, mostly girls who went a lot to the Golden Salamander, dancing with foreigners.

The orchestra was playing a tune from the film, *Gulliver's Travels*, and Bessie was humming it when Lily nudged her and whispered: 'Get a load of that lovely French sailor. Isn't he gorgeous!' And while Bessie was craning her neck to see the one to which she had referred, Lily glanced round to see that Teddy hadn't heard and hummed: *Home again, sailor man. . . .*

As the dance ended, Lily watched the direction in which the French sailor went. Then she rose and said: 'Comin', Bess? I want to go upstairs for a minute.'

Lily led the way to the ladies' cloakroom. 'I wanted a breather,' she said. 'I feel I need a rest from Teddy for a bit. He's that damned jealous. Every time he sees me lookin' at another felly he gets ravin' mad.'

'Y'know, while we're here, there's somethin' I want to ask you,' Bessie said. 'I've been worried about it for weeks.'

'Joe?' Lily said. 'You haven't been and gone and done anything you shouldn't have, have you, Ferret?'

'No, it's nothing like that at all,' Bessie flushed. 'It's Mabel.'

'Mabel?' Lily tilted her head and looked at herself in the mirror through the smoke of her cigarette. 'What's that old cow been up to now?'

'Well, it's like this,' Bessie said, and then the words came in a rush.

'What!' Lily exclaimed. Her cigarette fell from her mouth on to the floor and she stopped to retrieve it. 'Mabel! Really, and her a married woman with two bairns. Honestly, Bess, it's not decent. She should be tarred and feathered.'

'I don't know what my Da'll say,' Bessie said.

'Tarrin' and featherin' 's too good for the likes o' her,' Lily cried, heaving with indignation. 'Really, I never heard the like. It's a wonder to me that the rest o' the folk in the street put up with it. She should be hounded out.'

Lily would have seethed with indignation for longer, but she remembered that she had something more important than the second Mrs. Hipkiss on her mind. 'Well, come on,' she said. 'We can't stand here all night talkin' about your good-for-nothin' steppy.'

'I wonder?' Bessie said, and she hesitated.

'What's wrong with you now?' Lily cried irritably.

'I'm a bit feared to leave Mrs. Irvine's shawl here in case . . .' Bessie said. 'I think I'll get it. Now that we have a table I can aye leave it with that nice auld Polish colonel when we're dancin'.'

'It would be safer here,' Lily said. 'However——' she shrugged. 'If anythin' happens to it, don't say I didn't warn you.'

While Bessie was getting the shawl from the attendant, Lily went out. When Bessie reached the top of the stairs she found Lily speaking to the Free French sailor who had taken her fancy. Bessie stood for a minute, thinking: Well, I must hand it to Lil, she knows how to pick them. He was a very attractive young man indeed; smooth dark hair, good-looking white face, and although not tall he was very well built and solid-looking. His sailor's uniform was very tight, showing practically every muscle.

Bessie hovered about, uncertain what to do. Lily saw her and waved. 'Hoy there, Bessie!'

'This is my friend, Miss Campbell,' she said.

The sailor smiled, showing a row of small pearly teeth. 'Raoul,' he said. 'Raoul Lefebre. I am charmed to make your acquaintance, mam'selle.'

He turned to Lily. 'You will dance, mam'selle?'

'Madam,' Lily said. 'Madam Gabanski. The Countess Gabanski.' And she inclined her head regally.

'Ah, Madame la Comtesse!' He bowed.

'I am here with my husband,' Lily said. 'But'—she shrugged in what she imagined was a woman-of-the-worldly way—'that . . . that does not matter.'

'Perhaps later?' he said.

Lily nodded. 'We are sitting at a table over there.'

The sailor bowed and stood aside to let them pass. 'I will come and make your husband's acquaintance, madame.'

'I don't know what it is about sailors,' Lily said. 'But they aye get me. They look that go-ahead—I think that must be what it is!' She giggled. 'And they're aye ready for any kind o' fun!'

Joe Pole, Gabanski and the elderly Colonel were deep in conversation when the girls returned. They sprang up, clicking their heels, and almost at once Teddy swept Lily on to the dance-floor. He danced very well and obviously took great pride in his accomplishment.

Bessie folded the lace shawl carefully and put it on the couch behind her when she sat down between Joe and the Colonel. Lily returned from the dance with heightened colour, and Gabanski looked moody.

'It is very nice for an old man to watch the young people dance,' the Colonel said, picking his words carefully, but speaking in excellent English. 'I am, alas, too old for the dance, but it is nice for young people.' He smiled and launched forth into stories of days when he was young in Warsaw and the world had been gay and wonderful. Bessie sat with open mouth, enjoying every word, but Gabanski played with his cigarette-holder and yawned every now and then, though he pretended great deference to his superior officer. Lily kept uttering little giggles and gasps and said 'Och away!' or 'You don't say!' at the end of every story. She and Gabanski danced several more times, and Bessie and Joe danced once, then Gabanski suggested that they all go for a drink.

'Nice pub outside,' he said, and he shepherded Colonel Feliks Pietras with them. Bessie was so intent on wrapping the lace shawl carefully around her and seeing that it didn't trail on the ground that she forgot to demur about going into a pub.

Once in the Saloon Bar, however, she shook her head and giggled when Teddy asked her what she would have. 'Nothin',' she said. 'No, I'll have nothin'.'

'Aw, for the luvva mike, Bess!' Lily turned her eyes to

the ceiling with exasperation. 'Be your age! You've *got* to have a drink.'

'Well, I'll just have lemonade,' Bessie murmured, shrinking close to Joe and looking around timidly at the other people in the bar.

Gabanski bowed as he handed her a glass of sherry. 'Lemonade for Bessee!' he grinned. 'Nice lemonade!'

'Oh, I shouldn't,' Bessie cried, but she took a sip.

Joe reached out and took it from her. 'Bessee must drink from Joe's glass first,' he said, and he held his glass to her lips, saying '*Nazdravja!*'

Bessie spluttered as a mouthful of neat whisky seared over her tongue and down her throat, and she was still coughing as the three officers and Lily clinked their glasses together with great ceremony, all bowing and bringing their heels together as they shouted '*Nazdravja!*'

The Poles threw their whisky back at one gulp. Lily sipped her gin and orange in what she thought was a ladylike manner. But Bessie's sherry was still practically untouched when the Colonel ordered another round of drinks.

The same performance was gone through, and then Joe bought a round. 'For Christ's sake, Ferret,' Lily whispered. 'Hurry up and drink those first two glasses. Mind, they'll not be pleased if you don't. Teddy's awful touchy about girls that refuse drinks. He says it's an insult.'

Bessie swallowed the first glass of sherry, but she boggled at the second. Then as Joe handed her another glass, Lily reached out and took it away from her, whispering 'I'll finish it for you.'

Bessie tried to drink as quickly as she could, but the three mouthfuls of whisky which Joe had made her take kept returning to sting her palate with every mouthful of sherry. Her cheeks were hot, and already her head was spinning slightly. The thick tobacco-scented air seemed to hang around her like heavy dust-filled curtains.

She tried to listen to what the Colonel was saying. 'When we left France we went to the Isle of Wight,' he said. 'The white island. You know? It is a peculiar name for an island.

is it not? Your English is very difficult sometimes. So many words have two, three, four meanings. It is very difficult for some of our men, the poor moujiks you know. How can they understan'?' He raised his glass to Lily and said: 'To your eyes, Miss Lily, to your beautiful immoral eyes!'

Lily giggled. 'Hear that, Bess! The Colonel says my eyes are immoral.'

'It means—it means you've got a temper,' Bessie hiccoughed. 'Joe told me.'

Colonel Pietras laughed. 'Yes, when we left Isle of Wight we were stationed in a great English school for girls. Near Brighton. Roedean? Yes, that is the name. Roedean! The girls, of course, had been evacuated.' He chuckled. 'A great pity!'

Gabanski said something in Polish, and the three officers laughed.

'But even without the girls it was charming,' the Colonel said. 'The Polish soldiers enjoyed themselves very much. But there was one thing they did not understan'. No, nobody understan'. In the dormitories where soldiers slept there were notices. Notices which said: "If you want a mistress in the night, please ring."'

The Colonel shrugged and spread out the palms of his hands. 'Poor soldiers ring, and they ring, and they ring, but—nobody came!'

Gabanski was buying another round of drinks, although Joe and Colonel Pietras were trying to dissuade him, when Raoul Lefebre came in with another, taller, French sailor. He bowed when he saw Lily, and when he got his drink he held it up and said: 'To you, madame! Best health!'

'Who iss that?' Gabanski asked coldly.

'Oh, just a fellow who asked me to dance,' Lily said.

Gabanski looked the sailor up and down, then he thrust back his shoulders stiffly and said: 'French! Pah! I do not like the French. They are not good soldiers. They are nozzing but traders—shopkeepers! Money, money, money all the time!'

'The French,' Colonel Pietras nodded gravely. 'They are

a clever nation, but as you say, my friend, they are too commercial-ized. There was that little matter of their forests in Normandy, remember? It was necessary to cut down the trees because of the war effort when the Germans were advancing so quickly. We Poles were being pushed towards the sea, and we needed to cut the trees. But the French—no, no, they would not allow us to cut their beloved trees! The French have no feeling for the army. The war to them is nothing. Let the Germans come and conquer them so long as their beloved trees remain uncut! They have the mentality of the serf.' He screwed in his eye-glass fiercely. 'Do you wonder that they were defeated?'

Gabanski scowled across at Raoul Lefebre, who drank and chattered vivaciously with his companion, unaware of the dark looks that were being cast at him.

'I hate the French,' Gabanski said, flinging his whisky down his throat. 'I almost prefer the Germans.'

'My friend,' the Colonel said, laying his hand on Teddy's shoulder as they left the pub, 'I do.'

Inflamed by the whisky, Joe swept Bessie on to the floor at once, whirling her through the crowd, giving great stomps every few steps. Bessie leaned against him, allowing herself to be dragged along. She felt dizzy and hot, and she kept wishing she could put something cool on her forehead. It seemed an eternity before the orchestra stopped playing, then, terrified that they might give an encore, Bessie disentangled herself from Joe and pushed through the crowd. And she sighed with relief when she reached the couch and sank down beside Colonel Pietras.

'You're lookin' kind of peaky, Bess,' Lily said, emerging from the dancers. 'Are you all right, hen?'

'Ay, I think it's the lights,' Bessie murmured. 'They're dazzlin' me a bit and makin' my eyes water.'

'Electric light is not good,' Gabanski said pompously. 'Electric light is too hard. I do not like electric light. At home, in Poland, I have nozzing but candles. All my great house is filled with candles.'

'Gee, it must take a bit of doing to light them all,' Lily

giggled. 'How d'you manage, Ted? Do you start to light them in the afternoon and then spend the whole night blowin' them out again?'

'I do not touch them,' he said, waving his cigarette-holder in a lofty manner. 'I have plenty of serfs. The serfs attend to all zose candles. It is a much softer light, very nice for the eyes, better zan electric light. I would prefer to have candle-light here.'

'Ay, but we haven't any serfs here,' Lily said.

'A pity,' Gabanski shrugged.

The orchestra was striking up another dance. Gabanski was languidly putting out his cigarette, preparatory to taking Lily on to the floor, when Raoul Lefebre appeared and bowed in front of her:

'May I have this dance, madame?'

'Okay,' Lily giggled and took his arm. 'D'you mind, Teddy?' And without waiting for an answer she started to walk away.

But Gabanski stopped her. 'Who is this—this gentleman?' he demanded. 'Do I know him?'

Seated between Colonel Pietras and Joe Pole, Bessie saw what happened next through a kind of mist. She was dimly aware that Gabanski had gripped Lily's arm and had pulled her away from the Free French sailor. She could feel Joe's thigh tensing against hers, then he sprang up as a knife suddenly appeared in Gabanski's hand.

'Teddy!' Lily screamed.

The Colonel rose, and he and Joe Pole blocked out Bessie's view. She got up unsteadily and groped her way between them.

Lily was standing with one hand on Gabanski's chest and the other on the chest of the sailor. 'Stoppit, Teddy, you bloody fool!' she was shouting. 'Put that knife away!'

'This dirtee French pig will apologize first,' Gabanski hissed. 'My woman will not dance with a Free French shop-keeper.'

'Cochon Polonais!' Raoul spat, and he, too, whipped out a knife and thrust Lily aside as he leapt at Gabanski.

Bessie joined Lily in screaming as Joe sprang away from her

and gripped Gabanski and the sailor by the arms. She made a move to rush forward, but Colonel Pietras restrained her.

The orchestra continued to play, dancers gyrated on the floor. A small crowd had collected around the protagonists. Bessie and the Colonel were pushed back towards the wall so that they could see nothing. Bessie put her hands to her hot cheeks and screamed in sympathy with Lily, who was hidden in the middle of the mêlée.

'It is all right, Miss Bessee,' Colonel Pietras said, laying his hand consolingly on her arm. 'Gabanski will be all right. Gabanski will be fit for any Frenchman.' He gave a sardonic laugh. 'The Free French! That is another of your peculiar English words that the poor Polish soldier finds it difficult to understan'. The Free French are too *free* with everything.'

Attendants and the manager appeared, and in a few minutes the *fracas* was settled. The French sailor was led away, gesticulating wildly. Gabanski pulled down his tunic and straightened his shoulders. He stood as stiff as a ramrod and lit a cigarette. Lily flung herself on the couch and burst into hysterical sobbing: 'Oh, Teddy! What if ye'd been killed! Oh, Teddy!'

Joe wiped some blood off his hand with a snowy linen handkerchief. 'It is nothing,' he assured Bessie, putting the handkerchief up his sleeve. 'It is just a scratch. Joe Pole iss veree good with knives.'

'We will go now,' Gabanski announced, staring disdainfully at the spectators who were loath to move away. 'Come, Lilee, stop weeping. It is not good. It makes circus for the *moujiks*.'

Joe took Bessie's arm and led her towards the stairs. Her legs were still trembling violently, and her head was swimming. The taste of stale whisky and sherry clung to her tongue and the roof of her mouth. She clutched Joe's arm thankfully. Then suddenly she cried:

'Oh, my shawl! My shawl!'

But the shawl was not where she had left it in the corner of the couch. There was no sign of it anywhere.

VII

'Now if anything happens to this shawl, Bessie Campbell,'
Mrs. Irvine had said as she and Joe were preparing to leave,
'I'll never forgive you. Don't you dare come back here without it. That shawl's very valuable. It belonged to my mother,
so it's got a lot of sentimental value for me. But apart from
that it used to belong to a very famous woman, a very famous
woman indeed.'

'Fancy!' Bessie said.

'Yes, it used to belong to Mrs. Fitzherbert, and I don't need
to tell you who Mrs. Fitzherbert was.' Mrs. Irvine drew herself up with mingled pride and scorn. 'Mind you, I'm not
saying anything in her favour, for she was a bad lot. She
was a bonnie woman, but she was a bad lot. However, she
had something to do with my family—not in a bad way,
mind you! Don't you run away with that idea!—but she had
something to do with it, and that's how I've got her shawl.
It's been handed down from generation to generation, and
when I die it'll go to Flora or Anna.'

'Not that I've any intention of dying yet,' she said.

'Too true!' Bessie giggled and clutched Joe's arm.

'I've had that shawl "read" by a medium,' Mrs. Irvine
went on, determined not to let them go until she had had
her say. 'And the medium—old Madame Delotti who's
passed over herself by this time—told me that this shawl
would bring me fame and fortune yet and would be the means
of placing me amongst the High and Mighty ones where I
belong. And my daughter, Anna—she's the one who takes
after me and belongs to the Faith—has seen it all in the
crystal. Yes, she's a great one for the crystal is our Anna
and never loses an opportunity to see what's what in it. Well,
she saw in the crystal as clear as clear could be that I was to
go to some great building—the House of Lords she thinks it
was—and there I'm to get papers that'll prove something. Anna
couldn't make out what the papers were supposed to prove,

but it's something important. And then she saw me going into another huge building, like a museum, and I turn to the right and go along a wide passage and then turn to the left and I stand in front of a portrait of a bonnie woman that's wearing this identical shawl. And underneath the portrait there's a panel and I'm to pass my hand over this panel until I find a secret knob, and I press that and the panel swings open and there's a wee cubby-hole with stairs leading down——'

'Fancy!' Bessie's mouth was wide open, but Joe Pole stood with an expressionless face, not understanding one word and wondering when 'Mummy' was going to stop and let them go.

Mrs. Irvine sighed. 'Unfortunately, Anna couldn't see any more in the crystal. But as far as I'm concerned she saw enough to prove that I'll go far up in the world yet. She says she thinks the portrait is Mrs. Fitzherbert. Well, I don't want to have anything to do with her, as I've said already, for she was just *nothing*. But I wouldn't mind having something to do with George IV.'

She drew herself up and nodded regally. 'Yes, Bessie my lassie, the day may come when you'll have to curtsy to me yet. And that day'll come, I know for a fact. I can feel it in my bones even if Madame Delotti hadn't told me.'

'So don't you dare let anything happen to that shawl,' she said. 'I can't think why I was so soft as to let that glaikit McNeill body get round me to loan it to you. But away with you—before I change my mind!' She waved them off. 'And pity help you if you come back without it!'

'And now the shawl's lost!' Bessie wailed. 'What'll I do?'

'Och, it must be around somewhere,' Lily said. 'For God's sake, Hippy, stop moanin' about it. The bloody thing'll turn up.'

'Do not worry, Bessee,' Joe Pole murmured.

Gabanski and the Colonel were mousing around, looking under tables and chairs, pushing their way through the crowd watching the dancers. Gabanski glared at everybody he brushed against.

'But it was on the couch!' Bessie cried. 'It couldn't have moved away by itself. Somebody musta pinched it.'

III

'Well, this is the couch we were sittin' on,' Lily said. 'And it's not here. So what are you goin' to do about it? You'll just have to tell auld Irvine that somebody lifted it. She can't do anythin' about it. After all, she can't blame you for somebody else bein' a thief.'

Joe Pole was standing with a pensive expression, making no move to join Gabanski and the Colonel in the search. 'But this is not the couch, Lilee,' he said. 'It was that one.' And he pointed to a couch where a RAF sergeant and a girl were clasped in a close embrace.

Lily sighed with exasperation. 'It was nothin' of the kind. D'ye think I don't know where we were sittin'! We were sittin' here right behind this pillar, weren't we, Bess?'

'Well, I——' Bessie frowned, trying to remember. There were so many couches, and now that she came to look at them they all seemed alike. And she was still dazed with the drink and the fight.

'I—I don't know,' she said.

'God!' Lily turned up her eyes and shrugged.

Joe did not wait for any further argument. He got down on his hands and knees in front of the couch and shoved one arm under it as far as it would go. 'Here, what the hell!' the airman shouted, coming out of his trance as Joe's shoulder pushed against his leg. 'What are you playing at?'

But Joe disregarded him. A look of triumph came over his face. 'Ah!' he cried. 'So!' And he muttered something in Polish and stood up, waving the shawl.

'Well, I hope this'll teach you to be more careful after this, Bessie Hipkiss,' Lily said as they left the Palais de Danse. 'Jesus Christ and General Jackson, it might have been somethin' far more important than this auld shawl—and then you'd 'a' been in the soup!'

Lily would have said a lot more in the same strain had not Colonel Pietras said: 'Please excuse me, Miss Lily, but may I offer you a ride home in my car?'

Lily fluffed up her hair and giggled coyly. 'It's awf'lly nice of you, Colonel, but won't it take you out of your road?'

They stood beside the large staff-car with its impassive Polish peasant driver, arguing about the best way to manage. Bessie and Joe were going in one direction; Lily and Tadeusz in the other; and the Colonel was billeted in a large mansion in Musselburgh, which was in a totally different direction from either. Eventually Joe said that he and Bessie would walk.

'Not far,' he said. 'Nice night.'

'Ay, we can walk through the Meadows,' Bessie said. 'It's no distance.'

'Well, don't you go and get up to any tricks in the Middle Meadow Walk and lose that shawl again,' Lily warned, settling herself in the centre of the back seat of the car and invitingly patting a place beside her for the Colonel. 'Forewarned is forearmed, mind!'

'No fear,' Bessie giggled. 'We'll go straight home.'

Once they had started to walk, however, Joe appeared disinclined to hurry. A nippy East wind had arisen, and Bessie shivered and pulled the shawl closer around her neck and shoulders. 'C'mon, get a move on,' she said, pulling Joe's arm. 'At this rate I'll be frozen to death by the time we get home.'

Joe laughed and pressed her against him. 'Joe will warm Bessee,' he said. 'Joe will warm Bessie good, yes?'

'C'mon, none o' your capers,' she said, and she pulled herself away from him and pranced ahead.

It was all right as long as they were on the pavements, she knew her way, and the movements and talk of other late-night pedestrians guided her. But once they had moved away from the main street and the few belated blackedout trams whirring along like enormous bats, and had turned into Bruntsfield Links it was more difficult; there was no moon and few stars, and the blackout swept over them like a shroud. In the open space, too, the wind seemed even more biting.

'Damn!' Bessie cried as she stumbled against the edge of the path and the grass.

Joe laughed and caught her round the waist. There was a strange, exultant note in his laugh, which combined with the pressure of his fingers on her stomach made Bessie sober up and become aware of herself and her surroundings. Suddenly she realized that this was the first time she had been out with Joe so late at night and so far from everybody else. They might have been walking in the wilderness. A feeling of terror overwhelmed her. Yet it was a pleasant enough feeling, like the tingle she got in her spine when she read a thrilling mystery story. And so she only said 'Stoppit!' when Joe pulled her against him and stopped.

'Bessee,' he murmured. 'Bessee kiss Joe, yes?'

'Och, I'm cauld,' she said.

But she made no resistance when he put his mouth against hers. She put her arm round his neck and allowed her body to curve into his. They stood for a few moments as though they were built from the same piece of stone. Then Joe became urgently sexual. He nipped her ears with his teeth and kissed her neck, burrowing his head into her shoulder. His right hand began to wander over her body, and Bessie would have shied back like a frightened colt had his left hand not gripped her firmly on the buttocks, pressing her against him.

'I lof you, Bessee,' he murmured thickly.

'Oh, Joe!' she cried.

He started to push her off the path, and when she felt the grass under her high heels she pushed Joe's chest. 'Not here, Joe, not here! Can ye not wait till we get home?'

But he was as stolid and rampageous as a young bull, and he half-lifted her and half-pulled her on to the ground. She gasped for breath and held her mouth away from his rapacious tongue. 'We'll get wet, Joe,' she whimpered. 'My frock'll get dirty. . . .'

The few stars suddenly dissolved into one enormous star of great brilliance and then the blackout became a greater blackout of warm, sensual ecstasy.

IX

'Hello, Bessee, my wee hen!'

Bessie gaped and held the door half-shut so that Dmitri Klosowski could not enter. He was forced to push it open for himself, and he said laughingly: 'Bessee got a fright, yes? Bessee is glad to see Dmitri?'

'Ay,' she mumbled. 'I suppose so.'

She huddled into the shelter of the door, clutching the handle as he made a move to kiss her. But he stopped with his face halfway to hers. 'Ah, Bessee has new hair!' he cried.

She grinned and took the opportunity to move away. 'D'you like it?' she asked, putting up her hand and fluffing it. 'Red suits me better, doesn't it?'

'Red veree nice,' he nodded. 'It makes Bessee look——' He spread out his hands expressively. 'What you say? More fas—cin—ating!'

'Och, don't you try and kid me!' She laughed and backed along the passage. 'I'll go and tell Mummy you're here.'

'Ah, one moment!' he protested. 'Just one moment, Bessee!'

But she was already at the kitchen-door shouting: 'Mrs. Irvine! Mrs. Irvine, it's Lieutenant Klosowski.'

'My goodness me!' Mrs. Irvine bustled out, dusting flour off her arms. 'This *is* a surprise,' she said, smoothing her hair. 'I got your post-card, of course, but I didn't expect you till Monday.'

Klosowski clicked his heels and bent to kiss her hand. 'Ah yes, I could have stayed three more days in Cupar, but——' He straightened up and slapped his chest gallantly. 'But Cupar ladies are not like Edinburgh ladies. Klosowski was lonelee for Edinburgh ladies. Mummee is glad to see me, yes?'

Bessie backed into the kitchen and left Mrs. Irvine to deal with him. Her legs were trembling, and she leaned against the sink for support.

Now what? she thought. She had known all along that he would come back, but, like Mrs. Irvine, she had thought there would be more warning. She had read the post-card that morning and she had thought: Och, there's still three days to think about it. Plenty of time to think up something. But now. . . .

She was terrified of him, terrified of what he might do about herself and Joe. Of course, she excused herself, he had no

115

business with her whatsoever. He had just given her that dress and then there had been *that* night. . . . He was just another Pole as far as she was concerned. And a Pole that she didn't like very much at that.

But her instinct told her that there was much more in it than that. His return was going to upset everything. . . .

She was still leaning against the sink, sunk in a black brooding mist, when Mrs. Irvine bustled back into the kitchen.

'C'mon, Bessie, show a leg there!' she cried. 'You'll have to hurry up and get the table set. They'll all be here before we can cough. It's a good job, isn't it, that Joe Pole's not coming in for his tea, otherwise we'd have been sunk. Lieutenant Klosowski can get his share of the fish. C'mon, c'mon! What's wrong with you, lassie? You're standing there as though you'd lost a shilling and found a sixpence. What's the matter with you?'

'Nothin',' Bessie said, and she hastened away to the dining-room. All the time she was laying the table she kept her ears cocked and looked every now and then at the door, terrified in case Dmitri would pop his head around it.

But he stayed in his room until she had rung the gong. As soon as she heard the quick patter of his feet on the stair, Bessie rushed to the kitchen. She waited until she heard Captain Van Klee and Lieutenant Leja go into the dining-room before she picked up the tray and carried it in.

Klosowski was standing with his back to the fire, gesticulating with his long cigarette-holder and talking volubly.

'Ah, in Cupar there are some wonderful girls,' he was saying. 'Beautiful Cupar girls! They all lof the Polish soldiers. Ah, they are so kind, so understanding, so——'

He waved the cigarette-holder again and grinned at Bessie. 'Bessee is looking very nice, yes! More nice than the Cupar girls!'

She shook her head numbly and busied herself in putting the plates of hot fish in the right places. Captain Van Klee gave a laugh which seemed to come from the depths of his great stomach, and he said as he sat down at the table: 'You haf had lots of nice adventures, Lieutenant? You tell me,

116

and perhaps I go to this Cupar, too. We will make Bessie jealous!'

'So what?' Bessie giggled and darted away with the empty tray. In the passage, however, the giggle died into something like a sob, and a shiver trickled down her spine.

Usually she left the kitchen-door open so that she could hear the voices and laughter of the boarders while they ate, but this evening she shut the door and only restrained herself by an effort from locking it. If it had not been for Mrs. Irvine she would have done so. And it was long after she had heard the sounds denoting that they had adjourned to the sitting-room that she took a tray and crept cautiously along the passage to collect the dirty crockery.

She was in a state of tension throughout the entire evening, and she did not relax until she had heard the front door bang several times. It was only when the house was quiet that she allowed herself to settle beside the fire and picked up that week's copy of *Cynthia's Circle*. But she did not read more than a few lines. She kept glancing at the door, ready to jump up and put the table between herself and any intruder. And all the time she thought of Joe—Joe, who tonight of all nights was at a lecture on military tactics and would not be back before eleven or twelve. If only he would come to comfort her. . . .

x

Despite her fears, however, Klosowski did not go out of his way to molest her for several days after his return. At first she was very careful to keep away from him, making certain that other people were within earshot whenever he spoke to her. Not that he made any move to be more than mildly flirtatious in the way he would have been flirtatious with any girl. He was too full of his own importance for that. Apparently he had got promoted while in Cupar, and he was very proud of it. He was also proud of his conquests among the Cupar girls, and he talked endlessly about them, speaking about 'Meg' and 'Janet' and 'Eileen—ah, what a lovelee woman

Eileen is! You would lof Eileen, she is so big and strong—more big and more strong than Dmitri,' until Mrs. Irvine said: 'Well, I must say I'm getting a bit fed up with hearing about all these women he's been so friendly with. I don't like the sound of them at all. It strikes me that some of them were little better than . . .'

'Little better than what, Mrs. Irvine?' Bessie asked when the older woman did not finish her sentence.

Mrs. Irvine sniffed and said: 'I don't need to tell you, Bessie. I hope you know enough at your age. But I hope, too, that your knowledge is as far as you've got.'

'You know,' she said one morning, 'I'm real sorry for poor Joe Pole having to share a room with that Klosowski. He's such a blow, and he never knows when to stop talking. His tongue just goes like the hammerbone of a goose's arse—if you'll excuse me being vulgar!' She laughed. 'I don't know what it is, but Klosowski brings out all the bad in me. I'm real sorry now that I didn't write and tell him he couldn't come back here. But of course I *promised* when he went away that I would keep the bed for him. And I could hardly break a promise, could I?'

'No,' Bessie agreed. 'I don't suppose you could.'

'It'll be a lesson to me, though,' Mrs. Irvine said. 'A lesson never to make a promise to anybody again. So let it be a lesson to you at the same time, m'girl!'

'You bet!' Bessie said with greater fervour than she might otherwise have done. Although when she thought it over she could not remember ever having made any promise to Klosowski. He was just a man who had taken her out once, given her a dress and then. . . .

She shuddered and thought instead of Joe. Mrs. Irvine was correct when she thought that Joe did not relish sharing his room with the other Polish officer. 'It is so bad, Bessee,' he complained. 'So bad for you and me. You cannot come and sleep wis me any more. Joe misses you.'

Bessie sighed. She missed him, too. She had got used to being with him in the last few weeks, and it was galling to lie alone now in her own small bed, knowing that Joe was

118

turning and tossing in his while in the same room Klosowski was either snoring or keeping Joe awake by telling him about all his conquests in Cupar.

Something'll have to be done about it, she told herself fiercely. We can't go on like this.

But what? She was so busy thinking about ways and means, wondering whether it might be possible for Joe to slip up to her room—except that there was always the danger of Dmitri finding out where he had gone—that she got lulled into a state of false security as far as Klosowski was concerned. She began to forget her fear of being waylaid by him, and she became careless about meeting him alone in the house. Not that he appeared to bother about her. When they met he would tease her about her 'new hair' and tell her about the girls in Cupar. All the time he seemed to imply that he was no longer interested in her and that 'Meg' and 'Janet' and 'Eileen' were much more in his line than a little half-fledged servant-girl. And even once or twice when he might have kissed her he made no attempt to do so. It was only later that she realized how clever he was in this, how he had been waiting his chance like a cat playing with a mouse.

He had been back for over a week when she went into his room one night with clean towels for him and Joe. It was about eleven o'clock. The house was silent. Mrs. Irvine had said she had a headache and she had gone to bed early. As far as Bessie knew, all the boarders were either out or asleep. Joe was at another military lecture and would not be home until late. Otherwise Bessie herself would have been in bed by this time. She was waiting up, however, to see him on his return. He had promised to come to the kitchen to talk and drink tea.

She was so busy thinking about this, anticipating what she would say to Joe and what he would say to her, and dreaming of his love-making, that she opened Klosowski's door without knocking. Klosowski had gone to the lecture with Joe.

The room was in darkness. She switched on the light and went to the towel-rail. A slight sound from the farther corner made her turn in alarm.

119

Dmitri was lying on top of his bed, wearing only a bright scarlet silk dressing-gown. He sat up and grinned at her startled face. 'Ah, Bessee, you got fright, yes?'

She nodded, panting. 'I—I thought it was a mouse or a rat,' she said.

'Veree big mouse,' he grinned. He sat up and swung his legs over the bed, sitting on the edge of it. He picked up a short riding-crop that lay beside him and smacked the bed with it. 'Dmitri was asleep,' he said. 'Dreaming of Bessee!'

'Oh, yeah!' she said.

She put the clean towels on the rail. All the time she was aware of his dark, brooding eyes watching her. She folded the dirty towels slowly and far more carefully than she needed to, since they would be flung soon among the other dirty clothes. She sensed rather than heard him cross to the door with cat-like movements. And when she turned he was standing with his back against it, stroking his thigh with the whip. The top of the dressing-gown fell open, showing his broad chest fuzzed with short dark hair.

'Bessee has been a-void-ing Dmitri?' he said, his lips lifting to show his gold teeth. 'She is not pleased to see him again.'

'Och, what makes you think that?' she said. She felt her stomach turn, and she licked her dry lips for confidence. 'I've been that busy,' she said, 'I never seem to have had time to talk to ye.'

He grinned sardonically and swished the crop through the air. Bessie's stomach heaved again at the sinister sound.

'Well, I—I must get on,' she said, forcing herself to walk towards him. 'I've a lot of other clean towels to lay out,' she lied.

'No, Bessee,' he said, gripping her wrist. 'There is no hurry.'

'But I—but I must,' she cried, and she tried to pull herself away from him.

Dmitri smiled and said softly: 'Bessee is not like the girls in Cupar. Girls in Cupar were veree fond of Dmitri. Eileen was terr-ib-ly fond of Dmitri. Eileen loffed to *master* Dmitri!'

120

'Look, it's late,' Bessie said. 'I've a lot to do yet, and I must get away to my bed. I—I'll—we'll have a wee talk tomorrow, eh?'

'We will talk tonight,' he said, running his hand up and down her arm. 'It is a long time since we talked. Does Bessee remember that Dmitri promised to teach her to ride a horse? And Bessee promised to ride horse, yes? Re-mem-ber?'

'Uhuh,' she nodded, shivering with fear.

Dmitri smiled. 'You want to learn to ride horse, Bessee my wee hen?' His voice slurred on the Scottish endearment, and he laughed. 'Come, I teach you now.'

'But——' She stared.

'I will be horse,' he said. 'And you will be master.'

Suddenly he thrust the whip into her hand, and got down on his hands and knees. 'Come, Bessee!' he grinned up at her. 'Get on Dmitri's back.'

Bessie gave a hysterical giggle and backed to the door. 'Och, I'm ower auld for thae bairns' games,' she said.

'But Bessee, you promised!' he whined in aggrieved tones. 'Come, get on back! Come, my wee hen!'

'No,' she said, and she turned the handle of the door. She felt sick with terror when she found that it was locked, although she had already sensed that it would be and that Dmitri had the key in his pocket.

'Come, Bessee!' he commanded.

She would have cried out, but her tongue clove to the roof of her mouth. 'But—but it's so *daft*!' she protested in a weak voice.

He said nothing. Looking round at her with a half-smile, he sidled towards her until his buttocks pressed against her legs. 'Come, my wee hen!' he whispered.

Gingerly, Bessie seated herself astride his broad back. 'So!' he exclaimed. He grinned round at her and gave a little leap. 'Dig in knees, so!' he ordered. 'More firm. Press knees hard into Dmitri's sides, so. Now, use whip!'

'But——'

'Use whip,' he commanded.

Timorously she gave him a feeble stroke on the thigh.

'More hard,' he said, and he pretended to rear. 'See, horse will get fe-ro-cious if master does not whip him hard.'

Bessie giggled and gave him another gentle tap. 'Och, it's awful daft,' she protested. 'I thought we were goin' to practice on a real horse.'

'Dmitri is real horse,' he said.

And suddenly he reared in the air, causing her to fall on the floor. He turned and laughed: 'See what happens when horse is not punished. You must be firm, my wee hen. Veree firm with horse. Give him his licks, *hard*!'

He stood up and crossed to the chair where his clothes were folded. 'Put on these, Bessee,' he said, and he handed her his riding-boots and breeches.

'But I——' she said. 'But what would Mrs. Irvine say if she caught me?'

'Missees Irvine she has gone to bed.' Dmitri stared at her with smouldering Slav eyes. 'Put on riding-trousers.'

'But——'

She said no more. Oh God, she prayed to herself, oh God, if only something would happen to stop him. And she trembled as she pulled on the riding-breeches and shoved her feet into the boots. Let's get it over with *quick*, she told herself. He's mad! He's mad!

'So!' Dmitri grinned at her, then suddenly he threw off his dressing-gown and got down on hands and knees again. 'Horses not have clothes, so it is better to ride bare-backed from the commencement.'

XI

'What did ye do, Ferret?' Lily asked when Bessie told her the whole story the following evening.

'What do you think I did?' Bessie's breast heaved with indignation. 'I screamed the place down, of course. I just opened my mouth and let rip. God, what a shindy there was!'

'Quite right, too,' Lily said, equally indignant, although

there was a slightly jealous note in her voice. 'The dirty brute, wantin' you to do that to him. Really, I've met some funny tykes o' men, but I've never met one like this before.'

'Mind you,' she ruminated, 'I think if I'd been in your place I'd have taken the chance and given him lardy. I'd have made him no' able to sit down for a week.'

'Oh, it was terrible, Lil,' Bessie said. 'Really terrible. There he was kneelin' without any clothes and sayin' "Eileen she loffed to whip Dmitri." And there I was screamin' my head off.'

Bessie still shook with terror when she recalled it all. Dimly she had been aware of herself lying on top of the bed, having hysterics, while Dmitri kept saying: 'Be quiet, my wee hen! Be quiet!' And then there had been pounding on the door and voices.

And then Joe had burst open the door and come in with a rush.

'Joe!' she screamed. 'Oh, Joe!'

She ran to him and threw her arms around his neck. But he thrust her behind him and advanced on Dmitri, shouting in Polish. There was a knife in his hand.

'Joe,' she screamed again. 'Don't! Oh, Joe, don't!'

Lieutenant Leja, wearing a dressing-gown and with a woman's hair-net over his marcelled hair, was hovering in the doorway. Behind him the two French officers were gesticulating madly and chattering like excited parrots. Old Mr. McQuarrie was peering from his door, his red blob of a nose quivering with curiosity.

'What's going on here?' Mrs. Irvine, clad in a voluminous white nightgown and clutching a too-small dressing-gown round her ample figure, pushed her way through the group in the doorway. 'What's all this?' she cried.

'Now, Mummee, now, Mummee, please!' Captain Van Klee cried sheepishly behind her, tying the knot of his dressing-gown with one hand and putting the other on Mrs. Irvine's shoulder.

'What's this?' Mrs. Irvine cried again. 'What're you doing dressed up like this, Bessie Campbell?'

'I didn't—I didn't!' Bessie whimpered. 'It was Lieutenant Klosowski. . . .'

'Oh, I see.' Mrs. Irvine nodded and advanced into the room where Klosowski had retreated into a corner, holding his tunic between his own nakedness and Joe's thrust-out knife. They were snarling at each other in Polish.

'Will you kindly explain this, Lieutenant Klosowski?' Mrs. Irvine said in her most majestic tones. 'Perhaps you'll be good enough to tell us why you've disturbed the whole house at this time of night? Really!' She threw up her head and glared. 'Put some clothes on at once. I'll have you know that this is a decent house and we'll have no capers like this here.'

Bessie could not follow what was said next, it was so jumbled up, and she was so busy struggling out of the Pole's breeches and boots. But one phrase struck her, and that was Klosowski saying in a sneering voice: 'A decent house, did you say, Mummee? It cannot be a decent house when its mistress sleeps effery night wis Captain Van Klee.'

Mrs. Irvine's face purpled with rage, and she flung out one arm majestically: 'Out! Out of my house at once! How dare you, you dirty Polish swine!'

'And you, Joe Pole,' she cried. 'Put away that knife before anything happens to get us all into the papers.'

Lily sighed with envy when she heard Bessie's version of the scene. 'Really, Bessie Hipkiss, you do see life!'

'Huh, you can have my share of it,' Bessie said, but she held her head a little more proudly and waggled her hips a little more as she pranced along beside Lily. 'It wasn't any fun at the time, I can tell you, I was scared stiff. And it's a good thing that I didn't lose my job over the head of it.'

'Anyway, he's gone,' she said. 'Good riddance to bad rubbish!'

But even as she said it she wondered whether she had seen or heard the last of Dmitri Klosowski. She had an uneasy feeling that some day, some place, he would turn up again like the proverbial bad penny and cause her a great deal of heart-burning.

PART III

/

I

ONE morning a week before Christmas Bessie returned from the grocer's to find Mrs. Irvine entertaining Mrs. Moore to tea in the kitchen. 'Oh, it's you, Bessie,' Mrs. Moore said in her most genteel accent, and rather as though she had expected it would be somebody else. 'I've been waiting for you.'

Bessie said 'Uhuh,' and put her basket on the dresser. 'How are you, Mrs. Moore, dear?' she said, wondering as she put the ration-books in the drawer what had brought the old woman here at this time in the morning.

'Oh, I'm all right,' Mrs. Moore said, enunciating every syllable slowly and keeping an anxious eye on Mrs. Irvine, determined not to sully the good impression she had made already by lapsing into the doric. 'I never felt better in my life. As I was saying to Mrs. Irving here it's a good job that us old ones are able to take things in our stride and not let this awful war get the better of us. Goodness knows what would happen if the girls of the old brigade let themselves go.' She laughed and said: 'Isn't that so, Mrs. Irving?'

Mrs. Irvine sniffed and said: 'Some more tea, Mrs. Moore?'

'Yes, thank you, hen—er, I mean Mrs. Irving.'

Bessie got herself a cup, then added a saucer for appearances sake. 'You're surely out early this mornin', Mrs. Moore?' she remarked, watching Mrs. Irvine pour the tea.

'Ay.' Mrs. Moore coughed to hide her embarrassment. 'Yes, as I was telling Mrs. Irving, I had to come up and see

125

you. I felt it was my duty. I thought you had better hear the news from a close friend and not from some stranger.'

Bessie held the cup halfway to her lips. 'What news?' She replaced the cup in the saucer with a clatter and cried: 'It's not my Da? He's no' been . . . ?'

'No, your father's all right, Bessie,' Mrs. Irvine said.

'Yes, your father's all right,' Mrs. Moore agreed. 'Though goodness knows what he'll feel like when he gets the news. Poor man!' She sighed, then she resettled her bosom over her folded hands and said: 'No, it's not your father I've come to tell you about, Bessie. It's your stepmother.'

'Mabel? What's she been up to?'

Mrs. Moore looked at Mrs. Irvine, and both primmed their lips.

'Well, it's like this, Bessie,' Mrs. Moore said after a pause. 'You know that your Steppy's been chums a' bubbly wi' a Pole for quite a while now. A perfect disgrace it is, and her a married woman wi' a family to keep and her man in the army —puir Bert, I dinnie ken what he'll think when he gets her letter.'

'What letter?' Bessie cried.

'It's a disgrace, really it's a perfect disgrace,' Mrs. Irvine said. 'Such a callous trick! To leave those two poor little bairns alone and unprotected. . . .'

'Oh, there's no question of that as long as I'm there, Mrs. Irving, I'm perfectly able to protect them.' Mrs. Moore blew out her fat cheeks with gusto and swept on, determined not to let Mrs. Irvine get hold of the stage. 'It's like this, Bessie, Mabel's gone. She's skedaddled with her Pole.'

'She's what?'

'She's skedaddled with her Pole,' Mrs. Moore said. 'Yes, she's away with him and left yer poor Da and the bairns in the lurch. I was sittin' at my window last night, having a bit lookout to see what was happenin' in the street—even though it was the blackout and I couldnie see as much as I'd have liked—and I saw the bold Mabel come out of your entry with her Pole and two or three cases. "Oho!" I says to Dirty Minnie who was sittin' beside me, keepin' me company.'

'That's Miss Nimmo who bides in the next stair to me,' she explained to Mrs. Irvine. 'A very nice woman, too, and a good pal to both me and poor Bessie's mother that's away with it.'

Mrs. Irvine inclined her head regally.

'Yes, I saw them with their bits o' luggage,' Mrs. Moore went on. 'So I turned to Minnie and I says: "Oho, and where do you think they can be goin' to at this time o' night?" Well, we sat and talked about it for a while, and we decided that like enough Mabel was away up to the station with the Pole—Alix his name is—for we'd heard that he'd got shifted to a camp near Airdrie, and we were wondering what the bold Mabel would do about that, whether she'd get another Pole or not, or whether she'd take a turn to hersel' and remember that she was a respectable married woman. Anyway, we were sittin' there when we saw wee Jenny at the entry. "It's ower late for that bairn to be out," I says to Minnie. "It's high time she was in her bed." Well, she went in, and then after a good long while she came out again, and she was greetin'. "Goodness me," I says to Minnie, "this'll not do." Well, to cut a long story short we went out and spoke to Jenny, and she said she couldn't get in. So Minnie and I went up to investigate. The door was locked, and we were just goin' to come away, thinkin' we'd better give poor wee Jenny something to eat and then put her to bed in one o' our own places, when Minnie discovered that the key was under the mat. So we went in.'

Mrs. Moore paused dramatically.

'Yes, we went in,' she said. 'And there on the kitchen table were two letters. One that was sealed and addressed to yer poor Da—God knows what he'll think when he gets it! —and the other one was open and just had "To Anybody It May Concern" on it.'

Mrs. Moore reached over to Mrs. Irvine's side of the table and lifted a sheet of notepaper. 'Here it is,' she said, holding it out to Bessie. 'My God, but the woman that wrote that should be thrown into the tide and held down. Hangin's too good for her.'

'To whom it may concern,' Bessie read. 'I am sick and

127

tired of looking after these bloody kids, so I am away to Airdrie with the man I love. Bert Hipkiss can divorce me if he likes, I don't care. I will follow the man I love to the ends of the earth. Yours Truly, Mabel Hipkiss.'

Bessie swallowed, then she looked from Mrs. Moore to Mrs. Irvine.

'Yes, it's a blow, Bessie,' Mrs. Irvine said. 'It's a great blow, but it's something that war brings with it. Really, I can't understand what has come over some of the women nowadays. They just need to see a uniform and they lose all self-control. I always thought your stepmother was a funny one, but mind you, I must admit, I never thought she would stoop to the like of this. It just shows.'

'Ay, it just shows.' Mrs. Moore inclined her head in sympathy with Mrs. Irvine. And a pious note came into her voice as she added: 'It's a good job that some of us manage to keep sensible and not let these foreign sodgers sweep us off our feet. It would be a sad thing for the country if we all fell for their cheap-jack tricks and their hand-kissin' and all that palaver. Govey Dick, if one o' them tried any o' his daft capers on me, I'd give him a right good scud on the lug.'

'You never spoke a truer word, Mrs. Moore.' Mrs. Irvine sniffed with indignation in time with the other woman, then she turned to Bessie and said:

'Well, m'dear, what are you going to do?'

Bessie's mouth opened as she looked from one to the other. 'But—but——' she gasped. 'What can I do? Mabel's away, and—and——'

And then before any of them could say anything, realization of what was expected of her dawned on her. 'No,' she whimpered. 'Oh no, no, I couldnie.'

'You must, Bessie,' Mrs. Irvine said. 'It's your duty. Goodness knows I don't want to lose you—I don't know how I'll manage without you—but it's your duty, m'dear.'

'I won't,' Bessie cried. 'I won't.'

'Now, Bessie, don't be daft. You know perfectly well that it's your duty to go home and look after these two little motherless bairns.'

'I would look after them, hen, you know that fine,' Mrs. Moore cut in. 'But I'm an auld woman, and they're young steerin' bairns. I doubt they would be ower much for me. It's no' that I wouldnie do it for the sake of your poor mother that's dead and gone, but I'm just no' able.'

'Of course, Mrs. Moore, it would be nonsense,' Mrs. Irvine agreed. 'It would be absolute nonsense for you to go and burden yourself with them when Bessie's here—a young able-bodied girl.'

'But I dinnie want to go back to Calderburn,' Bessie snivelled. 'I'll not go back to Calderburn. It's not fair. I've never had a chance.'

'I know, Bessie, I know,' Mrs. Irvine said soothingly. 'I know you've never had a chance. But you can't look at it that way, m'dear. You've got to think of the poor wee innocent bairns. They've never had a chance either, and they're never likely to have a chance unless somebody that loves them takes them in hand and looks after them.'

'After all, it'll maybe no' be for long, Bessie,' Mrs. Moore said. 'After all, yer Da's a young man yet and if he's popped the question once he'll likely pop it again. So dinnie distress yourself, hen. It'll maybe just be for a wee while. There's sure to be a silver linin'.'

'But I dinnie want to go back to Calderburn,' Bessie wept, twisting her handkerchief between her fingers. 'I wanted to get away from it all. It's not fair, I tell you. It's not fair.'

And she flung herself across the table and wept hysterically, screaming: 'I've never had a chance, I've never had a chance. I'll not go! I tell you, I'll not go!'

'Of course, you'll have to go, Bessie m'dear,' Mrs. Irvine said, placing a sympathetic hand on the girl's heaving shoulders. 'I know it's hard on you, but it's hard on me, too, Bessie, for you were just beginning to be a right good wee help to me. But a Higher Hand than ours has ordained it all. And you mustn't forget these two poor little innocent children waiting for you to take care of them.'

'Tell me a story, Bessie.' Jenny Hipkiss stood inside the kitchen-door, kicking moodily at the panelling. 'Tell me a wee story out of your head.'

'Stop that row,' Bessie said, without looking up from her ironing. 'You're gettin' on my nerves. Away out of here and play.'

'I don't want to go and play,' Jenny said, scowling. 'There's nobody to play wis.'

'Well, go and play on yer own like a good girl.' Bessie smoothed out one of her small sister's dresses and flicked water over it to dampen it. 'Go on now, when I tell ye.'

'Tell me a story, Bessie. Or else——' Jenny gave the door an extra hard kick. 'Or else I'll get Hitler to come and drop a bomb on ye!'

'Away out of here when I tell ye!' Bessie cried, blowing on the iron before dunting it irritably on the dress. 'You're gettin' no story. I'm fair fed up with you.'

'I'm fed up wis you, too,' Jenny said.

'So you are, are you! My God, I wish it was time for you to go to the school.' Bessie breathed with exasperation and pressed the iron savagely into the folds of the small skirt. 'They'd sort you there, my fine lady. The school-teacher would knock some o' the nonsense out of ye.'

'I'm not goin' to school,' Jenny said. 'I'd kick the teacher and then I'd spit in her face and then I'd throw a stone at her and then——' She meditated for a moment, her small face puckered. 'And then I'd do a wizzy on my breeks!'

She looked triumphantly at Bessie, but her sister did not rise to the bait. Bessie folded the dress and laid it to one side, then she picked up one of her own underskirts and spread it out.

'And then——' Jenny's voice dropped to a conspiratorial whisper. 'Do you know what I'd do then?'

Bessie did not answer.

'Do you know what I'd do, Bessie?' Jenny cried insistently.

130

'I'd put my fingers to my nose and then—and then I'd *swear* at her.' She eyed Bessie malignantly, but Bessie was frowning over the underskirt, pressing the iron smoothly. 'Go on, tell me a story, stinky Bessie, or I'll swear at you, too.'

'Swear away,' Bessie said wearily. 'I don't care.'

She sighed and went on ironing, shutting her ears and her mind to Jenny's mingled whines and threats. Those bloody bairns, she was right fed up with them. From morn till night they went on and on. If they didn't want this, they wanted that, and there was no way of pleasing them at all. She'd been here for two weeks now, taking care of them, and still there was no sign of her father coming home. He was supposed to be getting compassionate leave, but it seemed that the Army wasn't in a hurry to let him go. Either that or he wasn't in a hurry to do anything about it. He was probably being jack-easy because he knew she was here to look after the bairns. Mrs. Moore kept telling her that he'd come soon and then he'd make 'arrangements,' but it didn't look like it. If it wasn't for Joe Pole coming to see her almost every evening she didn't know what she would do. She was that miserable she sometimes felt like shoving her head in the gas-oven.

Mrs. Moore and Dirty Minnie were driving her mad with their continual advice and interference. The way they went on about Joe coming to see her! Really, they had a bloody good nerve. What right had an old fat blowsy besom like Mrs. Moore to say: 'You know, Bessie, I don't think ye should have that Pole comin' to see ye. It's not decent. Especially after the way your Steppy behaved! What will the neighbours think?' It was jealousy, that was what it was. Just because they were too old and ugly to get Poles for themselves. If Dirty Minnie had been just a wee bit younger she'd have been away up to Princes Street at the toot, prancing along and grabbing Poles right and left.

She didn't even have Lily these days to console her and talk things over with. Lily never came to Calderburn, and she wasn't able to go up town and meet her because of the bairns. That Jenny was continually dragging along at her heels, and at night she daren't go out and leave them in case there was

131

a fire or the house got bombed or something. My God, if she even ran across the street to talk to somebody, Mrs. Moore and Dirty Minnie didn't let her hear the end of it for days. 'What would yer poor Da think, hen,' Mrs. Moore had said one night after she had gone to see Joe on the last tram, 'if he came home to find that the two poor wee ones had been burned in their beds, the poor wee lambs, because you were out gallivantin'?'

There had been a short silence from Jenny, but suddenly her voice was lifted again: 'Bessie! If you'll tell me a story, Bessie, I'll go for yer messages.'

'I'm perfectly capable of goin' for the messages myself,' Bessie said, and she folded the last of the ironing and carried it into the back bedroom. Jenny followed, whining and scuffling her feet. 'Tell me a story, Bessie, tell me a *true* story or else——'

'I'll tell you a true story on the side o' the head,' Bessie roared, pushing Jenny out of the way violently. 'Get away out o' my sight, you wheenging wee bitch!'

'I'll tell Daddy about you when he comes home,' Jenny snivelled. 'I'll tell Daddy about what you and Joe does when Billy and me's in our beds.'

'Get out of here!' Bessie screamed, tensing herself to spring at the child, but holding herself back by an effort. 'Get out of here before I murder you!'

Jenny backed to the door, sensing that her sister's patience was exhausted, but determined not to give in without a struggle. 'Yah, stinky Bessie!' she yelled. 'Stinky Polish tart!'

And she turned and fled.

Tell me a true story, Bessie said to herself. Tell me a true story! My God, I'll tell you a true story all right, you little bitch. I'll tell you a true story that'll make your hair stand on end. A true story about Lily and Teddy Gabanski. . . .

III

Bessie's thoughts were disturbed by the shrill blast of a

horn, which showed that the Store van had arrived in the street. She collected her ration-books, shopping basket and purse and ran downstairs.

Mrs. Moore and Mrs. Finlayson had already arrived at the van, and women were swarming towards it from all directions. They shouted friendly greetings to each other as they ran, though each of them was determined to reach it before any of her neighbours. About six women were there before Bessie, and she leaned against its side, resigning herself to at least a quarter of an hour's wait. She replied to the greetings she received, but made no move to enter into conversation with anybody. Moodily she traced with her forefinger in the dust on the van's side, making patterns beneath the huge letters *Edinburgh United Co-operative Society*.

Mrs. Moore was bandying words with the vanman. 'Now, listen here, Andy, I want decent eggs this week. The ones I got the last time near walked up to ma house on their own. My auld man had heart-failure when I dished them up to him. He says "Tell Andy that if I want to eat chickens I like them to be a wee thing aulder than this".'

'Ach, there was nothin' wrong with the eggs,' Andy grumbled. 'It's your imagination, woman.'

'It was not my imagination,' Mrs. Moore said. 'I ken a good egg when I see it.'

'She's such a bad egg hersel'!' Dirty Minnie guffawed.

'I ken it was big-hearted of you, Andy, to think o' givin' me chickens so cheap,' Mrs. Moore said. 'But I dinnie want any more o' them. I couldnie cope with a chicken this week.'

'Huh, if this war goes on much longer you'll be glad to eat all sorts o' things,' Andy said. 'You'll maybe be eatin' frogs and snails before long.'

This started the usual discussion about rationing, and they were all airing their views when a taxi swept into the street and stopped before the McGillivrays' entry. The women were silent. Taxis were an uncommon occurrence in this district, and they all gazed open-mouthed when Lily McGillivray got out.

133

'God Almighty!' Mrs. Moore said at last. 'Look what the wind's blown in!'

Lily wore a bright green waterproof, and beneath it they could see a smart black-and-white checked costume. On her head she had a black hat shaped like a Turkish fez, with a scarlet tassel hanging from the crown.

Mrs. Moore whistled softly and put her hand to her head. Several women giggled, and Dirty Minnie said: 'Ay, I must get one o' these. My, but I'd be a dabber out walkin' on a Sunday!'

Lily teetered on the edge of the pavement, paying the taxi-driver with great ostentation. She knew that she was the centre of attraction, but she never looked once at the group around the Store van. It was just as the taxi drove off and she turned to go into the entry that she appeared to notice them, then she waved gaily and cried: 'Hello, folks!' And as she went in the door she shouted: 'I'll come over and see you in a wee while, Bess. Have a cup of tea ready!'

'Set her up,' Mrs. Moore said. 'You'd be gey daft, Bessie Hipkiss, if ye waste your tea-ration on the likes o' her.'

'Did you notice the way she was riggit out?' Mrs. Finlayson said. 'My God, but these clothes would cost a bonnie penny!'

'It's easy seen she's got hold o' some daft auld Pole with more money than sense,' Mrs. Moore sniffed. 'A colonel no less! Before that she was supposed to be bidin' with a Count. It's a wonder she has the nerve to show her face before decent folk.'

'God help that poor simple sammy-dreep o' a sailor she's married to,' Dirty Minnie said. 'I'm real sorry for him.'

'Och, he's no' the only one,' Mrs. Finlayson said. 'Lots o' men'll come home from this war and find their wives have hooked it wi' somebody else.'

Bessie huddled against the side of the van, not looking at any of them in case they started to speak to her. They must guess that she knew all about Lily and Gabanski and Colonel Pietras. She pretended to study her Store Book, remembering that night she had met Lily at the Wellington Monument and Lily had almost floored her by saying: 'Well, I've left Teddy.

He told me he was a Count, but it turns out that he's not a Count at all. It was Colonel Pietras that told me. It seems he knew Teddy's people in Poland and they were just gutter-snipes. Fancy, the cheek of him! Tryin' to deceive a poor simple lassie with tales like that. My Christ, I fairly told him where he got off. Honestly, Bess, you should 'a' seen his face when I let him know I knew! Oh, I fair turned watery at the knees, he looked that fierce. And when he picked up a knife——'

'Oh, Lil, he didn't?' Bessie breathed.

'He did that.' Lily gripped her arm so hard that Bessie had a black-and-blue mark on it for days afterwards. 'Ay, he picked up a knife and he came rushing at me with his hand held up. God, Hippy, I just took to my heels and ran and locked myself in the bedroom.'

'Of course, he came and started to greet at the door,' Lily said after a pause. 'He wept and roared like a muckle bairn. Honestly, it would 'a' made you sick. "Forgeef me, Lily," he kept saying. "I do not mean to do this to you. Forgeef me, my little flower, and ve vill go and make whoopee. Ve vill get drunk," and a whole lot more like that. But I wasn't havin' any. I packed my case, and when I came out with it he burst out cryin' again and got down on his knees and tried to kiss my feet.' Lily half-giggled, half-snorted with indignation at the memory. 'But I just told him he'd had it,' she said. 'And so I walked out on him and went straight to see Colonel Pietras. He's a gentleman and knows how to treat a young lady. The Colonel's been after me for ages, anyway, wantin' me to break things up with Teddy and go and bide with him.'

'Bessie!'

'Hey there, Bessie Hipkiss, are ye deaf?'

Bessie shook herself and grinned weakly. 'Ay?' she said.

'It's your turn, hen,' Mrs. Moore said. 'It's a good job that we're all honest folk here, or you'd ha'e missed your turn in the queue. Standin' there in a daydream! What were ye thinkin' about, lassie?'

'Nothin',' Bessie mumbled, and she put her Store Book and

the ration-books on the counter of the van and said: 'The rations, Andy, please, and a pound o' semolina.'

'She'd be thinkin' about her lad likely!' Mrs. Winter suggested.

'No' her, she's got more sense than that, haven't you, Bessie?' Dirty Minnie nudged her. 'You'd be thinkin' about clothes, hen, weren't ye?'

Bessie nodded, feeling this was the simplest way out.

'Ay, I suppose the sight o' Lady McGillivray set you off,' Mrs. Moore said. 'You'll be appearin' in one o' these funny wee hats next.'

'Ach, well, it's all the lassie's chance,' Minnie said. 'She might as well make hay while the sun shines. I just wish I was young enough to make hay again myself. I'd show some o' them a thing or two. I wouldn't see half o' these young ones in my road.'

'Don't tell us you're goin' to follow Lady McGillivray's example, Minnie!' Mrs. Finlayson giggled as she stowed her purchases in her black oilskin bag. 'Jings, but you'll be comin' out with a flourish one o' these days!'

'Well, some folk are flourishin' all right with this war,' Minnie retorted. 'So I don't see why I shouldnie follow suit. A lot o' them got fur-coats and pianos in the last war, but there'll be no holdin' them back after this one. It'll be motor-cars they'll all be wantin', so I don't see why I shouldnie flourish wi' the rest o' them. Hope springs eternal, ye ken!'

'Ach, folk like us never flourish,' Mrs. Moore said. 'Look at me. I never even got the smell o' a fur-coat in the last war, so I'm no' likely to get anythin' in this one, wi' my auld man not bein' able to work or anythin'. Can ye picture me in a fur-coat?'

'My, ye'd be a toff!' Minnie giggled, and she nudged Mrs. Moore with her folded arms.

'Talkin' about fur-coats,' Mrs. Finlayson said. 'Do ye see that auld Mrs. Symington's got one?'

There was a moment's silence, and Bessie said: 'Oh, and I'll take a pound o' prunes, Andy, if you've got them.'

'Mrs. Symington!' Dirty Minnie exclaimed. 'Mrs. Symington with a fur-coat! Her that hasn't got two halfpennies to rub together!'

'I must say this beats all,' Mrs. Moore said. 'I'm that flabbergasted ye could knock me down with a feather.'

'I saw her wi' my own eyes last Sunday,' Mrs. Finlayson said. 'Mind you, it wasn't one o' these up-to-date coats like dyed squirrel or mink or anythin' like that. It was just plain sealskin—and gey shabby sealskin at that! But it was a fur-coat for all that.'

'Really, and to think o' the things I've given that woman, thinkin' she was a puir auld cratur' and harder-up than myself,' Mrs. Moore said. 'The sleekit auld bitch that she is never to breathe a word about it. You know, I give her a small gift every Christmas. She gets my papers for me every Sunday, so it's a way o' payin' her back like. But she never even sends me a Christmas card. If she can afford to buy a fur-coat you'd think she'd be able to spend twopence on a Christmas card, wouldn't ye?'

'Some folk have no gratitude,' Minnie said. 'It's just not in them. Take all and give nothin'—that's their motto.'

'Well, it's the last thing auld Symington'll get from me,' Mrs. Moore said. 'I'll never mention it, mind. The words fur-coat'll never pass my lips. But I'll remember it to my dyin' day.'

'Och, it would be a terrible world if we were all alike,' Mrs. Winter said. 'Maybe auld Mrs. Symington doesn't ken any better.'

'She kens fine,' Mrs. Moore retorted. 'She kens how many beans make five all right. But it'll be the last thing she'll ever get from me, I'll warrant. Fancy, I took up two pies and a plate o' chips to her only last week, and she never even said she'd got them. If I'd taken her up a nip o' whisky she'd ha'e thanked me quick enough, though!'

'I'd nip the drunken auld bitch,' Dirty Minnie said. 'Where she'd feel it most!'

'Ach, ye wouldnie get much grip there, Minnie!' Mrs. Moore laughed, her good-humour returning. 'She's all skin and bone, and I dare say the puir auld bitch needs the

fur-coat to keep out the cold. She's no' as well padded as you
and me!'

IV

As soon as she got inside Bessie put on the kettle, then
she ran to the bedroom, clambered on a chair and raked on
top of the wardrobe. She kept watching the door in case Jenny
should appear suddenly. She had hidden a tin of biscuits here
out of the children's way. She opened the tin quickly, put
half a dozen biscuits on a plate, and she had just got back
to the kitchen when the bell rang.

'It's me,' Lily said. 'I'm just down for a flyin' visit before
I go to London tonight.'

'London!' Bessie gasped.

Lily smirked and pranced into the kitchen, where she hoisted
herself on to the edge of the table. 'Ay, London,' she said,
putting a cigarette in a long black and gold holder. She held
out her cigarette-case to Bessie, then struck a match. 'Yes,
Hippy, me and Feliks are hittin' the trail for the Great Big
Bad City tonight. D'ye not wish you were comin' with us?'

'Gosh!' Bessie breathed. 'You have all the luck!'

'Feliks has got some kind of position with the Polish Embassy in London,' Lily said, swinging her legs and admiring
her sheer silk fully-fashioned stockings. 'So I'm not half goin'
to cut a dash I can tell you!' She held up her cigarette-holder
elegantly and blew little clouds of smoke. 'I bet these gossipin'
auld bitches in the street had somethin' to say when I appeared,
hadn't they? They're a shower!'

'They just took notice of your clothes,' Bessie said, making
the tea.

'New ones Feliks bought me,' Lily said. 'He says I must
be properly turned out and do him credit. Honestly, Feliks is
a scream sometimes. He's that auld-fashioned and has such
funny notions about what women should wear and how they
should behave. Did I tell you he has a wife already?'

'Has he?'

'Ay, it seems he left her behind in Poland when the war

138

started, but she's managed to get to Lisbon and she's there now.' Lily shrugged. 'I must say Feliks is a cool one. He never once mentioned wife to me all that time when I first knew him and he was nag-nag-naggin' at me to leave Teddy and come and be his little friend.'

'What if his wife turns up in London?' Bessie said. 'What would you do then, Lil?'

'Och, she's not likely to turn up.' Lily took the cup of tea Bessie handed to her and sipped it fastidiously. 'Feliks says she's not likely to get a visa or somethin' for at least another six months—and who knows what'll happen in six months! I might as well take the chance when I get it and see some life. I've aye wanted to go to London.'

'But what about Tommy?' Bessie asked.

'Tommy?' Lily frowned. 'What Tommy?'

'Tommy—you know fine what Tommy I mean,' Bessie said, her eyes wide with amazement.

'Oh, Tommy Hutchinson! My husband!' Lily giggled. 'Ach, I'm not worried about him, and I don't suppose he's worried about me. I don't care what happens to him or what he thinks as long as I get my allowance regular.'

'No, I've plenty on my mind at the moment without worryin' about Tommy,' she said, popping half a biscuit in her mouth. 'All my attention's taken up with Feliks and his daft notions about the way nice women should behave. Honestly, Hippy, you'd die sometimes if you heard him! He keeps goin' on and on about his wife. He says "My vife, she does not paint her face and my vife she does not smoke," and he keeps tryin' to get me to follow her example. He even cuts up rough when I paint my nails. Says his wife has never painted her nails in her life, and he disapproves of me doin' it.'

'What an auld sap!' Bessie exclaimed.

'Ay, he's tryin' to reform me.' Lily laughed raucously. 'Jesus Christ and General Jackson, he's got some hope!'

She giggled and spluttered so much that crumbs of biscuit flew out of her mouth. 'If he thinks I'm goin' to act all quiet and ladylike he's got another thought comin',' she said.

139

'What does he think I'm goin' to London for? It's not for his bonnie blue eyes!'

'I wish I was goin' to London, too,' Bessie sighed.

'Ay, it's a pity. We'd fairly paint Piccadilly red, wouldn't we, Bess!'

'Too true!' Bessie sighed again. 'But I've got to stay in this bloody place and look after these two bloody kids. I'm fair fed up with it.'

'Och, cheer up, it can't last long,' Lily said. 'You're lookin' all right, I must say. Gettin' away from that auld nark, Mrs. Irvine, seems to agree with you.'

'Huh, does it!' Bessie sniffed sulkily.

'You're lookin' fine. In fact, you're puttin' on beef, Bess.'

'What?'

'Ay, you're puttin' on beef,' Lily said. 'You're lookin' kind of hefty.'

'Ach away and no' be daft!' Bessie said.

'Right enough,' Lily said. 'I'm not jokin'. You're a lot stouter. In fact——' She paused and regarded Bessie critically. 'Are you sure you're all right?'

'Of course, I'm all right,' Bessie snorted. 'I'm just fed up. I get that tired o' these bairns and no' bein' able to move one foot without all these gossipin' auld bitches gettin' on to me.'

'I don't mean that,' Lily said, pursing her lips. 'I mean—are you *all right*?'

'Well, I—I suppose so.' Bessie hesitated. 'I sometimes feel a wee bit sick in the morning, but otherwise——'

'Aha!' Lily sat up triumphantly and asked a few more intimate questions.

She whistled slowly as she ground out the end of her cigarette. 'Well, I must say, Ferret!' she said at last. 'I must say that it looks to me as though you're going to have a baby.'

V

'A baby!'

Bessie couldn't believe it. 'A baby, Lil?' she repeated.

'It looks like it,' Lily said. 'If you're not five months gone already, then I'm a Dutchman.'

140

'Oh, Lil, what am I goin' to do?' Bessie wailed. 'Five months. . . . Oh, Lily!'

'Stoppit, Ferret!' Lily said sharply. 'I must say I can hardly credit that you'd be so daft as not to ken for yourself. Honestly, you take the bloody biscuit. What else can you expect after all these high-jinks with Klosowski and Joe? I never thought you were so innocent, or I'd have done somethin' about it.'

"But I never thought . . .' Bessie wept.

Lily clicked her tongue with exasperation. 'Well, it's high time you did. You're not a bairn any longer.' She patted Bessie's arm with clumsy affection. 'Och, cheer up, hen, everything'll be all right. You'll see, it'll all come out in the wash.'

'But my Da—what'll he say?'

'Time enough for that when he comes home,' Lily said. 'Maybe we could get somethin' fixed up before that. Is it Joe's? Could you not get him to marry ye quick?'

'I dinnie ken if it's Joe's or not.' Bessie rubbed her eyes with her fist, sniffling. 'I just hope it is—I couldnie bear it to be like Dmitri Klosowski.'

Lily took a fresh cigarette, and so great was her agitation that she forgot to put it in her new cigarette-holder. 'God, I just wish you had asked me for a few tips, you silly wee bitch. I might 'a' known you'd go and land yourself in the soup.'

'What'll I do?' Bessie wailed again.

'Search me,' Lily said, walking up and down, hands on hips, frowning in concentration as she had seen film stars act in slightly similar situations.

'I'm too young to have a bairn,' Bessie wept. 'I dinnie *want* a bairn.'

'You should 'a' thought o' that sooner,' Lily said. 'Now, stoppit, Bess,' she ordered sharply. 'There's no sense in makin' such a mollygrant about it. The thing's done now. What we want to do now is to find some way out o' it.'

'But how?'

Lily sighed. 'I dunno. I wish I did.' She inhaled deeply. 'God, I wish I wasn't goin' away tonight,' she ruminated. 'I don't like to leave ye like this on your own.'

141

Bessie threw herself in a chair and burst into fresh sobs at the thought.

'Now listen, hen,' Lily said, bending over her and patting her shoulder. 'You've got to pull yersel' together, Bess. Nobody knows about it but you and me—at least I hope not. None o' these nosey auld bitches have said anythin', have they? It's a wonder that auld Mrs. Moore hasn't had a word to say— her that's got eyes in her backside.'

'No,' Bessie whimpered. 'No, she's never said a word.'

'I can hardly believe it,' Lily said. 'She's the kind that's aye first to notice a thing like this. Of course, seein' you every day maybe nobody would see anything extraordinary. You're such a wee thing and don't show much. I don't suppose I'd 'a' noticed myself if I'd been seein' you every day. But I haven't seen you for weeks and weeks, and it fair hit me in the eye.'

'Did Mrs. Irvine no' twig it?' she said suddenly.

Bessie shook her head. 'I don't think so. No, I'm sure she couldn't. I havenie seen her since before Christmas.'

'Well, that's only a week ago, and I'm sure it was stickin' out a mile then,' Lily said. 'Hell, I wish I wasn't goin' away tonight. I've half a mind to tell Feliks I'll follow him down in a day or two. In fact, I think I will.'

'Aw, Lily, you cannie do that. I'll be all right.'

Lily sighed. 'Are ye sure, hen? I'll stay if you like. I wouldnie hesitate about it, except that I dinnie trust Feliks no' to get hooked up by some philanderin' bitch in London when he's on his own. And besides, our seats are booked, and you know how difficult it is to get seats on the trains just now when there're so many folk travellin'.'

'I'll be all right,' Bessie snivelled. 'Don't worry, Lil.'

'Now, you must speak to Joe about it at once,' Lily said. 'Just you tell him point blank that he's got to do somethin'— and he's got to do it quick. I think you'd better get married to him right away.'

'Married?' Bessie tensed with agitation at the thought.

'Ay, married.' Lily threw her cigarette-end in the sink where it fizzed and spluttered for a moment and then went out. 'Why not? I'm married, amn't I? Why should you no' be married as well as anybody else?'

'But, Lil, I'm ower young to be married yet.'

'Och, you're only a year younger than me. Why should ye not get married, I'd like to know. Might as well be in the fashion as well as everybody else!' Lily tried to laugh jauntily, but there was a nervous tremor behind the laughter. 'And, anyway, you'd better be married if you're goin' to have a bairn.'

She lit another cigarette and puffed it rapidly. 'I tell you what, Bess,' she said after a pause. 'Why not go and see Mrs. Irvine? She's an auld bitch and she doesnie like me any more than I like her, but she's quite straight about things, and she's been good to you. I think you should go and see her.'

'Oh, I couldnie,' Bessie exclaimed. 'I'd—I'd be fair ashamed.'

'Och, forget it,' Lily said. 'This is no time to go beatin' about the bush. You go and see Mrs. Irvine, hen, and just tell her exactly what's happened. She'll likely go up in smoke, but you'll just have to put up with that. She's not a bad auld bitch, and I bet she'll do somethin' to help you. I'd feel easier in my mind, anyway, if I know you've got somebody like her to depend on when I'm not here.'

'Oh, I couldnie,' Bessie repeated.

'Don't be daft,' Lily ordered. 'You go and see her at once. In fact, I think you should go straight up to see her this afternoon.'

'Och, it's ower late now,' Bessie said. 'I've got these bloody kids on my hands. They'll be in roarin' for their tea in a wee while. No, I'll think about it and maybe I'll go and see her tomorrow.'

'There's to be no *maybe* about it,' Lily said. 'You go and see her when you're told. After all, she can't bite you.'

'All right,' Bessie sighed. 'I'll speak to Joe tonight when he comes and see what he thinks is best.'

'It's not what Joe thinks is best,' Lily said. 'It's what Mrs. Irvine thinks is best. You do what she tells you, hen. I bet she'll make Joe come to heel pretty quick.'

'Still, I'd better speak to Joe first.'

143

'Okay,' Lily said.

She peered at herself in the mirror above the sink, patting her blonde curls into place. 'I suppose I'd better go,' she said. 'I still have my auld man to see. He'll raise Cain when he hears I'm for off to London tonight.'

'Aw, Lily, I wish you werenie goin',' Bessie wailed.

'So do I.' Lily put her arm around her, and for a moment they clung together. Then, shamefaced at allowing herself to show such emotion, Lily pranced to the door, saying: 'Well, cheeribye, Ferret! I'll send you a post-card with the address. Now, be sure and write to me. Let me know what happens after you've seen Mrs. Irvine.'

'Ay, I'll go and see her as soon as I've spoken to Joe,' Bessie promised.

VI

But Bessie never got a chance to speak to Joe, for her father arrived home that night and the issue was forced upon her. She was trying to persuade the children to go to bed when Joe came, and at the sight of him Jenny and Billy decided that it meant that they could stay up for another hour or two.

'Hya, pal!' Billy cried. 'What about tellin' us a story, Joe! Tell us what you did at Warsaw.'

'He'll do nothin' of the kind,' Bessie snapped. 'You've heard about Warsaw hundreds of times. You're goin' straight to your beds, both of you.'

'Ach, we are not goin' to our beds,' Billy said, putting on a manly voice. 'We're goin' to stay up as long as we like and listen to Joe. You pipe down, Ferret-face.'

'I'll pipe down you!' Bessie cried. 'Away to yer bed at once, or I'll scud your ear.'

'You and who else?' Billy laughed boastfully and looked at Joe for admiration.

But there was no man-to-man friendliness in the stolid look which the Polish soldier gave the dirty-faced imp. Joe stretched himself to his full height, fingering his belt round his middle, and he sat down and said:

144

'It is better that you do what Bessee tells you.'

'Ach, c'mon!' Billy cried. 'You can tell us just one story.'

'Just one story,' Jenny repeated, leaning against Joe and preparing to get on his knee.

'No.' Joe pushed her away. 'It is bed-time for little children. Bessee and I wish to speak wis each other.'

'Aw, nuts!' Billy jeered. 'Ye're just wantin' to get us out o' the way so that you can canoodle with each other.'

'Billy!' Bessie cried.

Billy grinned derisively and, keeping a wary eye on Joe, he backed to the door. 'Who's afraid of you?' he said. 'You're not the boss in this house.'

'No, Daddy's the boss,' Jenny chimed in.

'Come on,' Bessie said, and she picked up Jenny, who started to kick and scream, and carried her by main force to the bathroom, pushing Billy in front of her. Billy turned to make for the front door, but seeing Joe give him a menacing look he went into the bathroom. As soon as the door was shut, however, he said:

'Who does that big Joe Polonay think he is, anyway? Comin' here and tryin' to boss everybody. Does he think he's still in Warsaw? I don't believe he ever shot ten Jerries off his own bat. If he saw a Jerry he'd dive under the bed with fright.'

'You'll dive under your bed and it'll not be with fright if you don't get your clothes off and get washed double-quick,' Bessie shouted. 'Come on now, before I lose my temper!'

It was over half an hour, however, before the children were washed and in bed, and by that time Bessie was exhausted by their whining and wheedling. She sighed with relief as she closed the door of their bedroom behind her, thinking that now she would have peace and a chance to speak to Joe about what had been uppermost in her mind since Lily's visit. But before her hand had left the door-handle a shout from Jenny stopped her.

'Bessie, can I come and sleep wis you and Joe if there's an air-raid?'

'There'll be no air-raid tonight,' Bessie cried. 'Go to sleep now like a guid wee lassie.'

'How do ye ken there'll not be an air-raid?' Billy yelled. 'Did Hitler tell ye? Or did Joe Polonay tell ye?'

'If you don't hold yer tongue I'll get Joe Polonay as you call him to come and give you a good belting,' Bessie screamed. 'Shuttup now, both of you.'

She could feel herself trembling with exasperation and rage, and she went into the bathroom for a moment, in order to try to collect herself before going into the living-room to face Joe. She was powdering her face when the door-bell rang.

'Damn!' she muttered. 'If this is Mrs. Moore I'll soon give her the bum's rush.'

But the belligerent look faded from her face when she saw her father bowed under an enormous soldier's pack.

'I had to ring,' Bert said, shouldering past her. 'I couldn't find my key. What a hell of a time ye took to answer the bell.'

'I—I was in the lavvy,' Bessie stuttered.

'What about somethin' to eat?' he said, dumping his pack with relief and pushing back his forage-cap to wipe his sweating brow. 'I'm fair starvin'. I couldn't get a bite on the train, and it was that packed I had to stand all the way. God! Talk about dyin' for your king and country! My feet'll die before the rest o' me if I have any more o' these long train journeys. It's a bloody scandal the way they shove us all into wee auld-fashioned trains like a lot o' cattle.'

Bessie shut the door slowly, staring at her father as though in a trance. 'I—er—I didnie expect you so soon,' was all she could find to say.

'Och, I meant to send you a wire, but I hadnie time,' he said. 'I just heard at the last minute that I could get leave, so I got packed and scooted for the first train.' He blew out his cheeks with weariness. 'God, I'll be thankful to get this uniform off and my feet into somethin' softer than these muckle boots. It's all right for some o' these young ones, they can take it, but I doubt I'm ower auld to make a good soldier.' He laughed and said: 'Well, what about a cupper char and somethin' solid to fill my belly? It's rumblin' like an auld traction-engine.'

'I—er—I've got a visitor,' Bessie mumbled.

But before she could say any more her father, who was looking quizzically at her, said: 'Here, what've you been doin' to your hair? It's an awful bright red. Good God, lassie, is it no' about time you stopped plaisterin' with it and let nature take its course?'

He opened the living-room door. 'Hello!' he said. 'Who the hell's this?'

Joe sprang up from his lounging position on the sofa and stood to attention, clicking his heels. 'Rolewicz, Josef,' he said, and he gave a little bow.

'A Pole, eh?' Bert Hipkiss advanced slowly into the room and leaned on the table.

'Joe's a terribly nice fella and him and me are keepin' company,' Bessie gabbled, scarcely aware of what she was saying. 'He's just down to see how me and the bairns are gettin' on. He bides with Mrs. Irvine, and he's an awful nice fella and . . .'

Bert leaned on the table, looking the Polish soldier up and down. Joe relaxed from his stiffened position and smiled. 'You are Bessee's papa, yes? I am veree pleased to meet you.'

'You're the only one,' Bert said.

He thumped the table with his clenched fist. 'So you're goin' with a Pole, are ye, my lassie? As if we hadn't had enough truck with bloody Poles in this family already!'

'But Joe's all right,' Bessie whispered. 'He's an awful nice fella and . . .'

'He may be all right, but I don't care,' Bert cried. 'He's a Pole and that's the end of it. We're for no truck with Poles in this house, and the sooner you learn that the better, my lady.'

'But me and Joe are gettin' married.'

'Married!' Bert threw himself into a chair and glowered from one to the other. 'So you're goin' to get married, are you? Now that I've had a closer look at you, you brazen wee bitch, I can see that it's not before time. Married. . . .'

Joe, who had been looking from one to the other, not quite understanding what was being said, but comprehending that something was the matter, moved towards Bessie and said: 'Joe Pole is veree fond of Bessee. Joe Pole lofs Bessee.'

'Love!' Bert laughed savagely. 'Don't make me laugh! What do your kind know about love? You're all out for the same thing, and you won't rest till you get it. All this kissing of hands and bowing and clicking your heels! Maybe it takes a trick with the women, but it'll not take a trick with me. Playin' about with silly wee craturs like this! Do you call that love?'

'Of course Joe loves me,' Bessie cried. 'Don't you, Joe?'

The Pole put his arm around her waist and drew her against him. 'Joe lofs Bessee veree much. Joe wants to marry Bessee.'

'See!' Bessie cried triumphantly.

'O.K.' Bert shrugged. 'Have it your own way, but don't say that I didn't warn you. You've left this house once before, so you can easy leave it again. But mind you, my lassie, this time you're not comin' back. If you make your bed you'll have to lie on it. Don't come whinin' to me for sympathy when you find you've made a mistake.'

'I'm not makin' a mistake,' Bessie said, beginning to weep. 'I love Joe and—and——' she gulped, 'and he loves me.'

'Well, get to hell out of my sight, both of you,' her father said wearily. 'But before you go, give me somethin' to eat.'

'What a welcome for a tired and hungry man,' he said, bending to unlace his boots.

Joe sat down uneasily on the sofa. Bessie wiped her eyes with her knuckles and said: 'Will sausages be enough, Da? It's all I've got in the house. Or if ye like, maybe Joe could run out and get some fish 'n' chips.'

'Sausages'll do fine,' Bert said. He leaned back and eyed Joe up and down. 'I must say you've picked a not bad lookin' specimen,' he said conversationally, taking out his pipe and filling it. Joe sprang forward with outstretched cigarette-case, but Bert waved it away. 'No, thank you.'

He puffed his pipe and stared stolidly at the younger man all the time Bessie was frying the sausages. Every now and

148

then Joe attempted a conciliatory smile, but Bert ignored him. When Bessie put the meal on the table, he drew up his chair and said: 'Well, they say you should never judge a sausage by its skin, but foreign sausages are just beyond my comprehension.'

'Mind you,' he said, his mouth full of sausage and fried potatoes, 'I'm all for Internationalism. I think that it's only by marryin' folk from other countries that wars'll eventually stop. The only good thing I can see about war is that it lets folk see that folk from other countries are much the same as themselves. All the same, I don't hold with the Poles.'

'Well, I do,' Bessie said defiantly.

'Have it your own way then,' her father said, picking up the evening paper and propping it in front of him. 'There's no sense in goin' over all this ground again. I could easy have this one up for wantin' to marry you under-age, but I can't be fashed. I wash my hands of you. Beat it, both of you, as long as I've still got my temper.'

PART IV

I

ONE morning in the summer of 1942 Bessie Rolewicz was awakened by the shrilling of the alarm-clock in her attic bedroom in Pixie O'Malley's boarding-house in London. She lay for a moment, wondering if it was another air-raid. Then gradually she realized that it was not the siren, but a signal to get up and get ready to meet Lily McGillivray who was being released from Holloway Gaol.

She buried her face in the pillow, longing to sink again into deep sleep. But the alarm continued its wail until it finally whirred into a little splutter and stopped. Bessie raised herself on her elbows and yawned. It was six o'clock and already there was a steady rumble of traffic down Gower Street on its way to Covent Garden. Bessie rose, twitched back the blackout-curtain, and put her head out of the window. She leaned for a few minutes on the sill, staring at the tall outlines of the University College and the green dome of the British Museum, while she tried to collect her scattered thoughts.

Ay, Lily was coming out of jug this morning after doing her six weeks for shop-lifting. Lily was a right mug to go and get herself caught like that. Any fool could have known she'd be lifted. But of course, Lily had aye been a bit of a fool. Only a fool would have gone back to Teddy Gabanski after the way he had treated her. Lily was a great one for laying down the law for other folk—she was aye saying things like 'Now just you listen to me, Bessie, and you can't go wrong'—but she was a real simpleton when it came to the bit. Only a simpleton would have let old Colonel Pietras slip

151

through her fingers. What if his wife had come here from Lisbon? Lily had more or less got herself firmly settled with him, hadn't she? All she had needed to do was say: 'Now, look here, Feliks, you've got to choose between your wife and me. After all, you've been living with me for nearly a year and you haven't seen your wife for over two. Is it to be her or me?' But no, Lily had been that daft that she had upped and left him right away, without waiting to see if he really wanted to go back to his wife or not.

Bessie sighed, remembering that day when Lily had come to tell her the news. Lily had been laughing fit to burst. Laughing, mind you, when it was no laughing matter. 'You should see her, Bess!' she had giggled. 'You mind how I told you that Feliks said to me "My vife, she does not paint her face and my vife, she does not smoke." Well, honest to God, Hippy, you'd die if you could see her. She's painted and powdered to the eyes, and she smokes like a chimney. And her nails! You should see them. You know how Feliks is aye going on about mine bein' so long and pointed. Well, you should see hers. They're like bloody talons and they're painted a terrible bright scarlet. My Christ, she certainly hasn't been sittin' quiet all this time in Lisbon, mourning for her beloved Feliks.'

'And what are you going to do, Lil?' Bessie had asked.

'Do! What can I do?' Lily had shrugged. 'I've done it already. I've left him. You can't picture me and him and her all living together in peace and quiet, can you? No, I just packed my bags and came away. Och, don't worry about me, I'll soon land on my feet again.'

Bessie turned away from the window and began to dress. Poor Lil. She had landed on her feet all right. She had jumped straight back into the arms of Teddy Gabanski. Jumped right up to her neck in trouble, in fact. Gabanski was attached now to the Polish Embassy and he had got to know Lily's whereabouts through Colonel Pietras. He had been pestering her for ages and ages to leave the Colonel and go back to him, so he was quick to take his chance when the real Madame Pietras came from Lisbon. Oh yes, he had been quick to take his chance all right. The way he had pleaded and pleaded with Lily, saying: 'Come back to me, my little flower. We will haf no more trouble, no more quarrellings. We will lif together like little doves in a nest.' It was right laughable. Lily, the daft besom, had believed every word of it, and she had gone to live with him in a wee flat in a narrow street in Holborn. And, of course, they hadn't been together for long before it all started again. Lily was all right as long as she was interested in the flat and painting it and one thing and another. She was in her element when she was in air-raid shelters and shop-queues, queening it and telling everybody she was the Countess Gabanski. She was all right, too, as long as Teddy kept taking her dancing and to the pictures and theatres. But after a while either he got tired or really was as busy at the Embassy as he said, and Lily was left with more time on her hands than she knew what to do with. And that was when the real trouble started. There was an awful lot of American G.I.s in London, and of course Lil had aye been a great one for the boys, so what does she do but go gallivanting along Piccadilly and places like that. Mind you, Lily had every right to get up to high-jinks if she wanted to, but there was aye Teddy and his jealous temper to be reckoned with. Time and time again Bessie had warned her: 'I tell ye what it is, Lil, you'll go stravaigin' once too often and then the fat'll be in the fire. Either a bomb'll land on you or somethin' else'll happen. And then where'll you be?'

As she brushed her hair, Bessie wondered why she should let Lily's troubles fill her mind to such an extent. God knows she had troubles enough of her own. She hadn't had a letter from Joe for nearly a month. Of course, Africa was a long way and it took time, but surely she should have heard from him before now?

She dabbed her face with powder and smoothed it in, then she made up her mouth the way Pixie O'Malley had shown her. Really, she had learned an awful lot from Pixie! She had learned far more from her than she had ever learned from Lily when you came to think about it. Pixie was a right good spud, and it was awful nice of Mrs. Irvine to have put her in touch with her when she came to London. Mrs. Irvine was a real pal—even though she had raised the roof that time when Bessie had told her that she was going to have a baby and that she was marrying Joe Rolewicz. 'Really, Bessie!' she had cried. 'The whole trouble with you is that you just can't say "No".' And then, after she had given her a terrible flighting, she had asked why hadn't she come to her for advice. 'For you know, Bessie, that I just feel like a mother to you.' And then she had waded into Joe and arranged everything for them getting married. Oh yes, Mrs. Irvine was a right pal all right.

They had been married only about a month when Joe got drafted to North Africa, and Mrs. Irvine had been an even greater help to her then. 'I think you should go to London or somewhere and have your bairn there, Bessie,' she had said. 'You know how narrow-minded some of the folk in Edinburgh are.' And she had given her Pixie O'Malley's address, and so she had come here.

Bessie gave herself a last look in the mirror, touching her blonde hair which was swept in a high pompadour off her forehead and hung shoulder-length, with the ends curled up. It was getting kind of streaky again. She'd need to pay another visit to the hairdresser's. Thank goodness she could afford it now off the allowance she got as a lieutenant's wife and off the pay she got for working for Pixie.

She clattered downstairs, her six-inch high heels tapping down the five flights to the basement. Mrs. Newlove, the charwoman, had just arrived and was folding her shabby brown coat and laying it over the back of a kitchen-chair. 'Mornin', Mrs. Roley,' she said. 'Another quiet night, thank Gawd. 'Ow d'yer feel this morning, love?'

'Not bad,' Bessie said, filling the kettle. 'How do you feel yourself?'

'Could be worse, ducks, could be worse.' Mrs. Newlove extricated the long skewer which held her black felt hat on to her little grey bun. She smoothed the overall over her ample stomach and said: 'They was over Bristol again last night. Somethin' cruel it must 'a' been. Them pore people, 'ow they must be suffering. And all because of That Man! Oooo,

154

but I wish I could get 'im 'ere for just five minutes. I'd give 'im what's for in no uncertain way. I'd take me 'at-pin and I'd . . .'

But what Mrs. Newlove would have done to Hitler was cut short by the entrance of Pixie O'Malley.

Miss O'Malley always made entrances or exits. She was an ex-chorus girl, a tall willowy woman of forty-five with faded blonde hair, which she got 'touched up' periodically. She had been married in the first World War, but her husband had left her 'flat on my beam-end, darlin',' she had told Bessie. 'But I didn't sit down and weep. That would've been futile, and I've never been one to weep about spilt milk. Anyway, my Spirit Guide told me I'd make good after crossing a lot of water, so I went across to the States and hoofed it there for a while. Dear God, darlin', those road companies in the States are the bloody end. You're in Baltimore one week and you're almost right across the continent in some one-horse town in Ohio the next.'

'Morning, Bessie,' she said now. 'Morning, Mrs. Newlove. Everything okay?'

'Everythin' in the garden's lovely,' Mrs. Newlove said, going to the sink and preparing to wash the large pile of dishes which had been left from the previous evening's supper.

'What time are you going, Bessie?' Miss O'Malley said.

'After I've laid the breakfast. And I want to take Mr. Powys up his breakfast before I go.'

'You spoil that old divil, darlin'. If it was left to me he wouldn't get so much attention, I can tell you,' Pixie laughed. 'No, I'd be telling him just where he and all those old books of his got off. Him and his precious books! Mother of God, he thinks more of them than many a mother thinks of her kids—or many a girl about her boy-friends!'

'Och, he's a nice old man,' Bessie said.

'Nice old man my foot! If it wasn't for you cleaning up his room whenever you get the chance—and the dear God knows it's not often the old divil can be got out even to take a breath of fresh air!—he'd be living like a pig in his own dirt. Nice old man says she! A more futile, feckless old

155

blackguard never drew breath. Though it's a clever man he is, I've no doubt,' Pixie said. 'With his old bald head stuffed with all that dirt he gets out of books. I suppose in the heel of the hunt he's happier than any of us.'

'He's aye very nice to me, anyway,' Bessie said, beginning to lay Mr. Powys' tray with extra special care as if to make up for Miss O'Malley's tirade, good-humoured though it was.

'Well, don't make yourself late, darlin',' Pixie said. 'And don't be after rushin' back here as though a hundred of Herr Hitler's storm-troopers were after you. Though why in God's name you should be bothering yourself to go and meet that silly bitch, Lily, beats me. I'd be inclined to leave her to paddle her own canoe.'

'Och, I couldnie do that,' Bessie cried. 'Poor Lily. It wouldn't be fair after all she's gone through.'

'She brought it on her own head, darlin', so she's nobody to blame but herself. Maybe it'll be a lesson to her not to play fast and loose with Poles and Yanks—with Yanks, anyway,' Pixie added quickly. 'If she'd only come to Mother for advice I could 'a' told her they were a no-good lot of villains. They all look alike to me, anyway, with their yellow faces and their big fat backsides.'

'Oooo, Miss O'Malley!' Mrs. Newlove was shocked. 'The things you do say, love!'

'Well, it's right enough. I simply can't bear the way they all have their trousers stretched so tight across their hams. Walkin' along with their hands in their pockets as though they were all so proud of them. Sometimes in Piccadilly when I see them, standin' around like a lot of lost sheep or amblin' along as though they were God's own gift to the girls, I'd like to take a big stick and . . .'

'Coo now, Miss O'Malley love, you just wouldn't 'ave the 'eart,' Mrs. Newlove said. 'After all, they didn't ask to come 'ere any more than our pore lads asked to go to Egypt and India and them other wild foring places. They're all some-body's kids—bless 'em.'

'Oh, I suppose they are,' Pixie shrugged. 'All the same,

I can't bear them. I just think back to the rotten time I had in the States, and every G.I. I meet makes me see red.'

'Och, they're not all alike, Pixie,' Bessie said. 'I've met one or two not bad ones.'

'Now don't you be going and following in that Lily McGillivray's footsteps,' Miss O'Malley said. 'One of her kind's more than enough.'

'Trust me,' Bessie grinned. 'I'm not that daft.'

II

Of course, Pixie was all wrong about the Yanks, Bessie thought on her way to Holloway. She had a bee in her bonnet about them. They did not all have yellow faces and fat bottoms. Maybe some of them looked like that, but there were a lot of lovely fellows amongst them, too. Oh yes, there were really some lovely fellows. Like that one who had helped her and been so nice that time she'd had trouble with the baby. . . .

Standing in Euston Road, waiting for a bus, it all came back to her with greater vividness, for it had been near here that it had happened. Over a year ago it was now, not long after she came to London. She had been fairly far gone in pregnancy and Pixie kept insisting that she shouldn't work, but should just take things easy. Pixie wouldn't let her out on her own either; she said that she must always have somebody with her. But one day old Mr. Powys had wanted tobacco from the little kiosk where he always got it near Euston Station, and Bessie had volunteered to get it for him. 'Let the old divil go for it himself,' Pixie cried. 'The lazy old blackguard! Sitting up there so crafty amongst his books and wantin' a poor girl that should be sittin' with her feet up to go and do his dirty work for him. If he's sore needing his tobacco he'd be glad to go and fetch it for himself.'

'Och, I don't mind going,' Bessie said. 'It's not far, and the walk'll do me good.'

'I don't like you going out on your own, darlin',' Pixie said. 'What if your pains started comin' on or there was a

157

raid or a bomb dropped near you? Holy Mother, I'd never be able to forgive myself—or that good-for-nothing old divil upstairs!'

But Bessie just smiled and went. It was a clear, sunny morning, and it was pleasant walking up Gower Street and down Euston Road. She had just passed the traffic lights and was gazing idly into a shop-window when suddenly above the rumble of the traffic came the heart-turning shrill of the sirens. 'Oh, God!' she exclaimed, and she turned to look for the nearest air-raid shelter.

It was about a hundred yards away, and already people were rushing into it. Bessie started to run. Keep calm, you fool, she told herself, but she could not prevent her heart pounding and the wild beatings in her temples. The drone of aeroplanes could be heard now above the final wails of the sirens. At the back of her mind something told Bessie that these were British fighter-planes, but, although her bodily burden made it difficult, she lumbered on.

'Steady, lady! Steady! There's no great rush.'

The voice behind her made her turn, but she did not stop. 'But the bombs!' she cried. 'The bombs!'

'Okay, lady. Time enough for them. Jerry's not over yet, so you take it easy. You'll make the shelter in good time.' And the tall American in the drab olive-green uniform took her arm, saying: 'Just you leave it to me and I'll see that you're okay.'

Bessie was relieved to lean against him and to have her steps directed. 'Oh, what awkward times they choose to have their auld raids,' she gasped. 'Can they not come at a reasonable time!'

The G.I. laughed. He had a pleasant brown face and short black hair, and his eyes creased into a lot of tiny lines at the corners when he grinned. He had very blue eyes, Bessie noticed later, and his black lashes were so long and thick that they made them seem even darker; at times they looked almost navy-blue.

'Well, here you are,' he said at the entrance to the shelter. 'You'll be okay now.'

158

'Oh, are you not comin' in?' she cried. 'You'd better.'

'Aw no, I might as well stay outside and see what fun's going,' he grinned. 'Probably just a false alarm, anyway.'

'But——'

'You'll be all right now, lady,' he said. 'Plenty of dames in there. They'll look after you. But you be a good girl after this and don't go window-shopping on your own.'

He saluted her and was turning away when Bessie cried: 'Just a minute! I wonder if you'd . . .'

What she had been going to ask him to do she did not know later when she came to think about it. For just then she fainted. She remembered only that her heart was palpitating and that she was terrified he'd go and leave her to the mercy of strangers. . . .

When she came to she was in an ambulance being driven to hospital. The G.I. and an air-raid warden were sitting on the bunk opposite. As she opened her eyes, the G.I. grinned and said: 'You sure took a quick powder, sister. Are you all right?'

'Lucky for you 'e was with you, missis,' the air-raid warden chipped in. 'Coo, there was so much excitement inside the shelter—lot of old gals all cluckin' like agitated hens—that I might never 'ave known you was lyin' on the doorstep if 'is nibs 'adn't come and fetched me.'

Bessie smiled wanly and whispered: 'I—I think I'm all right.' And the last thing she saw before she again lapsed into unconsciousness was the G.I.'s lean brown face and sympathetic blue eyes.

A week of pain and misery followed. The baby was born prematurely and lived only a few hours. In a way Bessie was glad and relieved; she did not want the burden of a child. Though at the same time she was disappointed—for Joe's sake most of all, since he wrote about the child in every letter—and she had steeled herself during the past few months to the inevitability of it, and now that it had come and gone she felt cheated in some fashion. To have borne so much pain and inconvenience, to have had so much worry . . . and all to come to this! 'I've never had a chance,' she whimpered to Pixie

O'Malley, 'so maybe the poor bairn wouldnie ha'e had a chance either.'

Besides Pixie, she had visits from old Mr. Powys, Lily and the G.I. sergeant. She was especially glad to see Mr. Powys, who had been fretting and blaming himself for her plight. 'Och, don't worry,' she told him. 'It's all for the best. If I hadnie gone for your tobaccy, I might have slipped down the basement stairs or somethin'. 'What's the good of worryin'? I'm just as pleased. I'm too young to be saddled with a bairn.'

'But a young life, my dear!' Mr. Powys said. 'When so many lives are being taken just now in all this bombing and horror we need all the young lives we can get. The world must go on.'

Mr. Powys brought her some books, but Bessie could not interest herself in them at all. There had been a time when she could have sunk herself into them and been oblivious to everything else; but now there was so much to see in the ward, so many people in beds around her, so much to think about, that books were no longer necessary as a means of escape. Even though two of them were *Rebecca* and *Gone With The Wind*, which she'd been wanting to read for a long time, she did no more than glance through the pages, unable to focus her attention on them. 'Och, I'll read them some time,' she said to Lily. 'I'll maybe get time after the war's finished.'

Lily picked another book from the top of Bessie's locker, looked at it, and threw it back with disgust. '*The Poems and Sermons of John Donne!*' she cried. 'I help my God, Hippy, don't tell me you've been tryin' to read that?'

'I've just looked at it,' Bessie said. 'I cannie make head nor tail o' it. I think Mr. Powys must have left it by mistake. I should think it's a book he's been readin' himself.'

'Huh, if he reads books like that, no wonder he's such a queer auld fish,' Lily said. 'It's enough to put years on anybody!'

The day that the G.I. called he, too, picked up the books and looked at them. He had already phoned the hospital several times to ask about her condition, and Bessie had learned

from one of the nurses that his name was Norman Gantz. He
sat shyly beside her bed, twiddling his service cap between his
long brown hands. 'Tough about the kid,' he said. 'Still,
you're only a kid yourself. Maybe . . .'

'It's all for the best,' Bessie said.

'I tried to get in sooner,' he said. 'But they wouldn't let
me. Say, they sure are strict in these hospitals. One starched
piece asked me if I was the father!' He grinned and picked
up a book to hide his embarrassment. He flicked through the
pages while Bessie watched, as perplexed as he was for a subject of conversation. 'You readin' this?' he asked.

She shook her head. 'I've looked at it, but . . .'

'Queer kinda book,' he said. 'All those funny spellings.
Out of this world! Not that I'm a bookworm.' He frowned
at a page, then he read aloud: 'The world is a great volume,
and man the index of that book; even in the body of man,
you may turn to the whole world; this body is an illustration
of all nature. . . .'

'What d'ya make of that?' he said.

'I dunno,' Bessie said. 'It's beyond me.'

Gantz mouthed a few sentences soundlessly, scratching his
head. He turned the book over and looked at the spine. 'John
Donne,' he said. 'Never heard of him.'

'What else does it say?' Bessie said, liking the sound of his
soft nasal voice.

'They said in their hearts to all the world, Can these bodies
die?' he read. 'And they are dead. Jezebel's dust is not
amber, nor Goliah's dust terra something or other . . . Latin,
I think. . . .'

'Jezebel's dust is not amber,' Bessie repeated, looking at the
way his hair grew in a widow's peak on his forehead. 'What
does it mean?'

'Search me, sister,' he said. 'I was just gonna ask you.'

'I must ask Mr. Powys some time,' she said.

But she never had, she reflected as the bus jolted towards
Holloway. She'd never had time. It was funny how busy
she seemed to have been since she came to London. What
with all the work in Pixie's boarding-house (Pixie's Bear

Garden as Miss O'Malley herself called it) and all Lily's troubles and writing letters to Joe, she never had a minute. And when she did have a minute she usually sat as she was sitting now, thinking about this or that—sometimes about Joe, but mostly about that American sergeant.

It was awful, she thought, but she couldn't remember the colour of Joe's eyes at all. While she remembered the Yank's eyes as clearly as though he were standing there in front of her. It was really terrible, for she was in love with Joe. Of course she was in love with him. Weren't they married and all that, and hadn't he been right good to her? Why in God's name she should keep thinking about Norman when she had only seen him twice in her life was beyond her. It was fair uncanny, but she seemed to know him even better than folk she had lived with all her life. It was a real good job he was stationed at some camp in Lancashire and that he'd never been back in London since that time. He had written to her once or twice—not that there was anything in his letters, mind you, that anybody could take any offence at. If Joe had been here she could have handed them over for him to read. No, there was nothing sleekit or underhand about them at all; they were just ordinary letters to say how was she and he hoped she was having a gay time and that it was pretty dull in his camp and that he remained her sincere friend, Norman Gantz.

Gantz . . . it was a funny name, wasn't it? Of course, when you came to think about it, Rolewicz was a funny name, too. Bessie giggled softly to herself as she remembered how she used to hate her own name, Hipkiss. And now here she was married to a man called Rolewicz, and folk kept calling her Mrs. Roley-Poley and daft-like things like that. What would they have called her if she was Mrs. Gantz?

Aw, stoppit, you daft besom, she admonished herself, rising as the bus approached Holloway. What's the sense in thinking a lot of daft rot about a tall thin Yank that you're never likely to see again in your life? He's probably no good, anyway, and writes letters to lots of girls.

III

'Hya, Ferret!'

Lily McGillivray's greeting was as jaunty as her appearance as she stepped through the gaol gates. She wore a tightly-belted scarlet coat and high-heeled black suede shoes. A white silk scarf with red markings was tied in Russian peasant fashion over her peroxided hair. She gave a mock salute to the gateman and cried: 'Cheerio, chum!'

'I'll be seein' you,' he called after her.

'Not if I can bloody well help it!' Lily laughed and cleeked her arm through Bessie's. 'Well, Bess, how's tricks?'

'I'm all right,' Bessie said, looking in an ashamed way from right to left, avoiding the glances of passers-by. 'Are you all right yourself, Lil? How did you get on?'

'Och, I'm okay,' Lily said. 'It wasn't too bad. It was a nice rest.'

'You can have my share of it!' Bessie tried to emulate Lily's jaunty tone.

'No, it wasn't too bad,' Lily said. 'But I'm damned glad to get out all the same. It sort of cramped my style in there.'

'Really, Lil, what made you do it?' Bessie asked as they waited to cross the road.

'I dunno.' Lily shrugged. 'I just thought I'd take a chance. It looked that simple, and I wanted the stockings. Teddy was that mean that he wouldn't buy me any. How was I to know that yon bloody floorwalker was watchin' every move I made? My Christ, if I ever run up against him I'll claw his smarmy face for him. The idea! He had been bowin' and scrapin' and sayin' "Yes, madam" and "No, madam" and "This way madam" to me just two or three minutes before he called the store detective. What a bloody twister! Leadin' innocent folk up the garden path like that!'

'Still, they say that you should have all the experiences you can get in this life,' Lily said as they got on a bus.

'Well, it's an experience I don't want to have,' Bessie said. 'If I can help it!'

'You never know the moment!' Lily giggled.

'Too true,' Bessie said, but she said it soberly, thinking, as she said to the conductress: 'Two to King's Cross, please,' that Lily was quite right when she said you never knew the moment when something would go wrong and then maybe through no fault of your own you would get into trouble. It's like what Robert Burns said, she thought, the best laid schemes of mice and men. . . .

'Are you deaf, Bess?' Lily demanded.

'No, no, I was listenin'.' Bessie started guiltily.

'I was sayin' I suppose I'll have to get a job somewhere,' Lily said. 'One thing I know: I'm not goin' back to Teddy. Not after the way he behaved in the court. The cheek of him to say to the magistrate that I was unreliable and that it was only his influence that had kept me out o' gaol before! When had I ever been in trouble before, I'd like to know!'

'Ay, he had a right nerve,' Bessie said.

'But I'm finished with him,' Lily said. 'Yes, he could go down on his bended knees, but I'd never have anything to do with him again. I'm going to get myself a job and then I'll be independent of the bastard.' She sighed and drew luxuriously at her cigarette. 'God, what a relief it is to have a fag again!'

'Y'know, Bess,' she said a moment later, gazing dreamily at the conductress, who was chaffing a large stout man at the front of the bus, 'I wouldn't mind gettin' a job as a bus-conductress. Lookit the variety you would get! Just think of all the different fellas who'd get on your bus that you might get a chance to click with. What a rare time I'd have!'

'Aw, Lily!' Bessie was horrified.

But Lily just giggled, and she leaned forward and hailed the conductress: 'I say, ducks, how do you get a job on one o' these buses?'

She was still getting the details and listening to the conductress' stories and warnings when Bessie cried: 'C'mon, here's King's Cross. We've got to get off.'

164

They pranced into a Help Yourself and picked up trays at the end of the long snack counter. Lily led the way, peering at the racks of food. 'Is there nothin' but beans on toast, love?' she asked one of the assistants behind the counter. 'Och, what a mouldy dump this is! You don't bother to cater for your customers at all. It's a wonder folk come here.' She picked up a cake, then put it down again. She fingered several, oblivious of the glares of the assistant, before she found one to please her. 'It's not much cop, but I daresay it'll have to do,' she said, pushing her tray along to the cash-desk. 'Hurry up, Bess, I'm fair starvin'.'

Lily picked the most prominent table in the restaurant and sat down with a regal air. 'We can see everythin' fine from here,' she said, shovelling a forkful of beans into her mouth. 'My Christ, it's a relief to be feedin' in a civilized way again. I got bloody browned off in there when I used to look at all their sourpusses.'

'Was it awful bad, Lil?' Bessie asked sympathetically.

'Och, it was all right.' Lily tossed her head. 'Let's forget it and enjoy ourselves while the goin's good.' She nudged Bessie. 'Get a load o' that G.I. in the corner. Isn't he a smasher!'

'Ay, I suppose he's all right,' Bessie said, glancing at the large beefy Yank in the too-tight uniform.

'Suppose!' Lily giggled. 'Of course, he's all right. I could go for that fella in a big way.'

'You're welcome to him.'

'Och, what's come over you, Bess? You're that stand-offish about fellas these days. You'd think you'd joined the Salvation Army or somethin'. It's high time you snapped out o' it. You're only young once.'

'I'm not interested in anybody but Joe,' Bessie said. 'After all, I'm a married woman.'

'Well, so am I!' Lily laughed raucously. 'And do you think I'd sit and mope about Tommy Hutchinson? Catch me! Joe's thousands and thousands o' miles away. D'you think he's sittin' there, calmly, thinkin' about you? Not on your life! I bet he's havin' a good time. So why shouldn't you do the same? Have a good time as long as the goin's good is my motto!'

'Ay, and look where it landed you,' Bessie sniffed.

'I'm sorry, Lil,' she added quickly. 'I didnie mean that. You know I didnie. I just—well, it's like this: I don't seem interested in other fellas these days.'

'Ah, well!' Lily shrugged. 'You can do what you like, but I'm not goin' to sit still and make an auld maid o' myself before my time.' She turned to eye two other G.I.s who had just come in. 'Not bad,' she said.

'Are you wantin' anything else to eat?' Bessie asked.

'Ay, I believe I could go another cake,' Lily said. 'In fact, I could go two! My belly's never stopped rumblin' for weeks and weeks.'

'I'll get them,' Bessie said, and she rose and went to the counter.

When she returned with the cakes, Lily nudged her and whispered: 'See that lassie at the next table with the blackie!'

Bessie glanced at the girl with the Negro G.I. and said: 'Ay, what about her?'

'I'm maybe not all I should be, but I must say I'd draw the line at a nigger,' Lily said in a louder voice, conscious of her own virtue. 'My God, yes. East is East and West is West and never the twain shall meet like it says in the Bible.'

'Och, c'mon drink up your tea and let's get weavin',' Bessie said, avoiding the glare of the girl with the Negro.

'What's all the hurry?' Lily demanded. 'I'm enjoyin' myself if nobody else is.'

Somebody had turned on the radio, and Lily sang in time with it: 'You are my sunshine, my only sunshine. You made me happee when skies were grey. . . .'

'Did I tell you I had a letter from Mrs. Irvine?' Bessie said, anxious to change the subject.

'No, you havenie told me any o' your news.' Lily tried to look bored. 'What's she sayin' to it, the auld bitch?'

'Well, do you remember Lieutenant Leja?' Bessie said. 'Remember the Pole that used to wear the hair-net and was aye eatin' oranges in his bed?'

Lily nodded, tapping her foot in time with the jazz from the radio.

'Oranges!' Bessie sniggered. 'It just shows what mugs me and Mrs. Irvine were. If he'd had somebody like Pixie to deal with out he'd have gone on his neck at the toot. He didnie eat oranges in his bed at all! D'you know what the stains were?' And she leaned over and whispered in Lily's ear.

'Naw!' Lily was genuinely shocked. She sat bolt upright in her chair. 'Fancy that! It's a good job that none o' us ever had anythin' to do with him. Of course, I couldn't bear him. He was such a sissy.' And she began to imitate Leja's affected voice and mannerisms.

As she watched Lily's impersonation, Bessie remembered how, when she was a little girl and she imitated anybody, her mother used to say something which for a long time she thought was 'Mockin' scratchin',' but which later turned out to be 'Mocking's catching.'

'Mockin's catchin', Lil,' she said now, for Lily, tired of Leja, was making a few catty remarks about Mrs. Irvine. 'Stoppit, for goodness' sake. You maybe don't like Mrs. Irvine, but she was good to me, and I'll hear nothin' against her.'

Lily's mouth fell open with surprise. 'Honestly, Hippy, what's come over you?' she said in injured tones. 'I never saw such a change in anybody. I feel as if I'd been away for six months instead o' six weeks. You used to be aye ready for a bit o' fun, but nowadays you go about with a face like a flittin'. You're that meek and mild. Talk about bein' more holy than godly!'

'Well, I don't see anythin' to laugh about,' Bessie said.

'Ach, I suppose you're right,' Lily said. 'We've had enough o' Poles—both o' us. So let's forget them. All the same, I can see it's high time I took you in hand again,' she said, rising. 'C'mon, let's get out o' this dump. Let's get crackin' and collect my duds and then we'll go to the pictures. I'm just dyin' to see a good picture. Have you any idea what's on?

IV

Despite Lily's pleas, Bessie would not go to the cinema with her. 'No, I'll maybe meet you tonight,' she said. 'But I've got to get back to Pixie's now.' And as soon as she had helped Lily to pack her belongings from the flat in Holborn, she returned to the boarding-house.

'Bessie darlin', there's been a phone-call for you,' Pixie cried when she went into the kitchen. 'You'll never guess who!'

'I dunno,' Bessie said.

Pixie winked at Mrs. Newlove, and both of them laughed.

'I took one look at you and then me 'eart stood still!' Mrs. Newlove sang, striking an attitude at the sink. 'Coo, Mrs. Roley, but you are a one and no mistake!'

'Who was it?' Bessie cried. 'Not—not Joe?'

Pixie shook her head. 'Don't be so futile, darlin'. I know they come from Africa pretty quick these days, but they don't come just as quickly as all that.'

'It was your American beau,' she said. 'Norman Whatsisname.'

'Fancy!' Bessie gasped. 'Fancy, I was just thinking about him this morning.'

'Aha!' Mrs. Newlove cried. 'I thought you 'ad a far-away look in your eyes, ducks!'

'Well, he's here in the flesh,' Miss O'Malley said. 'He's going to ring again at three o'clock. He wants you to go out with him tonight.'

'Och, I can't,' Bessie said. 'I half promised Lily. . . .'

'And why not? Don't be a fool, darlin'. It's not every night you get the chance of being taken out by a handsome young man—even though he is a Yank, and God knows Yanks are two a penny in London these days.'

'But I promised Lily,' Bessie said.

'Oh, Lily!' Pixie snorted. 'D'you think she'd pause to consider a date with you if there was a man in the offing?

168

Don't be a bee fool, darlin'. You go out with whatsisname and have a good time and forget Lily.'

'But——' Bessie hesitated. 'But I don't think I really want to go out with him. He's awful nice and all that, and I like him, but . . . well, I don't think that Joe would like me to. . . .'

'Holy Mother of God!' Pixie looked at Mrs. Newlove. 'Did you ever hear such balderdash in all your born days? Would you be after worryin' about your lawful wedded if a nice young man asked you out?'

'Not me,' Mrs. Newlove said, patting her stomach and trying to pull it in. 'Not on your life I wouldn't! Chance is a good thing—that's wot I say. I'd seize the hopportunity with both 'ands, and I'd never, I'd never let go!' she carolled, breaking into a popular song of her youth. And she gave a few grotesque skips as she carried some dishes from the sink to the table. 'Face me up, Biddy!' she giggled to Miss O'Malley.

'Get along, you silly old so-and-so!' Pixie chuckled. 'You drop one of those dishes and you'll get your marching orders.'

'Seriously though, Bessie,' she said. 'What's to hinder you from going to meet this boy? He seems a nice enough fellow—as Americans go—so why not go out with him? He's on the level okay.'

'No, Joe wouldn't like it,' Bessie said.

'Ah, to the divil with Joe!' Pixie turned up her eyes and sighed. 'What do you think we should do with her, Mrs. N?'

'I told yer,' Mrs. Newlove said. 'I said to yer, didn't I? I said yer should just 'ave told 'im to come round and then when 'e was standin' on the doorstep she couldn't't've done nothin' about it. Cor, them young ones! The chances they miss, just because they think they should remain faithful to their true loves. I was just the same meself, mind! Yes, in the last war when Newlove was away, and a smashin' 'Ighland sergeant with a kilt asked me to go and see Mary Pickford with 'im, I got ever so 'oighty-toighty and not one foot would I budge. Coo, I've regretted it ever since.'

'You see,' Pixie said to Bessie. 'You take advice from people that've had a roll in the hay before you.'

'Oh, roll me over in the clover, roll me over and do it again!' Mrs. Newlove sang, and she dissolved into helpless giggles. 'Coo, that 'Ighland sergeant was a one and no mistake! D'yer know wot 'e said to me one night when 'e'd 'ad a drop too much?'

'I can guess,' Pixie said.

'I don't know what to do,' Bessie said. 'Mind you, Norman Gantz is a nice bloke, but . . . well, I just don't think it would be fair, me bein' a married woman and all that. . . .'

'You can always lose your weddin' ring, ducks,' Mrs. Newlove said. 'Go on, it'll do yer good. 'Ave a nice night out.'

'I don't see any harm in it,' Pixie said. 'It's not as if you were a flighty piece like that Lily. You've got your head screwed on the right way and you're not likely to come to any harm. After all, it's very nice of this boy to ask you when he might have asked dozens of other girls. In fact, it just shows that he is a decent sort of man, because he knows you're married. He just wants to be friendly. He doesn't know anybody in London, I expect, and he was really very good that time you were taken to hospital. I think it would be terribly ungracious to refuse to go out with him.'

'Well,' Bessie sighed, 'I'll think about it.' She took off her coat and draped it over the back of a chair. 'There's plenty of time to make up my mind before three o'clock.'

'Yes, but see and 'ave your mind made up good and proper, ducks,' Mrs. Newlove advised. 'A bird in the 'and in London is worth two in the bush in Africa them days. And wot a bird! If I was in your shoes I'd . . .' She broke off and ran to the door. 'Here's the postman comin' down the area steps! Coo, but you are late today, 'andsome!' she greeted him. ''Ere was I pinin' because me boy-friend 'adn't sent me no letters. You just came in the nick of time to keep me from shovin' me 'ead in the gas-oven.'

'Keep a place beside you for me, Ma!' The elderly postman sighed as he handed her a bundle of letters. He shifted his postbag to his other shoulder and wearily pushed back his cap from his sweating forehead. 'I'm proper browned-off with all this footsloggin'. I wish I was safely back in the sortin' room again. Before the war me missus was always at me for not gettin' enough fresh air, but now I get too ruddy much of it. Fresh air! Fresh air be damned! I'd rather be back in the sortin' room 'avin' a friendly game of Nap with the other lads.'

'God be with the old days,' Pixie said piously, looking through the letters. 'One for you, Bessie darlin'.'

Bessie grabbed it eagerly. 'From Joe!' she cried when she saw the Service Air Mail envelope, then her mouth slacked open. 'No, it's from . . .'

Pixie O'Malley looked up quickly from her rummage through her boarders' mail when she heard Bessie's queer little cry. 'What is it, darlin'?'

'It's—it's Joe,' Bessie gulped. 'He's been wounded. This is from a friend of his to say he can't write himself. He's— he's in hospital and isn't allowed to write.'

'Dear Mother of God,' Pixie said, putting her arm around the weeping girl. 'If it's not one thing it's another.'

'Cheer up, love,' Mrs. Newlove cried, patting Bessie on the shoulder. ''E'll be all right. Don't you worry. Like as not 'e's all right by this time—sittin' up and takin' a little nourishment—the top of father's egg!' She giggled. 'If they're gettin' eggs in Africa. Don't you worry, ducks. Only the good die young. That's why I 'aven't been called to the 'Eavenly Mansions long before this!'

v

When Norman Gantz telephoned, Bessie was in the middle of writing a long letter to Joe. 'I don't think I want to speak to him,' she said to Pixie. 'Could you not . . . aw, tell him I'm not well or somethin'.'

'Go on!' Pixie jerked her head towards the phone. 'Don't be so futile, darlin'.'

Bessie took the receiver and said 'Hello' in a toneless

171

voice. Pixie nudged Mrs. Newlove who was hovering anxiously at the top of the basement stairs. 'I'd like to take a stick to her,' she whispered.

'Oh, I'm not bad,' they heard Bessie say. 'I daresay I could be worse. . . . What? Aw, I don't think I could. . . . No, I'm awful sorry, but I can't. . . . Eh? . . . Well, maybe some other time, but not tonight. No, I just couldn't. . . . Okay. Cheeribye!'

'Well, I must say,' Pixie exclaimed when Bessie hung up. 'You're the absolute end! You sounded like a wet cold fish. That poor fellow!'

'What did 'e say, love?' Mrs. Newlove asked.

'He said he'd ring me again in a day or two. He's got shifted to a camp near Reading, so he says he'll be in town oftener.'

'Well, I wouldn't be surprised if this is the last you hear of him after the reception he got,' Pixie said. 'I must say, you are a fool, Bessie. Brushin' off a decent young man like that!'

'Well, I couldn't go out with him and Joe lyin' there in hospital, could I? It wouldn't be right.'

'Ah, you'll change your mind in a day or two, ducks,' Mrs. Newlove said. 'The next time 'e rings up you'll say yes, and then out you'll go to meet 'im all dolled up to the eyebrows.'

'I don't think so,' Bessie said, and she went back to the writing of her letter.

She sat and stared at what she had already written: two and a half Air Mail sheets full of love and messages for Joe's quick recovery. What else could she say, she wondered, picking up her pen. How could she show him that she loved him and him only. Oh, Joe, Joe, if you were only here. . . .

It would be so much easier. It was awful to think that he was all that distance away, lying in a strange bed with God knows what wrong with him. His friend had been very vague about the wound. His English was bad and the letter had evidently been written with great difficulty. He just said Joe had been wounded and that he had asked him to send her his love.

What else can I say? Bessie wondered. She had told him

172

about Lily and she had sent him loving messages from Pixie and Mrs. Newlove and Mr. Powys (even though they hadn't actually sent them she knew that they would have done if they had just thought about it). But what else? There was still a half-sheet of paper to fill, and she was determined to write down to the end.

Frowning, with tongue sticking out of the corner of her mouth, she wrote: *Do you remember the nice American that helped me that time the baby was born, well he phoned today and asked me to go out with him, but I said no. I just couldn't have gone with him, Joe dear, knowing you were lying there thinking of me the way I am thinking of you. Get well soon, darling, and let us hope the war will be finished soon and then you will come back to me. Love and XXXX Your Loving Wife, Bessie.*

She was adding a few more crosses to fill in a gap when Mrs. Newlove shouted: 'Mrs. Roley! Ahoy, there, Mrs. Roley-Poley! Are you deaf, ducks? Telephone!'

'Gosh, who is it this time?' she said. 'Not . . . ?'

'No, it ain't 'im, ducks,' Mrs. Newlove said. 'Pore young feller, you can't expect 'im to phone so quick after the way you spoke to 'im. No, it'll take 'im two or three days to come round again. But 'e will, of course, 'e will. 'E'll just take 'is time. No, it's that Lily wot wants yer!'

'Hello, Lil,' Bessie said.

'My, what a time ye've been,' Lily screamed across the wires. 'Where have ye been?'

'I was writin' a letter to Joe,' Bessie said, and she told her all about it.

'Och, poor Joe,' Lily said. 'Still, he'll soon be all right again. I wouldnie worry, if I were you, Hippy. Worryin' never did anybody any good. Well, now, what about the pictures?'

'Och, I can't, Lily. I couldn't go with Joe lyin' there. . . .'

'Why not? Mopin' at home'll not do Joe any good. I never heard the like. Are you in yer right senses, Bessie Hipkiss?'

'I can't go, Lil, and that's flat.'

'Aw lissen now, Bess. Be your age! What's the sense o'

sittin' at hame like a weepin' widdy? C'mon and see *Casablanca* with me. Or if you like we'll go and see Marlene Dietrich in *Destry Rides Again*. I've seen it already, but I wouldnie mind seein' it again.'

'I'm not goin',' Bessie said.

'Aw, for cryin' out loud! Really, Bess, you take the bloody biscuit. A jaunt to the pictures'll do you good. I'll meet you at Piccadilly Tube Station—at the Shaftesbury Avenue entrance—at six o'clock, and then we'll go and see Marlene. I'm just fair dyin' to see her again and to see her scratchin' Una Merkel's eyes out. My, what a rare fight yon was! And when Marlene sings: *See what the boys in the backroom will have and tell them that I'll have the same. . . .*'

'I'm not goin', Lil.'

'And tell them I died!' Lily sang. 'And tell them I died on the game!'

'I'm not goin',' Bessie said.

'You are so goin',' Lily said. 'Honestly, I never heard the like. I'll meet you at six o'clock, and don't you be late. Cheeribye!'

And she clicked down the receiver before Bessie could protest further.

VI

That night when Bessie returned to the boarding-house about eleven o'clock she found a telegram to say that Lieutenant Josef Rolewicz had died of wounds received in battle.

PART V

I

'A VISITOR for you, Bessie.'
She looked up listlessly at the sound of Pixie's voice. For
the past fortnight, ever since the news of Joe's death, she had
sat every afternoon, as she was sitting now, in the sitting-room,
staring with lacklustre eyes at the street. In the mornings she
did a certain amount of work, but so aimlessly that Mrs. Newlove often had to do it after her. Pixie and Mrs. Newlove
kept telling her to snap out of it. 'After all, darlin', you're
still a young woman—Holy Mother of God, you're little more
than a child—so you shouldn't let it get you down like this,'
Miss O'Malley said. 'You've got all your life in front of you.
I know how you feel, darlin'—I felt the same when my man
left me—but you can't just sit down and let it get the better
of you. You'll be after going into a decline if you're not careful.' But all their pleadings and warnings passed over her
head. They meant less to her than the dronings of the
aeroplanes which sped continually through the sky above
London. Perhaps it was a bomb from a plane like those which
had been the means of killing Joe. . . . She had had no
details.

'Here's a visitor, darlin',' Pixie repeated, and she turned and
beckoned to someone behind her.

'Hello there!' Norman Gantz said, sliding his tall body
past Pixie. 'Hope you don't mind me calling, but I was around
these parts and I thought——' He grinned and smacked the
palm of his hand with his folded service-cap. 'Well, I thought
it would be kinda nice to see you again.'

175

'Hello,' Bessie said, rising.

She smiled as they shook hands. 'How d'you do?' she said mechanically.

'Aw, I'm okay,' Gantz said. He sat down, his long legs wide apart, and leaned his elbows on his knees. He looked at her for a moment, then he looked down at the pattern of the carpet between his feet. 'Say, I was mighty sorry to hear the news about—about your husband. Miss O'Malley told me what a swell guy he was. It's tough luck.'

'Uhuh.' Bessie pleated the skirt of her black dress between her fingers.

'Smoke?' Gantz held out a packet of Chesterfields, shaking one loose.

'Thanks,' Bessie said.

He stood up like a spring uncoiling and bent over her with a lighter.

'Thanks,' Bessie said, inhaling.

'I phoned two or three times,' Gantz said, lighting a cigarette for himself. 'But—well, I guessed it was better not to disturb you, so I just left a message.'

'Yes, Pixie gave me them,' Bessie said.

'Say, she sure is a swell dame. One of the best, I reckon.'

'Ay, she's awful nice. She's been right good to me. I don't know what I'd've done without her.'

'It's mighty nice to know nice people,' he said. 'You sure are lucky.'

He got up and walked to the window and stood there, hands thrust deep in his pockets, looking out. Then he turned and took a few steps round the room. Bessie watched the smoke from her cigarette. She could think of nothing to say.

'Nice room,' the American said. He sighed as he sat down again and gave a deep pull on his cigarette. 'That's something you get lonesome for in the army. A nice room, nice furniture, nice people. . . . The army's okay, I guess. One gets around. One sees things. But it's kinda—well, it's kinda cramping, if you see what I mean. I often wish I was back home among the folks I know, doin' things I want to do.'

'I know,' Bessie said.

And suddenly she felt a rush of sympathy for him. Despite his size and loose-limbed toughness he was so much like a small lost boy. His eyes had a clear innocence that sat oddly against the hard-bitten lines around his mouth. And she wondered again how old he would be. Twenty-two maybe? Twenty-five?

'Ay, you're like me,' she said. 'You've been for a hurl in the barrow.'

The lines at the corners of his eyes crinkled. 'How come?' he said. 'I don't follow.'

Bessie laughed. 'It's a Scottish expression. It means you've been taken for a ride.'

'And how!' Gantz stood up and squashed his half-smoked cigarette into an ash-tray. Watching him, Bessie was horrified at such extravagance. Really, when cigarettes were so scarce and not only scarce but dear. . . .

'Yeah, I guess I have been for a what d'you call it—a hurl . . ?'

'A hurl in the barrow,' Bessie said.

He grinned. 'I reckon you'll have to teach me Scots. An idea, eh? You teach me Scots and I'll teach you real honest-to-God American. That a bargain?'

'Och, away!' Bessie started to giggle, then she stopped. She had not laughed for days and days. Somehow it didn't seem right.

He was walking about the room again. Can he not sit still? she thought, watching him pick up photos of Pixie's Irish relations and lay them down again. He stood with one in his hand while he said slowly:

'It's kinda funny, but the last time I saw you it was just after the baby. And now your husband. . . . Strikes me maybe I got a sorta jinx as far as you're concerned. Maybe I shouldn't of come to see you. Maybe I'd better light out now. . . .'

'No,' she said. 'Why should you? It's awful nice of you to come. . . .'

Her voice trailed away, and to hide her embarrassment she stubbed her cigarette in the ash-tray, although normally she would have smoked it to much nearer the end. This was a nice man, she realized, a man like Joe. And with the realization she saw Joe again. Although he had never been out of her mind for the past two weeks she had never been able to picture him. She had tried desperately, but she had never been able to conjure up just how he had looked or what his voice sounded like or any of his ways or facial expressions. But now, like a sudden flash of lightning, she saw his close-cropped blond hair and his rather sullen face. The deep scar on his forehead was so striking that she wondered how she could ever have forgotten it. And his eyes . . . those deep-set Slavonic eyes. . . .

She stared at the American, her mouth slightly agape. It was odd how he should have reminded her of Joe, for they weren't really alike. The American was so dark and he was at least two inches taller than Joe, and he was much thinner. Joe's shoulders had been broad and his waist had tapered in as though he were corseted; but Gantz was almost the same width all the way down. . . . No, she saw that although not as broad and chunky as Joe's, his shoulders were really quite wide, and his hips were narrow. It was the cut of the blouse of his uniform that made him look the same width. But it wasn't his face or his figure that reminded her of Joe. It was something about his manner. . . .

Suddenly Bessie found herself crying. She hid her face against the back of the couch and sobbed as though she would never stop. She had not been able to cry like this since she had heard that Joe was dead. And although she searched frantically for her handkerchief, she knew that it would be useless. The tears just flowed in a pain-easing torrent.

'Easy there, easy!' Gantz murmured.

But he made no move to touch her; and when at last Bessie was able to sit up and dab at her eyes she saw through the mist that he was looking out of the window. 'It's okay now,' she said to his straight, tall back. 'I'm sorry, but——' And she gave a final sniff.

'I guess that was a load off your mind,' he said, and he turned and gave her a quick, small boy's smile.

'Uhuh.' She gave her eyes a few more dabs and then tucked

her handkerchief away. 'Gee, I must look a sight,' she murmured.

'No, you look okay,' he said. 'I'll lay my money on you any time.'

Bessie went to the mirror above the fireplace and smoothed her swollen eyelids with the tips of her fingers. 'Excuse me,' she muttered as she took out her compact and dabbed her face with the powder-puff.

She was embarrassed, but not as embarrassed as she might have been, she reflected. If it had been somebody else she would have been fair ashamed. But somehow or other she did not mind so much with this man, stranger though he was. She knew instinctively that he would never be a stranger as far as she was concerned. He had been *in* on two of the greatest emotional experiences of her life. She knew, too, that she had found a new friend. And that was something which, deep inside, had been troubling her for the past two weeks. With Joe dead she had felt completely alone and friendless. It was true that she always had Lily and Pixie and old Mr. Powys, not to mention Mrs. Irvine and all the others she knew in Edinburgh, but without Joe she had nothing to cling to, nobody to lean against. Now, she realized, that maybe there was somebody in the world who might care a little about her. . . .

II

The air-raid warning went as Norman and Bessie came out of the cinema. 'They sure are early tonight,' Norman said. 'Well, what about it, kid? Will we make for the tube?'

'It'll be awful crowded,' Bessie said. 'But I suppose we'd better.'

They ran along Coventry Street and joined the crowd jostling down the stairs into the Piccadilly Underground. Waves of stuffy heat surged up into their faces. Inch by inch, step by step, they moved down into the depths, Norman gripping Bessie's arm tightly. She was glad to lean against him; she felt suffocated by the crowds and the stale smell of humanity.

The regulars who brought their bedding every night to the tube had taken up their positions long ago. Bessie and the American were forced to step over rolls of blankets and mattresses arranged for the night. 'Tough going,' he said, pulling her after him into a small corner where they could stand and watch other struggling for a vacant space. 'Roll on, peace!'

'You've said it, sarge!' a voice said at his elbow.

Three young G.I.s, little more than boys, were huddled together, service hats pushed to the backs of their short-cropped heads, jaws working overtime as they chewed gum and gazed with vapid faces at the milling crowd.

'Where you from, sarge?' one of them asked.

Bessie did not listen. She knew that Norman's reply would be: 'Willow Creek, Wyoming,' and that the other would probably say: 'Never heard of it, bud. Now me, I'm from Kansas, little town called . . .' She had got used to it by this time. After all, this was the fifth time she had been out with Norman. The fifth, or was it the sixth? She counted, and decided it was the fifth. The first time, that day he had called after Joe's death, didn't really count, for she hadn't gone out with him; he had just stayed for supper. But five times, every week-end since, when he came up from Reading, she had met him and he had taken her to a cinema or a theatre. Only five times, and yet she felt that she had known him for years. . . .

A raucous Scottish voice shrilled above the crowd of chattering, bird-like cockneys: 'Mind ma stockin's for any favour! Can ye no' watch yer big flat feet?'

Bessie craned her neck, and almost at the same moment Lily McGillivray pushed through the crowd, clinging to the arm of a large, over-fed American. 'Lily!' she cried. 'Hey there, Lil!'

'Why, Bessie Hipkiss!' Lily could not have been more surprised if she had not seen Bessie for three years instead of three days. 'What are you doin' here?'

'I've been to the pictures,' Bessie said.

'Fancy! So was I,' Lily said. 'We were at *The Forty-Ninth Parallel*.'

'So were we,' Bessie exclaimed. 'Funny we never saw ye!'

'Wasn't Leslie Howard lovely?' Lily said, shifting her chewing-gum to her other cheek. 'I could go for that fella in a big way. Though, mind you, Laurence Olivier wasn't bad after he shaved off his beard.'

'I'll give you beard, sister,' her huge American said. 'In a big way!'

'Ach you!' Lily giggled and slapped his chest. 'Lissen, Bess, this is Nat.'

'Hya!' Nat said.

Lily was peering past Bessie at Norman. 'Is this him?' she said.

Bessie nodded and plucked Norman's sleeve. 'Norman, this is Lily McGillivray. You've heard me speakin' about her. And this is Nat.'

'Hya, bud!'

'How d'you do, Sergeant Gantz?' Lily said in her most polite voice. 'I've been *dying* to meet you. As I said to Bessie here, I knew you'd be all right, for Bessie knows how to pick them. She's never picked a dud yet. Have you, Bess?'

Bessie flushed, wondering what ill chance had blown Lily and her boy-friend into this particular tube station. She was relieved when, after smiling and shaking hands, Norman turned and continued his conversation with the three young G.I.s. Nat squeezed his enormous bulk into the corner beside them and joined in, and the two girls were left free to talk. Lily was bending down, smoothing a tear in her stockings with wettened forefinger.

'Isn't this damnable?' she said. 'My new nylons that Nat just gave me. I could scream, really I could. Some folk just never watch where they're goin'. Of course, I must say I was in a fair panic and wasnie lookin' where I was goin'. Thae sirens aye make me go all haywire.'

'I thought you were on duty tonight, Lil?'

'I was, but I got put on another shift at the last minute. God, ay, I'll have to be up at half-past five the morn's morning. I must say bein' a bus-conductress isn't as much fun as I thought it'd be. Still'—Lily looked at Nat's large back and rolls of thick neck—'I'll maybe be able to give this job the heave one o' these days.' She sniffed. 'I must say I wish I was you, Hippy. Leadin' a lady's life. You're laughin' kit-bags, you that's got a widdy's pension and all.' She giggled. 'Fancy, at your age! I used to think it was only auld wives that were widows.'

'I don't see anythin' to laugh at,' Bessie said. 'Poor Joe, every time I think about him. . . .'

'Och, what are you worryin' about, Ferret?' Lily cried. 'You cannie help Joe gettin' killed any more than he could help himself. Anyway,' she sniffed, 'as far as I can see you're doin' all right for yoursel'—widdy's weeds or no widdy's weeds!'

Bessie glanced down at her black frock. Every time she put it on she could not help thinking about Joe. Tonight, before coming out with Norman, she had wondered whether she should wear it; it seemed so sort of . . . well, pointed. Yet she knew that Norman did not mind. He was completely in sympathy with her about Joe, and never once had he tried to take any advantage of her. He just wanted her company. Never in any way had he tried to make their relationship of the kind that Lily was hinting at. His hand on her elbow when crossing a street, or a brief handshake before parting—that was the nearest they ever got to touching. But Bessie knew that they didn't need to touch each other physically; there was a close bond between them that was stronger than any bodily contact.

'I see you're chewin' gum like everybody else,' she said. 'I wonder at you, Lil. It's so common.'

'Ach, what's wrong with it?' Lily pouted. 'It takes the bareness off your face.'

'I aye knew you were a bare-faced liar,' Bessie giggled. 'But this is the first time I've heard you admit it.'

'Well, really!' Lily drew herself up majestically. 'You're a fine one to talk, Bessie Hipkiss! You that's a bigger liar than anybody I know.'

'Me!' Bessie tossed her head and gave her hair a fluff up

from her shoulders. 'When have you heard me tellin' lies, I'd like to know?'

'Oh, I've heard ye all right. Absolute whoppers! You forget sometimes that I've got a long memory. The way you've been goin' on ever since Joe was killed you'd think you had never said a word against him. He's everything that's wonderful now, but I remember the time when you said you wished you'd never met him. And the things you said about him when you were goin' to have the baby—Jesus Christ and General Jackson, you forget half o' them! But I don't.' Lily resettled her coat over her shoulders and plucked Nat's sleeve. 'Och, how long are we goin' to stand here, big boy? I've no intention o' spendin' the rest o' the night in this stinkin' tube. Let's get crackin'.'

'Okay, sister, hold your breath a minute,' Nat said without turning from the animated discussion about Russia's chances against the Germans in the Ukraine.

'You and your auld Russians!' Lily exclaimed. 'I hear about nothin' else. If the Russians can just hold them at Stalingrad! Of if the Russians can do this or the Russians can do that! I'm fed up wi' the sound o' the Russians. I mind fine when the Russians weren't so popular, when nothin' was bad enough to say about them. But now even auld Churchill goes about spoutin' about them and wavin' the Red Flag!'

'Aw, pipe down, Lil. For Chrissake talk about somethin' you know somethin' about,' Nat said wearily, and without looking round he drew a packet of chewing-gum from his breast-pocket and held it in Lily's direction. 'Shove that in your gob and shuttup.'

'Well, I like your cheek!' Lily cried, but she took the gum and broke open the packet. 'Have a bit, Bess?'

'No, thank you,' Bessie said, brushing some specks of dirt off the white silk jabot that frothed down the front of her dress.

'Aw stick!' Lily guffawed and put a piece of gum in her own mouth. 'I'm loaded down with this stuff,' she said. 'Guess I might as well give some o' it away. Here, sonny, want some gum, chum?'

A little boy who had been sitting on a mattress, watching

them with goggle eyes, sidled forward at Lily's invitation and took the packet. He fumbled at the paper with dirty fingers, watching them all the time as though fearful it might be snatched away from him again.

'That's no' the way to open it, stupid!' Lily said. 'Here, let me open it for ye,' and she took off the paper and pushed a piece of gum into the child's mouth. 'That fine, eh?'

He chewed stolidly and nodded. Lily grinned, then overcome with generosity she rummaged in her bag and brought out her purse. 'Here's a penny for ye,' she said.

'Och, a penny's not much good, Lil,' said Bessie, opening her own bag. 'What can the poor bairn buy with a penny these days? A penny was all right when you and me were bairns. It was a real fortune. But a penny's not much good now. What could he buy with it?'

'Ach, I suppose you're right.' Lily took out another two-pence and handed it to the child. At the same time Bessie gave him a threepenny-bit. 'That's enough to buy him some sweeties,' she said. 'If he can get the coupons!'

Another little boy—evidently a brother—had nosed into the group, seeing gifts being distributed; and Bessie rummaged and found another threepenny-bit. The first little boy wriggled his way through the crowd and shouted to a large stout woman: 'Look, Ma, look at wot them lidies gave me!'

'Ladies!' Lily giggled. 'My, we're gettin' up in the world, Bess!'

The fat woman thanked them profusely and took the opportunity to complain about That 'itler and being forced to spend their nights in air-raid shelters or tubes. 'It ain't right, that's wot I say,' she said. 'All squeezed together in 'ere like Farmer Brown's cows. It ain't decent.'

Suddenly a look of horror came over her face. ''Enry!' she shouted.

But she was too late. The elder of the two little boys had pushed his way past Lily and Bessie and was trying to push into the group of G.I.s. Seeing the enormous expanse of Nat's bottom in front of him, he put out his hand and pinched it in the softest part.

Nat jumped with a yell. But before he could grab the boy, the mother got him first and gave him a resounding slap. 'What've I told yer?' she shouted. ''Aven't I told yer time and time again that yer mustn't do things like that to gentlemen. Really, the trouble I 'ave with 'im,' she complained to the giggling girls. 'I dunno where 'e learned it, I'm sure. It must just be the natural badness in 'im comin' out. 'E did it the other day to a policeman. 'Struth, that copper did create! 'E was bending over inside a car when 'Enry was passing, and before I could grab 'im it 'ad 'appened.'

'Well, I suppose the temptation was too much for him,' Lily giggled. 'I know I don't blame him for pinchin' Nat. I've often thought of doin' the same myself.'

''Enry, you're a bad wicked boy,' his mother shouted. 'If I catch yer doin' that again I'll whip the skin off your be'ind. Somebody said I should take 'im to one of them psycholergists,' she said to Lily. 'But I dunno. I don't trust 'em. Just meddlin' with nature, that's wot I think they do. Like as not 'Enry'd be worse after seein' them than 'e 'ad been before.'

She would have talked on and on, but Lily turned away after a while and plucked Nat's sleeve again. 'Lissen, big boy,' she said. 'If you're meanin' to stay in this stinkin' hole all night, I'm not. I've got to get home, anyway, and see if I can get some sleep. C'mon, get up them stairs!' And she giggled ribaldly.

Nat grumbled, but he and Norman dislodged themselves from the discussion on Russia. The four stood for some time, talking amongst themselves, then they went their separate ways. Norman took Bessie by tube to Tottenham Court Road, then, glancing at the sky every now and then and listening to the drone of planes and the faraway thuds of bombs, they walked towards Gower Street.

At the door of the boarding-house, Norman held her hand in his for longer than usual. 'Well, so long, kid,' he said at last. 'I'll give you a ring tomorrow. Okay?'

'Okay,' Bessie said.

She put her key in the yale-lock, but she did not open the door until he had disappeared into the blackout. And then suddenly as a bomb thudded in the distance she had a terrible desire to rush after him and throw her arms around him. . . .

III

For a long time after she was in bed Bessie lay awake. The All-Clear had sounded and there were no more distant thuds. She heard an occasional plane high overhead, but these were commonplace and nothing to worry about. It looked as though it would be a quiet night. All the same, she could not stop worrying about Norman. What if something happened to him on his way back to the Allied Services Club? What if he never phoned her tomorrow?

Oh God, she couldn't bear it if he didn't. Not after losing Joe like that. It wasn't that she felt for Norman like she'd felt for Joe, mind . . . it was just that she wanted to have him around. He was that nice and sensible. And such good company. Somebody she could depend on. It would be terrible if something happened to him now that they had got so pally. . . . And things did happen to folk so suddenly these days. One minute they were here, and the next they had been blown to smithereens by a bomb. Every time you went out into the streets you saw great gaps where houses had been standing the day before. . . .

If only things were like they had been before the war. Not that she wanted to go back to Edinburgh, mind. London was all right if only it wasn't for the bombs. Funny when you thought about it, what a lot had happened to her since those days before the war. Of course, she had been only a lassie then—and a daft skate of a lassie at that! All those ideas she had had about being a French princess. What a lot of havers! As though things like that could happen to the likes of her! Still, things *had* happened to her right enough. Here she was in London, five hundred miles away from Calderburn and the tenements, from Mrs. Moore and Dirty Minnie: five hundred miles away from her Dad and the bairns. . . . She had had a bairn herself and now she was a widow. And still she was only eighteen this month. . . . Jings, what a queer life it was when you came to think about it. Who could have known only two or three years ago that she would be lying here now in this bed thinking about a tall Yankee that she had seen only six or seven times in her life?

It was long before Bessie fell asleep, and when she awoke she started to think at once about Norman. All the time she was preparing the boarders' breakfast she kept listening for the telephone. Several times it rang, but it was always a call for somebody else. And when finally Gantz did ring at ten o'clock, Bessie had almost given up hope.

'Are you all right?' she cried.

'Of course, I'm all right,' he said. 'Why shouldn't I be?'

'Och, I just——' she laughed with relief, 'I just wondered. That's all.'

'Sure I'm okay,' he said. 'I was wonderin' if you'd come out with me this afternoon?'

'Och, I couldn't,' she said. 'I really couldn't.'

'Aw nuts!' he said. 'Of course, you can come. It's Sunday and it's a lovely day. God's in His Heaven and all's well with the world. Of course, you'll come.'

'But I have the boarders' teas to see to,' she protested. 'I really couldn't. I couldn't leave Pixie on her own.'

'Aw, c'mon! I got to go back to camp tonight, and I won't be able to see you until next week-end. Have a heart!'

'But——'

'You go and tell Pixie I want to speak to her. If you haven't got a heart, I bet she will. A large Irish heart at that!'

'Och away!' Bessie giggled.

'Tell her I want to take you for a walk in the park. A blow of fresh air'll do you good. You're lookin' kinda peaky.'

'Och away!' Bessie said, but she shouted to Pixie and told her. 'Well, what are you waitin' for, darlin'?' Pixie cried. 'None of your shenanigans now! Just you tell him you'll be there. A little canoodle in the park's the very thing the doctor ordered for you.'

'Well, really!' Bessie said, and she returned to the telephone with heightened colour.

'All right,' she said. 'I shouldn't come, mind. But—well, seein' you're not everybody, I will.'

'Can you make two o'clock?' Norman said. 'Or earlier? What about havin' lunch with me first? I just discovered a swell little restaurant in Soho.'

'No,' she said. 'I'll meet you at half past two and not a minute earlier.'

'Okay, can you meet me at Marble Arch tube?'

'Right,' she said. 'I must fly now. Cheeribye!'

A few minutes later, Mrs. Newlove, who came for only a few hours on a Sunday morning and who was dressed in her best in preparation for going to her 'local' for a drink, nudged Pixie and said: 'Listen to that, ducks! Ain't 'eard 'er sing since it 'appened.'

They grinned at each other and listened to Bessie humming *Underneath the lamp-post by the barracks gate there's a girl awaiting da da da da di dee. . . . We'll meet again by lantern light . . . My own Lili Marlene. . . .*

The ringing of the telephone broke into the song and her thoughts. Giving the banisters of the stairs a flip with her duster she clattered on high heels towards it.

'Is that you, Bessie?'

'Ay, hello, Lily!'

'What are ye doin'?'

'Oh, I was just dustin',' Bessie said. 'What are you doin' yourself? Where are you? I thought you were on duty.'

'I was, but I'm not any longer. I've just walked out. I've just told them they could stick their auld buses up their back-sides for all I care. Honestly, Hippy, what a mornin' I've had. The cheek I've had to put up with! There was an auld geezer got on my bus about nine o'clock and asked for Piccadilly Circus, so I just said "This bus doesn't go within a mile o' Piccadilly Circus, mate." He says: "Oh, does it not?" I said: "No, this bus goes up the Strand, mate. Better get off and get another bus." He says: "Well, can you tell me which bus I get for Piccadilly?" I says: "Search me, mate, I don't know. All I know is that this bus goes up the Strand. Are ye gettin' off or are ye not? Because if you're not I want yer fare. What d'ye want? A three halfpenny?'" "I want Piccadilly," he said. "Stop this bus at once." "I can't till we get to the next stop," I says. "Hold tight there!" just like I'd been told to say. Well, d'you know, Bess, he raised blue bloody murder. Told me I was impedin' the war effort and God knows what else. So I just said to him: "Listen, mate, by the look o' you we're not impedin' any war effort. All your war efforts must 'a' been done in the Crimean War." Oh, and then the band played! He took my number and got a polisman, and then it turned out he was Sir somebody or other, some high up general or somethin' in the War Office. I ask you! How was I to know? And he was fair livid because I'd called him "mate." So the upshot was that I just told them they could stick their bus!'

'Fancy!' Bessie said.

'Yes, me and buses have had enough o' each other,' Lily said. 'So I'm off on the randan for the day now. What are ye doin'? Can ye meet me at two o'clock?'

'No,' Bessie said.

'Och, why no'? Surely to God Pixie can let you off for a half-day. I'm goin' to meet Nat and I want ye to meet a friend o' his. A lovely fella that I know ye'll like.'

'I can't,' Bessie said, 'I'm goin' out with Norman.'

'Oh, him!' Lily said.

'Yes, I'm goin' to meet him at half-past two.'

'Och, give him the bum's rush,' Lily said. 'What're you wastin' your time with him for? He'll never do ye any good.'

'And why not?' Bessie demanded.

'Och, he's all right, I suppose,' Lily said. 'But I don't know. He's sort of—well, he's sort of quiet and sleekit-like, isn't he? He doesn't say enough for my taste. I must say, Bess, I was terrible disappointed with him. He's not the right kind o' bloke for you at all, Bess. I never trust those quiet, sly kind. And he's awful snooty. The way he looked me up and down last night! Well, really, I felt like sayin': "Have you got a smell under your nose or somethin'?" No, I wouldn't have anythin' to do with him, if I were you. Now, this pal o' Nat's is an awful nice guy and he's fair loaded down with nylons that he's splashin' left and right——'

'I don't care,' Bessie said. 'I'm meetin' Norman at half-past two. So there!' And she banged down the receiver.

Really, Lily had a right nerve, she thought, polishing the hall table vigorously with her duster. What right had she to interfere? Her and her friend of Nat's. He could have all the nylons in the world for all she cared. Really, Lily took just too much on herself. She hadn't forgiven Lily yet for all the things she'd said last night about her being a liar. She was *not* a liar. It was Lily that was the liar. Really, the way Lily *twisted* things. . . . She had never in her life said anything bad about Joe. Mind you, she *had* complained about having the baby once or twice. But that was understood. Even Joe knew that she didn't want the baby. Not at first, anyway. But she had got used to the idea and she had been fair broken-hearted when the baby didn't live. But she had never once said a word against Joe, and Lily McGillivray was a right bad hat to suggest such a thing. . . .

IV

Just before the news of Joe's death Bessie had bought a new wine-coloured dress with white polka dots. She had used the last of her clothing-coupons to get it, and when Joe died she had got coupons from Mrs. Newlove to buy a black dress. Getting ready to go and meet Norman Gantz, Bessie fingered the new dress, wondering if maybe this once she could wear it.

It didn't seem right to be always meeting Norman wearing her black dress. And it was a lovely sunny day. She might as well give the new dress an airing while the good weather lasted.

There! She stood back and admired the effect, smoothing the thin morocain over her hips. She looked very nice in black —Mrs. Newlove said she looked a perfect little lady—but it needed something warm like this to set her off. She pulled the white silk collar straight and picked up her white gloves and the white handbag which Pixie had given her for her birthday. She was ready.

She hesitated for a moment, wondering if she should take a coat, but decided against it. 'Well, I'm away, Pixie!' she shouted down the basement stairs. 'I don't suppose I'll be that long.'

'No hurry, darlin', Miss O'Malley called. 'See and enjoy yourself and don't do anything I wouldn't do!'

When Bessie arrived at Marble Arch tube station she was rather early and there was no sign of Norman. She went up the steps into Oxford Street and stood for a few minutes, watching the Sunday afternoon crowds stroll past. But twice she was accosted by G.I.s and a man, leaning against a window, reading the *News of the World,* kept glancing at her, so she decided to go downstairs again and wait beside the ticket-machines. She looked at the clock. Norman was five minutes late. It wasn't like him at all. However, she mentally shrugged, he had probably been delayed. She watched the people going up and down the escalators.

'Excuse me, plees,' a voice said at her elbow. 'Vill you direct me ze vay to Hampstead?'

A short, dark, good-looking Free French soldier was grinning at her.

'Ah, but yes!' Unconsciously, Bessie's voice took on a foreign intonation, and her hands fluttered with vivacity. 'You take ze Central Line and change at Tottenham Court Road, and zen you take ze Northern Line.'

'Merci,' he bowed, and broke into a torrent of French.

Horrified, Bessie gaped at him. She felt herself flushing. 'But I am not French,' she said, unable to keep the guttural accent out of her voice. 'I am Poleesh. My 'usban' he was Poleesh officer. I am so sorree.'

'Ah, la Polonya!' The Frenchman bowed again.

'He vas keelled,' Bessie said dramatically and she pressed her hands to her breast. 'Two monce ago!'

'Ah, mes condolences, madame,' he said. 'You are vaiting for somebody, no?'

'But yes, I am vaiting for a frien',' she said, and just then

191

she was glad to see Norman running down the stairs towards
her. 'Adieu!' she said quickly, and crying: 'Make ze change
at Tottenham Court Road!' she hurried towards the American.

'So you were gettin' off, were you!' Norman grinned. 'You
can't trust you dames! I reckon if I'd been another coupla
minutes you wouldn't of been here.'

'Och, it was just a poor wee Frenchie asking the way to
Hampstead,' Bessie said.

'I bet he knew all right without you tellin' him,' Norman
said, laughing as he put his hand under her elbow. 'I don't
trust these French wolves. If you're wantin' to play around
with wolves, sister, you stick to the American brand.'

'You bet!' Bessie giggled.

'You're looking pretty swell today,' he said. 'That sure is
a snappy frock.'

'Like it?'

'Sure, it's keen,' he said, piloting her through the crowded
pavement of Oxford Street. 'But whatever you wear, you're
always okay by me.'

'Och away!'

He said nothing else as he steered her across the wide space,
towards the entrance to Hyde Park, but the pressure of his
fingers on her arm made Bessie tingle as she had not tingled
since Joe had . . .

But she mustn't think of Joe, she thought, trying to fit her
short high-heeled steps into line with Norman's loping gait.
Poor Joe was dead, and that was an end of him. She would
aye remember him, of course, but she was too young to spend
the rest of her life thinking about him all the time.

Although it was a clear, sunny afternoon there were few
people in the park. Those who were out were keeping religi-
ously to the streets, eager to see and be seen, determined to get
as much out of life as they could in case death came quicker
than they expected. The only ones in the park were couples
like themselves, walking arm in arm or sitting on chairs with
their arms round each other. Bessie turned her head away
from the sight of a G.I. and a girl lying under a tree. The
girl's skirt was suspiciously high, and so were the G.I.'s

movements. She was just on the point of saying: 'Well, I think they might get farther away from the open street,' but she checked herself in time. It was the sort of thing that Lily would have said in her loudest possible voice. And anyway it wouldn't look nice if she drew Norman's attention to it.

Norman had seen nothing. He was bending his face towards hers. 'Yup, you're looking a heck of a lot better,' he said. 'You got some colour in your cheeks now. I like a dame with some colour. I hate to see a dame all plastered with powder like your friend Lily.'

'Oh, what did you think of Lil?' Bessie asked.

He gave a short laugh. 'Not much. She's too tough a babe for me.'

'Oh, Lily's all right,' Bessie said. 'There's nothing wrong with Lily.'

'Maybe not,' he said. 'But she's not my line, that's all.'

'Poor Lil,' she said. 'She's never really had a chance. She's been pushed from pillar to post all her days. Like me. No wonder she's a bit . . .'

'She's more than a bit,' Norman said. 'She's rank poison. I reckon you shouldn't be seen around with her too much. I guess it's none of my business, but a nice kid like you's bound to get contaminated by the likes of her. You give her a wide berth, kid.'

'Och, I couldn't do that,' Bessie cried. 'After all, I've known Lily all my life. We grew up together and went to the school together, and she's aye been a good wee pal to me.'

'Well, maybe,' he said.

He said nothing more as they scuffed their feet through the dead grass littered with soggy brown leaves. 'Guess we'll sit down, eh?' he said.

'Right,' she said.

They sat on two chairs under a tree and looked at the sunlight glinting on tawny foliage and on the ripples of the Serpentine. 'Pretty here,' Norman said at last. 'Kinda nice and quiet after the rest of London. It reminds me of the river near us back home.'

He had never told her much about himself. She knew that

he came from Wyoming and that it was sage and cattle country. Norman had been a cowpuncher for a short time, 'but it's nothin' like you see on the films with Gene Autry,' he said. Before he joined the army he had helped his father to run a small agricultural implement business.

'When I was home,' he said now, 'I used to think I'd like to get away from it. I got kinda loused up dealin' with small-time jerks of farmers and wished I could get into the big league. But now I'm not so sure. I reckon I'll be glad to be back home, just sittin' on the front porch at nights and not worryin' about what's gonna happen tonight or tomorrow. No worryin' about bombs fallin' or gettin' drafted or wonderin' which side's winnin'. Just sittin' tight, me in one chair and a nice wife sittin' in the other. And then when it's time she'll go in and cook me a nice supper, and then we'll hit the hay and sleep peaceful, knowin' we ain't gonna be rushin' like wildcats to the nearest shelter. Roll on peace!'

Bessie sighed in sympathy with him. 'I know,' she said. 'I used to feel like that, too. I was just crazy to get away from Edinburgh and go places and do things. But now I'm jack-easy. I just want a quiet life.'

'A good home with nice people!' Norman grinned. 'Aw, you're just a kid yet. There's no call for you to talk like an old grandma.'

'Well, who's talkin' like grandpa?' she said.

They laughed, and he took the opportunity to reach out and hold her hand. Bessie sat silent. She would have been content to sit like this for ever, if necessary, but Norman went on:

'Maybe I'm talking out of turn, but I was wondering . . .' He hesitated. 'I guess I'm a heel. It's maybe not the thing a regular guy would do, but, well, a bomb might fall and a guy's got to take a chance. I want to settle down with a nice girl, and I was wondering if . . . You wouldn't come over to the States with me when the war's over, would you, Bessie?'

'Oh, Norman!' she cried.

'I don't want to rush you,' he said quickly. 'I reckon it's a bit early after all you've been through. But if you'll think

194

about it maybe, if you'll think whether you could put up with a guy like me. . . .'

Bessie said nothing. He was holding her hand tightly, but she was able to move her forefinger and stroke his thumb gently.

'Of course, I'm a lot older than you,' he said. 'I guess maybe I shouldn't . . .'

'How old are you, anyway?' she said.

'Twenty-six. Maybe . . .'

'Aw, Norman,' she said. 'It's only eight years.'

'Yeah, but eight years is one helluva difference,' he said. 'That was what Lois said—only it was five years, not eight. Guess I've never told you about Lois?'

'No,' she said, staring at a couple who were walking hand in hand along the bank of the water.

Norman fumbled in his breast-pocket and brought out a packet of cigarettes. He frowned as he handed one to her and took one himself, and he flicked his lighter several times before he got a flame.

'Lois was a girl I met on a ranch I worked on. I was kinda green, just twenty-one, at the time, and I fell for Lois a lot harder than I should of done. She was the foreman's daughter and she was kinda cute and, well, it was like this—there weren't many dames around that part, and most of them were married anyway. You know how it is. Well, I made a play for Lois and before I knew where we were we were hitched up.'

Norman tossed his lighter from one brown hand to the other. 'Of course, an older guy than me would of known it wouldn't work out,' he said. 'Lois was only sixteen and, hell, she wasn't long out of school. She didn't know anythin' about keeping house or any of that sorta thing and—well, one thing led to another, and so finally we decided to call it a day. She went back to her folks and I went back to mine. I let her put a divorce through a while back. Mental cruelty.' He gave a short bark-like laugh. 'That's what they called a few bust-ups and Lois always naggin' me because I was five years older'n her.'

He leaned back in his chair and relaxed, having got it off his chest.

'D'you remember sayin' once that we'd both been for a—what d'you call it?—a hurl in the barrow?' he said. 'Well, that was mine.'

'Aw, Norman,' Bessie said softly.

They sat for a few seconds in silence, then Bessie put her hand on top of his. He swivelled round in his chair and muttered: 'Bessie. . . .' And suddenly he threw away his cigarette and lowered his face to hers, and their mouths met. At first their kiss was a floundering of lips against lips, then gradually as they became more certain of each other they relaxed and the kiss became a long communion of promise and trust.

v

Bessie went around in a haze of delight for several days, thinking of nobody but herself and Norman, dreaming of their life together in a pretty cottage in Willow Creek, Wyoming. Scenes from all the cowboy films she had ever seen passed through her memory in a cavalcade of sweeping plains, rugged mountain passes, shacks sheltering beneath willows on the banks of a rushing river, great herds of cattle and wildly whooping Indians on horseback: a swiftly moving series of pictures out of which she tried to choose the spot where she would like to live. But as one fantasy crowded on top of another, making it so difficult to choose, the ties of the outer London world tugged hard and made themselves felt. She was reminded that she must do something about Lily. It wasn't fair not to let Lil in on her secret, she decided. After all, Lily was her best friend and all that, so she had better be told. It was funny that Lily hadn't phoned before this. Of course, she *had* cut her off that last time. . . . Still, it wasn't like Lily to be in a huff.

'Oh, it's you, is it?' Lily said coldly when Bessie telephoned.

'Ay, it's me,' she said.

Lily's sniff at the other end of the wires was like spittle sizzling on an iron. 'Huh, I thought you'd been bombed or somethin',' she said. 'You might have been for all I'd 'a' known. Nobody ever thinks o' tellin' me anythin'.'

'No, I'm all right,' Bessie said. 'Are you all right yourself, hen?'

'I could be worse,' Lily said.

Bessie made a clucking noise of sympathy, but Lily did not rise to the bait. The line was silent.

'How's Nat?' Bessie tried again, hoping this would encourage Lily to burst into a babble of speech.

'I've no idea,' Lily said.

There was another pause.

'What d'you mean?' Bessie said. 'I have no idea! Are you and him not pally any more?'

'No,' Lily said.

She sniffed, and again there was silence. Desperately, Bessie made another effort.

'What happened?' she cried. 'Did you and him quarrel or what?'

'Well, we did and we didnie,' Lily said. 'I'll maybe tell you about it sometime.'

'Well, when will I see you?' Bessie asked.

'I dunno. Please yoursel'. I'm more or less a lady o' leisure. Give me a ring sometime.'

'Well, what about tonight?'

'I've got a date.'

'Well, what about this afternoon?' Bessie said. 'You wouldn't like to go to the pictures, would you?'

'I can't be bothered.'

'Och, Lily, are you still in a huff? It's not like you to be in a huff, hen.'

'And why should I no' be in a huff?' Lily cried. 'Really, Bessie Hipkiss, you've got a right nerve. After tellin' me to go to hell you ring up as sweet as pie and expect me to say nothin' about it.'

'What?' Bessie exclaimed. 'When did I tell you to go to hell?'

'When did you not! The last time you were speakin' to me on the phone and I said somethin' about your precious Norman or whatever his name is you cried "Go to hell!" and cut me off by the winkers.'

'I did nothin' of the kind, Lily McGillivray.'

'You did sut,' Lily screamed. 'You forget that I've got a good memory, Bessie Hipkiss. I remember your exact words. You said: "Go to hell! I'm meetin' Norman at half-past two. So there!" And then you cut me off. Jesus Christ and General Jackson, can ye wonder that I'm in a huff?'

'But I never said that, Lily.'

'Och, stop tellin' lies. You know fine that you said that. As I've told ye time and time again, liars should have good memories. The whole trouble wi' you, Bessie Hipkiss, is that you say things and forget what you've said two minutes after.'

'But I'm sure I never said that, Lil. I mind I was in a bit of a paddy when you said somethin' about Norman, but I never told you to go to hell. I'm sure I never——'

'Well, I am,' Lily snapped.

'Are ye sure?'

'Of course, I'm sure. D'you think I'd say it if I wasn't sure? Honestly, Bess, you fair take the cake sometimes.'

'Och, I'm awfully sorry, Lil. If I said it, you know that I didnie mean it. I wouldnie dream o' sayin' anythin' like that to you. It must 'a' slipped out or somethin' . . .' Bessie frowned, trying to remember what exactly she had said. After all, if Lily said she had said it, then she must have done. 'I really am awful sorry, Lil, you know I didnie mean anythin' . . .'

'Och, that's all right,' Lily said, mollified.

'Well, what about the pictures?' Bessie said. 'Can you go this afternoon?'

'We—ell, no, I don't think so,' Lily said. 'I've got a sort of a date. It may not come off, but I don't want to miss it in case it does. What about meetin' me for a drink about six o'clock? Meet me in the Dragonfly. I've got to meet Hank there at half-past six, so we can have a drink and a wee crack before he comes.'

'But, Lily, you know that I don't like goin' to pubs.'

'Och, it's high time you snapped out o' those daft notions,' Lily said. 'I used to see your point when we were in Edinburgh, and your Da bein' in the trade and all that, but you've got to remember we're in London now, and when in Rome do as the Romans do. Anyway, a wee drink never did anybody any harm.'

'But I dinnie like pubs.'

'Well, if you can't meet me in the Dragonfly at six, I'll no' be able to see you till the end o' the week,' Lily said. 'I'm a busy woman these days. I don't see why you can't meet me at six, and then you can wait and meet Hank when he comes at half-past.'

'Who's Hank for any favour?'

'Just a fella. You'll see him for yourself at half-past six.'

'All right then,' Bessie said.

'But mind!' Lily said. 'As soon as Hank comes I want you to skedaddle. Hank wants to see me and nobody else. So don't you stay and play gooseberry!'

'All right then,' Bessie said.

VI

Lily was sitting at a table in the corner of the Dragonfly when Bessie arrived. A glass of gin and orange was in front of her. Her tweed cream coat was slung over her shoulders, and a little green hat with a long pheasant's feather was stuck jauntily on the back of her head. 'What are you goin' to have, Bess?' she said, uncrossing her nylon-clad legs carefully so as not to knock them against the leg of the table.

'I think I'll just have a lemonade,' Bessie said.

'Aw, be your age, Ferret!' Lily said in a disgusted tone. 'Have a gin. Be reckless for once in your life!' And she finished her drink at one gulp as if to show that this was the way to do it.

'All right,' Bessie said, and she sat down and watched Lily mince to the bar. Really, she thought, taking in every detail of Lily's appearance from her expensive black shoes to the large pink pearl studs in the lobes of her ears, Lily was fair dressed to kill and no mistake.

'Well, cheers!' Lily said, lifting her own gin and taking a good slug.

'Cheers!' Bessie said, taking a sip and putting the glass quickly on the table.

'My, I must say, you're lookin' like a cat that's just pinched the cream,' Lily said. 'What's happened to your widdy's weeds? You haven't been long in goin' out o' mournin'.'

'Well, I thought,' Bessie hesitated, 'I thought I'd better. After all, I cannie go on wearin' black forever. So I just thought. . . .'

'Ach, you're quite right,' Lily said. 'What's the sense in goin' about with a face like a funeral! You're only young once.' She took another slug of gin and said: 'How's whatsis-name? That Yank—Norman is it?'

'Oh, he's fine,' Bessie said. 'He's—oh, Lil, you'll never guess! He's asked me to marry him.'

'What?' Lily put down her glass with a clatter on the table.

'Ay, he asked me to marry him and go back to Americy with him after the war.'

'Well, I must say!' Lily took another drink. 'I must say!' she repeated and leaned back and stared at Bessie. 'It takes some folk! Really, some folk have all the luck!'

'He's really awful nice,' Bessie said. She took a packet of cigarettes from her handbag, but she gazed dreamily at them and made no move to open the packet, so Lily reached forward and took a cigarette for herself.

'Well, I must say!' Lily said, striking a match. 'Words fail me!'

'And what did you say?' she demanded, blowing a cloud of smoke through her nostrils. 'Did you say ye would?'

'Well, I haven't exactly promised yet,' Bessie said. 'He told me to think about it. He said I wasn't to rush into it or any-thin'. But I've made up my mind I'm goin' to say "yes" when he comes up again at the week-end.'

'You'd be a fool if you didn't,' Lily said. 'Gosh, I wish

I could get a chance to go to Americy. I'd be away at the toot. There'd be no holdin' me back. But of course, I can't. There's that bloody Tommy Hutchinson still alive and kickin'.'

Lily glared moodily at the tip of her cigarette. Her sailor husband had been in Pacific waters for a long time. She had not seen him for over a year, and every letter she sent him was written with great difficulty and her ingenuity was taxed to the uttermost to find excuses for her various changes of address.

'The only good thing about him is that I get my money regularly from the Post Office,' she said, and she drained her glass and banged it down on the table. 'I don't wish Tommy Hutchinson any ill, but sometimes I wish . . .'

'Oh, Lil, what a like thing to say!'

'Well, what's the odds?' Lily said. 'What good is he to me, anyway? Lookit you. You're laughin' kit-bags. A widdy's pension and now a Yank wantin' to marry you. Huh, you're in the money all right, Bessie Hipkiss!'

'Oh, Lily!'

'Ach, don't sit there "Oh Lilyin'" me. Drink that up for ony favour and get some more drinks. I must have another before Hank comes. And you can well afford it!'

'But I don't want another drink,' Bessie said.

'Well, I do.' Lily pushed her coat back from her shoulders and sat bolt upright. 'So get weavin', chum! There's nobody between you and the bar!'

When Bessie turned round after buying a drink for Lily a tall G.I. was bending over their table, between herself and her friend. She could see only his rear and his massive back. But as she approached the table she suddenly halted and stared. The gin slopped over slightly. Bessie looked at the black hands gripping the edge of the table, and then her gaze travelled slowly upwards to the black grinning face.

'Bessie, this is Hank,' Lily said. 'Hank, this is Bessie Rolewicz.'

'Hya, Bessie!' the giant Negro said.

VII

'Really, you could 'a' knocked me over with a feather,' Bessie said, describing it to Norman the following Saturday as they sat in the park. 'Lily didn't need to tell me again to skedaddle. I got away as quick as I could.'

'Why?' he asked lazily, toying with the ends of her hair. 'What was wrong with the guy?'

Bessie gaped at him. 'But he was a blackie!' she said.

'Well, that's nothin' against him,' he said. 'There are millions of blackies, as you call them, in the States. Nice guys, too, most of them.'

'But——' Bessie frowned, biting her lip. 'But it doesn't seem right. I mean, fancy if Lily was to want to *marry* him or somethin'.'

'Oh well, I reckon that would make it a bit different,' Norman said. 'Although I don't see why she shouldn't if she wanted to. After all, it's her business.'

'But——' Bessie stumbled again on what she was trying to say.

'I don't say I altogether approve of it,' he said. 'But at the same time I've nothin' against it. It all depends on the people themselves, I guess. If a Negro and a white girl want to get hitched up, that's their affair. It's only when they have kids that the trouble starts. It seems to me to be kinda hard on the kids. I've known a lot of nice darkies. Some of them are a darned sight nicer than a lot of white folks I could mention. Still,' he shrugged, 'it's none of our business. We got other things to think about. You and me for instance. Are you gonna marry me, kid?'

'Oh, Norman!' she cried. 'You know that I am.'

'All I wanted to know,' he said, and he bent down and kissed her.

'I got to go away to Devon on a three weeks' course,' he said some time later. 'D'you think we could get hitched up as soon as I come back?'

202

'Uhuh.' She snuggled against him.

'I wish we could get it done before I go,' he said, rubbing his cheek against hers. 'But I reckon we haven't got time now. I just heard about this course yesterday—some kind of commando trainin' or somethin' they call it—and I kicked about it. But I got to go. You'll take care of yourself, won't you, kid, till I come back?'

'Of course,' she said.

'I got to speak to Pixie about you,' he said. 'I got to tell her to keep an eye on you. I don't want to lose you now that we got really going.'

'Aw, Norman,' she sobbed, 'I don't want to lose you either.'

The first few days that Norman was away Bessie felt almost as she had felt when Joe was killed. She went about with a wan face, not eating, and seldom smiling. 'Really, darlin',' Pixie O'Malley said. 'You'd think he wasn't coming back. It's high time you snapped out of it and saw about your trousseau if you're goin' to be a G.I. bride.'

Bessie tried to do as she was told, but all the time she kept worrying about Norman down in Devonshire. What if there was a bad raid down there? What if some accident happened on this commando course?

She was quite relieved one afternoon when Lily phoned and asked her to meet her. It would maybe take her mind off Norman a bit. Lily was such a gas-bag, she would be sure to have a lot to talk about, and maybe it would cheer her up. It would help to pass the time, anyway, until Norman came back.

They met in a restaurant because Bessie had flatly refused to go to a pub. 'I must say,' Lily said, 'I don't see why ye should be so stuck-up about pubs. Everybody down here meets in pubs. It's not like Edinburgh where if a woman goes into a pub everybody thinks she's a bad one. Down here even women like ma mother goes into pubs. However——' She shrugged and picked up the menu. 'What are we goin' to have? I'm fair starvin'.'

'I don't want much,' Bessie said listlessly, eyeing Lily's appearance. 'I'll just have a Vienna steak and a cup of coffee.'

'Och, I want tea,' Lily said. 'Don't tell me you've started trainin' already for goin' to Americy? All the Yanks I've met are just crazy about *cawfee*. Give me good old tea any time!'

She glanced at herself in a mirror opposite. 'Like my new hat?' she said, touching the white tulle which was festooned around a small pill-box of navy-blue felt. 'Hank gave it to me before he went away.'

'Hank?' Bessie said.

'Ay, don't tell me you've forgotten the big blackie you met in the Dragonfly?' Lily giggled. 'My Christ, Hippy, you should 'a' seen your face that time! You couldnie get out the door quick enough. I don't see why. He was such a nice fella, and he was fair crazy about me.'

'I suppose he was all right,' Bessie said.

'Of course, he was all right.' Lily stuck her tongue in the corner of her mouth and rolled her eyes. 'Mmmm, Bess, give me a blackie any time! And how! There's somethin' about a blackie. My Christ, once you go with a blackie you never want to go wi' anythin' else. Just wait till I tell you,' and she leaned forward and whispered.

'Really, Lil!' Bessie was horrified.

Lily laughed ribaldly at the expression on her companion's face. Then she said: 'I don't see what ye're so shocked at. After all, you're not such a saint yoursel'. If your beloved Norman only knew the half o' it!'

'What for instance?' Bessie said coldly.

'Oh, I can think o' lots o' things,' Lily said. 'Lots o' things that happened before you met Joe. And lots o' things that've happened since! No, no, Bessie Hipkiss, I could tell a fine tale if I liked. A tale that would make yer beloved Norman's hair stand on end. One o' these days when him and me get together he'll learn a thing or two.'

'Don't you dare, Lily McGillivray!' Bessie clenched her knife and fork and leaned forward.

'Keep yer hair on!' Lily laughed gaily. 'I never said I would, did I? I just said *maybe*. . . .'

A lump of Vienna steak stuck in Bessie's throat, and she had to take a drink of cold water to shift it.

'I must say I miss Hank,' Lily said, picking up her handbag and looking at it reflectively. 'It's a pity he had to go away back to some outlandish place in Yorkshire. I bet the Yorkshire girls'll no' appreciate him like me. I miss him in more ways than one. He gave me this lovely handbag as well as the hat. It was nice o' him, wasn't it?'

Bessie said nothing. She chewed her Vienna steak for a while, then she said: 'Are you not goin' to get another job, Lil?'

'Och, why should I? I manage all right. Why the hell should I work if I can find mugs o' men that are willin' to pay for me?'

'Oh, but, Lily——'

'Ach, be your age, Ferret. After all, I'm no' the only one, not by a long chalk.'

'But if Tommy ever found out. . . .'

'Tommy!' Lily's face twisted in a sneer. 'I don't suppose Tommy'll ever come back, and if he does—well, that'll just be too bad for him. He'll get the air all right.'

'But it doesnie seem fair to him,' Bessie said.

'Och, what's fair in this world?' Lily laughed raucously. 'And if you're thinkin' about sayin' anythin' about my private life to Tommy Hutchinson, Ferret-face, well—I can think o' a few things I can say to a certain stuck-up Yank. Things that'll maybe make him think twice about takin' you back to Americy with him.'

'I never said I would say anythin' to Tommy,' Bessie protested.

'I never thought you would,' Lily said. 'I was just warnin' you, that was all.'

She glanced at a short blond G.I. who had sat down at a table opposite. 'Nice,' she murmured. '*Very* nice.'

Bessie did not answer, nor did she look round.

'By the way, I met Teddy the other night,' Lily said casually.

'Teddy?'

'Ay, Teddy. How many Teddies do we ken, you dope? Teddy Gabanski, of course.'

'Oh, Lil!' Bessie's eyes widened with horror. 'What did he say?'

'What would he say?' Lily laughed. 'He asked me how I was, of course. And I told him I was fine. I must say I aye liked Teddy. There was somethin' about him. I don't know what it was, but he was such a gent. He had such nice manners when he opened doors for you and things like that. Mind you, I'm not sayin' anythin' against the Yanks. They're all right. But when it comes to little wee things like kissin' your hand and bowin' you out and in the Poles have it every time.'

Lily lit a cigarette and watched the blond G.I. through the smoke. 'Teddy asked me to go back to him,' she said.

'What?'

'Oh, it's all right,' Lily said. 'Keep your shirt on! I didn't say I would go. I told him I would think about it. I've been tryin' to figure out whether it would be better to have a safe bet like him or just to have ships that pass in the night like Nat and Hank.'

'But, Lil, I thought you said you were never goin' to have any more to do wi' him.'

'What I said and what I'm goin' to do are two entirely different things,' Lily said. 'Not that I *have* said I was goin' to have anythin' to do with him, have I? I just said I was *thinkin'* about it. Now, if that G.I. at the next table was to say the same sort of thing . . . Mmmm, he's cute, isn't he?'

'Really, Lil, you're terrible,' Bessie said. 'You keep away from Teddy Gabanski, Lil. He's a real bad hat. Lookit the way he treated you the last time. He could easy have done somethin' to keep you from goin' to the nick, and——'

'I beg your pardon?' Lily said icily.

'I'm sorry, Lil.' Bessie flushed. 'That just slipped out.'

'Well, don't let me hear it slip out again,' Lily said. 'Or else I can open my mouth a bit wider too.'

'I wouldn't trust Teddy Gabanski an inch,' Bessie said quickly.

'Ah well, we'll see. After all, it's my business. By the way, he asked about you. Asked how you were, so I said you were goin' to marry a stiff-necked Yank. I don't think Teddy was any too pleased about it. He was aye awful fond of Joe.'

'Well, that's *my* business,' Bessie said. 'And Teddy Gabanski can keep his nose out of it.'

VIII

Norman Gantz would be in Devonshire only for another three days and already Bessie had cast aside her gloom. She was full of plans for his return. In order to get suitable clothes for her wedding, she had bought clothing-coupons from Mrs. Newlove. She had also bought some from a friend of Mrs. Newlove's, who said: 'She's a lidy with a large family, ducks, so the pore dear can't afford to buy clothes. It takes 'er all 'er time to feed 'er brats, ducks, so you be warned!' While hunting through the shops Bessie lived in a day-dream such as she had not had since those day-dreams of long ago in Calderburn, when she was a helpless, feckless girl of fourteen, burdened on her mother's death with a house and three small children to look after. But now her day-dreams were different from those dreams of royal palaces and Madame Royale, Duchess de Bourbon-Parma, Princess of France, who ruled over kings and statesmen. Now her dreams were of life with Norman—sometimes in a small cottage in the backwoods of Wyoming, sometimes in a pent-house in New York, but most often of a tiny flat in Reading. She supposed they would have to stay in Reading when they got married. Unless Norman could get shifted to London, of course. Not that she really wanted that. No, London was just a bit too dangerous. London was all right, but what with all those air-raids and one thing and another she didn't want anything to spoil their happiness. It would be awful, wouldn't it, if they got married and then one of them got bombed. . . . Or if Norman got drafted overseas and got killed like poor Joe. . . . They would be better in a nice wee flat in Reading. Norman said it was a swell place, and it was near enough for her to come up sometimes to London for the day to see Pixie and her other friends.

After all, she wasn't so gone on London as she once had been.

She was thinking of this one evening after returning from an exhausting afternoon in Selfridge's. Her packages were still lying unopened on her bed, and so soon as she had helped to give the boarders their supper she went upstairs to unpack. She had just opened the parcels and was admiring her purchases when Pixie shouted:

'Bessie! Here's a visitor for you!'

There was something in the sound of Pixie's voice which made Bessie's heart leap. She glanced hastily at herself in the mirror and saw that she had gone white and was going slowly pink again. She put her hand to her heart to try to still the little jumps it was giving. Was it Norman back sooner than she expected, she wondered as she ran downstairs. Or was it somebody to say something had happened to him?

Almost fearfully, she halted outside the sitting-room door. She touched her hair and wet her dry lips before pushing open the half-shut door.

'Hello, Bessee, my wee hen! How are you doing, ducks?'

Dmitri Klosowski was standing in front of the fireplace. He grinned at the expression on Bessie's face, and he bowed and clicked his heels together.

'You are surprised, yes?' he said, coming forward and lifting her hand to his lips. 'My wee hen! How nice, how charming it iss to see you again. It has been such a *long* time. Poor Dmitri has been heart-broken for his wee Bessee.'

'How—how did you get here?' Bessie stammered.

Klosowski shrugged and gave his hands an airy wave. 'Ah, it iss a long story. Dmitri will tell you sometime. I am in a pub and I meet Lilee, and Lilee tell me where to find you. Beautiful Lilee—more gay than ever! So happee to be back once more wis her Tadeusz.'

Bessie's legs had suddenly gone so weak that she was forced to sit down on the arm of an easy-chair. 'I—I—— But Lily had no right . . . She knew that I . . .'

'Lilee iss a *good* pal, yes?' Klosowski threw away his
208

cigarette-end and put another cigarette in his long amber holder. 'Cigarette, *my* dear?'

Bessie took it mechanically.

'You are not *pleased* to see Dmitri?' he said, as he flourished a cigarette-lighter.

'Oh, well——' Bessie inhaled and stared at him as though mesmerized. 'I never expected to . . .'

'Ah, but you did not think Dmitri was *dead,* did you, my wee hen?' He laughed, showing more gold teeth than ever. 'You must have known, Bessee, that your Dmitri would come back to you sometime, no? We were veree good pals, yes? Always I haf been thinking of you, always! And now when I meet Lilee, and Lilee tells me about Josef Rolewicz—well, I just *fly* to see my wee Bessee and say 'ow sorry I am. *So* sorry.'

'Well, I wouldn't 'a' thought that by the way you behaved to him the last time . . .' Bessie's sudden courage failed her, and she broke off. She shivered, wondering if she could scream loudly enough for Pixie to hear if Klosowski tried any tricks.

The Pole, however, sat down in a chair opposite and crossed one elegant riding-boot over the other. 'Ah, that was unfortunate, but 'ow unfortunate,' he sighed. 'It was veree stupid. Stupid of me, stupid of you, stupid of Josef. It wass all so—so unnecessary!' He gave his hand a flourish and, taking a white handkerchief from his sleeve, he flicked his boots.

'You will forgeef me, Bessee, my wee hen?' He smiled suddenly with ingratiating charm. 'Josef—poor Josef—iss dead, and life iss short. Life iss too short to be angry wis each other, yes? You un'erstan', my wee hen, Dmitri wishes you to forgeef him and be *pals* wis him again.'

'Well—I—er——' Bessie faltered.

'So!' Dmitri smiled and stood up. 'We will shake hands, yes?'

'A—all right,' Bessie mumbled, and unwillingly she put her hand in his.

'Ah, now!' Klosowski expanded his chest and grinned. 'Now, you must come to see Lilee. Lilee iss ill and she has asked me to breeng you to spik wis her.'

'Lily ill?' she cried. 'What's wrong with her?'

209

'Ah, it iss not bad.' Klosowski spread out his hands. 'A leetle thees, a leetle that—some pain in the tummy. I do not sink it iss much, but Lilee vishes to see you.'

'Where is she?' Bessie asked. 'She's not—she's not in hospital, is she?'

'Oh no, no! She is wis Tadeusz. In the flat. She goes back to live again wis Gabanski.' Klosowski sighed sentimentally. 'So beautiful it iss to see Lilee and Tadeusz together again. So beautiful. . . . Lilee has cried and laughed so much to be back that she has gifen herself the—you un'erstan'?—the *coleec*.'

'Och, is that all?' Bessie stood up and threw her cigarette-end in the fire. 'Well, tell her I'll come along and see her tomorrow some time.'

'Ah, but no, no!' His tone was piteous. 'Tonight! Lilee wishes to spik wis you tonight. It iss very importan'—you un'erstan'?'

'But I don't think I can. . . .'

'Ah, but yes, Bessee! Yes, you mus' come for Lilee's sake. She will be so disappointed. She will cry and cry and cry and zen——' He opened his eyes wide and there was such a look of misery on his face that Bessee started to giggle.

'So!' He grinned. 'You will come?'

'Well, I really shouldn't,' Bessie said. 'But—all right, I will.'

She put on her coat and went in search of Pixie. 'Is that a friend of Joe's?' Miss O'Malley said. 'He's a grand figure of a man, isn't he?'

'Oh, he's all right,' Bessie said. She had never told Pixie about Klosowski, and she had no intention of doing so now. It was better to let bygones be bygones. What was the sense of raking up a lot of dirty linen? 'He's come to take me along to see Lily,' she said. 'Evidently she's no' very well. She's back livin' with Teddy Gabanski, so of course that explains everythin'.'

'Holy Mother of God!' Pixie cried. 'Some women never learn sense. I didn't think they were born so dumb as that Lily McGillivray. Not these days, anyway.'

'Aw, poor Lil, I suppose she can't get Teddy out of her system.'

'I know what I'd do to her system,' Pixie sniffed. 'A damned good dose of castor oil. That would shift her! She wouldn't be after havin' time then to flit from one man to another.'

'Well, anyway, I'll go and see her,' Bessie said. 'I shouldn't be long. About an hour, I'd think. I really shouldn't go, but, well, I daresay Lily would do the same for me.'

'She would!' Pixie sniffed. 'Don't be after deceivin' yourself, darlin'.'

She followed Bessie into the hall where Klosowski was waiting. 'Are you sure you'll be all right?'

'Of course. It's just as far as Holborn and back. What could happen to me?'

'You never know!' Pixie shrugged, and she smiled at Klosowski and said: 'Now, be sure and bring her straight back, Lieutenant. No shenanigans, now!'

'Shen. . . ?' Klosowski looked puzzled. 'Please.'

'Ah, it's just a joke!' Pixie laughed. 'A wild Irish joke that has very little blarney left in it. Now, away with you!'

IX

As soon as Pixie shut the door behind them, cutting off a welcome shaft of light, Bessie experienced a sudden spasm of fear. She shivered when Klosowski took her arm, and she drew away from him, crying: 'It's all right, I can manage.'

'I see better in the blackout when I'm walkin' on my own,' she said in order to mollify him. 'If you're takin' somebody's arm you're likelier to bump into folk.'

'So!' he chuckled softly. He made no further move, however, to come near her, and they kept about a foot apart as they walked towards Great Russell Street. But when they were going into Southampton Row, he moved nearer to her and said: 'Bessee, it iss better to take my arm. It iss *dangerous* around here—you un'erstan'? Do not be afraid.'

'I told ye I'd rather walk on my own,' she said, and she quickened her steps to keep the distance between them. In her haste she bumped into a lamp-post and gave a startled cry.

'So!' Klosowski laughed. 'Did I not tell you, my wee hen? It iss better to take Dmitri's arm.'

Bessie sighed with exasperation, but allowed him to grasp her elbow. 'It's not far now,' she said, to reassure herself.

He had been in Palestine and Egypt since she had seen him, and talked all the way about the various girls he had met. 'Beautiful girls in Cairo,' he said. 'Lofelee girls, but none of them was as *goot* as you, Bessee. All the time I haf been wondering about you. My heart it was pining for my wee Scotch hen. I was so glad when I met Lilee and she told me where to find you.' Bessie did not answer. She walked as quickly as she could, straining away from him like a dog on a leash. And she was thankful when they reached the narrow street where Gabanski had his flat. She disengaged herself from Klosowski's grasp and ran up the dark stairs ahead of him. He followed more slowly, feeling his way cautiously, but still talking of his amours in foreign countries. Relieved at having got here without any unpleasantness, and as though to show him that she was not interested in his Arabian beauties, Bessie started to hum: *Tonight my heart will sing the sweetest song of them all . . . Ta da di da. . . .*

'Bessee is happee, yes?' Dmitri reached the landing and she could hear him groping on the ledge above the door. 'Lilee iss in bed, so we must find the key. Ah, so!'

She heard him fix it in the lock, then he switched on the light. *'Entrez!'* And he stood aside to let her in.

'My goodness, Lily,' Bessie cried, clattering towards the bedroom. 'What's this I hear? Fancy you bein' in bed!'

She flung open the bedroom door. The room was in darkness, so she switched on the light. The bed was empty.

'W—what?' She stood with her mouth open, then she turned round quickly.

Klosowski grinned at her. 'No Lilee?' he said softly. 'No Teddee? Bessee iss disappointed, yes?'

'Where are they?' she cried.

He spread out his hands and hunched his shoulders. 'Ze birds haf flown!' He flashed his gold teeth at her. 'But my little bird is here, yes? My little bird will not be able to fly away thees time.'

He gripped her arms and pulled her against him. 'Stoppit!' she cried. 'Stoppit! Less o' yer tricks now! Where's Lily? I thought you said she was in her bed.'

'Bed? Ah, no! The bed iss empty. The bed iss waiting for Bessee. . . .'

His arms clamped firmly around her and she was pressed against his chest. 'Do not be afraid, *moja kochana*,' he murmured. 'You are quite safe wis Dmitri. Lilee will come back some time. But first we haf a little time to ourselves. We haf much to say wis each other. Many things to talk about. . . .'

'Lemme go!' she cried, and she pushed her fists against his chest. 'Lemme go! You tricky wee bugger!'

'Ah, that iss not nice, that iss not friendly.' His tone was aggrieved, but his embrace remained firm. 'Come, my wee hen, take off coat and we vill sit down and be goot pals again, yes?'

'No!' she cried. 'No! I'm goin' home.'

She struggled and broke away from him. He laughed as she rushed to the door and rattled the handle frantically.

'It iss locked,' he said. 'Dmitri has the key in his pocket. Safe!' And he slapped his thigh.

'You—oh, you wee——'

Bessie ran into the sitting-room, but before she could shut the door after her, Klosowski was at her heels. She ran to the fireplace and stood with her back to it, glaring at him. There was a self-satisfied smirk on his face, and as he advanced into the room, Bessie reached down and lifted the poker.

'Just you come near me,' she shouted. 'Just you come one step near me and I'll brain ye wi' this!'

'Ah, Bessee,' he purred in conciliatory tones. 'Do not be foolish, my wee hen. Dmitri iss not going to harm you. Dmitri wishes to be pals wis his wee Bessee again. Come, let us talk! Let us be *straight* wis each other.'

'No, I've had enough,' she exclaimed. 'Gettin' me here

213

with a dirty trick like this! I should 'a' known ye weren't up to any good. I should 'a' had the sense to know that ye were just tellin' lies.'

'Lies! Ah but no, Dmitri does not tell lies,' he murmured. 'Dmitri said Lilee was ill, and Lilee *iss* ill. She has a pain in her tummy. But she has gone out for some drinks wis Gabanski never-the-less. She said it would help her pain.'

'Well, I'm goin' home,' Bessie said. 'You stand away from that door and let me pass. Or else——'

'Dmitri has the key in his pocket,' he said, and he took out his case and put a cigarette in his holder. 'You would like a cigarette, yes?' And he held out the case.

'No, thanks,' she said, gripping the poker firmly.

He shrugged and sat down. 'Nine o'clock,' he said, looking at his watch. 'The pubs do not close until eleven. We haf two hours. Two hours for Bessee to be *nice* to Dmitri.'

'Oh, you——!' Bessie narrowed her eyes with rage.

The Pole lit his cigarette and sat down on a divan near the door. He smiled and stroked the military ribbons on his breast. 'Dmitri can wait,' he said softly. 'Dmitri has often waited for what he wants. This ribbon, this medal, was gifen to Dmitri because he waited and waited—and then *pounced* on his enemy at the proper time. You un'erstan'?'

Bessie lowered herself slowly into a chair beside the fire, keeping her eye on him all the time. She still kept a firm grip on the poker. If he can wait, she thought, well, so can I. I can sit here for a couple of hours, too, without budging.

'Lilee has told me you are friendly now wis a Yank, wis an American,' Klosowski said. 'Lilee says *perhaps* Bessee will marry him and go to America, yes?'

'Yes,' she said. She licked her lips, but her throat remained dry, and a nerve was beating madly in her neck. She put a finger on it to try to stop the steady beat, beat.

'He iss nice, your American?' he said.

She nodded.

'Nicer than Josef Rolewicz?' he said. 'Nicer than Dmitri?'

'Yes,' she said.

'He knows about Joe?' he said.

214

She nodded.

'He knows about Dmitri?' he said softly.

Bessie caught her breath and swallowed. Klosowski's lips quirked with amusement at the trapped look on her face.

'So!' He grinned. 'Your Yank does not know that his wee hen hass been goot pals wis me, no? *Veree* goot pals!' He twiddled a large signet ring round and round his finger. 'Perhaps Dmitri will meet this Yank,' he murmured, 'and then he will tell him about Mrs. Irvine and Edinburgh and what goot times Bessee and me used to haf together. . . .'

'You wouldnie!'

'But why not?' Klosowski spread out his hands, palms upward. 'It iss not a secret, iss it?'

'Don't you dare!' Bessie cried. She had started up with fury, but she sank back again, still clenching the poker. 'Anyway, you're not likely to meet Norman, so it doesnie matter.'

'Ah, but yes! Dmitri can easily meet this Yank. Lilee will tell him where he iss to be found.'

'Oh, you——' Bessie clamped her mouth tightly. 'Och, he wouldn't listen to you,' she said. 'I can easy tell him what a liar ye are.'

'Of course, I might not tell him,' Klosowski said. 'Perhaps if Bessee—perhaps if my wee hen was to be *nice* to Dmitri once again, I might forget that we ever knew each other *so* well in Edinburgh. No?'

'No!' she cried. 'No!'

'Come, my wee hen,' he said cajolingly. 'Be nice wis Dmitri once more. Let us be friends, yes? It iss not nice to quarrel.'

And suddenly, before she had realized his intention, he had bounded across the room and was kneeling beside her chair. The poker dropped with a clatter, and he kicked it out of reach behind him. 'Bessee,' he whispered, taking her hand and kissing it passionately. 'Bessee, you still lof Dmitri? You still remember. . . .'

'No! No!' she cried, and she tried to push him away and stand up.

But his arms were held firmly across her knees, and before she could prevent him he had pressed his face into her lap.

'Forgeef me, *moja kochana,*' he moaned. 'Forgeef me!'

'No,' she screamed, clawing furiously at his face.

'Beat me, my wee hen!' he slobbered. 'Flog me! I am a *bad* mans, and I must suffer. I *want* to suffer.'

'Stoppit!' she yelled. 'Stoppit!'

'I *must* suffer!' he cried. 'Bessee must whip her Dmitri and then he will go away and not trouble her again. She must! She must!'

'Stoppit!' she screamed. 'Norman! Norman!'

But she knew that her screams were futile. She was being pressed back further and further into the chair and the lithe, muscular body of the Pole was almost upon her when the door was flung open and Lily McGillivray cried: 'Here, what's goin' on? What're ye yellin' the place down for?'

x

'Is it no' enough for me and Teddy to have a row without you two joinin' in the chorus?' Lily shrieked. 'Jesus Christ and General Jackson, we could hear ye at the other end o' the street.'

She flounced into the room and stood in the centre with her hands on her hips. Tadeusz Gabanski slouched in the doorway, a sarcastic look on his face. He made an ironical little bow towards Bessie.

'Thank God ye've come!' Bessie cried, jumping up. 'I was just gettin' ready to brain this one wi' the poker.'

'Huh, it's nothin' to what I'd like to do to that one,' Lily cried, turning to Gabanski and flaring: 'You Polish bastard, I'll strangle you one o' these days. I'll wipe the silly grin offen yer face, even if I have to swing for it.'

'Do not be foolish, Lily,' Gabanski sneered. 'Try to control yourself.'

'Control myself! Control myself!' she shrieked. 'D'ye hear that, Bess? The impiddence o' the brute!'

216

'It iss more ladylike to control yourself, my dear Lily,' he said. 'But of course!' He shrugged and gave a short laugh. 'But of course you are not a lady, my dear. You are just a common tart.'

'What!. D'ye hear that, Bess? He has the bloody nerve to stand there and call me a tart. *Me* a tart!' Lily raised her eyes and blew her breath sharply with martyred indignation. 'Well, of all the bloody nerve!'

'Perhaps you would prefer me to call you a prostitute, my dear?' Gabanski said, lounging elegantly into the room and saying something in Polish to Klosowski.

Klosowski was still kneeling where he had been pushed away by Bessie. Before the arrival of Lily and Tadeusz he had taken off his belt. It lay like a brown snake in the middle of the room. He buckled it on now, saying piteously: 'Ah, Bessee. . . .'

'Well, I'm goin' home now,' Bessie cried. 'I wish I'd never listened to that wee trickster. He told me you weren't well.'

'Neither I am,' Lily said. 'I've got an awful bellyache. That's what we went out for—to see if two or three drinks wouldnie shift it. But it hasnie. If anything, it's worse. All this commotion has fair put my nerves on edge. I must have a cup o' tea. You'll stay and have a cup, hen?'

'No, I'm goin' home.'

'Och, stay and have a cup,' Lily said. 'C'mon.' She pranced into the kitchen-cum-bathroom, and Bessie, after hesitating for a moment, followed.

'Oh, what a smell in here!' She stood in the doorway and held her breath. 'No wonder you've got a sore belly, Lil. The stink in here's somethin' terrible.'

'Ay, it is kind o' heavy. I dunno what it is,' Lily said, putting the kettle on the gas-stove. 'It's been like this ever since I came back, but I haven't had time to do anythin' about it yet. Teddy's such a dirty pig. Lookit the mess everythin's in. I've been meaning to tidy it up, but, well, what wi' one thing and another. . . .'

'And ye used to have it lookin' so nice,' Bessie said. 'When you were here before this kitchen was a fair wee gem.'

'Ay, but just see what two or three months o' Gabanski on his own has done!' Lily laughed harshly and lit a cigarette.

Bessie wrinkled her nose with disgust at the piles of dirty crockery littering the sink and the top of the dresser. A filthy tarpaulin covered the bath, and she lifted one corner of this. '*Feech!*' she cried.

'My Christ!' Lily peered over her shoulder, and both girls held their noses. 'I wondered where the stink was comin' frae.'

The bath was full of empty and half-empty milk bottles. The empty ones were unwashed, and the milk in the half-empty ones was green and soured. 'My God!' Lily exclaimed, and she started to count. 'One, two . . .'

'Seventy-seven bottles!' she cried. 'No wonder the man in the dairy gave me such a funny look this mornin'.'

'And what's this?' Bessie lifted the cover of a soup-tureen and disclosed a piece of meat with a fungus several inches thick. She put back the lid quickly. 'Well, when ye think of so many folk starvin'! It's fair criminal.'

'Ay, it takes these Polish aristocrats!' Lily said. 'Aristocrats my arse! Of course, Gabanski thinks he should have serfs waitin' on him all the time like he had in Poland. Serfs! The cheek o' the bugger! But he doesnie need to think he's goin' to make a serf out o' me. I've had enough. After what I had to put up wi' tonight in the pub! And now this!' She tossed her head. 'No, me and Teddy's partin' company again pretty damned quick.'

'You should never have come back to him,' Bessie said. 'I told you!'

'Ah well, I've learned my lesson this time,' Lily said. 'It just shows what these dirty Poles are. Tryin' to make mugs out o' simple lassies like us. I wish I'd never seen a bloody Pole. I wish they'd all go away back to their own country. Really, the way Gabanski went on in the pub the night because I just happened to look at a G.I. Honest to God, Hippy, I was just *lookin'* at the fella, but Teddy went straight through the ceiling. He ranted and roared so much that I just downed

218

my drink and walked out. If it hadnie been for that we wouldn't 'a' been back yet.'

'Gee, I'm thankful you are,' Bessie said. 'Ye just arrived in the nick o' time.'

'I'm sorry about Klosowski, hen,' Lily said. 'I gave him your address without thinkin'. I just opened my mouth and let it out. I never thought he would try any tricks.'

'Och, it's all right. Let's forget it.'

'Well, let's have our tea and then we'll get on wi' it. Will ye help me to pack, hen? And then I wonder—d'you think you could put me up for the night?'

'Well, you'll have to share my bed,' Bessie said. 'It'll no' be that comfortable.'

'It'll be better than sharin' a bed with that Polish swine.' Lily made the tea and started to rake amongst some tins on a shelf. 'I thought there was some biscuits somewhere. . . .'

'You haf made the tea, Lily?' Gabanski stood in the doorway, thumbs hitched in his belt, a half-smile on his face.

Lily did not answer. She tossed her hair back from her eyes and opened another tin.

'Haf we no coffee?' Gabanski said. 'Klosowski and I would prefer coffee. It iss unfortunate that you Scotch are so fond of tea.'

'Well, you can make it for yourself,' Lily said without looking round.

'Lily,' he said. He leaned against the lintel of the door and tapped his foot. 'Lily, I asked you to make coffee for myself and my guest.'

'Well, I'm not makin' it,' she said. 'And that's flat. Do your own dirty work.'

The corner of Gabanski's mouth curled menacingly. 'Lily,' he said quietly. 'Lily, there are certain things which a vife must learn in Poland.'

'Well, we're not in Poland, and I'm not your wife,' she cried.

Gabanski shrugged. 'Ah, perhaps not. But you must remember, my dear Lily, there are certain things which I know about you, which would be very unpleasant for you, if I spoke about them. You un'erstan'? There is a question of allotment-money from your real husban'. I do not think the police would look very kindly upon you. And there are clothes here which . . .'

Lily turned from her search among the tins. She straightened up and put her hands on her hips. 'What d'you mean?' she demanded.

Gabanski gave a slight shrug. 'There is a dress which you brought from a shop only yesterday—a dress which you omitted to pay for, my dear. It was very stupid of you, was it not, to tell me about it when you had had two or t'ree drinks? I am surprised at you, Lily. T'ieves should be more cunning.'

Bessie shrank against the sink, looking from one to the other. Lily lifted one arm and swept her hair back from her forehead, staring at Gabanski all the time. He lounged against the door, a sinister smile on his face. 'Yes,' he said, tapping a cigarette on his case. 'There iss this dress, and naturally there are other things. . . .'

'You bloody——!' Lily's upper lip lifted in a snarl.

'Don't listen to him, Lil!' Bessie cried. 'Drink up your tea and let's go.'

'You t'ink you are very clever, Lily,' he went on. 'But it iss not so. Gabanski could make things very *awkward* for you.'

'So you're threatenin' me, are ye?' Lily cried. 'You dirty Polish bastard! Gerrout! Gerrout!' she screamed. 'Gerrout or I'll wipe that silly grin offen yer face. I'll *murder* ye before I let you say anythin' to anybody about me!'

Bessie cowered between them, holding her coat tightly around her. She looked quickly from one to the other, terrified at the looks on their faces. 'Lily!' she cried. 'Let's go, Lil! C'mon!'

'I'll murder ye first,' Lily repeated, enunciating each word slowly, and she leaned towards Gabanski and hissed: 'Don't you think, you bloody dope, that I'll let you get away with it. I've just had more than enough o' you and your high and mighty ways, my man. I wish to God I'd never seen ye. Gerrout o' here!'

Gabanski laughed sarcastically. 'So! You will get tough,

yes? Two can play at that game, my dear.' And he moved towards her menacingly.

'Get back!' Lily shrieked. 'Get back! Or I'll——'

But he moved slowly and relentlessly towards her, his fists clenched, the self-satisfied smirk on his face changing to brutal sullenness.

'Get back!' Lily screamed. 'Get——'

Bessie's scream mingled with Lily's as she saw the knife flash upwards and then swoop towards Gabanski's chest.

'Lily!' she screamed. 'Oh, Lil, what've ye done?'

Her scream was cut off suddenly, and she stared from Lily to Gabanski who had slumped against the table. 'Lily!' she screamed again. And she turned and fled through the sitting-room, past Klosowski, and ran shrieking downstairs into the street and straight into the arms of a policeman.

EPILOGUE

'C'MON, Mom, tell us a story!'

Mrs. Bessie Gantz sighed. Honest, those kids were the absolute end. They wouldn't give her a minute's peace.

'Can't you see I'm busy, Normie,' she said. 'I got all this darning to do before Pop comes home. I'll tell you a story before you go to bed.'

'Aw, for Pete's sake!' Normie scowled and stuck out his stomach and his lower lip. He was a sandy haired child of seven with dark blue eyes like his father's. 'Why can't ya tell us a story now? You're jest sittin' there. You can easy talk while you're darnin', can't ya?'

'Sure she can,' Marlene said, and she sat down and leaned her dark head against her mother's knee. 'C'mon, Mom!'

Bessie sighed and looked from one child to the other, realizing that she was trapped. It was a good hour before Norman was due home from the store, so she could not make the excuse yet that she must see to the supper. Anyway, the kids knew that Grete had already prepared that. She was trying to think of another excuse when the door burst open and five-years-old Truman rushed in, yelling: 'Capture this bunch you guys! We gotta make 'em talk before we mop 'em up. Zooop!' And he rushed at his mother and brother and sister, pointing his toy machine-gun. 'Tie up this doll, guys!' he shouted, throwing himself on top of Marlene.

'Truman!' Bessie cried. 'How often have I got to tell you, Truman Gantz, that I won't have you using that word *doll*? It's only common little boys from across the tracks that use it. If I hear you say it again I'll get Pop to speak to you.'

Marlene, with the dignity of six years and a superior strength, pushed away her small brother, saying: 'Be quiet, Butch! Mom's going to tell us a story.'

'I don't want a story,' Truman shouted. 'I want to go to the movies to see Alan Ladd. The Keating kids are goin', and I want to go with them. Give me a quarter, Mom.'

'I'll give you a quarter on the side of your head,' Bessie said. 'You've already been to the movies this week. Once a week is quite enough for a small boy. And, anyway, I wouldn't let you go with the Keating kids. How often have I told you to keep away from them? I will not have you playing with the janitor's kids. I'm going to speak to Pop about you.'

'Aw nuts!' Truman said. 'Pop won't say nothin'. Pop likes the Keating kids. He gave them a ride to school on Tuesday.'

'C'mon, Mom,' Normie cried. 'Don't listen to him. Get on with the story. If Butch don't want to listen, tell him to get out.'

'If I can't get to the movies,' Butch cried, 'I want to watch Hopalong Cassidy.' And he moved to the television set and began to tinker with it.

'It ain't time for Hopalong yet,' Normie said. 'We're all gonna watch Hopalong when it's time. But right now Mom's gonna tell us a story.'

'Tell us about when you were a little girl in Scotland, Mom,' Marlene said.

'Aw, not that story,' Truman said. 'I'm sick and tired of that story. Tell us about the bombs in London, Mom.'

'No, tell us about what Pop did in the war, Mom,' Normie said. 'You don't tell it as good as him, but I reckon you'll have to do.'

'You keep away from that television set, Butch,' Bessie exclaimed. 'Or else I'll get Pop to talk to you. Pop paid a lot of money for that set, and he doesn't want it broken by a nosey wee boy.'

'C'mon, Mom!' Marlene tugged her skirt. 'Don't pay no attention to Butch. Get on with the story!'

Bessie sighed. Sometimes she found her responsibilities as the mother of three children and one of Willow Creek's

224

prominent young matrons just more than she could bear. What between attending to the flat, the children and her husband, keeping an even balance between friendliness and the status of an employer with Grete, the hired help, trying not to snub Keating the janitor too much, and entering into the social activities of all the other young matrons, life was very crowded, and often she wished she could just sit back and dream. This afternoon she had hoped that she would be able to do this while darning. But now. . . .

'Well, once upon a time there were two young ladies,' she began. 'One of them was called Lily, and one of them was called Elizabeth, and Elizabeth was really a princess in disguise. Elizabeth's father was really a king in exile——'

'Aw, I don't like stories about kings,' Truman cried. 'I want a story about Hopalong. What's in exile mean, anyway?'

'Shuttup and listen to the story,' Normie said. 'If ya don't, I'll . . .' And he glared menacingly at his small brother.

'Was Lily a princess, too?' Marlene asked.

'No, Lily was not really a very nice girl,' Bessie said. 'Lily was, well, Lily was kinda jealous of Elizabeth because Elizabeth was going to marry a handsome prince, and she plotted with a Polish count to kidnap Elizabeth and hold her to ransom. . . .'

It all seemed so far away, she thought, as she mechanically told a story she had told the children so often. And yet, at the same time, some of it was as clear as though it had happened yesterday. Although eight years had passed since that day in the court when Lily had created such a scene, it was so vividly imprinted on her memory that sometimes Bessie Gantz awoke crying in the night, having had a nightmare about it. And then it was reassuring to find Norman lying so solid and sensible beside her, and to curl up against him, putting her arm over him for comfort. Would she ever forget that day, she wondered, that day after Lily had been sentenced and she herself had walked in a daze from the court, holding on to Pixie and Norman, and then outside had collapsed weeping into Norman's arms and had heard him say: 'It's okay, kid. What're you worryin' about? You got me, haven't you? You

225

and me are gettin' hitched right away, and then you can forget about all this. It won't be long now before we get to the States and we'll be able to settle down good and proper.' She had clung to him, weeping, unable to take in the full meaning of his words, realizing only that she was safely out of the court, away from the horror of it all; seeing only the wild look on Lily's face and hearing her screams as she was led to the cells. 'Poor Lil,' she kept saying. 'Oh, poor poor Lil!' The flashing of a press photographer's bulb made her jump. Behind him she saw Gabanski and Klosowski hail a taxi, Gabanski with his arm in a sling. As he slammed the taxi-door behind him he seemed to look straight at her again with that sneering expression he had directed towards her so often during the trial. And she shut her eyes tightly: trying to shut out that look, trying to shut out Lily's face, trying above all to shut out the Judge's voice when he said: 'Mrs. Rolewicz, I'm afraid you are a very unsatisfactory witness.'

Oh, that Judge! And, oh, that prosecuting counsel! Even yet Bessie Gantz went cold when she remembered the sound of his voice. It had sent shivers down her back as soon as she was called to the witness-box and she heard him say: 'Now, Mrs. Rolewicz, I want to hear your description of this unfortunate incident.' Bessie was terrified because of Lily standing there in the dock, Lily, who was even yet trying to be jaunty and putting on a bold front, her hair marcelled and her nails polished, lips larded with lipstick, and powder smeared thickly over her wan cheeks. But Bessie was even more terrified at finding herself in such a position; she felt so prominent standing there with strangers gaping and all these policemen; and she could only lick her dry lips and stammer: 'I—er—I——'

'Now, don't be nervous, Mrs. Rolewicz,' the Judge said. 'Speak up.'

Bessie gripped the edge of the witness-box and looked wildly round the court. Pixie, who was sitting between Norman and old Mr. Powys, gave her a reassuring nod. Bessie looked again at the Judge, going over in her mind the words she had already repeated so often to others. She drew her breath and said: 'She said, "You Polish something, I'll strangle you one of these days. I'll wipe the silly grin off your face, even if I have to swing for it." '

'Oh, what a flamin' lie, Bessie Hipkiss!' Lily screamed, leaning over the dock. 'I never said anythin' o' the kind. Really, I never heard the likes! You can't believe a word that lassie says, your lordship. She's aye been an unholy liar.'

The Prosecutor held up his hand. 'Please, Mrs. Hutchinson,' he said. 'You will get a chance to tell your version of the—um—incident in due course.'

'Continue, Mrs. Rolewicz,' he said.

'Then Lily said to me we would have some tea, and when she had made it Teddy—Lieutenant Gabanski—came in and asked for coffee, and they had a row and Teddy shook his fists at Lily and—and——' Bessie halted and wet her lips again.

'According to Lieutenant Gabanski's evidence, Mrs. Rolewicz, he was standing in the doorway when Mrs. Hutchinson lifted the knife and sprang at him.' The prosecuting counsel's long fingers flirted along the bench and he watched them as though they were dancers doing an intricate movement. 'Is that right?'

'No, your honour, he—he shook his fists at her and went right at her, and I thought he was goin' to hit her.'

'That's right,' Lily cried. 'He came straight at me, and I was that feared that I lifted the knife—I dunno how it got there, it was just lyin' handy—and I——'

'Please!' the Judge said in a pained voice. 'If the prisoner interrupts again, I shall have to adjourn the court.'

'But I was just——'

'Silence!' the Judge cried, and the policewoman beside Lily gripped her arm.

'It all happened that sudden,' Bessie said. 'One minute Teddy was springin' at Lily, and the next he was leanin' against the table and there was blood all over the place.'

Even now in the middle of telling a story to her children, a story she could have told with her eyes shut, no matter how tightly she shut them she could still see the blood. It was a good job for Lily that the knife had glanced off the fleshy part of

227

Gabanski's chest into his arm. If it had just gone the other way, well. . . . But as it was, it bled and bled and bled. Bessie shuddered now at the remembrance and she stopped speaking. A sharp tug from Marlene brought her back to the present.

'Go on with the story, Mom! What happened next?'

Continuing with the story which any of her children could have repeated backwards, Bessie's memory returned to the highlights of that older story, that story she would have preferred to forget. Lily had tried to twist everything that was said, and not once, but many times, during the trial she had accused Bessie of being a liar. But she had not been able to twist round the Judge. Even though he had said Bessie was an unreliable witness, he had given Lily a dreadful dressing down in his summing-up, calling her 'a painted Jezebel' and 'a menace to society,' and he had given her what everybody said was a stiff sentence.

A number of papers had had photographs of herself and Lily and bits about 'the morals of the younger generation.' Mrs. Irvine had written a long letter to say that she had always known that Lily was 'a bad hat' and would come to no good; and even Mrs. Moore had written a wee note to say that the whole of Calderburn couldn't get their *News of the World* quick enough that week.

Oh, they had been in the news all right! Though Bessie had had her photograph in some of the Edinburgh papers later on when she married Norman and then again when she sailed for America: *An Edinburgh G.I. bride, Mrs. Norman Gantz, leaves for the States with her two-years-old son, Norman, and her baby daughter Marlene. Mrs. Gantz was formerly Miss Bessie Hipkiss of Goldengreen Street, Calderburn, and before her marriage to Captain Gantz, she was married to Lieutenant Josef Rolewicz, who was killed in North Africa.*

But it wasn't what the newspapers had said that Bessie remembered most clearly. It was what old Mr. Powys had said that evening when they were all sitting in Pixie's sitting-room, Bessie still stunned at the verdict and still weeping quietly about Lily. 'Poor child,' Mr. Powys had said. 'It isn't her we should judge. It's society that's to blame. If they will

228

have wars, they must put up with the troubles that wars bring in their wake. A short life and a gay one! Can we blame the unfortunate girl for wanting to have a good time while she could? Nothing in temporal things is permanent, and nobody is perfect.' And then he had gone on to say that if the war hadn't happened the Poles would never have come to Scotland. . . . Ay, and if the Poles had never come to Edinburgh, Lily would have stayed married to Tommy Hutchinson—or if not him, she would have married somebody else, for she had married Tommy in a hurry because of the war. She might have been flighty for a while, but she would have settled down all right, the way Bessie was settled down now. She might have had some bairns by this time instead of being God knows where. Bessie had no idea what had happened to her. Often she had wondered, and she had prayed that her stupid one-time friend had not been fool enough to go back again to the arms of Tadeusz Gabanski.

But you never know, Bessie reflected. Lily was a daft bitch in many ways, and she didn't really stop to count the cost. Poor Lil, she had never had a real chance. Tommy Hutchinson had divorced her after all the scandal. That was the last news Bessie had had of her. Mrs. Irvine was not likely to mention her in any of her letters, and poor old Mrs. Moore was dead. Sometimes she thought that she would ask her father when she wrote and sent him a food parcel, but she knew that he would take no notice of it in his reply. He had aye been against Lily. It had taken him all his time, in fact, to forgive her, though he wrote occasionally and she knew that he boasted to people about ' my daughter in America that's done very well for herself. She's got three bairns and a nice flat and a motor-car. Her husband's a nice fellow and has a big store. Plenty o' money there all right! ' Maybe some day when she wrote to Jenny, she would ask her. . . . Ay, that would be the best plan. But not for a while yet. Not until Jenny was older and had the gumption to write a letter on her own, without telling her Dad.

It was a strange life all right, she thought. Maybe the war had made a queer-like mess of Lily, and there were lots besides

Lily in the same boat. But at the same time, if it hadn't been for the war she would never have met Norman and she wouldn't be sitting here now. In a way, it was just sheer luck that she hadn't been standing in that dock instead of Lily. She might have struck Klosowski with the poker. Probably she would have done if Lily and Teddy had not come back so soon because of the row in the pub. And then where would she have been?

'What're you cryin' for, Mom?' Normie cried. 'It's not a sad story.'

'No,' Bessie Gantz said. 'It's not a sad story. It has a happy ending. Elizabeth married her prince, who was a kind, good man who didn't care about all the things that had happened to Elizabeth before that. He said: "Don't you worry, kid, everything's going to be hunky-dory from now on." And so they got married and sailed across the sea and lived happily ever after.'

'But that's not the end of the story, Mom,' Marlene said. 'Is it?'

Bessie looked down at her small daughter, and as she said: 'No, that's not the end of the story,' she saw again another small girl with dark hair, her sister, Jenny, who in the same way had cried so often long ago: 'On and on and on with the story!'

Lightning Source UK Ltd.
Milton Keynes UK
10 December 2010

164200UK00002B/20/P